Praise

"Darby starts out grumpy but when his heart opens up watch out! Darby couldn't be a more perfect book boyfriend if he tried."

— EVELYN V., U.S. GOODREADS

"This book was fun of humour, romance, banter, and heartwarming moments as well as some really important chronic illness awareness. I love how Brooke writes and includes how chronic illnesses do not define you."

— CLAIRE C., ENGLAND, GOODREADS

"A book about healing, faith, family, pain and love. I don't think my soul will forget it !!! ... I AM A FAN !!!"

— FEDY P., ITALY, GOODREADS

"I absolutely devoured this book."

— JENN C., NETGALLEY

"I lost the day to laughter and tears. I thank the author for not beautifying the pain, the insecurity and fears of any of the brilliant characters in the book. Only yesterday I spoke to my husband about our "Job moments", to see it referenced in this novel brought so much comfort"

— RACHEL M, AUSTRALIA, NETGALLEY

"I loved that it was more than just a contemporary romance and that it is such an advocate for those with illnesses that you can't necessarily see . . . Books have saved me and gives me something to do when I don't feel well and I'm so grateful for Brooke and what she is doing to bring light to those that need it."

— RACHEL P, US, NETGALLEY

"This was such a wholesome read! As an Irishwoman myself, I laughed so hard at some of the references . . . These characters are developed well and the storyline is simply beautiful, and very educating. I can't wait to see what else this author has in store.

— AMBER Z., NETGALLEY

"I love reading stories where spoonies get their happy ever after and find a genuine romantic partner that loves them for them. It's a book that's good for the soul and full of vulnerability that will leave you feeling cozy and hopeful!"

— SIERRA R., NETGALLEY

"The Irish Fall is a true love letter to spoonies. This story is a breath of fresh air and a true marvel of writing."

— TOMI TABB, AUTHOR OF THE GREAT AUSTEN ESCAPE

"In The Irish Fall by Brooke Gilbert, the author deals with a relevant topic not often touched on in the romance genre...It is seldom that a character in a book has real-life issues that are not mainstream. With a focus on Crohn's Disease and endometriosis, the author has reached a new audience. Being a chronic illness sufferer, it was comforting to read an authentic take on what it means, with all the issues around diet and physical exhaustion."

— REVIEWED BY DELENE VREY FOR READERS' FAVORITE

Also by Brooke Gilbert

The Paris Soulmate: A Sweet Romance Novel

Reeling from the reality of turning thirty soon, Christine decides to take a trip that has been on her bucket list for years. She has dreamed of going back to Paris, but since being diagnosed with several rare autoimmune disorders, she never imagined she would get the chance to return. Now, she finds herself on the way to the city of love with an unexpected surprise... An extremely handsome British stranger seems to have mysteriously fallen onto her path. Is it just a coincidence that they are both traveling to the city of love at the same time? It all seems too good to be true.

The Irish Fall

SOMETIMES YOU HAVE TO FALL TO RISE

Written By
BROOKE GILBERT
Edited By
CAITLIN MILLER

Copyright © 2023 by Brooke Gilbert

Cover Image License provided by Canva Pty Ltd. Cover design by Brooke Gilbert. Original Cover design copyright © 2023 by Brooke Gilbert. Edited by Caitlin Miller.

The following is a work of fiction. All people, places, names, events, and situations are a product of the author's imagination or used in a fictitious manner. Any resemblance to a person, dead or living, is completely coincidental, and is not to be taken as reality.

Library of Congress Control Number: 2023911009

First Edition

Paperback ISBN: 979-8-9872622-1-4
Amazon Paperback ISBN: 979-8-9872622-0-7
Amazon Hardback ISBN: 979-8-9872622-3-8

All rights reserved. No part of this publication may be reproduced, copied, transmitted, or distributed in any form without the author's written permission.
www.brookegilbertauthor.com

Dedication

For every woman who has ever felt the loss of a child or the opportunity to ever have one.

And for Chad, you're a "Free Bird" now.

Also, to those whose chronic illness has affected their ability to do the things they love. May your dreams evolve with you so that you *can* pursue the ones that have always been waiting for you.

As I have had the privilege to meet more chronic illness and mental health warriors on my writing journey, I have witnessed firsthand their strength and beauty. The way they embrace each other and uplift one another is a beautiful example for the world to see. They're always celebrating differences while connecting over similar struggles. It is a wonderful community, and I thank you for accepting me into it. I finally feel at home. It is my wish that this story helps you believe that you can still pursue your dreams, whatever they might be, and wherever they may lead you.

"Your feet will take you where your heart is."

-Irish Proverb

Contents

Travel Map   xvii
Sight References   xix

Content Caution   1
Irish Slang   5
Spotify Playlist   7
Prologue   11
1. Darby   13
2. Darby   17
3. Eyre   22
4. Eyre   27
5. Eyre   31
6. Eyre   37
7. Darby   46
8. Eyre   55
9. Eyre   65
10. Eyre   73
11. Eyre   81
12. Darby   91
13. Eyre   101
14. Darby   112
15. Darby   120
16. Eyre   128
17. Eyre   136
18. Eyre   153
19. Darby   160
20. Darby   163
21. Eyre   178
22. Darby   192
23. Eyre   204
24. Eyre   219

25. Eyre	230
26. Darby	241
27. Eyre	256
28. Darby	267
29. Darby	275
30. Eyre	283
31. Eyre	288
32. Eyre	294
33. Darby	306
34. Darby	311
35. Eyre	316
36. Eyre	327
37. Eyre	334
38. Eyre	343
39. Darby	351
40. Darby	362
41. Eyre	376
42. Darby	394
43. Eyre	400
Epilogue	407
Movie List	417
GF Fish & Chips	420
Gf & Df Tartar Sauce	422
Autoimmune Paleo Diet	424
Discussion Questions	426
Author's Note	431
Acknowledgments	439
About the Author	445
Also by Brooke Gilbert	447
Chapter 1	448
Chapter 2	454
Sneak Peek	461
Dear Doris	463

Cary | Atlanta, Georgia | 1969

Travel Map
FOR REFERENCE

Sight References

FOR REFERENCE

1. Attribution: Bob Linsdell. https://commons.wikimedia.org/wiki/File:The_Browne_Doorway,_Eyre_Square,_Galway_-_panoramio.jpg
2. Attribution: Gerd Eichmann. https://commons.wikimedia.org/wiki/File:Galway-18-Claddagh_Rings-2017-gje.jpg

3. Attribute: Bob Linsdell. https://commons.wikimedia.org/wiki/File:Galway_Hookers_Fountain,_Eyre_Square,_Galway_(506259)_(26294583000).jpg

Content Caution

Hello Lovely Reader,

    First, I would like to thank you for picking up my novel. I know there are so many books out there for you to select from and the fact that you picked up mine means the world to me. You are the reason I keep writing. With that in mind, I wanted to make sure to take a moment with you to discuss the content of my novel.

    Nothing infuriates me more than novels without content warnings, so I am going to try my best to provide them here without giving away any spoilers! There are mild medical episodes that include descriptions of pain associated with esophageal Crohn's, arthritis, migraines, and endometriosis. There are also discussions of infertility and suicidal thoughts in relation to endometriosis & Crohn's. This disability representation is written by an author who also battles autoimmune and chronic health disorders herself. The journey I have begun with my own female health problems and my mother's endometriosis was the inspiration for the main character to have this condition.

This novel also features mental health episodes and will include anxiety and panic attacks. They will be fairly descriptive. Themes of forgiveness and loss are present throughout.

Please be kind to yourself and if now isn't a good time to read this novel, then I will definitely understand. Perhaps there will be a better time in the future. And if you would like modifications, there are chapters you could always skip, and I'd be happy to discuss those options with you. Or if you have questions and specific triggers in mind, know that my door is always open. I'm available through Instagram (@enchantingbrookevoiceover) and brookegilbertauthor@gmail.com.

This is a clean novel. Descriptive kissing only. No cursing.

THE IRISH FALL

Faith conversations included.

I hope you enjoy your time in Ireland! Can't wait to discuss this novel with you :)

Love, Brooke

Irish Slang

Learning more about Irish slang was one of the most fun parts of my research for this novel. I'm going to be incorporating them into everyday speech. Lol. Here is the list of Irish terms and definitions used in this novel for reference.

Gobdaw (idiot)
Slag (to tease)
Lashing (raining)
Dopes (idiots)
Dosser (someone up to no good)
Gobdaw (stupid person)
Lobbing the gob (kissing)
Shifting (kissing)
Kip (dirty)

Murder (very difficult)
Youngfellas (young boys)
Eejit (idiots)
Shattered (exhausted)
Manky (dirty)
The jacks (toilet)
Grand (great)
Gombeen (dodgy man)
Gowl (idiot)
Boyo (adolescent)
Jammy (lucky)
Make a bags of it (ruin it)
Give it a go (to try)
Gombeens (chancers/dodgy person)
Donkey's year (in forever)
Bunk off (flake or disappear on someone)
Crack on (move on)
Earwigging (eavesdropping)
Ossified (drunk)
Langers (drunk)
Babhdóir (Irish matchmaker).
I was scarlet (embarrassed)
Bucketing down (pouring)
Good on you (good for you)
Oye (oh, boy)
Clown (dislikable person)
Manky (dirty)
Craic (fun. An alternative meaning is gossips)
Messages (groceries)

Spotify Playlist

Listen to *The Irish Fall* playlist on Spotify while you read this book. It includes music mentioned in the novel and/or music I listened to as I wrote this novel. Enjoy :)

- Best of You- Andy Grammar, Elle King
- Missing Piece- Vance Joy
- Wildfire- Seafret
- Be Slow- Harrison Storm
- My Sunny Day - Ted Fresco, Lyn Lapid
- I Lived- OneRepublic
- Tenerife Sea- Ed Sheeran
- Mess is Mine- Vance Joy
- In Your Arms- Chef's Special
- Horse to Water- Tall Heights

- Hold My Girl- George Ezra
- Someone to You- BANNERS
- Galway Girl-Ed Sheeran
- Daisies for Dara-Ben Sands
- Addicted To You- Picture This
- Bloom-The Paper Kites
- Come Thou fount of Every Blessing- Open Blue Skies
- The A Team-Ed Sheeran
- Dreams-The Cranberries
- She-Ben Abraham
- Clair de Lune, L.32-Claude Debussy, Martin Jones
- This Side of Paradise-Coyote Theory
- Gone, Gone, Gone- Phillips Phillips
- Amazing Grace- Melody Lake
- Sparks-Coldplay
- Dancing in the Moonlight- Toploader
- Fast Car-Tracy Chapman
- Shoulder-Ed Patrick
- Someone Like You-Noah Kahan, Joy Oladokun
- Grow as We Go-Ben Platt
- Coastline-Hollow Coves
- Wildfire- Cautious Clay
- The Leprechauns in Ireland- Ola Melander
- Crazy Love-Van Morrison
- Danny Boy- Bamford Stevens
- Cough Syrup-Young the Giant
- Haven- Novo Amor
- Deux Arabesques- Claude Debussy, Nikolai Lugansky
- Spirit Cold- Tall Heights
- Stay With Me-Sam Smith
- You Are the Best Thing-Ray LaMontagne

THE IRISH FALL

- Scarborough Fair-Bjørn Lynne
- Nocturne No.2 In E Flat, Op.9. No.2- Frédéric Chopin, Maurizio Pollini
- Electric Love- BØRNS
- Stubborn love- The Lumineers
- Sleep on the floor- The Lumineers
- Somewhere Only We Know- Keane
- Still Rolling Stones- Lauren Daigle
- Bloom- LULLANAS
- Of Foreign Lands and Places- Robert Schumann, Glenn Morrison
- Castle on the Hill- Ed Sheeran
- Clocks-Coldplay
- Love Grows-Edison Lighthouse
- Earth Angel- Joseph vincent
- Can't Help Falling in Love- Kina Grannis
- Every Side of You- Vance Joy
- Just Begun- WILD
- Lease on Life- Andy Grammer
- Free Bird- Lynyrd Skynrd

Spotify Link: bit.ly/theirishfallplaylist

Prologue
DARBY

Luck had nothing to do with it. I may be Irish, but I still believe there was something else happening. But I didn't start out believing that way. No, my heart started out much differently. It started as stony as those Irish cliffs that brought her to me.

ONE
Darby

The Cliffs of Moher were weeping with extra vengeance today, mocking the beautiful woman standing all alone on the edge. Teetering dangerously close to the rocky brink. So close that I was beginning to worry the steep chasm would reach up, consume, and swallow her whole. From my vantage point, it looked as if that might not only be a real possibility but judging from the look in her sad eyes, a preferred choice. Her sorrowful eyes were going to haunt me from this day forward, no matter the outcome.

As I stared mesmerized at the woman, another blasted tourist was rambling on in my ear. I swear these tourists were like herding cats. I didn't get paid enough for this job. I honestly didn't know how I even kept this job. My surly attitude and lackluster demeanor should have gotten me fired by now. Maybe it was because the owner had known me since I was a wee lad. Maybe it was because the tourists thought I was absolutely adorable. They seemed to think surliness was part of my "Irish charm," which only aggravated me more. I can tell you quite frankly that there is nothing *charming* about me. Take away the Irish accent and you're left with a cynical curmudgeon. But for some reason these ladies found it especially appealing.

Right now, I just wanted them to leave me alone. I had been completely drawn into the world of this stranger. I needed to know what she was thinking. I'd give anything for a glimpse into the labyrinth of her mind . . . *just give me a tiny opening.* A high window, a vent, even a crack in an old wall. *Anything,* I'd make it work. Believe me, it was unusual for me to be this interested in . . . well, anything. But from the moment I'd seen her, I'd been captivated and I'd steadily moved closer and closer to her.

An older woman was using her cane to tap on my stupid–cockeyed–leprechaun hat. Yes, provided by the company. No, I didn't provide it myself. I wouldn't even wear it for extra tips. And yes, that was something that my co-workers did. They had no dignity apparently. They were more than happy to lean into the Irish stereotype. I had standards. *Seriously, when did this leprechaun thing get started? And when was it going to end?* Has any tourist yet to see one of those ridiculous green buggers? I didn't think so.

Great, now they were tag teaming me. The lady's friend was tugging on my obnoxiously bright green Irish tour guide shirt. *Also* provided. The leprechaun body was printed on the front of the shirt in all of its glorious form, forever commemorated in ink. The words *"Ask me anything, I'm Irish your service"* plastered on the back. No, I'm not making this up. I promise you, I couldn't. Or at least I sure hope I couldn't.

But the harder the ladies tapped and tugged at my shirt—skillfully hanging on to their umbrellas at the same time—the firmer my eyes stayed fixed on the mysterious woman. She appeared to be inching her way to the edge. And my imagination amplified the heartache in her eyes. She had turned so that her sight line was devoid of people. She was completely alone now and I hated it. At least earlier, she had been turned enough for me to see the expressions on her face. But now—being unable to see her eyes—this was agony.

What I wanted to know was why no one else seemed to notice her, why only I seemed to see her and sense her distress. And I wasn't usually a particularly observant guy. As the women continued to chatter in my ear, the last thing that seemed of importance at this moment was answering questions about the height of the cliffs or some other query I had already answered a zillion times. *Oh, how I hated this job.* The feedback from the cursed employee evaluation survey was right in politely suggesting that I needed to work on my people skills. Well, now seemed as good a time as any to start.

I turned toward the group of ladies and quickly said, "Excuse me, ladies. I'm sorry, but there is some extremely important and urgent Irish tour guide business I must attend to. You all are the best of the group. I leave you in charge. It's a great responsibility, but I know you can handle it. I temporarily deputize you ... Irish." They beamed so brightly that you would have thought they had found the pot of gold at the end of the rainbow. *Tourists,* I thought sarcastically, *you gotta love 'em.*

As I turned, I rolled my eyes in relief—glad they hadn't sensed my sarcasm—and I started moving quickly toward her. I couldn't stand not being near her any longer. And I couldn't handle not knowing what had brought her so much heartbreak.

TWO

Darby

Scurrying away from the women as quickly as I could—while I still could—I stared at the beautiful woman ahead of me with anticipation. There were fireflies lighting up my insides with every step. *What was I planning to do? What was—*

"Miss, the tour's about to leave. I'd hate to see you left behind. This view is incredible, but it gets pretty cold here at night. Lonely too." The words flew out of my mouth without any conscious recognition, just as my hand landed on her arm in the same unconscious fashion. I looked down in surprise when I saw it there. I yanked it back as if scolding myself for my inappropriate action.

She turned with a startled abruptness that actually made me jump, but I was also caught off guard at how beautiful her hazel eyes and golden brown hair were up close. She had been so still before, as if completely lost in a trance. And not one caused by the mesmeric cliffs, either. I'd seen hundreds of tourists stare at these captivating cliffs, and her reaction was not the typical one I usually saw. There seemed to be something else that had enveloped her mind, putting her in a hypnotic state, one full of darkness. In some futile hope that I could block the darkness, I unfolded my umbrella and held it over her as she continued to stare at me with unsure and uncertain, hollow eyes.

The rain stopped pelting her, and the umbrella offered some reprieve finally, but she seemed to prefer the rain hitting her skin since her brows knitted together. Not exactly the reaction I'd been expecting. Maybe she liked feeling *something*. Or maybe she didn't have an umbrella over her head for the same reasons as me–she thought she deserved to be standing out in the rain, open to whatever punishment it had to offer.

With a sudden gush, words escaped her mouth as if she hadn't intended to speak either. "I'm not with your group. Sorry to waste your time. Thank you, though." She began to turn back toward the cliffs, stepping even closer to the stony edge.

And to my astonishment, I found myself grabbing her arm again. *Personal space, Darby. Remember, that thing you never have to worry about invading.* I found myself saying, "Well, all the tour companies know each other. The owner wouldn't be happy if I didn't help another tour's guest. I'll find you a ride to whatever village you're staying in when we get back. I'd be happy to let you finish your tour with us." I looked around. "It's late in the day. I don't think you're going to be seeing many more tours coming through, and probably not one from the area where you're staying." I let my hand fall again, but much more slowly than it had found its way there.

"No, I'm not with any group. *Sorry.*" This time she turned with a definite movement to signal the end of our conversation.

As I continued to let the umbrella hover above her, I decided with the same precision and determination that it was indeed *not* over.

"Well, I wouldn't forgive myself if I left a gorgeous woman stranded alone in the pouring rain. I'd be a *gobdaw* for sure." And the last thing I wanted to be in front of her was an idiot. Then I took a very large pause before speaking again. "Are you sure you aren't part of one of the tours?" I asked, cocking my head, trying to put my best beguiling Irish charm on it.

She slowly turned, like she was moving heavily through water. She had to be freezing, I couldn't help but think. Who knew how long she'd been standing out here in the pouring rain.

"Maybe." Indecision seemed to mark every crevice of her beautiful face as happiness started to spread over mine. Something that those deep, darkened places within me weren't accustomed to feeling anymore.

I dared to venture, "Well, I'd feel very lucky if that was the case. And trust me, I don't have much luck. That's just an Irish myth. I think you should definitely join our group." Her eyes started to gain a little more light in them, so I boldly continued. "Well, meet your new tour guide. Lucky for me, they left you behind. I'm Darby, not to be confused with Darcy."

A smile crossed her face–a genuine one. As it spread, there was a heat that simultaneously grew in me at the same rate, feeding off her reactions at the same exponential speed.

"Does that need clarifying?" She laughed, and it was a sweet, sultry sound that made my eyebrows raise.

"Yes, it does. Do you know how close we are to the land of Austen? Doesn't matter how many times I say it on the tour–the tourists are pretty insistent. One customer even complained to my boss, said that I was making fun of them and that Darby wasn't a 'real' name. I finally just stopped correcting them. Apparently, an Irish Darcy is even rarer than catching a lucky leprechaun."

"Ok, I believe you, *Darby*," she said, pronouncing my name slowly and accurately, finishing with a bite of her lower lip. *A nervous habit or something else?* She had a little flourish of laughter in her tone as well. For a woman that had looked so lifeless a few moments ago, she sure had a wonderful palette of personality. I was already massively intrigued and completely captivated.

I stood awkwardly, feeling like a fool, holding the umbrella as I waited impatiently for something more from her. At last, she offered, "I'm Eyre." There must have been a confused look on my face because she quickly added, "With an 'E.'"

"Oh." A laugh escaped me. Then it dawned on me as I said, "Seems like someone is playing a cruel joke on us. Some wicked literary forces are at work. Have you made the literary forces mad lately, Eyre?"

Now there was a smile creeping on her face that I loved to see. She also seemed to have warmed up a bit after the respite from the pelting rain.

"Well, Darby isn't Darcy, so I don't think that's the case. Doesn't seem like we have anything to worry about. If I were named Elizabeth, you should probably just walk away."

Another hesitant soft, lyrical laugh escaped her. And my lip couldn't help but quirk upward as I listened to the sound of her melodious laughter. *How were those eyes even more beautiful up close?* And the very last thing I wanted to do was walk away. I hadn't felt this way in a very long time. I felt a little spark of life—of fight—flame inside myself.

"The whole village calls me Darcy, on occasion, just to *slag me*—tease me," I said, feeling the need to explain. "Can't really stop them. Tourists are always getting my name confused so it's just stuck. They must really think it's funny. Plus, I'm like the least romantic person ever. I'm the antithesis of Darcy. So they think that's hilarious. That 'b' really makes all the difference."

"I don't know, maybe they just haven't gotten to know you well enough yet," she replied.

THREE
Eyre

He kept eyeing me like I was going to change my mind and head straight off the cliff like a character from a *Looney Tunes* cartoon or whatever the equivalent was here. But he seemed to be watching me because he cared—not out of some duty, pity, or morbid curiosity. More than that, it seemed like he genuinely wanted me to be a part of this very eclectic group of people. Well, actually, a group of women. Okay, really just older ladies who were all staring at him and hanging onto his every flawlessly accented word. I guess they sure knew a fine Irish specimen when they saw it. And they weren't just hanging onto his words either, they were physically hanging on to him as well. It was like he was an attractive adult Irish jungle gym.

After we'd made our way slowly back to rejoin the tour, in between bouts of silence and small talk, I'd gotten to witness for myself how "hands on" his tour really could be. This was definitely a tactile group of ladies. I wanted to laugh out loud every time they touched the ridiculous leprechaun on his shirt or the absurd hat on his head (that trick was just for the ones that hadn't shrunk yet and could still reach it). It was seriously like a *Golden Girls* convention had come to town and in true Sophia Petrillo style, these women weren't holding back. As if they were channeling Betty White, none of them had forgotten their be-dazzlers or their tracksuits. I was starting to get a little bit of amusement from my Ireland trip, especially from their comical antics. I could even feel a hint of a smile trying to form on my face.

I was beginning to wonder how all these older women had ended up on Darby's tour, but then again, maybe the tour company was just insanely smart. If I had a tour company, I'd definitely put all the older ladies with Darby. Although, I was beginning to think that was a bit of a gamble. He didn't seem like he had a very long fuse for this sort of thing. I mean, I think the apparel alone was perhaps pushing things a little bit too far. He appeared to be somewhat cynical and a little sarcastic from just the few sentiments we'd exchanged. I thought the tour company was very brave but also a little stupid to be rolling the dice with a tour group stacked with this many older ladies. He looked like the overwhelmed dad who had one too many kids tugging on his arm. An inappropriate giggle did actually escape me at that point. As hard as I'd tried, I couldn't contain it.

Darby was already looking at me, but now his eyes widened. He had been looking at me with sheer humor–being a really good sport–but I think the giggle may have sent him over the edge.

"Alright, ladies," he said. "That was the last question for the day."

"Aww." A unison of sorrowful protests broke out and my heart fell a little, seeing the disappointed looks on their faces.

"Darcy, it feels like we just got here. Time moves so quickly with you. Don't you know how precious time is for an old woman that doesn't have that much left?" said one of the youngest looking ones in the bunch.

His eyebrows rocketed upward as he cast them in my direction. The giggle fit only grew and was now becoming pretty uncontrollable.

The group of women shot me angry looks as my uncontrollable laughter cut through the silence. It was like a rabid pack of seagulls all turning their heads at once, zeroing in on their target. I had to bite my lip so hard I thought I was going to draw blood. But it didn't help. My muffled laughter continued in a weird heaving sound. It was so much worse. I guess the stress that had built up inside of me had now decided to expel itself as inappropriate laughter and it wasn't helping the situation.

The one eyebrow he pointed at me and his lopsided upward curved lip had a sexy aura to it. He was mostly intrigued and amused. Challenging me to make my next move and tangle with his flock.

"I just joined the tour so I missed everything. I didn't get to hear anything about this beautiful place." I replaced the laughter with a pathetic pout, but it did little to hide my amusement.

Darby's face fell into a cold, stony stare. A mouth click told me I was in for it, and gone was that glorious, sexy expression. Although this fierce stare was still pretty attractive. Now all the *gulls' heads* swiveled back towards him with big grins plastered on their faces.

THE IRISH FALL

He cleared his throat. "Well, we wouldn't want you to miss out on anything, now would we?" The staring match between us hadn't broken, and I didn't think a winner was going to be able to be declared.

"No," a high-pitched chorus chimed in.

He called out to the bus driver, who was not dressed in the company uniform. Probably a good call. He was more of a "rough and tough" kind of man. I would probably fear for my safety if I handed him a shirt with a caricature of a leprechaun on it. The all-black look suited him much better.

"Oye, Shamus. Will you take the ladies back to the tour office? Please take good care of them. They're all precious treasures. I have some extremely important guide business that popped up here. It's pretty urgent."

Shamus just nodded and grunted his response.

The death glares came at me like dominoes and when the final one fell, I wanted to find a hole to bury myself in.

I pretended like I didn't realize what was happening and proceeded with the ladies back to the large industrial white and green striped shamrock bus that looked way too large and out of place in the bucolic Irish countryside.

Darby took a few very long strides toward me and grabbed my arm. "Oh no, ya don't."

I looked up at him with an alarmed hesitancy. "I thought the whole point of me joining the tour was to be able to get a ride back to a village. How am I supposed to do that if the bus is leaving us?" I asked with incredulity.

"I have a cell phone. You brought this upon yourself." He leaned down and whispered. "Just wave at the ladies nicely. They can—and *do*—bite."

I watched as the women reluctantly loaded onto the bus

and drove away. Their crestfallen faces looked at Darby for as long as possible while they sailed past.

"That wasn't cute, ya know." He turned to look at me as soon as they were out of sight. "Do you really want a tour of this place? Because from what I saw, it seemed you'd had enough of it. I've got something much better in mind."

"Better than the Cliffs of Moher?" I looked at him skeptically.

"Yeah, walk with me. Just be happy it stopped *lashing*." He looked up at the sky, and it was only then I realized the rain had stopped. "Come on then, better get a move on if we're gonna get back to the village before dark."

FOUR

Eyre

"You can't be serious. I haven't seen any towns close to here. Why did you send the bus away?" I asked in irritation.

"First lesson in Ireland." He looked at me pointedly. "Never anger an Irishman. We do have tempers. That's not a rumor like the leprechauns. Second lesson in Ireland: there's not anywhere bad for walking in this countryside, especially if it gets you away from a busload of tourists."

"Wow, you really do hate your job, don't you?" I asked as he removed his hat and tossed it over a crumbling stone wall on the side of the road. "That's littering, you know."

"No, it's not. Some child will think it's a pot of gold. I'm making their day," he said flippantly.

"Isn't that your uniform?"

"Well, unfortunately, I happened to have lost it rescuing a damsel in distress," he mused.

"Yes, somehow I don't think anyone is going to believe that," I said, looking at him skeptically.

"Watch it, or I'll take more of it off, and then they won't let us into *any* of the pubs," he said with mock seriousness.

"As long as you don't remove the shirt. We wouldn't want you to lose your glorious leprechaun physique. *However will* you attract the ladies?" My sarcastic tone bit more than usual. "You'll have to rely on wit and charm alone. And that just won't do."

A silence stretched on before us like an endless desert. Not a single hint of water in sight. Finally, he cleared his throat. "Ahem. Ya gonna tell me where you're staying, or are we just gonna walk in silence like a pair of *dopes*?"

"I don't have a place," I said quietly. Darby looked over his well-defined shoulder out to the cliffs. At least the rain had stopped before he'd given Shamus his marching orders. At least, I hoped he had known the bad weather was going to continue to hold off when he sent the bus away. As he looked out upon the cliffs, they seemed just as mysterious and brooding as he did. The mist that was rising up to meet them was wispy and ethereal in an enigmatic way.

Darby began to sort through his thoughts. "Ok, so let me get this straight. You came all the way here without a place to stay—without any luggage, I presume—and what, just to look at the cliffs, and leave?"

I was most certainly not telling him why I had gotten on an airplane . . . or what had led me to those cliffs. Truthfully, I'd chosen the first flight out of Nashville that looked appealing to me. I felt like John Wayne in *The Quiet Man* who fled to Ireland to forget his past in America. At least I'd had a lot of time on the plane to Google tourist sights. And as soon as I got here, the cliffs spoke to me. They had beckoned me closer and closer to their edge. Absolutely none of these events were going to be shared with this sarcastic, cynical Irishman–certainly not the one who was now having me *walk* home. When there wasn't even a home to walk to.

"I wanted to be spontaneous," I managed.

"You don't look like the spontaneous type. You look more like the type A perfectionist who plans every moment with a Google calendar and a backup paper planner."

"You know this *how?*" I asked, offended.

"Oye, come on. I give tours for a living. I can spot types."

"Well that certainly diminishes a person, don't you think? Putting people into types and categories, *Mr. Leprechaun*," I bantered back.

Fire sparked in those handsome, mossy green eyes as he retorted back to me, "You're about to get a really good view of the countryside as you walk through it *alone*. Now, where do you want to go?" His voice had started to rise, but there was still an edge of compassion in it. He hadn't completely given up on me and he still seemed intrigued by my situation.

I couldn't keep the exhaustion out of my tone. "Just take me somewhere, *please*. The closest place where you think I can find a decent room. This trip was such a mistake. I shouldn't have taken the first flight that looked good to me."

He looked at me with continued amusement. "Well, that's a start."

"What?" I said in disbelief.

"To you actually saying something that's real and honest ... From here, the walk is about an hour and twenty minutes to Doolin. That's where I'm from, and I'll help you find a place to stay. Liscannor is the closest village, but I can keep an eye on you at Doolin and you'll have a better chance at finding lodging. But it's gonna cost ya. Toll is at least some friendly conversation for the rest of the way." He abruptly started walking down the road.

My mouth hung open like a rusty gate that wouldn't latch.

"Ya coming?" he called as he continued down the winding road. I scurried up to him so as not to be left behind by my most attractive but infuriating guide.

FIVE

Eyre

"Are you actually capable of friendly conversation?" I asked, as I hurried up to him. Poking the grumpy leprechaun may not have been my smartest idea yet, but I couldn't help it. There was just something about him. He was an enigma that I was hoping to unwrap, and it seemed the more I poked him, the better chance I had of unraveling that handsome wrapping. I don't know if it was his surly, sarcastic attitude mixed with my feeling that there might be a soft heart hidden away in him, or if it was something else entirely, but I was finding myself drawn to him like a moth to a bonfire. And I'd seen way too many of them "dive bomb" right into the flames. It was a glorious exit out of this world and made quite the impression, but it wasn't really how I wanted to go. A part of me felt like getting involved with him would be dangerous, not that I thought he'd ever open up to me enough to get to that point. I wasn't going to be able to crack through his bad boy's apathetic exterior, and I was already too tired to try. *So why not have some fun?*

Darby heaved a sigh of exasperation. "Really? Didn't I just get done telling ya, like a minute ago, that you were gonna be walking home alone? Do you ever listen? I think I'm being pretty generous, taking a complete stranger to my hometown."

"Well, generous would have been kindly escorting me onto the warm bus with the sweet old ladies," I scoffed.

"Ha, you need a new definition of sweet," he said with an eye roll.

I glanced over my shoulder at the rolling hills of the countryside that created a sea of pastoral beauty. I wanted to swim in the essence they created of a simpler life. I could get lost in their shadowy blanket of simplicity. One where mother nature created the timetables, instead of our artificial fast-paced, media-focused society. It was like my own version of *Leap Year* sprawled out before me. As I absorbed the lush greens and idyllic nature unfolding before my eyes, I instinctively knew Ireland would be good for a wounded soul like mine in ways no other place could be.

I let the calm soak through me before I turned to glance back at Darby. "Those ladies didn't seem too bad to me; that is, until their near geriatric revolt when I was about to become their new Marie Antoinette."

That finally received a laugh. *Good.* A chink in that cynical coating. I could handle that. I liked a man that laughed at my jokes. I hadn't had one that laughed at mine in a while. The one I left behind hadn't laughed at mine in quite some time. And this Irishman's laugh was glorious. I promise it was like the sun appeared upon hearing the first notes of his laughter, as if I could actually see the sun's rays shining through the dreary weather. The overcast skies and remnants of rain were brightening in its wake. The depth of color made my bones warm. Their deep aching was actually ceasing for the first time in what seemed like forever.

I continued speaking as I looked at the puzzle beside me. "So you don't like your job, I take it? Not a fan of all the attention? Here I had you pegged as meeting your wife on one of these tours and then becoming happily *ever after* married. You do seem to do so well with a *certain* age group of ladies. You mean you don't knit all weekend long to provide clothing for the whole entire village? And then go out together with your wife, clad in your matching hand-knit sweaters, to distribute your knitted apparel among the people?" I was joking, but secretly I would have loved to have that kind of bond in my life.

"Ahmm." He cleared his throat again as if I had managed to physically irritate it. A little twitch accompanied the sound, something that I hadn't noticed earlier but now I thoroughly enjoyed. *Oh, this was delicious.* Yes, I was going to quite enjoy myself. We were getting along in Ireland about as well as that bantering couple in *Laws of Attraction*. As long as I didn't come back accidentally married like them . . . Darby penetrated my thoughts. "No, I know you'll find this *extremely* hard to believe, but I'm single. And I don't like dating."

"What?" I said in mocked surprise. "You're not a romantic?" I stopped in my tracks, feigning total disbelief.

He reached out and literally grabbed my arm, yanking me along. "I'm beginning to think I should have left you at those cliffs." But there was a smile on his lips that told me otherwise. He continued, "Yeah, no . . . ok, no surprise, I'm not a romantic. But within two minutes of meeting me, you *don't* have me all figured out."

I let out peals of laughter that kinda sounded devious but I was actually thoroughly amused. "Oh, ho ho, but I think I do. Let me see . . . You can stop me any time I go *too* far off the mark." He looked at me with raised eyebrows. I took his expression as a challenge to proceed. "Let's see . . . You're completely cynical. Not only about love but pretty much in regard to your whole worldview. You build on that cynicism and turn it into sarcasm, so you have a nice little protective shell. And that coating doesn't allow any romance in your life, which you like–actually prefer. But I'm guessing that only makes you more attractive to the ladies, even though you say you don't have a romantic bone in your body."

He looked at me as if he couldn't believe I was speaking to him in this way. Part of me couldn't believe it either. Never in my life had I been so bold, so brutally honest, with a stranger. He snorted out a sound that I don't think I'd ever heard before, his tall frame gravitating closer toward me. I paused for effect. "That about covers it, except–"

"Except?" There was a glimmer of hope in his eyes. Yes, it definitely looked like hope.

"Except there's so much more to you. Maybe you should consider actually letting someone–at least *one* person see. You've proven that today. And I'm not buying any of the rest of the stuff I just said about you because . . . well . . . I think it's *all* a show."

Darby looked at me sternly. "Just because I was intrigued by you doesn't mean there's more to me."

I looked at him. His eyes echoed the colors of the enchanting pastureland. Their green hues were almost too beautiful to be real. And looking into those greens, I could tell he didn't believe what he had just said for a minute. In fact, I don't think he believed in the persona he projected at all.

"You wouldn't let those older women have so much fun at your expense if you didn't have such a good heart. You can't hide something like that, hard as you may try. Your heart has no choice but to show itself–expose itself. You can try running, disguising, distracting, or even burying it, but that will never work," I said with precision.

"I think it's just part of my job," he said curtly. Then with a stare that bore deeply into me, to a place that I thought had died, he said, "My turn." His eyebrows raised wickedly.

"What?" I questioned, a little afraid to ask.

"What, you just thought you could say whatever and an Irishman wasn't going to have a rebuttal? I don't know how they do it over where you're from, but men and women are equal here. *My turn.*"

I heaved a gasp of disbelief, but I was secretly excited by his refreshing response. "Please, *equalize me.*" I waved my hand out before me in a "be my guest" gesture.

"Oh, I thought you'd never ask." The look from him woke up feelings inside of me that I thought had vanished. A feeling of being desired, something that had been lost some time ago and I'd come to accept was my fate to live without. A feeling that I believed I was no longer going to possess or be capable of inspiring. Sparks shot off inside me as these feelings were resurrected. And my mouth ran dry as I wasn't sure what to do with these unexpected gifts. Once you resign yourself to the fact that you will be without something and make your peace with that fact, it's kind of difficult when it's just placed at your feet so unexpectedly.

I was awakened from the bubble of my thoughts with his words. "I didn't think you'd be so eager. I misjudged you." His lips quirked upward in the most adorable way. More stone was being chiseled away from his exterior. I could hear the imaginary rubble hitting the ground around my feet. "Well, you didn't deny the perfectionist personality–never letting your britches fly free–so I'm gonna gloss over that bit."

"How kind," I scoffed.

"But the perfectionist personality runs deeper than that. You have to be in control of everything, even our conversation. I'm guessing those two things have kept you pretty single, as well. So why in the world would you jump on a plane without a plan? You have a lot of heart. I can see that already, but maybe too much. I think you feel everything and you can't rein it in. That's a trait that spells disaster when it comes to love. Yet, you're not irrational, so I don't believe you got on that plane because of a man. It wasn't a breakup. No, it had to be something else . . . something that destroyed all the structure in your life and took every last ounce of control away from you." He looked at me to assess the impact of his words–to scale the damage done–in order to help him with his evaluation of me.

"Correct. *All correct.*" I gulped back my emotions. I did feel it all and my heart was never going to learn to contain itself.

"That's it? You're not going to tell me what happened?"

"Would *you*?" I asked incredulously.

"Probably not." He smiled, relenting.

SIX
Eyre

After a journey that involved way more walking than I thought possible, I finally started to make out some other colors in the sea of Irish greenery. As we strolled down the hill, there were suddenly bright splashes of color that invaded my field of vision and seemed to clash with the natural hues of the Irish landscape. Even though the colors of the village shops presented quite a jarring contrast to the natural greenery of the Irish countryside, their happy shades were a welcome sight to my weary eyes. It was as if I could hear Irish fiddles welcoming me, a rendition of *Danny Boy* playing in my mind. The village was a beacon, signifying that rest was near. This safe haven came just in time since my bones were aching like never before, and that was truly saying something. The combination of the plane ride, my emotional visit to this country, and now the very long walk with an infuriating stranger left my body exhausted and screaming. My muscles and joints howled at me, and the words they shouted were not family-friendly.

As we neared the village, the outline of cottages with thatched roofs came more clearly into view. My new craving for the Irish world urged me to focus my attention on this spot so as to forever ingrain it in my memory. Doolin was reminiscent of a Wes Anderson film. That vibrant *Grand Budapest Hotel* pink color caught my eye immediately as we started to walk toward a row of colorful shops. This must be their main street. Each building displayed a new vivid color that my eyes hungered to see.

I looked at Darby, expecting him to say something.

"What?" he said, looking at me. "I got you this far. You seriously need me to hold your hand the rest of the way?"

I looked at him with my mouth slightly open, dropping even further in his silence.

His next comment unnerved me even more. "Really, how were you going to make it in a foreign country?" My eyes widened in response, and then he laughed. "Alright, alright. I wasn't ever gonna just leave you. Calm down. Hold onto your knickers."

He took my hand for the first time, and his touch caught me completely by surprise, especially after the words he had just uttered. A warmth melted over me. Darby used his touch to direct me down the road toward the stone bridge. And while his hand was calloused and rough, his touch was surprisingly gentle and warm. Not what I had expected, but it seemed to echo his personality. My vision wandered over the peaceful stream flowing under the bridge that led to a vast expanse of open water in the distance. It was absolutely glorious. I couldn't decide what to explore with my eyes first. Darby seemed to notice the change in my mood. He tightened his hold on my hand in appreciation of my response.

THE IRISH FALL

"This is Doolin, my hometown," he said with a slight gleam of pride. "I need to stop by the tour shop first. The owner will certainly know better than I about a place for you to stay." He continued to look straight ahead, but there was a sign of compassion on his face that was undeniable. *Chink.* The sound resonated in my mind.

"Thank you," I said, more quietly than I'd meant to say. His face automatically turned toward mine and his smile found me. Our feet continued to strike the pavement as we passed shops filled with Irish charm and whimsical mementos. I scanned their windows with excitement, the reality of yesterday's decisions finally catching up to me. My right shoulder ached and complained with each step I took. The oversized purse I used to carry essentials dug into my shoulder with a wicked bite.

"Almost there," Darby said as if he could sense my growing discomfort. I was beginning to wonder if he'd noticed my waning energy on our walk. I was hoping he hadn't noticed my struggle to keep moving. Although, I'm not sure how he could have missed it. He couldn't be that unobservant. Truthfully, I was already in pain when we started our journey. Now, I was in need of a bed. *Urgently.* I was praying there was one available in this village.

We stopped in front of a lime green shop. It matched the color of Darby's t-shirt. Every nuance of the village seemed to scream whimsy, from the cottage-shaped shops and curly fonts on the hanging signs to the hobbit-like thatched roofs. Doolin was definitely filled with plenty of character and joy. Something I desperately needed. I couldn't have landed in a better spot if I'd been trying. Darby, however, scoffed at the traditional green leprechaun color and appeared to be allergic to anything promoting leprechauns and their legends. Perhaps, he was even allergic to himself.

Darby turned to me with a stoic countenance. "Ok, I think this is *never* gonna happen . . . *But,* will you please let me do the talking? This is my boss that I'll be talking to."

"Of course, Darby. Whatever would give you the impression—" I began sweetly.

He held up a hand in front of my mouth. "Ok, save it. Don't waste it on me. I'm sure it's a very precious and limited reserve." I let out a deep belly laugh just for him. This caught his attention and a smile crept across his face that he couldn't hide, letting me know he thoroughly enjoyed it.

"*Right*, let's just go in," he said as he ushered me inside. The wind chimes sang out their pure, melodious tones as we entered the shop. "Makenna? Mak?" he called out. "I guess he must be in the back," he said to me as he took me by the arm and led me further into the shop, talking to me in softer tones. He was close to my face as he spoke. His breath was just as soft and soothing as the Irish breeze on the cliffs today. I was getting lost in his scent when a figure popped up from behind the counter. We both jumped and I grabbed onto Darby, who, I'm sure in a lapse of judgment, chivalrously wrapped his arms around me.

"Mak, you're going to give me a heart attack. Don't be a *dosser* like that!" I looked at Darby a little unsure and confused as to what that could mean, but based on his tone, I could tell it wasn't a compliment. Also, I was a little bewildered that his arms were still around me, hugging me tightly around my back and waist.

The older gentleman wiggled his extremely bushy eyebrows. He looked like an adorable older elf, only slightly taller. His white hair was wiry and unkempt. He was dressed in red flannel and suspenders, with a no-nonsense country flare about him. He reminded me of the older man from the classic film, *The Luck of the Irish*. "Darce, I see you're still out wooing the ladies. At least now I know what you've been doing today. Although, I must say, she's about fifty years younger than the ones you were supposed to be wooing. Unless she's a granddaughter of one of 'em, I'm not impressed."

Darby started to open his mouth to speak, but he didn't get one syllable out before the older man continued his lecture. "Now, Darce, do you know what my evening was like?" he asked in a worn-out tone.

"I–" Darby began, but Mak held up his hand.

"Let me stop you right there, you *gobdaw*. While you were *lobbing the gob*, I was back here with a bus full of fiery, unhappy senior citizens wanting to know why the tour with their *favorite* Mr. Darcy was cut short. They were asking not only for a full refund but also for a complimentary replacement tour. A special, *extended* tour to make up for the disappointment of their day."

Darby let out a groan that rolled through his entire body and onto me. "Mak–"

"No, no indeed, you will give those ladies a new and extended tour. And you're gonna be so "Darcesque" that it will hurt *just* a little bit. Look hard and find that one romantic bone hiding in your body. You're sure gonna need it."

"Mak, will you *please* let me explain?"

"Why? You two are so close to each other, I can practically envision you *shifting* right before my eyes. At least have the decency to leave the lass outside, so your excuse is more believable. I was pretty irate, but now I'm happy to see that you might actually be capable of romance. So I'm gonna take it easy on you and let you off with just the extended tour. But only on the condition that you first introduce me to this mythical creature who unearthed a romantic soul hiding under that rough exterior."

"Mak!" Darby stepped away from me so abruptly that I stumbled out of his warm arms. He looked down with apologetic eyes and steadied me. Snickers emanated from the older gentleman as Darby's arms quickly shot out to anchor me. He rolled his eyes back to Makenna. "This is Eyre–"

"As in . . . Well, isn't this just the most fated romance–" Mak's amusement had escalated to new heights.

"Mak!" Darby was steaming. The older man was beyond snickering and had to support himself on the counter. Percussive sounds echoed throughout the shop as he continued to slap the counter. I stood in shock and complete amusement. I already loved this man and his antics.

Then suddenly, the hand slapping stopped with only the echoes to keep us company. "What happened to your hat? You know we have a strict uniform policy here," Mak said as soon as his eyes caught sight of Darby's bare head. This proclamation cut through all his laughter.

"27.50 Euros. I know. I'll pay it again," Darby said exasperatedly. *Again? How many times did this happen?*

"The shirt looks a little *kip* too, Darce. You know these women aren't paying to see a second rate, sloppy Darcy. I pride myself . . ."

"Mak, whatever. Will you just listen?" Darby was about to blow that short fuse again. The older man just rolled his eyes but managed to silence himself. "Eyre just arrived here without a place to stay—"

Mak exclaimed, "*What* is she doing in Ireland without a place to stay? You can't come in the busy season without a place to stay!" I could see the old man was getting very worked up.

"Ok, Mak, you're gonna have to let me speak more than a few words or this is not gonna work. Do you want to make it to the pub tonight or not?" Mak sat with a thump on a wooden stool behind the counter in utter defeat. His silence was clearly his reply. When Darby said nothing, Mak looked at him like he was an idiot for not speaking. "Right, so Eyre needs a place to stay. She came to Ireland spontaneously—"

"Spontaneously?!" Mak burst out, obviously not able to help himself as he jumped off the stool.

"So, I was hoping you knew of a place where she might be able to stay," Darby finally finished. After several long minutes of a stare-down between the two, Mak finally spoke. Darby's eyes had willed him to do so. Maybe there was a grandson-like plea in them and Mak took some mercy.

Mak responded, "It's going to be *murder* to find a place to stay. There's not a single place that's gonna be vacant. Our little village has very few spots available, and the surrounding villages are just about the same. You could travel to a bigger city like Dublin, but it will take a bit of time to get there. This is the peak tourist season. What would you like to visit while you're here?"

I didn't know how to respond, so I looked at Darby with a pleading expression that asked him to be gracious and kind.

"Mak, she's here to be . . . spontaneous. That's the whole concept. It's all new to her, and unplanned, so I think that means she doesn't know." Well, it would have to be good enough. Beggars couldn't be choosers. I sure wasn't going to explain to Mak why I was here, either.

I looked down at the floor with nervous embarrassment, and when I looked back up, there was a softness in Mak that I didn't think he would be capable of possessing. He cleared his throat. "Sweetheart, Ireland is good for the soul. You need to see as much of it as you can. You probably don't want to waste time traveling at this time of night, and I can also see that you're tired." *Was it that obvious?* The pain was probably pretty apparent, too. Mak's voice cut through the white noise of my mind. "You're never going to find a place to stay at this time of night, and we do have an extra room. Why don't you stay with us? We live just up the hill. It's country living, but you're welcome to join us. And it'll be nice to have a woman around. We've forgotten what one looks like." He gave a small laugh.

We? Did Darby live with this man? Was this his grandfather? I looked at Darby with confusion, hoping he'd enlighten me.

Darby spoke up right away. "Wow, you sure took it easier on her for disrupting the tour than you did on me." He looked at Mak with a stern gaze. One that said he should have run this little proposition by him first. "I'm out there rescuing damsels in distress, and then I get geriatric tour guide double duty. Hardly seems fair."

"Well, when you look like that," he said, pointing at me, "then we'll talk."

"I wouldn't want to impose," I said, speaking for the first time. Their eyes both flashed over to me at hearing the sound of my voice. "You're so very kind, but I'll take a taxi to the nearest place you think will have accommodations. While I appreciate your offer, it's too much to ask of you. Thank you, though."

Mak slowly looked from Darby to me and then back to Darby. His eyes landed on him, assessing the situation. His eyebrows slowly raised with mischief. "No, I insist. You shouldn't deny an old man his wish."

SEVEN
Darby

The last thing I needed was this woman staying in the same house as me. *What did Mak think he was doing?* I recognized that impish look in his eyes. It was pure Irish mischief. Passed on for generations and honed for centuries. And Mak embodied it better than anyone. The curved smile that twitched at his lips so knowingly was telling me that he thought there was most definitely something going on between the two of us. Maybe he didn't think we were out *lobbing the gob* all day, but he sure did think there was a spark. Mak, for all his good humor and his jests, was a bit of a matchmaker. One wouldn't think it by looking at him, though. He certainly seemed like the last person in the world that would be hung up on romance. I'd even seen him fall asleep with a romance novel on his lap from time to time.

I, on the other hand, didn't get the appeal of romance, whether in books or real life. *At all.* And that's why it was best not to get this woman's hopes up. I wasn't good at romance. Period. And I didn't deserve to be. To my chagrin, the older ladies on the tour weren't the only women interested in me. Apparently not being interested in romance made you really appealing to women–or at least that's what I'd been told. Like cynicism and a jaded heart emitted some high frequency that only they could hear. A "fix me, bad boy" siren call of sorts. That was certainly not my intention. I really just wanted to be left alone. And the few women that did get past my cynical exterior–well, they were really disappointed when they weren't able to actually get to know me, and then they were left without a call or a follow-up date. Unfortunately, my predictions were always accurate, so I was left just as jaded and uninterested. Also, ironically, even more lonely.

And I had no intention of disappointing this woman because she was different from the others. I was actually interested in this one. More than just interested, I felt some sort of connection to her. But just because I was broken didn't mean that she needed to be, too. She didn't need to get involved with someone like me and get damaged in my wake. Everyone seemed to get hurt by my uncontrollable vortex of misguided instincts. I already knew I didn't deserve a shot with her. The fact that my cynical heart was interested told me that much. And I needed to stop showing interest in her because she was going to get the wrong idea and end up hurt. Now Mak had just made that ten times harder to do. Because for the first time in my life, I didn't know how to turn my feelings off, and I didn't want to.

Eyre began to speak again. "Well, when you put it like that . . ." Her words halted the thoughts in my brain. I was relieved to have a break from them. I was also glad to have an excuse to look at her again. My hands were still firmly connected to her arms, I didn't care what Mak thought, I enjoyed them being there. And I was leaving them there for as long as was acceptable. She seemed to think for a while and then began again, "I am exhausted. My body is pretty—" She stopped. "Maybe just for a night. Thank you so much. Just until I can make accommodations. I promise I usually do plan. I'm normally *such* a planner. Believe me, people actually try to stop me from planning because they get so annoyed by it." Then she started laughing.

Mak responded, "It's no trouble at all. Really, I insist. And if you enjoy spending the night here, then you should just stay with us the whole time you're here. No use wasting your precious vacation time moving around." Mak looked at me with weighted meaning in his eyes. As if he was doing me the biggest favor in the world. "And Darby here is an excellent tour guide. He can show you around. Actually, as his boss, I insist on it." Then he gave me such a stern look that I knew it wasn't up for debate.

I wanted to say something more, but Mak wasn't only my boss, he was also like a grandfather to me, so I kept my mouth shut. Our grandfather-grandson type of relationship had always made us close. His grandson had been a few years younger than me, and we'd been good friends when we were *young fellas* growing up together. Mak had always been like a grandfather to me. Even closer than my biological grandparents. And when they passed away, Mak was there for everything they couldn't be.

When Mak spoke again to Eyre, he used a gentler tone. "The house is pretty cozy. It's a farmhouse, but there's a few extra rooms. Our guest room is upstairs, right beside Darce's room. And there's a bathroom the two of you can share." He grinned at me. "Darce will play nice, I promise, or else he'll have to answer to me." Then he looked at Eyre seriously. "You don't know us, but I promise that you'll be safe staying with us. Darby really is a good guy, just a bit hopeless with women, but always respectful. You can ask anyone at the pub or anyone in town if you like. And if you don't feel comfortable staying with us, then I am happy to figure out some arrangements for you in Dublin. I think you'll have much more success there."

Eyre just looked at Mak. She had become wide-eyed at the mention of my room, as if the idea of being so close to me had not crossed her mind and was more than a little daunting. And I was completely unprepared for this change of events as well. I looked at her. Really taking her all in. Her tall, willowy frame seemed to have movement even while standing still. Her curves looked as if they should always be in motion, adding a graceful elegance about her that intimated me. A beauty that made me want to say things to her that I knew I shouldn't. Made me think of things that cynical Darby would most definitely ridicule and mock. There was this quiet strength about her that intrigued me. I didn't know how long she was going to be staying, but I already knew I didn't want her to leave. And these were thoughts I shouldn't be having.

I looked at my hands still placed on her arms. Our points of contact blended together seamlessly. My eyesight scanned down to her small bag. There was no way clothing was in there. *What was she even going to sleep in? What was she planning to do for the week?* Thoughts of lending her one of my oversized t-shirts to sleep in raced through my mind.

Then images of her in said tee, standing in the doorway of our little farmhouse, made my face turn crimson. I did not blush. This was *not* a Darby thing to do. But the stubborn, vivid images would not leave my brain. Her long legs were seared inside it now, making the heat on my face grow. And fanning them was Mak's laughter.

"Oh, Eyre, this is going to be the best week of my life. I've never seen Darce blush before. Those must be some pretty good thoughts ye be having. Care to tell us about 'em?" Mak said with a sing-song, teasing tone.

I gave him a death glare–one that told him to mind his own business–and then finally let my hands drop from Eyre, which simply made it more obvious that the thoughts were most definitely about her. She looked up at me with those big innocent eyes. *Who knew hazel was going to be my undoing?*

Mak chuckled. "Right, well, while you collect yourself, Darce, I'm going to get everything ready and closed up for the night. We can take Eyre down to the pub and let her meet Sinead before we head home. That is, if Eyre isn't too tired. We can make it quick and get a bite to eat. Afterward, we can get her all settled in. I'm sure you'll be the *perfect* host," he said in such a jesting tone that it made me frown at him from the corner of my eyes. Mak turned to Eyre. "How do you feel, Eyre? Are you up for it? Sinead is an old friend from childhood who owns the pub. She'll make sure you get something good to eat. But only if you're not too tired," he said with concern.

"That sounds wonderful, thank you," Eyre said genuinely, which was met with a large smile from Mak.

As soon as he'd scurried into the back, she looked at me

curiously, "'lobbing the gob?' 'shifting?' What did your boss think we were out doing, Darby?"

My eyebrows raised quickly, not really sure I wanted to explain those Irish terms to her. "Uh . . . those would be kissing terms, Eyre." My face flamed enough for the both of us and it really annoyed me that I couldn't turn it off with this woman—not that this had ever been a problem before. But for once she looked way more embarrassed than I did. I guess it was a good time to discuss the other uncomfortable subject. "Eyre, I'm sorry about all this. You don't have to stay after tonight if you'd rather not. I'll help you find another place to stay. It can't be all that difficult. He's probably just making it sound worse than it really is."

I looked at her, hoping by some miracle she would say something to make me feel better about this situation. I already felt like a royal *dope* as I continued to babble. My eyes met hers, willing her to take the lead and help me out here. I wasn't used to feeling this way. The upside to cynicism was that you came off cool and collected in your apathy. I think I preferred that to looking like a blathering fool, while crimson gave away my attraction to a complete stranger.

Finally, she threw me a bone and spoke. "I think I'm really going to enjoy staying with you. Both of you. Mak seems to have a lot of knowledge to share." She eyed me with a raised brow, and I knew the "knowledge" was about me. I sighed helplessly as she continued. "And where else am I going to get a free tour guide who is in such high demand? I want the complete *Darcy* experience. *All. Week. Long,*" she said with pauses in between words for extra emphasis.

"Well, you should have gone to England then, lass, because here we don't have Darcys. Only *Darbys*. You're out of luck. You booked the wrong flight . . . And no, my name was not a mistake, as so many people try to point out to me."

She cocked her head before she spoke. "Are you sure? 'B' seems like it could very easily be confused with 'C.' They are right next to each other in the alphabet. Sounds like one of those mix-ups at the hospital. Your parents just probably didn't want to tell you."

"Yeah . . . no, definitely not. There's a huge distinction," I said emphatically. "I'm nothing like him, so don't get your hopes up."

"Really, not to burst your bubble, but isn't Darby like the Irish version of Darcy? I think you should just stop fighting it. Sounds like it's your fate." She was getting that glow on her face, and as much as this conversation annoyed me—now more than ever since this Darcy nonsense was coming from her—I loved seeing that glow in her expression. She added, "Plus, the ticket to Ireland was cheaper—"

I cut her off. "Right, so you would prefer to be in the land of Darcy, but you'll just have to settle for this second-rate version of it."

She looked me over slowly before proceeding cautiously, "Wow, you're really sensitive about this, aren't you? I was *joking*. The tickets were the same price. This was my first choice." She looked at me with meaning. "I also prefer the 'b,'" she said with decisiveness.

She was the first woman to ever say something like that to me. And then the waves of crimson were back, just like the red hues in an Irish sunset, bursting forth unexpectedly and taking over. I guess I was in my *Picasso Red* period. Well, at least it was a better period than the *blue*. Maybe something had finally gotten me out of that one.

Mak let out a clipped laugh followed by another abrupt noise that sounded like his walking stick had skidded out from under him. He obviously couldn't contain himself. We didn't realize we had an audience. For how long, I had no idea. Mak was never quiet. I didn't know he was capable of it. The crafty little bugger certainly was, though. Where was this quality when he was snoring like a freight train blaring through quiet pasture land at two in the morning or yelling out "Darcy" at the top of his lungs when I was trying to hide from a group of chatty women at the tour shop?

Mak let out a giddy noise when I turned to him. It was a sound that could only be rivaled by a child on Christmas morning. He was going to have to pull himself together or I wasn't going to be responsible for what I did next. I could have a temper. It went well with my "bad boy" persona. People didn't see it often, but where the apathy stopped, the low tolerance irritation began. There wasn't a lot in between. "Mak," I said through gritted teeth as a warning. I loved the man with all my heart, I truly did, and I respected my elders, but *this* was pushing it. Because I knew how far he'd go if I didn't stop his teasing right away.

"Eyre, is he bothering ya too much?" He sauntered over to her with his walking stick—the one he loved so much. As much as it helped him to get around better, it had also become a part of his identity. That was typical Mak. Who knew why he loved it so much: fashion statement, conversation piece, or old man privilege? We didn't know. He was eccentric that way. But as long as he needed it, he was going to make the most of it and find any "perk" possible. I'd actually thought he didn't need it at first because he loved the thing so much—which I felt badly about now, but I realized he was just owning it. One of the few people that would. And it made me love him even more.

    Mak got right in between us. I hadn't realized how close I still was to Eyre. I hadn't really left much space at all. I was feeling self-conscious about that now. He squeezed in between us, making a big production of it, as he looked up at me with his big light blue eyes and offered Eyre his arm. Locking their arms together, he started escorting her out of the shop as if he was the most debonair man that ever lived. You would have thought he was Sean Connery.

    "You coming, Darce? We're going to the pub. You know how to lock up. Or have you forgotten everything in the presence of this charming young lady?"

    My blood churned as I scrambled to close the shop and catch up to them. I was determined to stop Mak before any more damage could be done. There was no telling what he'd already been able to say with the mere head start he'd gotten.

EIGHT

Eyre

We sauntered down the charmingly beautiful Irish street toward the pub, which was only a few doors down. Mak scurried along while I just tried to keep up with him. My pain was becoming a little more demanding as were my chronic illnesses. They never allowed me to have a normal moment especially when I had pushed them past their flimsy breaking point. Mak had informed me that this was indeed Fisher Street, not Main Street as I had presumed.

Darby caught up to us as we reached a vibrant yellow storefront with natural stones on the entryway. It looked as colorful as Van Gogh's *Sunflowers*. It automatically made me happy, or maybe it was Darby's presence. In hindsight, it would probably have been better if Darby and I had gone inside the pub separately. As soon as we opened the heavy pub doors, the patrons looked up in greeting, and I could see grins spreading across their faces. Even the fiddle players stopped playing and waited expectantly. Right away, the crowd let out a raucous "Darcy." Glass beer steins raised in the air for extra emphasis at the jest. It appeared that Darby entering the pub with a woman by his side only spurred them on. He rolled his eyes and looked perturbed.

He grabbed Mak by the arm. I saw his body tense up, actually his whole body posture had seemed to change when we'd entered the pub. "Ok, you've stopped by. Just wave to Sinead. And now we'll get Eyre home. No time to dawdle, old man." That remark ignited a fire in Mak's glacial blues.

"Eyre, come on over to the bar and meet Sinead. We grew up together and she used to change Darce's diapers. She'll become one of your favorite people that you meet." Mak tossed a look over his shoulder at Darby.

As we moved further into the belly of the pub, my senses adjusted to the dimly lit atmosphere. The pub reminded me of the one from *Finding You*, especially the lively fiddle players and the energetic patrons. The woman in the film had gone to Ireland to renew her passion and dream. Maybe I could as well. The crisp crackle of fire roaring in the brick fireplace in the center of the pub brought me back to the current moment. The dark wood tones throughout the bar contrasted with the low curved arches of the bright, white-washed walls. There was a warm and comforting sense of camaraderie as the upbeat blanket of music resonating from the fiddles blended with the clink of glasses and raucous laughter from the pub patrons. The friendly and comfortable surroundings made me feel safe and warm, much like I was being wrapped in a cashmere dream.

Darby reached for me, trying to direct me over to a booth in a dimly lit corner, as far away from everyone as possible. But I quickly decided I wanted to follow Mak, so I eluded

Darby's grasp. Mak was headed straight to the bar where most of the patrons were clustered together. There was a look of trepidation in Darby's eyes, mixed with something else I couldn't quite identify, as I left him to follow Mak.

Within a few quick steps, we were already pressed against the bar. Mak had stopped abruptly, and his head was bobbing left and right. I presumed he was looking for Sinead. He looked like a tiny fishing lure lost in a giant sea. Suddenly, I felt someone's hand on my arm and my eyes looked back to meet Darby's eyes, realizing it was his warm hand that met me. I hadn't realized how close he was to me, and as I turned, our bodies were practically flush against one another, inviting his scent into my senses and causing a flickering that was still a surprise to me.

When his silent gaze made it apparent that he wasn't going to figure out what to say any time soon, I spoke first. "Sounds like you might want to rethink your stance on the whole name blunder at the hospital. It seems pretty clear what name you're supposed to have." Darby actually looked like a fish out of water in this place and banter was my way of getting him to loosen up. He looked kind of uncomfortable. Maybe he didn't want me to witness the town's interactions with him.

He leaned down so that our faces were even closer together. I could see the amber specks in his beautiful green eyes, like pieces of gold scattered throughout. Maybe that wasn't such a legend after all. It was there in his eyes, hidden among a green the same color as the Irish countryside that had already stolen my heart. There was just enough light in the pub to bring out the faint red tones in his soft brown hair as well. Darby's face turned serious as he said, "Like I said, you shouldn't get your hopes up. They're calling me that because it couldn't be further from the truth. I'm the antithesis. The least 'Darceseque' person you'll ever meet. Every time they say it, they're *slagging* me. They're making fun of me for being so hopeless with women. It started in secondary school. Our English teacher accidentally called me Darcy because she was teaching *Pride and Prejudice* to one of her other classes. The whole classroom broke out into laughter. And since then, it's only gotten funnier to the town. I suppose the tourists haven't helped matters . . . Nor has my romantic defect."

Darby's eyes stared deeply into mine. They seemed to be saying something entirely different from the words coming out of his mouth. Just before I started to speak, a few men's voices from the pub interrupted our moment. "Hey, *look*, Mr. Darcy has got himself an Elizabeth," one burly guy bellowed.

Another guy cackled, "Oye, lass, he's not the least like Mr. Darcy, not at all. More like Mr. Collins, this one here."

They continued their banter. "Yeah, I'd sure feel bad if we gave her the wrong impression of him. She would surely be sorry." They all started laughing at the last one's joke. I could tell they were already pretty drunk. I chose to ignore them and held Darby's gaze instead, allowing it to warm the deepest parts of me. Letting it reach down to those cold currents in the depths of my soul that no one could see.

"Fine, we were doing *you* a favor, but be rude then—" one of them said with a bite to his tone.

"Enough, Declan," Darby growled. He'd already seemed on guard, but this sent him right over the edge. My eyes instinctively drifted over to the men. There was a look of shock on their faces. Apparently they weren't used to this from Darby. At least, that was my guess. "Eyre is from America and she's going to be staying with us. I'm going to be showing her around . . . so try not to run her off. It would be nice if she went back to America without thinking we were a bunch of *eejits*. I know it's going to be hard not to act like complete idiots, but *try* your best."

Darby slowly turned back from them toward the bar and placed his hand on my lower back protectively, guiding me over toward Mak. I glanced back at the gobsmacked men. I heard one of them whisper, "Oye, who knew Darby could be such a gentleman?" Or at least that's what I thought they said.

Darby tapped Mak on the shoulder at the bar, and Mak slid down one stool so we could sit beside each other. He hardly looked at Darby, though. He was enraptured with the woman in front of him. This must be the infamous Sinead. I would wager they were around the same age. She'd let her hair go natural. It was a light silvery gray and flowed in loose, soft curls around her face. She was a beautiful woman. You could tell she was one of those women who had been, and would always be, gorgeous. Her light green eyes shimmered with life. If I had to guess, considering her animation and spirit, I'd say she had once been a fiery redhead. One that everyone wanted to be friends with. She looked bold, beautiful, and extremely comfortable in her skin. I was envious of that. Maybe some of her confidence would wear off on me. I could pretend well enough, but it wasn't the same as actually possessing that quality.

As I looked from Sinead to Mak, it was obvious that he was infatuated with her. I could see it in his eyes. His body language reacted to every move she made as if he had been in tune with her movements every day of his life and he would be lost without her. A *true love* dance of their bodies. A real "Johnny and Baby" partnership. And it was beautiful to see.

It made me wonder what had happened. I may not be good at reading men's body language when it comes to their interest in me, but I could certainly read it when applied to others. And I saw he was hopeless for her. *Did she not know how he felt?* I wanted to know the answer. I was extremely nosy when it came to other people's personal lives, and I would love to have been an old Irish matchmaker. Maybe I had missed my calling. I guess it wasn't too late and now could be a perfect opportunity to start. I just hoped I wasn't misreading the situation.

"Mak, stop flirting and introduce Eyre," Darby said. Well, that took the gusto right out of my sails. If he was teasing Mak, then Sinead had to know he liked her . . . or maybe I had read the whole situation wrong. Some detective I was. No "Strega Nona" here. Calling *not* missed. Darby called out louder, "Mak."

"Yeah, yeah," Mak said, looking at Darby out of the corner of his eye. Then he turned to me, his face lighting up as he spoke, "Eyre, I'd like you to meet Sinead. We grew up together. We've known each other since our first day of school. We were in the same year." As he turned to Sinead, his face lit up even more, and . . . *wow, that look* . . . well, it was exactly how I longed for someone to look at me. I had known that look existed and here was my proof. *Take that, Gabe.* My ex-boyfriend had thought my standards were impossibly high. Now, here was this sweet man showing me it indeed existed all along. I just hadn't been in the right place with the right person.

It was as if a bolt of lightning struck me as I turned to meet Darby's gaze. It couldn't possibly . . . there's no way I could be starting to feel that from him. But I'd been feeling something all day and it was only intensifying. *What was in the gene pool here?* Obviously, something that was missing back home. Whatever ancestors had that gene had surely missed the Mayflower boat.

"What?" he asked "innocently" looked at me.

I quickly spun back around to Sinead to avoid my confusing thoughts. "It's so great to meet you. I heard you have a lot of good stories about Darby." I grinned mischievously.

"Oh yes, dear. *Quite* a few. And I'd love to share them with you." She eyed Darby and he groaned from his stool. I could see his muscles relax a little bit with Sinead's teasing, which was the opposite of what I had expected.

"Can we get Eyre some food before you do that, please? She's been traveling all day." Darby turned, looking at me with care. "Sinead's food is amazing."

Sinead replied, "Of course, dear, how thoughtless of me. What can I get ya?"

"Oh, um, do you have steamed rice?" I questioned.

All of their heads snapped up together at the same time. They looked at me with questioning eyes.

"You're in Ireland and all you want is steamed rice?" Darby asked with concern. "Sinead's fish and chips are amazing. We're known for so much more than just rice. You've got to try our food."

"Yes, dear, I don't mean to brag, but the fish and chips

are really good, and you're all skin and bones. We'll take care of that—we're hearty eaters," Sinead said with a cheerful smile.

"No, that's ok," I said quietly. Darby looked me up and down with concern. I could tell he was taking in my skinny appearance and immediately I could tell what he was thinking—what they were all thinking: I must have some type of eating disorder. This wasn't uncommon with my conditions. I was extremely limited with what I could eat. I could spend upwards of five hours shopping online for groceries, looking at ingredients as I tried to find something that wouldn't make me sick to eat. And when I did finally find something I thought I could eat, it wasn't unusual to find myself too sick, or too nauseated, to eat my meal by the time I finally got it prepared. I had to make my meals from scratch since prepackaged foods usually contained preservatives. And after all that careful work and deliberation, there was always a chance the food would make me sick anyway, or I'd still have an uncontrollable flare. It all added up to a lot of weight loss, and I knew what it looked like to outsiders.

I was self-conscious about my weight since I knew how it looked—especially with the way I had to eat. I had initially thought it would be a bonus to lose weight, but now I honestly felt more unattractive. As if the weight loss was giving away how sick and out of control my conditions truly were at any given time. I felt I didn't have ownership of my body anymore. As if it had completely turned against me. My conditions were sacrificing so many important things in my life without my permission, and I didn't want to have to discuss it. Not again. I certainly wasn't ready to talk about it with strangers.

Darby's eyes focused on my face, willing my downcast ones to rise up to meet his. I didn't feel attractive with my conditions and talking about them was only going to make me feel worse. And someone as attractive as Darby, whose looks completely unnerved me, put every insecure thought I had about my physical appearance into the forefront of my mind. And not just passively placed there. No, they were all crying in unison, dying to be heard.

"That impossible American airbrushed standard isn't what's considered beautiful over here. Real women, that's what is beautiful," Darby said. "You know, the photo with the stretch marks from childbirth before they airbrush it. The one of the woman being whatever size she truly is and being comfortable in her own skin. The one with the scar on her face, or the slight gap in her teeth that gives her character . . . that's what we like here." Darby stated it so eloquently that I couldn't help but look at him in wonder.

"Darby," Sinead said in a harsh whisper, thinking he may have overstepped. But I just held his gaze. There wasn't anything but truth in his eyes. He wasn't saying it because society said he should or that it was what men were supposed to say to cover up how they really felt. No, it was all Darby. *Chink.*

And while he was saying it for different reasons than the ones that applied to me, I still really needed to hear it. But I wasn't ready to discuss my health with him. Not yet. But if he could let another piece of his guard fall away, then I could at least be brave enough to try this amazing food. It would be a victory, just not the one he thought it was. Maybe eating overseas would be different. Europeans had more restrictions with what they allowed to be added to their foods, as well as how their food was grown. I had heard, for some people, it did make a difference. I held his gaze as I spoke, "Well, okay. Thank you."

"Fish and chips it is. We'll all join you," Darby said with a grin, never letting his eyes leave mine.

"Yes, I'm starving," Mak said. I assumed he was still bewitched by Sinead, but I was too lost in the man before me. He was the first guy I'd met who actually wanted to help me with my low self-esteem and seemed to truly believe in natural beauty. He wasn't "parroting" a line or saying something that he had been taught to say. I could tell he truly believed it, and that was pretty life-changing for me.

I felt like beauty standards weren't something men were supposed to talk about. It was a taboo subject for them to discuss . . . and maybe they just didn't have the courage, or they simply didn't want to talk about it. But Darby . . . Darby didn't care. He would speak the truth the way he saw it.

He just continued to stare me right in the eyes with a look that hadn't changed at all. The same look that had seen my insecurities for what they were from the moment we'd met. And maybe he didn't know all of them, but he seemed to know their severity. And for reasons that could only be explained by my heart, I found myself staring back, owning every part of that perfect gaze that he bestowed on me.

NINE

Eyre

"This is the best thing I've ever tasted," I said, with my mouth full of fish. It was unladylike and completely unlike me.

"I told you so," Darby said with the biggest grin on his face. The soft gleam that had started to appear when he looked at me was only shining brighter now.

He reached over and slowly wiped a crumb from my mouth, letting his fingers linger. That pulsing feeling returned inside me, really overwhelming me again.

"Oh, so embarrassing," I heaved.

"No," he said, as he continued to shake his head slowly. "Really adorable." But his eyes were on my lips, and it wasn't for the first time today. Somehow I had a feeling it wouldn't be the last time and it shot a thunderbolt of electricity through me. How had I gone from feeling nothing–to feeling *this*? I'd never wanted to kiss someone so badly while eating. That was completely unappealing, but now . . . well, now it was all I could think about. The urge was really making it difficult to eat. And this fish was the best thing I'd tasted in a very long time. I planned to enjoy every bite. Except, the butterflies were taking up quite a bit of space in my stomach.

Mak had left us to our own devices, completely absorbed in Sinead and the happenings at the bar. Darby and I had turned our stools to face each other and were sitting with our feet on each other's bar stool, our legs interlocked to reach the other's chair. It felt like a '50s sock hop diner move or something from the musical, *Grease*. I was happy that Darby had relaxed now that we were in our own little world, tucked away in our little area of the bar.

When I slowed in eating, he asked, "Are you done? Do you want some dessert? There's a really great–"

"No, Darby, there's no way. Thank you, but no. Another time."

"I like the sound of that. As long as you're sure," he said with a most infectious smile.

"Yes, baby steps. This is all going to turn to sugar anyway. And I'm hypoglycemic." I really didn't want to press my luck. I was going to be fortunate if I could eat this and be okay. So far, so good, I thought . . . Maybe I really could eat differently in this country.

"Oh, I'm really sorry, I didn't know. I wouldn't have pushed–" he said apologetically.

"No, that doesn't have anything to do with–" I felt like I should just come out and tell him the truth about why I didn't want to eat much. I shouldn't let him just jump to conclusions.

Mak snuck up on us with an elf-like quietness, interrupting me before I got a chance to decide. "You lovebirds ready? Darby, stop making googly eyes or the lass isn't going to come home with us. You're going to scare her off. And it really would be nice to have a woman around the house, especially since ya scared all the others off that live within a five-town radius." Mak was obviously feeling happy after seeing Sinead, and he was now in top teasing form. Darby, on the other hand, was glaring at him. He had returned to his old self, with some extra prickly layers added on top for good measure.

"Right, well, I think we are ready now," Darby said through a tensed jaw. I began to get out my wallet. Darby and Sinead both went to stop me, but Sinead was faster.

Sinead began, "Don't you dare. It's on the house. Stop by every day for a good meal if you like. You're always welcome, especially if we get to see a smile on Darby's face." And with that, Mak cleared his throat and nodded a little too exuberantly toward her. They obviously had been planning something together. Sinead eyed Mak and said, "Say, Darby, how's that work going at the church?" There was a glint in her eye that I couldn't quite decipher its meaning.

Darby? . . . Church? . . . Work? There was no way all of those words belonged in a sentence together. "*What?*" I said before I could stop myself. I felt that I might have overemphasized the question.

Sinead looked at me and began again, "Oh, um, Darby volunteers at the local church. It's a restoration project. He's very talented with his hands, so–"

But Darby cut Sinead off. "Yeah, it's not so much me volunteering, and you know it. You shouldn't make it sound so good." His eyes had a hard edge to them. He wouldn't even look at me. Mak grunted behind me. I didn't know where to look, but Darby's words caught me before I could decide. "A historic church in our village burned down and it's been sitting vacant for a long time. I'm working towards restoring it. Some people seem to think that I'm good at carpentry."

Mak grunted again with a not-so-subtle sound. Sinead spoke up, "Well, Eyre, maybe you'd like to see Darby's work at the church. He spends a lot of time there, and since he's your tour guide and all—"

Darby's head shot up. His eyes landed on Sinead's with a disdainful look that I had yet to see from him. I was actually a little concerned now. He did seem to have a little bit of a temper, and it sounded like this church project had not been so voluntary. More like court-mandated or something. Things were starting to not look so good to me where Darby was concerned. Even *I* could heed that many warnings. Maybe I needed to find another place to stay.

I was just about to open my mouth when Mak spoke up, "Eyre, I think it would be really wonderful if you helped Darby with the church. And I think it would give you a true sense of Ireland and the community we have here." His voice was soft and gentle. This was followed by a staring contest between Darby and Mak, one that lasted an uncomfortable amount of time, but something changed in Darby as soon as Mak spoke. There was a solemn expression on Darby's face now, and he just nodded at me. That was as much of an invitation as I was going to get. Since Mak had done so much for me already and Sinead had been so welcoming, I felt if this was important to them, then I would certainly give it a shot. I wasn't sure how I could be of any help, but I would certainly do my best.

THE IRISH FALL

We left the pub with Darby in complete silence. I could tell he still wasn't over what had just transpired. I still didn't understand what had happened or its ramifications. All I knew was that there was some sort of unspoken struggle occurring between Darby and Mak.

I was trying to walk behind the pair, not only to stay out of whatever trouble was silently brewing but also because I had absolutely no idea how to get to Mak's house. Finally, to my relief, Mak broke the silence with his thick brogue. "Eyre, it's not too long of a walk to our home. I hope you'll be alright." He reached back and took my arm, glaring at Darby.

"Hopefully Darce didn't walk you too much already today. Less than twenty-four hours in our country and you probably already have blisters. It's not like there was a warm, dry tour bus waiting for you today. And ya know, it's not like his job is to escort tourists safely around our glorious countryside in one piece or anything. Oh, wait..."

The stare that ensued from Darby made me lose my footing, and even Mak's walking stick seemed to hitch as it got snagged amid the bumpy, uneven pavement of the sidewalk.

Mak continued, "As I was saying, we're about a fifteen-minute walk up the road and then up a hillside. I promise the views are worth it once you get to the top. Our little cottage isn't much, but the peaceful countryside and the grand views make up for it. Plus, no one wants to be around us. It's best for two old grumps to be isolated. This place seems to be the perfect fit for us."

I laughed at Mak's explanation and smiled as I said, "It sounds absolutely perfect. However, I don't think you need to be isolated at all. I've really enjoyed my time with you."

"Notice she said '*me,*' Darce. You've got some work to do." Mak winked at him.

Darby retorted, "Yeah, yeah, at your age anything is charming. You could probably tell everyone the world was ending and they'd just say, 'Aww, how cute.' You have a pass and you know it, old man. Doesn't hurt that you've somehow managed to make your walking stick into an adorable fashion accessory as well as a walking aid, either."

"Darby!" I said in shock, not able to contain myself, but a burst of deep belly laughter rumbling through Mak kept me from reprimanding Darby further.

Mak retorted, "We'll see. You'd be so lucky to be this cute in forty years, young curmudgeon. When it doesn't magically happen, then you'll know the truth. I'll be looking down, smiling then. You just remember that. You're gonna need a lot more than a walking stick. May I suggest a pipe and a fedora, too? Perhaps some oversized pockets filled with candy."

"I think you both will be equally adorable," I said, trying to calm the flames. However, Mak did not like that one bit as he quickly looked inquiringly at me. "Well, at least now you're both equally adorable." Now Darby was looking disheartened by my words. I really wasn't going to win here. "I'm excited to spend as much time as possible with both of you," I added quickly, correcting my faux pax. They both smiled at me. *Phew, that ought to fix it.*

THE IRISH FALL

Thankfully a car honked at us in greeting and disrupted the conversation. I was relieved, but I seemed to be the only one. The air tensed and in the moonlight I could make out that Mak also seemed to grimace. I would have thought that they both would have enjoyed a friendly car honk or greeting, but maybe it meant something different here. My eyes traveled to Darby and he seemed to be shaking slightly and breathing rapidly. Was he angry? Maybe they had some sort of feud with the person. But now Darby was hardly walking. He'd turned into a hologram of sorts. Mak gingerly backtracked and gently looped his arm with Darby's so that he was in between us.

"I feel like I'm Dorothy now and we're going down the yellow brick road," he laughed, pulling Darby along. I was trying to look around Mak to check on Darby, but Mak was positioning his body just right to disrupt me from doing so. "Actually, I'd be a really ugly Dorothy, you better take that one Eyre. I could pull off Toto though. And well, Darby, I don't know, he's probably a flying monkey."

He continued to fill the air and then shook Darby for a response. Finally Darby spoke. It took him a lot longer than it had earlier today to come up with a comeback. I was very confused as to what I had just witnessed. I really wanted to know who was in that car.

With Darby seemingly over whatever had bothered him, we walked the rest of the way to Mak's home in comfortable camaraderie. Mak, with his arm interlaced with mine, telling me tales about the village as we passed through different parts of it. Darby trailed off to the side, giving me glances I couldn't decipher. When we started up the hill, I really didn't think I had any energy left to climb it. I could see a flicker of guilt on Darby's face. I guess he could see the exhaustion that annihilated mine.

"You need a minute, lass?" Mak looked at me with concern and then over at Darby with a look of exasperation. "I could use one too. Actually, I insist on it."

I guess the look wasn't so subtle on my face. "You should carry the poor lass the rest of the way, Darce. You've only traipsed her across half the county. She could probably give a better tour now than you," Mak quipped. "And she's only flown across a whole ocean to get here. What's walking across part of the country, too?"

"Mak," Darby warned. They looked at each other and then at me. I'm not sure what they thought of me, but it seemed they thought there were some major issues that led me here. They weren't wrong about that. They also seemed worried about my stamina and health. Well, they weren't wrong to be worried about those things, either. I was quickly learning that the Irish were very intuitive. At least, that was true about this pair.

Suddenly, Darby's features softened, and he looked at me with care and concern. He started to come toward me without saying a word, and all I could do was shake my head. *No, no way.* He was not carrying me up that hill.

TEN

Eyre

It had taken everything in me to convince them to let me walk up the hill. It had also taken every last droplet of strength left in me to get up said hill. I actually wished that I'd let them both have their way by the time I reached the top. I was ready to literally crash into a bed. There was no way I'd be falling gracefully into one at this point.

But when I reached the top, I was in awe. Even though it was now dark outside, I could make out the water and shoreline in the distance through the ethereal moon and starlight. It took my breath away. The view seemed to stretch out in every direction that I looked, and I could tell it would be an even more marvelous view in the daylight. I couldn't believe this was real.

My eyes caught on a tall tower structure on the horizon. With the moon reflecting off the stone, it looked like a medieval spire. No big deal, there was just a castle in their backyard. The beauty of this country left me in complete awe. I was too moved to even speak. I just let the score of "Clair de Lune" play in my mind, a symphony conducting itself in the beauty of the night sky and casting moonlight on the water. The brightness of the stars and the clarity of the moon conjured up each note in my imagination.

"It's the Doonagore Castle tower," Darby said gently, interrupting my melodious thoughts. My eyes drifted over to his. I hadn't realized he was standing so close to me. I also hadn't realized his eyes were so fixated on me. My heart was stuck in my throat as I took in his complexion bathed in the moonlight. "The tower is part of the Burren National Park. I'll take you. It's really beautiful, I think you'll enjoy it. That is, if you'd like to go there," he added quickly.

Mak cleared his throat. "Of course, she'd like to go there. Take him up on it quickly, Eyre, before he changes his mind." He nudged me and then said to Darby, "*Beautiful*, Darce? Since when do you use a word like that to describe anything?" I could hear the cunningly mischievous tone in his voice that was no doubt aimed at Darby.

"I'd love that, thank you," I replied, not breaking my eye contact with him. The evening glow seemed to enhance the connection between us.

"It's settled then," Mak said, turning to go inside. "Alright, let's give you a tour and get you settled. There will be plenty to see tomorrow, but you need some rest tonight. You look *shattered*, I can see the exhaustion in your eyes."

I was more than relieved by his words and for his kindness. Mak took my arm with his and guided me to go inside. I was beginning to feel like he was my grandfather, too. He seemed to take up that role for everyone. Just a bighearted man that didn't take credit for being that way.

From what I could tell in the dark, the cottage was a small two-story home. The outside was white-washed with clean, straight, no-nonsense lines. As soon as we crossed the threshold, Mak scurried around, cutting on lights and trying to tidy up. Darby stood awkwardly beside me, not really knowing what to do.

"Mak, I really don't think she's that type of house guest. Let's just take her to her room, and then I'll help you straighten up. It looks worse this way. She can see how much work it takes to get things tidied up around here."

"We don't need her to remember how *manky* this place is. She'll think we leave things this dirty all the time." Mak said, glaring at Darby. But honestly, the place was pretty clean, especially for two bachelors. Mak was mostly picking up books and straightening blankets and the sorts. Maybe a few stray teacups here and there.

We walked straight into the living room, which had the most gorgeous, low vaulted wood ceiling and a stone fireplace. The woods encompassing the space were all composed of natural light hues. The room was exceptionally cozy with different colored fabric chairs and a quirky, patterned sofa. Everything was eclectic and, in my opinion, perfect. This place was a breath of fresh, welcoming air. The brown hues against the white walls were warm and inviting, and the accent colors made me feel happy. Not to mention the use of a variety of patterns in a way that felt so freeing. Patterns that normally wouldn't ever be used together, but yet here they were, daring you to mock them as they worked together in beautiful harmony. The picturesque home and location on this idyllic hillside felt like I'd stepped onto the set for *Wild Mountain Thyme*, especially considering all the unique touches. This was an actual home—in every sense of the word.

My eyes roamed over to the quaint stone fireplace, which was in jarring contrast to the one my boyfriend—former boyfriend now—had back in the States. His was supremely stark and modern. Living in the "big city of Nashville," as he liked to call it, he thought that everything needed to be "contemporary" and "cutting edge." That meant black-and-white furniture with no accent colors to add warmth. Nashville wasn't like that at all, though. The city—and the people that lived there—were homey and down to earth, even if it was a big city. That big city sentiment was just him. Everything had its designated place in Gabe's home and life . . . Even me.

Mak began speaking breathlessly as he scurried about. "Let me show you the kitchen in case you need anything, and then I'll take you upstairs." He led me through a narrow hallway and into a tight space. The sage green cabinets made me smile, and the butcher block counters displayed plenty of battle wounds in the form of nicks and scrapes that told me they had seen good use. "If you need water or anything, just come on in. Make yourself at home." A welcoming smile on his face told me he meant every word.

He pointed down the hall toward a bedroom on the way to the stairs, "That's my room. Come get me if you need anything. I mean *anything*." He looked at me. "Especially if Darce ain't behaving. I'll take care of him." He eyed him and laughed, then quickly escorted me up the stairs and pointed down the hallway. "There's a few rooms up here. *The jacks* is right down the hall. Just be careful because the lock to the bathroom is difficult to get to work. We need to fix it. And

Darce's room is right beside it. The room on the other side should be perfect for you" He grinned at me.

My face fell. I eyed the closed door at the opposite end of the hall, hoping there might be a bedroom there. Mak seemed to quickly pick up on my line of thinking. "Uh, that one's not ready. We can't use it." He quickly moved on. "Besides, this way Darce will be right next to you if you need anything, and he will promise to behave. *Won't you*, Darce?"

"Uh, huh," Darby said exasperatedly, rolling his eyes.

"There's a lock on your door," Mak whispered as he leaned over to my ear.

"I can hear you, Mak. You know you've never been good at whispering, right? You're too hard of hearing. So you should just stop trying," Darby said, not bothering to hide his exasperation. "I would never come into your room," he said as he looked at me earnestly.

"Well, never say never; she may invite you. Miracles do happen, you know," Mak said.

"Mak! Go downstairs, you rotten old man. I'm serious if you say another word–" Darby warned him.

"Alright, alright. I was just having a bit of fun. 'Twas only joking. Don't ever let him in your room, Eyre. Goodnight," Mak said with a wave of his hand.

And with that, he left us. I stared awkwardly at Darby, unsure of what to do. There was a look of complete humiliation that had spread to every crevice of his expression. We began to speak at the same time, which only amplified the awkward factor.

"Go ahead," I said, relieved he'd spoken.

"Sorry about Mak. He's a great guy, but he loves to say whatever he feels like saying. I promise I'm respectful. I know that doesn't give you any peace of mind because you don't know me from Adam, but I really like to think that I am. I promise this isn't the *Bates Motel*. *Grand*, now that makes it sound even sketchier because I brought it up."

I started chuckling. A little out of nervousness, a little out of relief, and a lot out of tiredness. "I believe you, Darby. I may be crazy, but I do." I smiled, and a look of relief washed over him. I could tell Mak's comments had really gotten to him.

He shifted from one foot to the other uncomfortably. "Can I get you anything? Um . . . Do you have everything in that bag that you need? It looks pretty small. I mean, what did you bring with you?" He hesitated, then quickly corrected, "I mean–I shouldn't have asked. I just meant . . . do you need some clothes for sleeping and toiletries? Things like that. I'm sure we have an extra toothbrush."

I blushed. I could feel my cheeks going rosy and betraying me. Truthfully, there were just the bare essentials in my oversized purse. I hesitated, knowing I was missing a lot. "I have a toothbrush, yes. And *a* change of clothes. I should have everything I need. I'm all set. The bare essentials are in here."

He just looked at me, sensing my hesitancy. "Toothpaste? Something to sleep in?"

"Yes, and not really," I said, looking down. "But I'm fine." Before I could finish, he'd already vanished into his room, leaving the door open. I couldn't help but peer inside, which I knew was a huge invasion of privacy. He'd just promised not to come into my room, and here I was gawking at his space.

The walls were simple and clean like the rest of the

home, and from what I could see, the room was modest. It looked like a picturesque, primitive cottage room, except for the dark navy tone accents. Masculine and bold, the accents were definitely not cottage-core. And there was a wooden bookshelf piled high with books–actually, it was stuffed with them. The mini library caught my eye immediately, and I was dying to see more of the room. I would never have taken Darby as a reader; rather I had assumed the room would be packed with sports memorabilia. And even more to my surprise, there were wooden carved boxes scattered around the room. I wondered if he had made them. Sinead and Mak did say he worked with his hands. I was just honing my snooping skills when he turned around and caught me. A smirk the size of Ireland crossed his face.

"You can come in." He laughed. "Not really anything to see in here," he said as I stepped into the room. He outstretched his hand to me with something in his grasp. "Well, I'm sure they'll be baggy on you, but at least it's something. You can always roll the shorts." As he handed the clothing to me, I realized the shorts were *boxers*. My eyes went wide. I was not going to be strutting around in Darby's boxers. Definitely not Darby's, of all people. Maybe Mak had something. I was about to say as much when he said, "You'll get long Johns from Mak. Better take that."

I bit my lip in indecision, looking at the tee and boxers. "Thank you, I really appreciate it. Sorry about all of this."

"Don't be sorry. I'm glad you're here." And I could tell it took a lot for him to say that. "Are you going to tell me why–"

"So the bathroom's down the hall? I'm really exhausted from the jet lag," I said, cutting him off.

"Oh, yeah, of course." He walked me out and pointed.

"Feel free to take a shower or whatever you need. I'll use the one downstairs."

"Really?!" I asked a little too excitedly. Warm water was one of the only things that helped with my body pain and cramping. Well, that and my heating pad, which, ironically, I did have in my bag. Hence the reason there wasn't a lot of room for anything else. The heating pad was a *much higher* priority. *Who needed a lot of clothes to wear when they were in that much pain anyway?* The heating pad was going to win every time. I couldn't sleep without it.

"Yeah," he said, looking a little confused about my excitement. "I've never heard someone so excited for—"

"It's the hot water," I explained.

"Ah. Well, in that case, there's a bathtub too. I don't know if you like . . ." But he stopped himself when he saw the look of sheer joy on my face. "You should take one. I think it would help with the jet lag. Just don't fall asleep in there if you do, ok?"

I smiled at those emerald eyes that were shining brightly back at me. They looked like they were doing a little jig, as if being able to do something for me made him happy. "Thank you. *Really,* thank you." And I meant it for so many things.

ELEVEN

Eyre

I left him and walked down the hallway to the bathroom with his t-shirt and boxers in my hand. My handbag seemed heavier than ever on my shoulder. It was getting to the point where I almost felt like I couldn't physically carry it any longer. My body was done. When I was finally able to unload the handbag on the bathroom floor, I felt a sigh escape me. My muscles started unclenching and relaxed ever so slightly.

The bathroom was a charming, retro oasis with its quaint black and white checkered tile, green cabinetry that was reminiscent of the 1930s, and wood paneling. But what caught my eye was the glorious bathtub and shower combination. I was home.

Usually, I would put salts in my bath—this is where I splurged and got creative. So much money in my budget was allocated toward trying natural remedies, especially for bath time. But tonight, I would go old school and be more than thrilled to have the purity of just the hot water. Hopefully it would ease some of the wear I'd been put through the past couple of days. However, my muscles and joints ached for some salts, and my abdomen cramped in agreement. But all they were getting tonight was hot water, so they would have to be satisfied with that.

After a little while, I slipped into the hot water like a mermaid returning to sea. I was particularly enjoying my *Splash* moment and thinking about how Darby would make a good Tom Hanks. Sighs escaped me that I couldn't control. I would need to thank both Mak and Darby in the morning. Their generosity was truly incredible. I was just about to block out everything that had brought me here and glide off into a blissful daydream world, free of worry, when I heard something.

My upper body bolted forward in the tub. Both of my hands grabbed at the slick sides, my head rotating like an owl trying to get a better look at its prey . . . Then suddenly, the door creaked.

"Eyre, um . . ." It was Darby's voice. *Oh my . . . was the door open? I must have forgotten to lock it. Or wait, didn't Mak say it didn't always lock well and to be careful? I should have checked it better. I wouldn't make that mistake again. Was that what caused the creaking sound?*

Darby's voice sounded again. "I thought you might like . . . I mean, I brought you some–" But he didn't get a chance to finish. "*Oye!*" he shouted.

All of a sudden, I saw this black-and-white blur race in front of the tub. I screamed, not knowing what was going on. My mind was racing too fast for me to process anything. Because, at the moment, all I was worried about was the possibility of there being a large feral animal in the house getting ready to attack me. Maybe that's why Darby had been at the door.

"Lucky! Lucky, no! Bad boy. Get out! Now! This is *not* your tub." Darby's voice was stern and raised.

Suddenly, I saw the most adorable dog sitting in front of me beside the tub. He was eyeing me with a look of helplessness. His black-and-white coloring was striking and absolutely gorgeous. He had to be either a Border Collie or an Aussie. Either way, he was too cute for words.

"Eyre, I'm so sorry. Ok, um . . . I can fix this. I'm not looking," Darby said frantically.

"What?!" I shrieked, spinning around in the tub while also trying to block any sight of my body with the side of the tub as I sank down. My eyes immediately zeroed in on Darby with a hand over his eyes and the other wrapped around a canister of something that was outstretched in front of him, trying to make sure he didn't crash into anything.

"I can't do anything with the bloody salts in my hand. Do you want salt? That's why I knocked on the door and then Lucky . . . He–"

"Lucky?" I questioned with sheer amusement. "Wow, there really aren't any women in this house."

"Don't even start, ok. I was younger and I thought it was ironic and cute, alright?" But I'd already begun laughing. "I knew this would happen when you met him." I could hear his eyes rolling in the tone of his voice.

"Does he have a matching uniform, like the one you were wearing today? Because I would pay big money to see that," I teased relentlessly.

"You know what?" His hand started to slide down his face, a crack of his closed lids exposed.

"Whoa!!!" I shrieked. His hand tightened on his face.

"Well, don't get me going like that then. Do you want some salts or not?" he questioned, losing his cool.

"Yes, please. Can you take like three more steps forward?"

"Yeah, why not?" he said sarcastically. I leaned against the back of the tub and grabbed the canister from him.

"Thank you. That was very sweet of you. Actually, extremely sweet of you. I always use salts in my bath at home." I couldn't believe he'd done that for me. I couldn't believe he'd even thought of it, actually.

"Well, you looked like you were in a lot of pain today, especially after I dragged you all over the countryside, as Mak put it. And . . . well . . . I thought salts would help. That's what Mak always says helps him. That's just table salt, though. Don't tell him I told ya, but Mak takes baths, too. He may even fight you for this tub. But he's asleep, and I have no idea where he keeps his salts. I don't know if these will work as a replacement." Darby was now on his knees, looking for Lucky. "Lucky," he gritted out in a whisper.

"Wow, thank you so much. I thought I heard something at the door," I replied.

"Yeah, well, that sound was probably Lucky before it was me. I didn't realize he'd been trying to get in. He usually claws at the door. He must have finally given up and then come back when he saw me. This is his spot. He thinks it's *his* tub. We leave the door closed a lot because it's not great for his joints being so hard and all. But he gets in here every chance he gets. He's a scaredy cat. He's terrified of the storms, and if we have bad weather, then we have to let him in. He'll claw the door down. Guess he thinks it's the safest place, and he's probably not wrong. It's where they say to go in a bad storm. He's a smart dog. One of the smartest, but sometimes he just gets scared out of his mind."

"Aww, well, he's adorable," I said, cooing at the dog, who seemed to be warming up to me in response.

"I'm glad. So does that mean you'll forgive us? I know I'm not adorable like him, but maybe his cuteness will make up for this?" His hands had finally found Lucky, but the dog just scooted farther away every time his hands got near him. It was a game of chase that Darby wasn't going to win blindly.

"Of course," I said with appreciation in my tone. "You can leave him. I love dogs, and I'd enjoy the company."

"Oh, but not mine," he teased. "Well, I would, but he's been known to try some things." I thought he was teasing, but there wasn't any hint of joking in his tone. I had no idea what that meant.

"I'll take my chances," I responded.

"If you're sure." Darby patted Lucky. "Looks like you are one lucky dog. You get to stay." Darby started crawling out with his eyes still covered.

"What in the name of all that is good and holy!!" Mak screamed out. Good thing I had brought my knees up to my chest and was turned against the side of the tub, using it like a shield. I was praying he couldn't see anything. Mak looked at me and then at Darby scrambling around on his knees. Darby's hand dropped from his eyes momentarily to stare at Mak, standing straight ahead of him in the doorway, and then he quickly slapped himself in the face to cover them. But he wasn't able to cover them before I had a chance to see that his eyes had taken on a giant, saucer-sized shape. They equally matched Mak's, whose mouth was as wide open as I thought physically possible. Finally, as if realizing himself, Mak slapped his hand to his face, too. It actually sounded painful. Almost as painful as Darby's had.

Mak began in irritation, "Oye . . . Darby! What are you doing lad? I told Eyre you would behave and you're making a downright fool of me, son. How is this *anywhere* in the vicinity of behaving? She's been here less than an hour and you're already creeping around her like a *gombeen* while she doesn't have any clothes on. This is worse than the *Bates Motel*, you couldn't be any more of a creeper. At least Norman had the courtesy to stay in a separate room while he did his peeping, you ole *gowl*. You're making us look like idiots!"

"Mak! Ow, *Oye!*" Darby had collided with Mak, sending him stumbling backward.

"For the love of . . . can't you do anything right? I literally just left Eyre in her room. All you had to do was say 'goodnight.' I didn't think I had to leave instructions for ya!!"

"Mak!" Darby was using Mak to help stand himself upright while keeping his eyes still covered. If I wasn't so embarrassed, the two of them talking to one another "blindfolded" would have been hilarious. However, I could tell they were not amused as their voices continued to rise. Darby tried to explain, "I was just—"

But Mak cut him off, "You were just . . . Don't even finish that. I knew you were attracted to her, but this is not the way, boy. No wonder you have so much trouble with women. Here I was peacefully asleep when I heard our guest screaming, and then I come up here to find you crawling on your hands and knees on the floor near our *naked* guest, like an imbecile. What is the whole village going to think of you now, Darce? Because there's no way this woman is going to keep staying here after your shenanigans. Do you think we'll be able to book any more tours? No one wants Norman Bates as their tour guide. *Congratulations,* your dreams have come true. No more tours for you," he said, with so much sarcasm I couldn't help but laugh. They both turned to look at me or rather *not* look at me, just instinctively facing me.

I finally decided to speak up and take some mercy on Darby. "Mak, Darby was just trying to bring me some salts for the bath and that's when Lucky came bounding into the bathroom and scared the dickens out of me. That's why I screamed like I did. Darby has been very sweet and promised he didn't see anything." I stared at him sternly and then remembered he couldn't see anything. "Right, Darby?" I said firmly.

"Yes, of course. I promise. I didn't see anything. *Absolutely nothing.*"

"Hmph." Mak let out a grunt as if he didn't believe it—didn't believe *any* of his story. "Did you not try to lock the door, Eyre? I did warn you," he called out to me in a joking manner. Then sternly, he reached out to Darby, swinging blindly at the air until he found him. He moved his hand up Darby's arm until he found his shoulder and squeezed it tightly in a death grip. "Ok, Darce, we are going *now*, before you make this any worse!"

"Mak, I—" Darby began.

"Now!" He grabbed Darby by the arm and led him down the hall. Their clashing voices echoed down the hallway as they went.

"Can someone close the door?" I asked in a whisper that trailed off.

Obviously not hearing me, Mak called from down the hall, "Sorry, Eyre. I'll take care of him."

When I came out of the bathroom with Lucky following close behind me, I stopped suddenly in the doorway when something caught my eye. My heart halted just as quickly as my feet. The sight of Darby leaning against the wall in the hallway had caught me totally off guard. I was not prepared for him to see me in his baggy tee and rolled-up boxer shorts. I was very aware of his clothing on me and just how ridiculous I looked now. They had felt sublimely comfortable–comforting, even–as I let his scent wash over me while I snuggled into them. But now I felt quite out of place, like a misfit toy.

The look on Darby's face didn't help matters. The usually cool and collected nature that emanated off of him instantly vanished. He stared at me and then quickly stood upright in a formal manner as if he were standing at attention for a roll call at school. And his face became fixated on me, *every* inch of me. Suddenly, I became extremely self-conscious, especially of the moon and star toe ring on my left foot.

He uncrossed his arms and quickly shoved his hands into his pockets. *This wasn't awkward at all.* Darby finally began to speak, "Uh, I just wanted to . . . I just wanted to apologize with my eyes open," he finally said. "I thought maybe then you could tell how sorry I truly am. And not just because Mak made me apologize." He laughed uncomfortably.

I wanted to walk over to him, but I couldn't. It felt like there was this whole ocean of awkwardness between us, and it was too uncomfortable to traverse. So instead, I spoke somewhat quietly, "I believed what you said to me before Mak came in. I promise. Thank you, though. The apology is definitely better with your eyes open." I let out a nervous chuckle.

He seemed to relax, but only ever so slightly. He kept drinking me in with his eyes, and the tension between us was palpable as he did so. I really couldn't figure him out. Maybe he thought I was still unsure and that I wasn't telling him the truth. Or maybe he thought I was concerned he might do something else that would make me equally uncomfortable. I just wasn't sure.

Finally, I started walking toward my room, realizing we didn't have anything else left to say. When I finally reached the door, he moved toward his room, our eyes remaining locked on one another, like a spotlight trained on each dancer, giving them their solo moment.

As I stood in my doorway, he spoke again. "If you need more blankets or something, let me know. Please don't hesitate to ask. I'm just right here. You can always knock on my door." I looked at him as he spoke, both of us poking our heads out of our doorways, trying to figure the other one out.

"Thank you. Again, I really appreciate everything you both have done for me. It's incredibly kind and generous. Not many people would have taken in a complete stranger. *Thank you.*"

"Yeah, well, people here are friendly and giving, and I'm sure someone would have taken you in. But I think we're lucky we got to meet you first. Sleep well, Eyre. I'll see you in the morning."

"Goodnight, Darby," I said, as I reluctantly went into my room.

TWELVE
Darby

I woke the next morning with the biggest grin on my face, and for the first time since I could remember, I'd actually slept well. The feeling of being rested was one that my body greeted as a most welcomed stranger. One I hadn't been acquainted with for a very long time.

I loved the idea of Eyre only being separated from me by a cottage wall. I also loved the idea of her wearing my oversized tee and boxer shorts. That soccer team logo had never looked so good. I still felt bad for scaring her last night–twice, I think–but seeing her wearing my clothing was worth it. I wished I could see her like that every night and every morning. She was truly beautiful. I didn't know how I would ever have the slightest chance of making something like that happen, though. I was going to have to savor this short experience and enjoy my time with her while it lasted.

I quickly wiped all those thoughts from my mind upon spotting something familiar. A light blue glow-in-the-dark star that barely still stuck to my bedroom ceiling reminded me that life wasn't always fair. That there weren't always happy endings, especially for people like me, because I didn't deserve them. And that's when the flashbacks started. A ceaseless barrage of memories covered all my thoughts, like unexpectant storm clouds, and sent a chill over my brain, as if it was being gripped by cold, clammy hands. And soon, my body was covered in a cold sweat. My pulse quickening, as if trying to keep rhythm with the sadistic movie reel in my mind.

I looked around the room quickly, trying to orient myself. My rapid breathing becoming too loud as it thrummed in my ears, a panic taking over every part of me. I bounded upward as quickly as my feet would allow, feeling the need to flee with my fear driving me. I needed to get to the bathroom and to the sanctuary of the cold water faucet. Sometimes splashing handfuls on my face helped.

The icy tentacles of the flashbacks started to release their grip as I made my way down the hallway. But to my surprise, the bathroom door was closed, and as I moved closer, I began to hear noises. Unpleasant sounds echoed through the door—intense retching sounds. And then there was a moan that sliced right through my soul. Nothing had ever been able to bring me back to the present so quickly, turning off the movie reel in my mind. Eyre was definitely in there. I probably should have knocked on the door, but I just wanted to get inside and help her. My shaky hand was already on the doorknob before even one thought of her privacy entered my brain.

"Eyre," I called as I turned the knob, but it wouldn't budge. Of course the lock would decide to actually work now. The one time I really needed it not to. There was no response. "Eyre," I tried again more forcefully.

"Go away, Darby. *Please*. I'll be fine. Unless this is the only washroom available, in which case, I'm not sure what to do."

"Eyre, that's not–it's not the only one," I said with irritation. "Please let me in."

"Please just go–" But she didn't get to finish.

"Alright, that's it," I said adamantly. I knew all too well how to get this door open. With one swift kick, I was in. I wasn't about to sit there and jimmy the lock like an *eejit*. The bathtub and sink were on the left hand side of the bathroom and the toilet was in the back right corner, so I knew the door would clear her. My eyes immediately found her crumpled over the toilet. My heart clenched to see her this way. She was chalk white, and for an Irish person to say that, well, that was really saying something. No color appeared, even when an absolutely mortified expression took over. "Eyre, I thought last night things changed for you. I thought . . . You don't have to do this–"

But she stopped me before I could continue.

"Darby, I'm sick," she said firmly.

"It's ok, Eyre. I know you have an . . . eating disorder. You can tell me. I know how I come off, but I promise you can tell me." I grabbed a towel and wet it, then slowly sat down beside her. The worn black and white checkered tiles greeted me with their cold touch. I started to press the wet towel to her forehead, but she pushed my hand away.

"No, Darby, I'm sick because of the food I ate at dinner last night." There was a mixture of shame and exasperation in her voice.

I just looked at her, utter confusion taking over my features. I was trying to mask it, but I knew I couldn't. I really wasn't good at hiding my emotions.

She looked at me with those hazel eyes that might have belonged to a Siren in another life. They must have lured thousands of sailors to the rocky Irish cliffs. I sure hoped hers weren't luring me anywhere because I felt myself falling. The fact that she was finally going to open up to me was making my heart race. And I was falling even more for this woman as I sat crouched on the bathroom tile floor.

"Darby," her voice whispered. "I'm gluten intolerant."

"Gluten intol–" I muttered. "Oh, gluten intolerant." I looked at her sincerely, then a smile spread over my face. "We don't have many of those around here, but we do get an occasional celiac visitor. Why didn't you say something? I feel like the biggest heel for insisting you eat that food for dinner last night. And your sickness is really all caused by the food? Eyre, you should have said something. Why'd you let me think? . . ." My face dropped.

"Darby, I'm sick," she reiterated in a soft voice.

"Well, I know that now." I looked at her, not understanding why she thought I was such an idiot. Well, I had completely jumped to the wrong conclusion last night, just like a goober. I'd never bothered to ask. I had just assumed. And I'd blustered like I was an authority on the topic. *Eejit. Complete Moron. Mansplaining, anyone?* Yuck, I didn't want to be that guy. Sinead had tried to stop me . . .

"No, it's–" She was hunched over the toilet again, violently heaving. I grabbed her hair in an attempt to help her. I felt completely guilty and totally helpless. I was wracking my brain for what I could do to help. I didn't want to leave her to go get something—we didn't even have a grocery store in Doolin. We really were a small village. I went to the sink and filled a cup of water.

"Here, drink this," I said, as I rubbed her back in what I hoped was a soothing and comforting manner.

In between sips, she said, "I have a condition called esophageal Crohn's, and that's why I can't eat certain foods. There are lots of foods that I can't eat. Really, there isn't a lot I can eat that doesn't make me sick, but even when I am careful with what I eat, I still have flares. It's just a vicious cycle. Diet has helped me control it to some degree, but I'm still learning. I'm just now starting to gain some weight back. I've finally started to learn what works best for me, and I'm beginning to see some progress in my quality of life. But that's why I'm so . . . skinny."

She hung her head over the toilet, letting it drop like a wilted flower that had been beat down by the harsh sun in shame.

"Eyre, why are ya looking like that? Why are you looking down? You have nothing to—"

"Oh, I don't know, Darby . . . Maybe because I'm throwing up in front of you, and I just told you I've got this life-threatening condition that I don't have under control. And I was trying to buy some more time to seem normal by not telling you the truth, which is even more embarrassing. And I let you believe something else was going on in order to do it."

"Eyre, you have nothing to be embarrassed about. That's what I was going to say. You're beautiful. I thought that from the first moment I saw you. You were too beautiful for me to ignore. I had to go over and say something to you. And I knew you were special. I was drawn to you." I looked at her. I could tell her physical pain was no match for the other type of pain she felt. And that really gutted me. I knew all too well about that other type of pain, and I wished she knew nothing about it at all. I looked at her deeply and reiterated, "I'm still drawn to you. It's just that—"

The shock in her eyes at what I'd just admitted was seared in my brain. But before I could worry about what to say next, I noticed something wrong. There was a bright red spot on my tee that Eyre was wearing. It stuck out like an off-pitch high note in the middle of an aria. It clung to her, and it was unmistakable. It was blood.

"Eyre . . . Eyre," I said with concern.

"What?" she asked, a little panicked.

"I don't want to freak you out, and I don't want you to look, ok? Just keep looking at me and I'll check it out, alright?" I tried to speak calmly.

"What?" she asked with more panic now.

"There's some blood—"

She did exactly what I said not to: looked down. She let out a mortified sigh. "I'm so sorry. I'll wash the shirt right away. It'll come out. I promise. As soon as . . ." She just looked at the toilet.

"Are ya joking? I'm not worried about my shirt. Please ruin the ugly thing. That's not what's important here. How could you even be concerned—"

I shook my head. What in her life could possibly have led her to have that response? Or was it me? Was I such a horrible person that she would think I'd be concerned about my shirt at a time like this? "Eyre, what's going on? Are you ok?" I heard more emotion in my voice than I'd heard in it for the last several years. I felt like her pain was mine. I wanted to carry it for her. I knew I wasn't strong enough to do that, though, and I suspected she was emotionally much tougher than me, but I'd gladly try if given the opportunity. Yet another thing I wouldn't be able to give her. Another way I'd never measure up.

"Can you please leave now? Please, Darby?" The ache in her voice was killing me.

"No."

"Darby!"

"No."

"I'm fine," she cried out quietly.

"Clearly you're not. People who are fine don't spew multiple types of bodily fluids. I don't know about where you're from, but around here, that's cause for alarm." She just looked at me sternly. I couldn't help but continue, "You're not even going to look?" She stared at me in shock. She'd left me no choice. "Right, well around here when someone is bleeding, we look. It's just an abdomen, nothing too hot. I promise I'll try not to get too worked up when I look," I said with mild sarcasm, trying to lighten the mood and make her feel better about the situation.

"Darby!" she shrieked. But before she could process what I was doing, I had pulled up the bottom of her tee and was staring down at a wound. There I saw a small incision, and the stitches that had been so neatly sewn at one time had torn. They must have ripped open when she started violently heaving.

Her head was in her hands. She wouldn't even look at me. I could barely process what I was seeing. "Right—so you let me walk you all over the countryside with stitches and after what . . . having just had a procedure? Eyre, what were you thinking? Then, you let me talk you into eating gluten? I'm seriously worse than a heel, but that's beside the point. What aren't you telling me? And how could you even fly here? This looks fresh. Eyre, talk to me."

"Please, go." It came out like a hoarse whisper, with her hands muffling her words.

"No," I said again firmly, pulling her hands down from her face. I looked her straight in the eyes. There was one thing I was good at being, and that was being tough in situations that called for it. I had plenty of practice standing firm with people–not letting their opinions bother me. She wasn't going to push me away. She could say whatever she wanted, and I was going to sit right here and look at her. I didn't get *slagged* every day without developing some benefits from it. "We obviously need to get you to a hospital, so they can look at you."

"They wouldn't know what to do with me anyway. They never do," she muttered, sounding completely defeated. Finally, she spoke again, and to my surprise, this time she held my gaze. "I have endometriosis. I had an outpatient procedure. No one knows I'm here in Ireland . . . Well, I have been calling my parents and checking in–after I arrived here. My ex-boyfriend is pretty persistent so I just told them I was somewhere in Ireland." She chuckled nervously. "I'm supposed to be home, recovering. Except I didn't go home from the hospital. Instead, I left and came here. And no, I probably wasn't supposed to fly. But when they released me, I took the overnight hospital bag I had packed and went to the airport instead. And I don't want to talk about any of it. I don't want to talk about my health or my life back home. I just want to be normal with you, if only for a week or two. That's all I wanted when I came here, and I'm really sorry I didn't tell you about my conditions. But I promise, as far as I know, those are all of them."

"Aren't you supposed to wait to make major life decisions after anesthesia or procedures?"

She laughed. "Yes, I signed a very long waiver stating as much. I was also informed of this several times. But it's ironic, don't you think . . . they tell you all of this, yet who's really going to be watching you to know? Maybe the paperwork needs to come with some sort of identification bracelet or something, so you can't do anything stupid before someone stops you. Because it was pretty easy to get on that plane. Actually, incredibly easy. All I had to do was stay awake until I boarded the plane. I was all determination and no inhibitions. It seemed like a fantastic idea at the time. The best idea I'd ever had. Propofol is really a marvelous thing."

I could feel my eyebrows continuing to rise. She looked at me and began talking again while she still could. "And don't feel too bad, that fish was so good, it was *almost* worth it. The trek across the Irish countryside wasn't too terrible, either. Although, the tour bus would have been a lot less painful . . . but not nearly the same."

I just looked at her dumbfounded. Out of all the women in the world, I would have to pick the one with the hardest head and the one that was the most difficult to understand. This was not good. I was already absolutely terrible with women. I would have failed with the most straightforward of the bunch, but this was undoubtedly setting myself up for abject failure.

But all I could do was look deeper into those captivating

eyes. There was a bravery in them that I admired and wished that I possessed. Maybe she couldn't see it, but I most certainly could. No one had ever opened up to me like this before. No one had ever trusted me or thought enough of me to do that. And in this moment, she became even more beautiful to me, which I didn't think was possible. Out of all the ways I didn't believe I'd be lucky enough to fall for someone, I'd never once pictured it being on the bathroom floor. But I couldn't imagine it happening *any* other way now.

THIRTEEN
Eyre

"You're going to take me to the vet?" I asked in total disbelief, looking at Darby with wide eyes. I had talked him out of taking me to the hospital, but I was afraid the alternative was looking worse.

Darby helped me down the hall and to my room. Well, really, he supported all my weight and pretty much carried me most of the way. He probably would have carried me if I'd let him. I was extremely thankful for the assistance because the aftermath of eating the wrong food wasn't just vomiting but also extreme pain. Every joint in my body screamed louder than the next, making me wary of putting one foot in front of the other, knowing the pressure was only going to make it worse. As if they were a group of radical protesters, all my joints swelled to show their displeasure, making me stiff as well. My hands felt like they belonged to the Tin Man and were in desperate need of some oil. Darby was my Dorothy as he picked up the pieces of me.

He put a towel on the bed to avoid stains and helped me

lie down. I didn't realize how weak I was from getting so ill. I was shaking from the food reaction, my angered conditions, and now low blood sugar. And Darby was definitely noticing. Lucky hopped up on the foot of the bed and laid his head and paw on my calf, looking up at me with soulful eyes. One brown and one blue eye drowned with concern. I looked from Lucky to Darby, and ironically enough, their facial expressions looked exactly the same. I guess people do really start to look like their dogs. They were both equally adorable, and I didn't know what to do with either of them.

I couldn't believe I was about to say this . . . "Darby, does this really need to be said? I'm not–" I looked at Lucky. "I'm not of the canine persuasion," I mouthed softly as if it were offensive to Lucky's ears.

"Yeah, Eyre, I'm pretty sure I realized that. Thanks for clueing me in." He quickly raised his eyebrows as if he couldn't believe *I'd* said it. "But the problem lies in the fact that the vet is the best option we've got right now. The nearest doctor is a town over, and considering we only have a bicycle, I think the vet is the way to go. Plus, he'll make a house call. He owes Mak a favor. He's the new, young vet in the village. He just returned after all his schooling and opened up on Main Street. We'll see if we can pull Dr. McDreamy away from the women with their 'pet emergencies.' Now we've got more pets than people in this village."

"What? Did you just say . . . ? I never thought I'd hear words like that out of your mouth." I started laughing a little too much, stopping when my side started to hurt.

"Right, well, McDreamy, McSteamy, Mc . . . insert whatever adjective you fancy, but that is how they describe the new vet."

"Ok, ok. It's alright Darby. Keep your knickers on." He eyed me with that warning look of his. I spoke again, this time without the joking tone. "I just meant that I didn't think you'd be saying those nicknames or even be aware of them. And I happen to think you are very much 'fill in all of those adjectives here.'"

This time Darby's blush wasn't subtle, and it wasn't slow to appear, either. It went up in flames like a match on kerosene. I watched him swallow nervously, his Adam's apple bobbing like a cautionary buoy in a storm.

He cleared his throat. "I'm going to see if Mak can call in that favor and then I'll make you something to eat, ok?" He went to the door, then pivoted and stood there, peering back into the room. "Uh, the question is, what am I going to be able to make you? I don't know if we have the types of food you can eat. And, like I said, there isn't a nearby grocery store. Definitely not a supermarket. Only a really tiny convenience shop. If I had known last night . . ." He trailed off, his face looking embarrassed that he'd brought it up.

I started to sit up. "I'll come down and figure something out. I'm really sorry for all this. I'm such an imposition. Really, this was incredibly stupid of me."

"No." He shot his hand forward and started moving toward me. Lucky sat up on full alert, head cocked. "If you start getting up, I'm going to have to restrain you. As much fun as that will be for me, let's see if we can do this the easy way. Lay back down. I'm fully capable of taking instructions and making whatever you need. I'm sure I can make an egg or something."

"That makes you way more McSteamier in my book." I looked at him a little dreamily.

"Ok, I'm starting to think you hit your head. Did you pass out at some point when I wasn't looking?" I laughed at his question. He continued, "Yeah, I think I actually need to know that information."

"Ow, stop making me laugh," I said in a painful burst of chuckles.

"So am I making an egg, or what?" he asked, trying to bring me back from my laughter. "Now, I wish you could come down to the kitchen with me. I'm actually starting to enjoy these descriptions now . . . even if it is because you bumped your head."

"I didn't bump my head, Darby. And yes, an egg please," I answered, and he looked at me for further instructions. "Any way you want to cook it. Surprise me."

Darby's face was serious as he looked at me. "Right, and absolutely no toast. And then I'll call the vet. We've got to get you checked out sooner rather than later." Then he turned from the room and quickly left.

"Darby," I called.

"Yeah?"

I called out through the open doorway, "Can you make enough to share?" The smile across his face was so infectious it made me momentarily forget my pain. "You know, for the dog," I said mischievously, with a nonchalant shrug.

"Right, princess. Coming right up." But he couldn't even get a teasing note to seep into his happy tone as he grinned widely.

Darby returned faster than I had thought it was possible to cook an egg. He began speaking as soon as he entered the room. "Mak called, and the vet will stop by today. I'm sorry, I'm not thinking too clearly, I need to at least put something on your wound until the vet arrives. Also, we should probably get you out of that shirt and into a clean one."

Darby walked toward me and Lucky bolted upright from his position beside me in the bed, making a little yipping noise as Darby approached us. Earlier, Lucky had snuggled into me, nestling against my side after Darby had left the room. He must have sensed how sick I was feeling. Lucky actually seemed really concerned about me, and it was so sweet. Just as adorable as Darby. However, Lucky now seemed a little worried about what Darby was going to do, and I had to agree with him.

I could see another shirt and a first aid kit in Darby's hands as he looked at me. I said swiftly, "Oh no, I'm fine. We'll wait for the vet."

"Well, I really don't want the shirt to stick to your wound and make it worse. Let me just put something on it temporarily." He'd already laid everything on the bed and was moving toward me. Lucky dashed off with his tail between his legs. I wished I could do the same.

He was already reaching for the hem of my shirt–his shirt, I don't know–when I scooted back away from him. His eyebrows drew together.

I quickly began, "Darby, we've really got to work on this. You can't just pull up women's clothing. Actually, you can't do anything to women's clothing without permission." His expression was stunned as his eyes found mine.

"Eyre. First, this is a medical situation. Second, if it wasn't a medical situation, I would be asking permission before I did anything to you *or* your clothing." His tone had a hint of exasperation while my face burned bright red. I bit my lip, feeling a little self-conscious. He took in my scarlet complexion and said slowly, "Eyre, do I have your permission to bandage your wound? That requires me to pull up your shirt."

Feeling embarrassed, I put my head in my hands, which he quickly pulled away from my face so he could look at me. "I have an egg boiling on the stove downstairs, and I'm not losing cooking points because you decided to go shy on me." I just looked at him. His eyes got a little wider, and he held up his hand gesturing to me in a *well?* motion.

"Oh . . . yes. Sorry," I replied, forgetting he was waiting for an answer.

"Don't apologize. I'm sorry for not asking. I tend to be overly pragmatic, and I just didn't think through the situation. I should always ask." He moved much slower this time and as he did so, I realized I definitely preferred his first approach. Fast and quick was much better. Feeling his rough, calloused fingers slowly graze against my skin as he found the hem of the tee and lifted it upward was so much worse. Because it felt *so good*. Every contact with him reminded me that I was indeed capable of having feelings for a man. Of wanting a connection—a relationship, even—and everything that went along with it. The chemical flares inside my body were making that quite clear by sending up an SOS wherever they could to let me know not to give up on this type of connection. Hope had been spotted and my cells were all celebrating in tandem.

Darby looked at me mischievously. "You know, I lied before," he said with a little sparkle in his tone.

"Huh?" I asked breathlessly, allowing his hands to work on me. Hands that were obviously used to hard labor yet very skilled.

He chuckled. "I lied when I said *"abdomens"* weren't hot and not to worry. I think I may even have a thing for belly buttons now."

I shoved at him, glad for the comic relief. However, the look in his eyes was anything but funny. His gold flecks were dancing, sparkling with intensity. How was it possible for a man to look this devastatingly handsome while taking care of you? Not only that but for him to look at you like you were beautiful when you had to be looking your absolute worst.

I sat up higher in the bed, propping myself against the pillows he had so kindly provided and meticulously arranged, so I could look deeper into those unbeatable greens. I wanted a better vantage point. The dreamy look in his eyes reminded me of the piano piece "Of Foreign Lands and Places" from Robert Schumann's *Scenes from Childhood*. The ordinary was becoming so extraordinarily beautiful. The peaceful notes glided through my brain and provided a soundtrack for this moment.

His hand slowly moved toward my face, hesitantly. He tucked a loose strand of hair gently behind my ear, lingering there as if he never wanted to leave. The music of my mind shifted abruptly, overtaken by Debussy. The romantic swell of his notes enveloped me, as if it wasn't clear enough what I was already feeling. My mind was telling me we were in an *Arabesque* moment, one of my favorite pieces by him. And then, as if Darby wanted to confirm my mind's musical choices, his face started swaying closer to mine. A dance of two expressions playing off of one another. Daring the other to ask for that connection. But there was no way, after watching me throw up all morning, that he had any intention of kissing me. *Did he? That was gross. So gross. Wasn't it?* I mean, I had brushed my teeth, *but still.*

My face was responding to his before I could even think about it. And somehow, our faces were closer than they'd ever been, inches apart. So close that I could see the wild Irish dance in his eyes. I was witnessing firsthand that he did, in fact, actually care. And as much as he tried to hide it, he had a huge heart. One that I was beginning to think possessed deep emotions within it that were more than he could handle. Maybe that's why he shut them down. And suddenly, the inches dwindled. This was really going to happen. *Oh my–*

"Darby!" Mak's yell cut through the charged air, slicing through all the electrons and protons moving toward each other in an undeniable attraction. "You're going to ruin these eggs. How long have they been boiling? Can't you do anything, lad?"

"Coming. Just cut them off," Darby called back. I heard a tea kettle screeching in unison with Mak's calls.

"Darby! What are you doing? The kettle's going off, too. How long does it take to put a bandage on? Good thing we called a vet. Obviously, you're hopeless. Seriously, lad. Just stick the bandage on the part that's bleeding. That's the red area. *Dope!*"

I just smiled at Darby. And while I expected him to be upset at Mak, he looked the happiest I'd ever seen him.

"Be right down. Thanks for that cutting-edge advice," he yelled back. Then looking at me in a gentle way, he said, "Well, I was going to help you change your shirt, but that seems like it might be . . . inappropriate now. But, um, I still can help. I can find a way *not* to look. I was always going to find a way not to look," he added quickly. I could see how flustered I made him. Something that seemed very un-Darby-like.

"Yes, I'd feel better if I just did it myself. Thanks for your offer, though," I said a little shyly.

"Ok, I'll be back. Fruit?"

"Anything without seeds. Thank you," I said as I sat up straight, preparing to change my shirt after he had left. I held another soccer tee in my hands with a woodsy scent to it that I already recognized as Darby's.

A few minutes later, I could hear Mak yelling at him in the kitchen. It was too hard to make out their banter, but it made me smile. No doubt he was grilling Darby about why it was so hard to dress a wound. Darby returned moments later, Mak's voice still trailing behind him. Mak wasn't giving up the ghost, but Darby was just ignoring him.

"He'll give up soon enough," Darby said as he sat a tray down on my lap. I'd never had breakfast in bed. Certainly never delivered by a man before, especially not one this attractive. And I had to admit it looked really nice. So wonderful, in fact, that I wanted to cry. Perhaps it was the low blood sugar kicking in. Although when I looked at the man in front of me, I didn't think that was the case.

"Will you sit and eat with me?"

"Oh, so I am the dog you were referring to. Or did Lucky just abandon you?" he teased.

"No, it was always you. Thank you for making extra. I was hoping you'd keep me company. I really enjoy being with you."

He smiled at my words. "You're the only one."

"That's not true." I looked at him. "But, ok, just more time for me."

He sat precariously on the edge of the bed, and I nodded with my head to the large vacant spot beside me that Lucky had abandoned. He walked around to it, and I pulled back the covers for him.

"Ah, a *real* breakfast in bed. The full experience. Now this I've never had," Darby said with a smile.

"Good, me either."

As if finding my words hard to believe, he said, "I'd think men would be lining up to do that job."

"No. They're lining up to run away from me as fast as they can. None of them would have stuck around if I had gotten this sick on them. I mean, I know you're kind of stuck with me at your house, but you still would have done the same thing for me even if I wasn't staying here."

"Well, after one date with me the women can't run away fast enough. So we're even."

I couldn't believe that was possibly true. I saw how all those women responded to him on the tour. No, he did something to make them run away. I was sure of it. And it made me very hesitant about finding out for myself what that might be.

"I don't believe it," I challenged.

"Well, believe it."

"I'll have to see it to believe it." My face flushed, but I didn't back down. I couldn't believe I'd said it. After all, I had just warned myself that I didn't want to find out what made women run from him. But the way he looked at me made me feel like I might be different. Or maybe that's how they all felt, too. Either way, there was something about him that made me unable to stop myself.

The uncontainable grin on his face was suddenly replaced by something else. "I promise you, Eyre. You don't want a date with me. I can't do that to you. You certainly deserve a lot better."

"I think *I* deserve to be the judge of that." When it was clear he wasn't going to say anything else, I speared a piece of fruit and started to eat.

We shared the tray and ate in what was an absolute luxury for me. This experience couldn't be touched by any other I'd had with a man. He joked with me and relieved my mind of its pain. And when we were finished, he set the tray aside and let me lean against his shoulder, where I found refuge in the sweetest sleep.

FOURTEEN
Darby

H ope. That's what this twinge was in my chest as this beautiful woman found comfort in me. Her head lay on my shoulder, and in her sleep she had drifted closer to me. Now her perfectionist barriers were asleep as well as she snuggled closer. I wondered if those walls kept her from getting close to everyone in her life or if she was just wise to be cautious. Something told me it wasn't just with me.

I was desperate–actually more than desperate–to know what had brought her here. I wanted to know all about her and everything she wasn't telling me. That incision haunted me. It looked painful, to say the very least, and my mind couldn't move on from it. She was like a puzzle with pieces missing. I was all too familiar with missing puzzle pieces, seeing as Lucky loved to eat any puzzle pieces that fell on the floor. I happened to think the same thing might happen here. If I allowed the pieces to drop, she'd make sure they disappeared, and I'd never get another opportunity to know about them.

I should have been more persistent. But she had looked so completely defeated. Whatever was happening in her life, it had pushed her to the breaking point. I was pretty sure that's what I had witnessed at the cliffs. I don't think that's why she originally came here or what she intended to do, but it seemed the thought was crossing her mind. And I wanted to take that thought away from her—whatever had caused her to get to that point—but I also felt like I might be the last person who could do that for her.

A sigh of contentment sounded from her as she nestled into my chest. She had slowly migrated down my body, and now she had her arms wrapped around me. A smile appeared unexpectedly on my face. I could actually imagine this woman being my happy place. The word "happy" and I were such strangers that it felt wrong for them to be in the same thought.

As I sat there studying her face, a knock sounded at the door, disrupting my current mood and the first peace I'd felt in a long time. Reality was here to drag me back down to earth.

"Come in," I said as softly as I could. A tuft of perfectly coiffed, blond hair poked through the doorway, followed by an immaculately dressed man. The vet had arrived, and I knew from experience he always made quite the entrance.

Mak, of course, followed behind Sloane, tiptoeing silently. I knew he wanted to make sure I didn't mess anything else up. But when he saw Eyre and me together, he got a shocked look on his face. He immediately began speaking to Sloane in an agitated manner. "The dog's not in here. So sorry, Sloane. Let me show you to the other room." And I immediately understood what he was doing. Seeing his apparent worry, I was now concerned, too. I had heard the way the whole village talked about this man with his kind bedside manner and his Adonis features–"every female's fantasy" was what they called him. It appeared Mak hadn't thought through this part of calling the vet. And the more flustered Mak became, the more I began to worry. Eyre was going to see she might need to think twice and next time she would know she better shop around for men in Ireland.

I looked from Mak to Sloane and felt the impending humiliation that was sure to follow. It felt like the universe was pouring salt on my open wound. It would be just my luck that I would be given a taste of what a connection like this could be like, right before it was swiftly ripped away because I was pretty sure that's what was about to happen.

Sloane cocked his head back in alarm, looking thoroughly confused at Mak's words. "I thought I was here to see a person. You never said anything about a dog." He looked at the sleeping Eyre with intrigue, and to my utter dismay, *interest*. It appeared Mak's worry had grounds for concern after all. Sloane could have any woman that he wanted . . . but Eyre was gorgeous. Nothing could take her beauty away, not even throwing up all morning and ripping her stitches wide open. Plus, she had the quality of a wounded baby bird, her colors shining even more brightly, and the grace with which she endured her conditions only made her look stronger.

"Now why would I call a vet to look at a woman? Sloane, I'm not daft. Not yet anyway. Come on." Mak was literally grabbing at the man. My eyes went wide. We did actually need to get Eyre medical attention. That was much more important than trying to keep her interest in me because that wasn't going to last much longer anyway, nor should it. She deserved to be with a man like Sloane, who had his life together. I eyed Mak with a look that told him as much.

Sloane dismissed Mak's words. "The lady looks like she's ill. Her coloring is off. Miss, are you alright?" Sloane took a step toward Eyre, but at the sound of his voice, her eyelids were already fluttering. *Great, they responded to Adonis. Why wouldn't Siren eyes respond to a Greek god?* This was just my luck. I was completely doomed. This was all a fated Greek tragedy . . . or comedy, depending on your perspective.

I practically rolled my eyes. Yup, the universe had done it again. Well, too late now. Sloane, being such a good lad, was going to make sure that he spoke with her. There was no way that Mak was going to be able to lead him out of this room now.

I could hear disgruntled sounds from Mak, and then he finally stormed out, saying something about getting the tea ready. I think he just didn't want to be privy to the inevitable. Getting overshadowed by an Adonis' *wasn't* going to exactly be a pleasant way to start the day.

"Miss," Sloane tried again as he stepped closer. He started to reach out to her, but I stopped him with my hand so I could explain the situation to him.

"Her name is Eyre. She's gluten intolerant, and she ate something she shouldn't have at the local pub last night. It's my fault. I convinced her to have the special. And then she got sick this morning and opened up the stitches on her abdomen. I bandaged them, but well . . . I thought you should look at 'em. I really appreciate you making a house call. I'm worried about her. She seems weak and fatigued."

"Ahh." Sloane nodded gravely, as if he could have sensed everything I said by just walking into the room. That was Sloane, though. I think the whole vet degree and Greek god thing had really gone to his head.

I looked down at Eyre a little too long, and Sloane cleared his throat impatiently. My eyes shifted back up to him with a look of annoyance, which I'm sure I did not do a good job of hiding. Then I bent back down and began to wake her. I gently started shaking her and saying her name.

Her eyelids started fluttering, and then she raised her chin to me with a pleasant sigh. A radiant smile overtook her sleepy features. Her mouth opened to say something when Sloane moved closer and cleared his throat yet *again. Was something stuck in it? Where was Mak with the tea?* Please get the man something to *bloody* drink. He'd ruined the moment, and now I'd never get to hear what was going to come out of those beautiful lips. Those delicately soft lips that I couldn't seem to stop thinking about. Sloane was starting to become more than an uncomfortable needle in my side. More like the whole scalpel.

Eyre, of course, turned toward the noise, and I'll never forget the moment their eyes met. And now it really was like I was in a Greek tragedy. Some *Tristen and Isolde* rubbish, for sure. In my imagination, I could hear a tragic aria playing in the background and see a dramatic spotlight vividly focused on them. It seemed like Sloane was absolutely smitten with Eyre. *Give me a break.*

"Uh... Um." He cleared his throat yet *again.*

"Sloane," I interrupted. "Mak is making some tea. Why

don't you go down and give Eyre a chance to wake up. I think you could use a cup. I'm sure you've been working hard all week and the last thing you needed was to get up early on a Saturday morning. Go rest." The annoyance couldn't stay out of my tone.

"Eyre," was all Sloane could say in a slightly *breathy* tone. She looked up at him dreamily in reply–although I was hoping she was just sleepy. Okay, this *Romeo and Juliet* nonsense was getting old. I would happily play the part of Paris and try to break it up.

Unfortunately, I figured it was time to introduce them. "Sorry, where are my manners? Sloane, this is Eyre. Eyre, this is Sloane." I looked at Sloane and spoke. "We really need you to check Eyre's wound and make sure that it's ok. She was able to eat something this morning and keep it down. Tea and an egg. A little bit of fruit . . ." But Sloane wasn't listening to a word I said. *Great*.

Sloane finally spoke–something more than a throat clearing. "Where are my manners? Hello, I'm Sloane." He reached out and ever so gently took Eyre's hand, and then he continued to hold it. Well, things were just getting worse. He turned his head toward me. "Darcy–uh–I mean Darby," he quickly corrected, which sounded incredibly weird to my ears. I hadn't heard him say my name correctly since grade school. "Can you go help . . . Uh . . . Mak. I need some time to consult with the patient in *private*. Before I give her a proper examination."

I'm sure he did. A lot of time and a real thorough examination to boot. My irritation was starting to get the better of me. "I think that's up to Eyre." I pointed my gaze at him. "She *is* in a foreign country. She's only been here a couple of days. She may want someone she knows to stay with her."

Sloane looked at me skeptically. "She probably should have picked a different local." The words were out of his mouth before he could stop them, and my eyebrows rose in mock surprise. Sloane was obviously driven and extremely competitive. I would just continue to take the high road and let him drive himself off of it.

Eyre was starting to pick up on the tension between us. She sat up straighter in the bed. Addressing Sloane, she said, "Darby has been nothing but kind and generous to me while I've been staying here. He has already looked after my wound, and I'm sure he'll be able to do it again if I need help, so I would like for him to stay." Her hazel eyes looked at me with such feeling. Something in my soul said it wasn't possible for her to look at the Adonis in the same way. She couldn't possibly look at another man in this way, *could she?*

I returned her deep gaze as I spoke, "Of course. I'm happy to help. And you're welcome to stay here as long as you like," I said with what I hoped was a reassuring smile.

Sloane interrupted our moment. "And I would always be happy to find you a place to stay, Eyre, if you like. But first, let's see how bad that wound looks."

Sloane seemed hesitant about how best to proceed. He kept eying me as if he wished I wasn't there. He moved forward slowly and crouched down, setting his medical bag beside the bed. I quickly rose and offered to bring over the large chair by the window for him. He graciously accepted. I didn't need to see Sloane's features, but I wanted to see Eyre's. I stood beside Sloane as he asked her questions and proceeded to examine her.

After he raised Eyre's shirt and saw her incision, he asked, "So, Eyre, how long have you been having female issues?"

Eyre's eyes opened wide at Sloane's blunt inquiry and her coloring paled. "Darby, I need you to leave," she croaked out quietly. "Please, Darby, now," she said a little more urgently.

Sloane turned with raised eyebrows. "Oh, and Darby, could you please check on that tea? I bet Eyre could use a cup right about now. I know I could."

FIFTEEN
Darby

I paced outside the door. *What could possibly be so bad that she wouldn't allow me to stay? How had we gone from "Darby is going to help take care of my wound" to "please leave?"* I didn't understand what was happening. I was hopeless when it came to women, and I was in way over my head. There was "over your head" and then there was "me"–one of those legends lost at sea. Mak finally came up with a tray of tea and saw me burning up the flooring with my back-and-forth pacing to expel my anxiety. Mak had taken his sweet ol' time. Obviously, he hadn't been motivated to see the ending of this Greek tragedy.

"What in the world, Darce? You let Sloane kick ya out? I knew you wouldn't win, but at least stay in the room, son." He eyed me with total exasperation. "How can you go totally spineless on me now? We're getting ya back in that room."

Mak went to knock on the door, but I stopped him. I took the tray from him. "Eyre doesn't want me in there. She did at first, but she had a medical procedure before her trip over here and she doesn't want me to know about it. Sloane figured that out quickly and he used it to get me out of the room. But it's ok. This was going to happen sooner or later. You need to resign yourself to the fact that Eyre deserves someone better than me."

"Like Sloane?" Mak huffed out.

"Well . . . maybe not Sloane. Although, he's an ok guy, I guess, but he plays a little dirty to get his way."

"Darby." My head snapped back at the use of my real name. "Ya are a much better man than Sloane could ever dream of being. You need to start realizing that. Sloane wouldn't have *dared* to sit on the bathroom floor with her this whole morning. He wouldn't have made her breakfast in bed and let her fall asleep in his arms. He'd have made some excuse and left to make veterinary calls."

"You don't know that."

"Oh, *but I think I do*," Mak said emphatically.

I just stared back at Mak and handed the tray back to him. "Here, you take the tea. They don't want to see me."

"Grow a pair, Darce." Mak shoved the tray back at me.

"Mak, I'm respecting her wishes," I said with defeat.

"Women don't always know what they want. That's for certain because the whole village thinks they want Sloane." He shoved the tray back harder this time.

Just then, the door opened. Sloane must have heard our whispered argument. He looked at us curiously. "Wonderful, I was hoping we might get some tea," Sloane said as he started to take the tray from us, but Mak stopped him.

"Oh, Sloane, no need for you to carry the tray. I'll bring it in for ya. You're the vet and our guest," Mak said in an exaggerated manner. I could see right through his tactics, but

Sloane's shoulders just rolled back as he thanked Mak. And with a wink, Mak vanished inside the room. I swore that man was going to be the death of me. He would at least be outliving me.

Now, it was just me, all by myself, on this side of the *bloody* door. *Why must it feel like I'm always on the outside?* In what felt like an eternity, Mak finally came back out, saying, "Well, I'm just an old man, so they let me hear some of their conversation. I was like a fly on the wall, and they didn't really seem to notice me. From what I can tell she has a condition that causes her a lot of pain, so she had to have a procedure. She's obviously really sensitive about it. Doctor "feel good" is in there right now, *comforting* her. Darce, you really need to get in there."

"It's not my place. If she doesn't want me to know, then I shouldn't know. You shouldn't have even told me—"

"Like ya don't want to know," Mak interrupted me.

He was right about that. I really did want to know. I had a feeling she wouldn't tell me, and I didn't think I could have a good understanding of her without that information. "Were . . . female issues mentioned? Sloane said something about them when I was in the room, and that seemed to be what caused her to change her mind about me being in the room."

"Oh, yeah . . . Well, he did say "fibroids" a few times . . ."

We just both looked at each other. We were way out of our element. That one health class in school wasn't going to get us very far, especially when it had been fifty years ago for Mak. There couldn't be a worse pair trying to figure out something like this. "Darce, what does that mean?"

"What?" His words snapped me out of my confused state.

Mak reiterated, "What do you think it all means?"

"It means I feel bad for digging. And we should stop." I walked down the hallway, feeling completely defeated, and closed myself up in the bathroom.

A knock sounded on the bathroom door. It felt like I'd been in this bathroom forever, but it really had only been a couple of minutes.

Mak's voice called through the bathroom door. "Darce, she's asking where ya went."

"Yeah, I'm sure she is. How'd you orchestrate that?" I said with disbelief in my tone.

Mak responded. "No, really. I told ya miracles happen. I was just starting to plot an elaborate plan when the door suddenly opened and Sloane asked if you were available. Now I swear, I'm not making this up, Darce. And good thing, too, because I wasn't coming up with much. My plan was more complicated than a Rube Goldberg machine and equally as superfluous, so I thought we'd lost for sure. It was looking like another Battle of Aughrim."

Mak continued, "Darby, don't be a fool. Take the gift. Ok? If a woman passes up the current, most eligible man in the village for you, take the gift and don't ask questions. I should know. And you know as well as I do that you could be one of the most eligible men in the village if you would just show some interest and work on that disposition of yours. You know, actually try to act a little romantic. Now get your–"

But I had already opened the door. I didn't want to listen to his lecture anymore. There was a big grin on his lovable face, along with his wrinkles from years of jokes and laughter at my expense. I had to admit, I loved seeing those weathered lines. I just nodded at him, not giving him any more satisfaction, and went to see what awaited me.

Sloane sat on a chair, impatiently waiting. He looked annoyed, like the Greek god Ares, who hadn't gotten his way. He looked up at me dismissively and then started organizing his instruments and speaking without looking at me. "Eyre and I have had a nice discussion, and now I'm going to sew up her wound. I offered to take her to the veterinary clinic, but she said it was fine to do it here–against my advice. She asked if you were still outside the door and if you were able to come back in."

I almost burst out laughing. The man couldn't bring himself to say the words "she asked for you." I think that– right there–just made my life complete.

"Oh, I see," I said, trying desperately to be the bigger man, but I had to literally bite my tongue as intermittent chuckles tried to slip out.

Sloane continued stoically, "All right then . . . well . . . I'm going to keep setting up, but first I need to ask Mak for something. I'll be right back." Sloane got up stoically– moving like a Michelangelo sculpture come to life. He left in a sulky mood. I was slightly concerned about what he was planning to do. I could have gotten whatever he needed, but

I guess he thought it would have looked bad for him to send me right back out the door again.

I walked over to Eyre, whose cheeks did have a little more color now. I was happy to see that, even if it was from the embarrassment of everyone knowing her private business. I looked at her and said, "How are you doing? I know Sloane can be a little much, but he really is a good vet. I just hope it translates to people. I don't think he can mess up stitches too badly. Mak probably could have even done it."

She laughed lightly and then paused, looking at me. "I'm sorry," she said softly.

"For what?" I asked.

"For making you leave the room. I feel bad about that. I just didn't know . . . I didn't expect him to . . . to say that. It took me by surprise. I thought he'd just treat the wound and be done with it. I just didn't expect it . . . I should have," she finished and gazed at me sheepishly.

"Well, it's nobody else's business."

"I'm sure Sloane was just trying to be thorough," she remarked.

"Yeah, *thorough*," I emphasized, and she looked at me, her eyebrows raised in curiosity.

"Darby, you've been so kind to me. I feel that I owe you an explanation. I just didn't want you to hear about it from Sloane. I wasn't sure what he was going to say."

"You don't owe me anything, Eyre. Why don't you just focus on getting better first, and then if you still want to talk about it, I'm here." I couldn't believe I'd just said that. I wanted to know more than I realized. I really didn't want to accidentally say the wrong thing or be insensitive by not knowing. And I excelled in that area. But even more than that, I just wanted to know Eyre.

She reached out and took my hand, speaking quietly. "I'm actually really scared of getting these stitches, Darby."

I looked at her with sympathy. "I would be, too." Eyre looked at me with disbelief. "I'm right here, though. I'll watch for you and make sure he does it right. I'll tie him in a Celtic knot if he doesn't."

Eyre let out a little laugh, her hand feeling warm and soft in mine. It was like slipping into the warm water in the bay. *What is it about this woman?* I had run from every American tourist I had encountered and now I was finally hoping one didn't run from me. Oh, the irony of my life.

She looked at me with laughter in her eyes. "There's no way that a Celtic knot is a real thing." Then quietly, she said, "I really do want to tell you, Darby."

"Ok, shall we start?" Sloane interrupted us as he returned with some towels in his hand. I swear it was like the man had perfect timing to ruin the moment. *What if she didn't open up to me again?*

I stayed in the room and held Eyre's hand while he stitched her up. And I did as I promised. I watched the whole time, making sure I kept an eye on everything–even if there was absolutely nothing I could do to help.

Eyre seemed to do okay especially since he numbed the area. But I was pretty sure she was very seasoned at putting on a good front. Already, I admired this woman who I had known for such a short amount of time. She continued to hold my hand after Sloane was done and I beamed with joy.

Sloane cleaned up and silently packed away his instruments. No doubt he was plotting his next move. I continued sitting on the edge of the bed, entranced by Eyre. I was content to sit by her side–holding her hand–in complete awe of the connection we had made.

At last, Sloane ventured to speak to Eyre. "I can come back to check on you tomorrow, but I really think it would be better if you came to the clinic. We're usually closed on Sunday, but I'm happy to make an exception. I know Mak and Darby only have a bicycle, so I can drive over and pick you up. It's a small car, so I only have room for one passenger. *Sorry,*" he said, looking at me.

"Right, because polluting the environment is so attractive." He eyed me. *Oh no, I'd said that one out loud!*

"It's electric . . . *Darcy.*"

"*Of course it is,*" I replied. And with that, Sloane took Eyre's other hand for one final goodbye, which I eventually had to cut short and then help him find his way out the door–I was too worried he'd been blinded by Siren eyes to find it. *Good riddance.*

SIXTEEN
Eyre

As soon as Darby left the room, I exhaled the gigantic breath I'd been holding. I couldn't fathom that I'd flown across an ocean to outrun my troubles and they'd hitched a ride along with me, anyway. It felt like the final scene in Disney's Haunted Mansion ride and my "hitchhiking ghosts" were staring back at me. Boy were they grinning.

Getting more involved with Darby meant opening that wound right back up. I'd literally torn open my physical wound today, but the figurative one was about to make an even bigger splash. And this was the reason I'd run. I couldn't face this one. I hadn't been able to have this conversation with my ex-boyfriend. I couldn't even tell my friends and family. If I uttered the words, then they were permanent. Then I was admitting my failure as a person–as a woman. And I couldn't bear it.

So I'd flown here to Ireland, to leave all that pain behind. To lock it in a deep, dark place and let the beautiful countryside of Ireland mend me. To be so surrounded by it that I had no choice but to be healed and restored. It was going to be a type of rebirth. An "Irish Renaissance." Because I couldn't face the alternative. I didn't want to know what my life looked like if I didn't find a way to heal.

I had prayed so hard, yet it seemed none of my prayers had been answered. At least, not that I could tell. The pain only got worse—both physically and emotionally—until I wondered what I had done to deserve it. Until one day, I hit rock bottom. And I didn't know if I should keep praying.

I was trying to hold the tears back when I saw Darby entering the room, grinning as triumphantly as Jude Nelson at the end of *The Breakfast Club*. I could almost see his fist raised in the air. A smile overtook me. There was something about Sloane that had really bothered him. Whatever it was, I was happy to see it wasn't there anymore.

I sat back up, shaking everything off, especially any trace of Sloane. I was happy that I was able to tell him about my procedure in private, but I hadn't really relished being alone with him. There was just something about him that made me uncomfortable, a gut instinct.

Darby's gait as he walked over to me was actually adorable. He looked like an extra in a Riverdance production as he sauntered my way. In my imagination, he was, and I almost burst out laughing. He sat down on the edge of the bed and crossed a leg over his knee.

"So..." he said as he looked deeply at me.

"Is he finally gone?" Mak asked, barging into the room, using his walking stick to push the door open with full force. I broke out in laughter.

Darby didn't look as amused. "Yeah, Mak, he's gone."

And then a realization dawned on Darby's face. "Mak, we totally forgot about the shop. Saturday's the busiest day." He made a move to get up, disheartened about this revelation and also seemingly disappointed to have our time interrupted.

Mak put his hand on Darby's shoulder and quickly pushed him back down on the bed. "Darce, I wasn't joking about giving you the week off. But I didn't give you time off so you could just sit here. You should either be taking care of Eyre or showing her the sights. I want you to give her the best Darcy tour ever. And by that, I mean Darcy at the end of the novel, not the beginning, please. You do tend to find these loopholes."

"Well, then, don't *you* need to be at the shop?" Darby replied.

"Hold your horses. I called and told them I was running late. Teagan is covering for me until I can get there. I thought we could all have a nice picnic down by Doolin's Pier, if Eyre's up for it. I'm not sure what Eyre can do, but I called Sinead and she said she could come. You know she doesn't have to go into the pub til' later. Then you can show Eyre some of Burren Park. I'll even get you a parasol so you can escort her in true regency fashion." Darby just glared at him. "Probably best to wear your uniform, too, so she doesn't feel cheated. It's good marketing, as well. I just received our company sunglasses. I haven't shown you yet. They're shaped like little pots of gold and the bridge is a rainbow. You're gonna love 'em, Darce. They weren't in the budget, but when I imagined them on you, I made room."

"How kind," Darby snorted.

"I'll just call Teagan and tell him he'll have to hold down the fort a while longer."

Darby turned to me with a concerned gaze. "We can always go another day, Eyre. Don't push yourself. We've got puzzles and board games here. I'm happy to stay home with you," he said with care. The fact that Darby had puzzles and board games gave me warm fuzzy feelings. This man playing a goofy board game seemed so out of character. This was something I had to see. And the juxtaposition made me bite my bottom lip at the attractiveness. I'm not sure why I suddenly pictured us curled up under a blanket by a fireplace, putting a puzzle together. It seemed so simple . . . so attainable . . . so incredible.

I shook my head to clear the bewitching fog and looked at those sparkling green eyes. "Yes, I'd love that. I'll just have to go slow. How much walking is involved?"

"Probably too much, but I could put you in the sidecar of one of our bikes. We have one for when Sinead's granddaughter visits," Darby said as he looked at me sincerely. "And I could pedal really slowly."

The serious look on his face was melting me. *Since when did he get so sexy?* Maybe I needed the Darby that irritated and infuriated me to come back. I was feeling way too many things. *And he was going to put me in the sidecar of his bike?* Okay, I didn't know how I was going to survive all this Irish attention—especially from a man who didn't normally dole it out . . . or so they said.

Mak grinned wildly. "Splendid, I'll go call Sinead back. She's halfway through packing the basket anyway." Mak skipped out of the room.

Darby leaned forward. My eyes widened in shock at his

proximity. But then he whispered to me, "I haven't forgotten you were going to tell me something. I would really like to hear it, if you still want to tell me. Whenever you're ready." The words barely made their way out. I could tell this—vulnerability—was difficult for him. Then he got up from the bed slowly and spoke in a normal tone. "You said you have a change of clothes. Do you need a jacket?"

I just looked at him like he wasn't real. "Yes, I do have a change of clothes, so I won't have to wear your baggy tee and boxers to the park, thank you," I said with a laugh.

"Well, that's just such a disappointment. We can go shopping later. I know a good place. I'll get you a jacket, just in case." He turned to leave. "Oh, and keep the boxers and tee. I wouldn't dare wear them again, knowing how good they look on you."

I didn't know how I was going to survive this picnic with him and not look like a total fool. He made me feel like a reckless teen again. Well, I guess *again* wasn't accurate. I hadn't been the rebellious type in my youth or one to throw caution to the wind. Darby made me feel carefree for the first time. And I was ready to lean in.

Mak took his bike and went to pick up Sinead from her house. I thought it was absolutely adorable that he insisted on going to her house to "pick her up," even though we were clearly closer to the park and he wasn't driving a car. But he looked like a schoolboy setting out to collect his first childhood crush. Maybe he truly was. His Irish tartan cap bobbed, and the faint sound of whistling wafted over to us as he walked his bike briskly down the path.

I turned to Darby, startled to see he already had a bike beside me. I had been too engrossed in Mak's movements to take notice. I looked at Darby, and there was already electricity pulsing between us. His fiery greens danced with new life and vitality, a growing attraction in them. His well-defined features, with just a hint of jaw stumble, were the perfect canvas for his gaze that was making my nerves raw.

"Have you ever ridden in a sidecar before?" he asked, breaking the silence but not the connection. I blinked in recognition that I was biting my bottom lip like an—what do they call it here?—*eejit*. "I imagine you don't use bikes in America as much as we do here." But it was hard to hear him when I was lost in thoughts of him almost kissing me earlier.

"Oh, no. This will certainly be a new experience," I replied. Somehow, I already knew everything was going to be new and exciting with Darby. *What had happened to me dying alone, a cat lady who would be devoured by her angry mob of hungry, furry felines?* And since I was a dog person, I'm not sure how the cats came into that scenario. *Crafty little buggers.*

The man in front of me was not what I thought my future held. He had come out of nowhere. I had safely resigned myself to the fact that no one was going to want me anymore. Before this trip to Ireland and meeting Darby, I was certain that I was destined to end up alone. I was convinced that I must have played the Old Maid game one too many times as a young girl and it had cursed me, branding me as a Charlotte Lucas at the ripe old age of seven. Before this trip I was certain that the game had been one hundred percent correct in its predictions. Because it seemed no one ever got that card, *but me*. Now, Darby was starting to prove that little "know-it-all" game wrong and I loved it.

Well, you haven't told him yet, now have you? But somehow, there was a part of me that thought he'd be different. Ironic that I thought this cynical man would be the one to be different. But I was starting to see a more authentic picture of him. He was like a painting that needed to be restored. Hidden underneath layers of dirt and debris that needed to be delicately rubbed away, one layer at a time, so as not to disturb the precious treasure underneath.

"Well, riding a sidecar is even easier than riding a bike." He smiled at me and positioned himself at the side of the bike. "Just turn around." And then, without warning, he picked me up–careful to put his hands low on my hips–and placed me gently into the sidecar. A squeal escaped me as he did so, and he chuckled.

"A warning, please, Darby," I said, aghast, looking back at him.

"Well, I figured you knew you were going to have to get in it somehow. Better to let me help you than you trying to get into it by yourself with your stitches. Or were you hoping Dr. McDreamy might come back and help you?" Darby said teasingly, but I could tell it was underlined with so much hope that it wasn't true. He paused and quickly said, "Nevermind, please forget it. Sorry, it's none of my business."

I responded right away, "Dr. McPerfect isn't so perfect. He's actually a little too forward and quite full of himself."

"Oh," Darby said, and I couldn't help but hear a hint of glee in his tone.

"Yes, and if you must know, I declined his dinner invitation."

"Wow, that was fast."

"Yes, pretty fast and unprofessional. Then I declined his tour guide offer. I told him that I already had the best tour guide in the village and that I was already booked with him for the entire week."

"Really? And you're sure you're not disappointed about that? I could give you a refund. I mean we want all our customers to be happy. If there's an upgrade available—"

"No, it would be a downgrade, Darby, and then I would have to give your tour office a bad review. But I'm happy to leave an exceptionally good review, if I get the full *Darby* experience. I want parasols, spinning shamrocks, and everything but the kitchen sink," I said with the biggest laugh. He fell back slightly against the bike, and it started to tip backward, taking me with it.

"Sorry," he said quickly, righting the bike, but I'd never been worried that we'd fall. "I'll make sure you have the best *Darby* experience possible. We Irish aim to please."

I looked back at him and smiled. His eyes had such a warmth to them that they reminded me of the warm summer pools of an emerald sea on the hottest day of the year. *Chink*. I was also aware that at this rate, Sinead and Mak were sure to beat us, and they probably had twice as far to walk.

"Well, when can I expect this tour to start?" I asked teasingly. But he just kept looking at me.

Finally, in a fluster, he said, "Now, definitely now. Sorry." And he began slowly pedaling.

SEVENTEEN

Eyre

As Darby picked up speed on the bike, the Irish countryside passed by quickly in a blurred mix of greens and yellows as we cycled down the picturesque, winding road. The bright blue sky was crisp above my head. I leaned my head back slightly to take it all in. I was like a kid watching a movie projector for the first time. Standing as close as possible to the large screen, trying my best to take it all in.

In the distance, the open water was endless in all directions, dancing and sparkling at a rate that far surpassed my heartbeats. The blues and greens were unmatched by anything I'd ever seen, except for possibly the green color of Darby's eyes, which I think I preferred even over this magnificent sight. The road quickly led us to our destination, and we started to gradually veer toward the shoreline. Darby slowed when we came close to the coast. There was a large grassy area between us and the ocean, and beyond that there was a large rocky area and a pebbled beach. The massive rocks would make it too difficult to have a picnic, so we'd have to settle for the grassy area further from the water.

As we drew closer to the shore, I was immediately met with the sounds of crashing waves and the wind whipping ferociously around me. The fierce sounds were intense yet comforting. Darby parked the bike, dismounted, and tenderly helped me out of the sidecar in a considerate and slow manner. I didn't think it was necessary for him to pick me up again, but I couldn't help but enjoy it. There was such a caring and protective way in which he did it, and I didn't think it came lightly from him.

He began speaking as he pointed out into the distance. "That's the Doolin pier and the ferry runs from there. And beyond that are some islands—that one right there is called Crab Island. We can take a ferry ride one day if you like, so you can be on the ocean."

His hand was still pointing out to sea, and I could see a boyish gleam in him that I'd never expected. As I looked out and saw the large cliffs in the distance and the stunning shoreline, I couldn't believe that this place was real, only a short distance from where he lived. I tried to take in all the scenery, but I was too overwhelmed. Darby, sensing my wonderment, slowly situated the bike as I tried to get a grip on my surroundings.

Darby returned to me and continued, "I think this will be the perfect spot for a picnic and a proper greeting for you from our village and Ireland. You haven't had the best welcome so far. We're going to fix that." He smiled with a warmth that reached my marrow, warming me completely with his care and concern for my happiness.

I saw Sinead and Mak coming toward us. I'd been so

captivated by the scenery that I barely noticed them walking off to our right. I was correct. They had beaten us here. I knew we had taken way too long at the house.

"Took ya long enough!" Mak smirked. I could see a picnic basket in his hands. "We were just trying to scope out the best spot. Come on. Don't waste any more time, Darce. You'll have time later to make googly eyes at Eyre once we get set up for our picnic."

I giggled and dared to look at Darby out of the corner of my eye. Darby had that look on his face that was only reserved for Mak. Turning to me, he said, "Come on, we shouldn't keep him waiting. He thinks he can get away with saying stuff like that because he's an old man." Darby laughed and slowly took my hand. There was such hesitancy in his movements with me. Like he was frightened by our connection, or maybe he was trying to fight it. I couldn't figure out which.

His fingers slowly interlaced with mine, one by one, as if trying on each one for size. Each finger seemed to fit better than the last. Darby's grip intensified at the surprising revelation that our hands fit so well together. I could feel the satisfied energy emanating from him when his fingers tightened together in one final grasp around mine. His rough calluses rubbed against my skin with a friction that gave me a heightened feeling of sensitivity in the best way possible.

When Darby didn't move, Mak called to him, "Come on, Darce. Do I have to drag you over here myself, like when you were a wee lad? I'm going to need to add a leash to your uniform pretty soon if ya don't knock it out."

Darby looked at me with apology while I clasped my lips

tighter together to keep from laughing harder. There was such a sweet softness in his eyes that it took my breath away, silencing the laughter. I was beginning to be thoroughly confused as to why the village people gave Darby such a hard time. He seemed pretty romantic to me. Maybe the other women had just never given him a proper chance. The attentive and caring man standing before me seemed like he would be any woman's fantasy.

I smiled at Darby as we strode over to Sinead and Mak. I was surprised that Darby didn't seem to mind if they saw us holding hands. I guess he figured Mak was going to give him a hard time either way, so he might as well do what he wanted. Holding hands didn't seem like something Darby would usually do. And yet, his sweet gesture felt so right.

Sinead greeted me with the warmest hug. "I'm so glad you're here. I could use another woman's help to keep these two in line. It's just been me for way too long. There's not enough X chromosomes in the world to combat their foolish Y ones. They're pretty hopeless." She chuckled. "Come on, come on. I want to hear all about you." She looked at Mak, who was just standing there, looking mesmerized. "Well, are you going to hold the basket all day or are we actually going to get a chance to enjoy it?"

"Oh . . . Uh . . . right. I was just about to–" Flustered, Mak started spreading out the blanket and scattering the basket's contents on it. I couldn't contain my laughter. It was hilarious that Mak could become both tongue-tied and bossed around by someone. I liked this dynamic.

Darby smiled and kept holding my hand. Sinead looked at Darby–no doubt about to say something to him about helping—but then I noticed her eyes fall upon our hands, and she stopped herself.

"Let me help ya, Mak," Darby said, taking pity on him. I couldn't help but notice how reluctantly Darby released my hand. Then he headed over to help Mak arrange the food items for our picnic.

"Well, you've already had quite the effect on him, I see," Sinead said softly as she moved closer to me. "This certainly isn't the Darby I know. I've never seen him hold a woman's hand before. *Ever.*"

"What? Really?" I asked, astonished.

"Darby isn't a demonstrative man. Well . . . I should explain. I think he feels everything. Don't let him fool you, but he won't show any of it. He's got the biggest heart under that stony exterior, but the last thing he wants to do is show it. Public displays of affection aren't for him. I guess it's a protective coping mechanism. And maybe it's smart, except for the fact that it's made him absolutely miserable and kept him completely alone. So tell me, how have you gotten through his tough outer shell?"

"I don't know . . . I didn't think I'd done anything. And I would hardly say I've 'gotten through.' I don't feel like I know anything about him," I responded, a little bewildered.

"Oh, if he's holding your hand and looking at you in such a special way, then you have. I promise you. That man is a fortress. The women in this village, and all the surrounding ones, have been trying to find out where his heart is located. And they can just forget about where to start looking for the key. They're all on a pointless scavenger hunt." She laughed at her analogy. "And he sure doesn't help."

"But the way he talks . . . you wouldn't think anyone was interested. That sounds more like how Darby talks about Sloane—"

"Ohhh, sore subject. Everyone loves to tease Darby. Have a little fun at his expense. But Darby is actually sensitive about it. I can tell you that he does compare himself to other men, especially men like Sloane. Darby's convinced he's like the image that the village has painted of him. You know—unromantic, completely terrible with women, rough—the anti-Darcy." She laughed a little.

"I don't understand. He's been so sweet to me. Nothing but considerate and compassionate. I'd rather have him than Sloane any day. I mean, Sloane seems very good at his job, and I'm sure he's nice, but he'll never be Darby." I glanced over to him seated on the picnic blanket. I noticed that his eyes were already on me, and it made my stomach twist. He didn't look away either but instead held his gaze steady. He wasn't ashamed to be looking at me or embarrassed by it. *Me,* the girl who had thrown up all morning and torn open her wound. "No, Sloane's definitely not Darby," I mumbled.

Sinead asked, "What was that, dear? Sorry, I'm going a little hard of hearing. The pub can be pretty noisy, and all those years take their toll on an old woman like myself," she said with a deep, sultry laugh. I turned and looked at her, seeing that same beauty I had noticed last night in the pub. She was even more radiant today in the few rays of sunlight that were brave enough to peek through the cloudy Irish sky.

I began again to explain. "Oh, nothing. Sloane just makes me feel a little uncomfortable is all. I don't know why there's even a comparison between the two."

Sinead looked at me cautiously. "I've never seen him behave like this with anyone else. And I've certainly never seen him agree to let someone see him work at the church. That's extremely special. Make sure you take him up on that. He's really talented." She paused. "I know you'll be going back to America soon, but while you're here, if you wouldn't mind being gentle with him, it would really be appreciated. This could be what we need to bring him back to us. He might seem like a fortress, but I promise it's built upon a foundation of fears."

Her words struck me as my eyes searched hers for more. I was just about to ask her to explain further when Mak called out, "Your Highness, I have everything ready."

"Well, it's about time. I don't think it even took me that long to make the food," she replied cheekily. I stood and let my eyes track Sinead as she sat down, still not believing what I had just heard.

My mind was processing, thinking of possibilities and hidden meanings, when I saw Darby's arm extend outward, inviting me to join them. I looked at the small group sitting on the picnic blanket, and it all seemed so picturesque: the people, this day, and this place. But I felt like there was a lot they weren't telling me. And as an outsider, I knew I didn't deserve to know, but I wanted to earn a spot inside this tight little circle. I couldn't even explain why I already felt so connected to them, but I did. Maybe it was because they were so welcoming, and I was confusing the two feelings. I was the girl from America who would be going back soon. I needed to remember that. I didn't need to disrupt this perfect symbiosis. An exquisite little harmony.

"Eyre, will you come sit beside me?" Darby questioned

in such a soft voice that both of the other faces on the picnic blanket looked over in wonder. Well, I certainly wouldn't be refusing that offer. Not that I'd ever planned on it. It was so heartbreakingly sweet like a Patrick Swayze bad boy turned good routine. And *oh*, it worked *so* well.

I walked over and took his extended hand without question, no hesitancy there. Not when he spoke to me like that. I went to sit down next to him, and his arm tugged me a little closer. I let out a chuckle. I couldn't help it. He was too cute. For all I knew this "bad boy finds a heart" persona was his go-to move. But when I finally took my seat–pretty close to Darby–the looks that Mak and Sinead continued to exchange told me otherwise.

He leaned back and propped himself up on his arm behind me. Okay, now he just looked like James Dean. Or whatever the Irish equivalent of that was. He was doing this on purpose. I couldn't take my eyes off of him. He just smiled and squinted his eyes in question. *Oh man, how did he not know what he was doing to me?* He *had* to know.

Mak cleared his throat. Apparently, everyone else could see the effect he was having on me. I quickly turned, feeling embarrassed about the exchange they had just witnessed, and started speaking. "Sinead, this food looks amazing. Thank you so much. You all have made Ireland so special for me."

She beamed. "I hope we have something that you can eat. Mak told me that you're gluten-free. I didn't know about any other food restrictions. So I just packed a variety of things I hoped you might be able to eat."

"Oh, it all looks great. I have–"

As I started talking, Darby sat straight up and quickly

interjected, "She just has to be careful, is all. She has a gluten intolerance. Right?" He looked at me. Giving me an out so I wouldn't have to explain my complicated—and painful—medical history.

I smiled at him. "It's ok." I turned back from Darby to them. "Darby is just trying to give me an out. I have several health conditions, and one of them is esophageal Crohn's. Less than one percent of adults have this condition because most people don't live long with it[1]. So I have to be really careful about what I eat. Diet is the only thing that's helped me so far. It has literally helped to save my life. I was really lucky to find a friend who had worked with a naturopathic doctor and a nutritionist to find a diet for his GI disorder. He was so kind in writing out his diet for me–a very detailed document. I promised I would pass it on to other people because that was the turning point for me. Everything changed."

"It wasn't overnight, but I started to see improvement, and after several years on the diet, I started seeing more quality of life. More than anything, I wasn't needing the procedures the doctors thought I would. And my prognosis suddenly looked completely different. One of the scariest parts of this journey was the powerful infusions used to treat Crohn's, called biologics. They were extremely expensive—some were comparable to buying a car before insurance adjusted their cost. Unfortunately, I was allergic to the biologics. They left me in crippling pain and unable to get out of bed for several weeks following each infusion. The doctors tried different types of biologics, but I was allergic to all of them. Actually, there were a couple of years when I was rarely able to get out of bed. After that, I was desperate to try anything. I was extremely blessed that my friend with the special GI diet was put in my life.

"Some of my doctors were able to find homeopathic medications for me, as well as prescribing other medications that could be compounded to avoid my allergens. I think this was the other missing puzzle piece for me. I'm already starting to see more quality of life, and I'm really hopeful. My arthritis that I had developed from my Crohn's had become so painful, along with the pain from my other condition, that I wasn't able to continue my job, which was disheartening to say the least. I think the Naltrexone that was prescribed for the pain, as well as my conditions, will be another miracle as well. It's already started to give me some relief."

Everyone sat in stunned silence. That was a torrent of medical information. I hadn't even touched on my endometriosis, and I wasn't planning on it. I hadn't gone into detail with Darby about my Crohn's earlier this morning, and this was my way of letting him know about its severity. Although it might be possible for me to have fun with Darby this week, I felt he deserved to know the truth about my health conditions. And for the first time, I really wanted to share this information with a man. I didn't want him to go any further with me–develop any deeper feelings–without truly knowing me. And while my illnesses don't define me, they are a part of me. They have shaped me into the person I am today. Every decision I make includes them. Like it or not, they're like an extra person whose feelings and needs I have to consider at all times. So it's best he knows he's getting that extra "person" as well.

It's not exactly the two-for-one special you'd want. Definitely not the kind of threesome most guys have in mind. But for some reason, I thought Darby was man enough to handle it. Maybe that's why I actually wanted to tell him. Perhaps that's why I couldn't wait for him to know. I wanted to be accepted. I didn't want to hide and wait to see if someone would actually like me. Because nothing mattered until they knew. Nothing they said about their feelings counted until they had that information–because it could change everything in a blink of an eye.

Darby leaned over slowly and whispered in my ear. His breath against my skin sent goosebumps down my spine. "I know you didn't have to share that. I know I'm not *exactly* the person most people want to share their feelings with. And I don't make it particularly easy, so thank you." He leaned back and looked at me. Those green eyes overflowed with meaning.

"Darce, you're acting like a *boyo*. It's like you're a lovestruck teen. There's a whole group here," Mak said, annoyed. But I was pretty sure it was because he was dying to know what Darby had said to me.

I decided to distract Mak from reprimanding Darby any further. "Sorry, that was really heavy. I should have just said, 'I have Crohn's.'" I laughed. "I just feel so comfortable around you three that I wanted you to know about my health. I promise I won't say any more about it. By the way, the chicken, rice, fruit, and veggies look amazing. Thank you, Sinead. So very thoughtful of you." But from their looks, they didn't look like they were ready to move on.

"Do not apologize." Darby's tone was stern. "We're very honored that you felt comfortable enough to talk to us about it. We're also glad we guessed right about the food. Or at least some of it."

"Yes, do not apologize," Sinead agreed. "I know it's not a typical picnic, but you said you could have steamed rice and veggies last night, so I figured this was safe."

"It's absolutely perfect," I said with a smile and looked over at Darby.

As we dished out the food, I couldn't help but be consumed by the scenery. Darby saw me taking everything in with eagerness and said, "I'll take you to the beach after we eat," as he leaned over to me.

"Thank you." I went back to focusing on the view and then on Sinead and Mak. I continued to watch their interactions with growing curiosity. This was a puzzle I wanted to figure out before I returned home. With my nosiness taking over, I asked, "So, how did you two meet? I mean, I know you said you were in school together, but what's the story?"

Mak and Sinead just looked at each and then began talking over one another. It was like each one wanted to be the first to speak. Like it was important whose side was heard first. Of course, Mak relented, allowing Sinead to speak before him. "Well, this fool here wasn't any better then than he is now." She gave a deep laugh. One that reminded me of Lauren Bacall. She certainly had the glamor. She even had a chiffon scarf tied around her head and neck that somehow stayed perfectly in place while my hair flew around my face with reckless abandon.

She continued on with an undeniable sparkle in her eye. "There's starting off on the wrong foot and then there's Mak. And, well, I don't think we talked much till we were older because of it. We were more playground rivals, *slagging* each other without mercy. Sometimes it was jokes, other times pranks. I once switched out his chocolate pudding for one mixed with mud."

"Well, that wasn't as good as the time I swapped the test questions on you for our English essay. Our teacher was visibly concerned about you," Mak lobbied back.

"Oye, still not sure how you pulled that one off. You somehow managed to see it ahead of time. You always were sneaky. Probably pretended to be the teacher's pet and got in her drawer . . . I was chosen to read mine aloud, too. We were supposed to be reflecting upon a serious poem and Mak gave me a really silly one. I looked like a moron, which didn't help my fear of public speaking. Everyone was laughing at me. One boy said he wished that he had some rotten tomatoes to throw at me."

"So what started everything?" I asked. "Sounds like this feud lasted quite some time."

They looked at each other. I could tell I'd asked the wrong question. It was probably over fifty years ago, maybe even sixty, and something that I obviously didn't need to ask them to rehash.

"Well, Mak–" Sinead began.

"We don't need to go into this." Mak interrupted.

"Oh, but I think we do. We were playing a game of cricket, and Mak here had been making eyes at me, and well . . . I'd been making some eyes at him. Just little curious glances. We were so young. It was just playground flirtation. I think it was my first time to try flirting with a boy. It was special. Well, I was really bad at cricket apparently–"

"I'd like the record to reflect that you said you were really bad at cricket," Mak chimed in quickly.

"I said 'apparently.' *Anyway* . . ." Sinead proceeded. "Mak rounded everyone up for a team huddle where he proclaimed that I wasn't allowed to participate any longer for the sake of the team. He said I hit like a girl. And ran like one too. He said that it was really hurting the team and we were never going to win at this rate. Oh, and that I shouldn't ever be allowed to touch the bat, either."

"Oh, Mak. Really?" I looked at him.

"I wanted to win. What can I say, we were gettin' demolished. She's as bad at sports as she is beautiful." Mak glanced at her and then quickly looked away.

Sinead blushed uncomfortably. "Well, that may be nice now, but back then, in front of everyone, it was humiliating. I'd always been the tallest girl with gangly, awkward limbs that I didn't know how to use. It just drew attention to me, especially my awkwardness. He wanted to win more than he wanted to protect my feelings. And to say I hit like a 'girl' . . . like being a girl was such a bad thing . . . yes, you better believe that started a feud," she ended triumphantly.

"So how long did this last?" I asked quickly. They had gone silent on the subject. How could they leave me hanging in suspense like that? This relationship of theirs was so intriguing and mysterious. It made me want to know more. Plus, they were so adorable together. Those playful and poised looks that fed off one another gave me hope for the future. They were so heated at times, too. It gave me hope that a spark could last a lifetime.

"Secondary School," they said in unison and looked at each other.

Sinead finally gave way to Mak. "That's when Sinead finally figured out I had a crush on her and that all this *slag-*

ging was my way of showing her," Mak said bluntly, looking at her with a challenge in his eye.

"Oh, I knew well before that. You're not so clever. And I'm not that daft. Well, maybe I was daft for most of the time, but I did *finally* catch on. I couldn't believe he liked me in that way, even when people told me he did. And I really didn't know what to make of this turn of events. All of a sudden, he'd changed his approach."

"Really?" I said, practically begging them to continue. Darby chuckled, leaning closer to me. I could feel his shoulder rub against the back of mine. I turned to glance back at him, currents of intensified feelings running through me at every brush of our bodies connecting together. And his smile only made the currents flow faster.

I turned back around as Sinead continued, "He started complimenting me, and I didn't know what to do with that. It was such a change. But when Mak is being sweet, he's pretty hard to resist. A sweet Irishman is dangerous, Eyre, don't you ever forget that." She looked over at me, then at Darby, and finally at Mak. *What was going on in this circle?* This was even better than American television. Why did everything seem so much more intriguing in Ireland? I was glued to it like an episode of *Bad Sisters*.

Mak took his turn to speak again, "Well, it would have been nice if you'd accepted the compliments or at least done something with them. Like, you know, acknowledged them or returned them. There was a dance where the girls ask the guy—"

"Like a Sadie Hawkins dance?" I interjected.

"Sure . . ." Mak said, with slight confusion as they all looked at me. "Well, word got around that she was going to ask me. I thought she was finally going to reciprocate. But then things got—"

Sinead interrupted before he could finish. "I guess he could tell I was going to ask him to the dance because I was so nervous. Before I could get a word out, he said his best friend was dying to go out with me. I took that as a not-so-subtle hint that I should ask his friend to the dance instead of asking him. He was obviously saving me from embarrassment." I looked over to Mak, and I could see more than a glimmer of regret in his eyes. Sinead finished the story. "Good thing. It would have ruined our friendship. My marriage didn't work out, and Mak has never been married, so neither of us has had any luck in love, but we've always been friends. We've practically known each other our whole lives. And this way we've gotten to stay a part of one another's lives. It's how it was meant to be."

"But—" My voice fell off as I looked at their faces. There was obviously so much more there, so much more to the story. Under that teasing nature was a deep love that had simmered and burned hotter than any other I'd ever seen. *How could it not?* The fire had been stoked for nearly sixty years. Now that was the slowest burn I'd ever witnessed, and I felt like I needed to step back from the flames.

What had happened? Why would Mak throw it all away? He'd been so close. He'd obviously pined for her all these years. And why put himself in purgatory by doing what he did, all for a close friend? And why didn't he ask her out later after she and his friend broke up? *And why had he let her marry another man without saying anything about his feelings for her? And he still wasn't saying anything?* I wanted to scream, and I'd only known them for two days. I wanted to shake the man. I just kept looking at them for any clues I might have missed.

"Stop thinking, Eyre, you'll never figure it out. They're more of an enigma than Stonehenge," Darby said in my ear.

---

1. htttps://www.sciencedirect.com/topics/pharmacology-toxicology-and-pharmaceutical-science/crohn-disease

EIGHTEEN

Eyre

After we finished the delicious lunch provided by Sinead, she encouraged us to go see the rocky shore by the water. Darby didn't need any more encouragement and he eagerly guided me that way. We left Sinead and Mak, and started our walk down to the water's edge. It was rocky, and I kept stumbling, but Darby held onto me the whole way. Always careful to grab low on the side of my hips to help me if I needed it. My breath caught in my chest when we made it to the pebbled shoreline and we looked out at the vast crystal blue horizon. The breeze on my skin rejuvenated my spirits and hopes. The horizon was filled with limitless turquoise blue water. Darby carefully put an arm around me, mindful to avoid putting any pressure on my stitches.

"Is that ok?" he asked gently, as he turned slightly toward me.

"Yes." I nodded slowly as his question brought tears to my eyes. He continued to hold my gaze as if he was waiting for me to say more–to finish what we had started earlier. I could not believe the cynical man that had picked me up from the edge of a cliff was now making me cry with the use of three little mundane words. I reined in my emotions and took a deep breath, looking up at him. I saw a strong, compassionate man. One who had been mysteriously hiding behind so many layers. I wondered if I would ever have a chance to get to know him. I also wondered if I shared myself and opened my heart, would I be the only one doing so? Would he reciprocate?

"I really want to finish telling you what I began to tell you earlier today." The words stuck in my throat.

He just looked at me and nodded. His jaw ticked with quiet concern, his eyes filled with a longing to help ease the pain of whatever I was going through.

"Darby." I could barely speak his name. It came out soft as the breeze and floated away just as quickly as it came. I looked him fully in the eyes, and it felt like I was finally facing my fears head-on. "I can't have children." It came out so quickly, in such a hushed tone, that it was almost as if I hadn't said it.

I stood there as he looked at me so earnestly. Just waiting, knowing there was more, and giving me room. My face contorted with pain. My foot was fidgeting, trying to distract my brain from sending tears to my eyes.

"I've had several procedures for my endometriosis and the doctors were worried that I wouldn't be able to have children. That's always their main concern and takes top priority. So I thought they would do whatever was necessary to make that happen. I never worried about it that much because it seemed that if I could endure the pain, having children would be a possibility. And frankly, at the time, I was more consumed by the physical pain. But then . . ." I bit my lip. "Well, one of the cysts on my ovaries burst—a chocolate cyst. It happened a few months ago, and then I got an infection. It was really serious. And things just got worse from there. That's when my doctor said I would need another procedure to clean me out and assess the condition of everything. That's what my incision is from."

I looked at him, hating myself for having to tell him this. But the green-emerald seas that shone back at me just beckoned me to continue. I turned more toward him and held on tighter, letting his eyes be my beacon—eyes that were filled with so much concern that Gatsby would have reached out to them. I sure needed them to help guide me now. So I let them serve as my true north and I grasped onto his arms.

"I went in for the procedure and expected to wake up and hear the same news as always: things weren't good, but they'd managed to remove the fibroids and the other places where the endometrium had adhered itself, etcetera . . . that they still believed there was a chance I could get pregnant, so all was well, and I could keep living my life. But that's not what I woke up to hear this time." I looked at him carefully, wishing I could tell what he was thinking. "And when you hear the doctor say that you probably won't be able to have kids . . . well, that really means you aren't going to be able to have kids, at least not your own biological ones. I already didn't know if I could have kids with my other health conditions—with my limitations and the worry of what genes I might pass on to them—but at least it was a possibility. But to have the option completely taken away—" I tried to collect myself enough to continue.

"I didn't tell anyone what was on the line when I booked the appointment. I already knew the doctors were really worried about my fertility chances. And then, after the procedure, I couldn't handle it. They only looked around and then decided to wake me up instead of going through the procedure. Because what they found didn't look good and they thought it might be time to give me the decision they had mentioned in passing before. Except this time it wasn't in passing. This time they wanted to know what I wanted to do about my options: reschedule the procedure to clean me out with knowing there's almost no chance I could have kids or go ahead with a oophorectomy and get relief. They kept me overnight for observation because I think they were worried about my mental state. I guess I was kind of unresponsive. There was no reason to keep me otherwise. They really hadn't done anything. But it hadn't really sunk in yet. Not truly. Probably because that propofol was still circulating in my system . . ." I laughed to try to ease the tension. "Early the next morning, when I called my boyfriend to drive me home, I just wanted to leave as quickly as I could. They won't let you leave without a driver. Actually, they make you sign paperwork that says you won't drive or make big life decisions for twenty-four hours after anesthesia. But there I went. I broke all the rules. I called an Uber while my boyfriend was waiting to take me home. So, technically, I did have a driver . . . just not the one I was supposed to have. They may need to widen that twenty-four-hour propofol window. Although I hadn't reached the mark when I hopped on that plane. So maybe that one was on me."

Darby's face was more than a little shocked. I let my awkward laugh subside and said, "All my boyfriend ever wanted was to get married and have kids. That's all he talked about after my cyst ruptured and the doctors were concerned about complications from the infection and the damage to my ovary. He actually wanted to get married right away so we could start a family as soon as possible. He knew that fertility rates were much lower with endometriosis already. And mine is no walk in the park. Nothing else really mattered to him."

"Eyre–" Darby began. There was a brokenness in his tone. But I had to continue while I could.

"Because what good is a woman in our society if she can't have kids, right?" I looked at him and swallowed hard. "You miss out on everything. Not only do you not get to be a biological mom, but then good luck getting a life partner. No one wants to date you. Even the first date conversation freaks people out," I said with a terse laugh. "You're 'a jerk 'if you don't tell them about your fertility issues, because then you've wasted their time, but if you do tell them, then you're considered 'a wacko' because that's not a first date discussion topic.

"It's not bad enough that I can't have kids, now they want to take parts of me too. Taking my ovaries is permanent. They told me they couldn't even harvest my eggs. And then they'll put me on bioidentical hormones to help with menopause . . . *menopause at my age*. I feel like a synthetic woman. And what if it changes me? What if I'm different without my hormones at this stage of my life? It's not how it's supposed to be. Nothing about me is how it's supposed to be."

"And then there's the fact that all your friends have kids. And you can't be a part of the mom club. You don't know all the secret tricks to soothe the terrible twos, or what helps with teething, or the best way to bottle feed. So you're completely left out of the discussion. And you can't have play dates with each other's kids and mommy time. It's a whole part of womanhood that you're completely left out of. A secret club you're never going to be a part of. It's the most isolating experience of your life. I think it's the most heartbroken I've ever been in my life. And I have multiple conditions. None of it compares. Nothing compares to this loss."

"And every doctor's appointment has become the same game: the doctors ask me about my age, conditions, and marital status. Then they try to figure out how to politely ask me if I want kids. But that's not the problem. Want is not the problem. It never was. Because there's already so much want when you're chronically ill. *Want* should never be a word used in that context. *Can*—that's the word missing from a chronically ill person's life. Because just when you feel like there's nothing left to take, your illness finds a way. And there's very few people left standing when it does."

I could hardly swallow with the lump in my throat, thick and heavy. The tears were really streaming down my face now. And I was mortified.

"Eyre." Darby's voice was as soothing as a still, calm sea. I could hardly see him through my burning eyes. Eyes that stung with failure and disgrace. He brought me back to face him, but I could only hold his gaze for so long until my head dropped. The salt of my tears dried on my face and pulled my skin taut like a mask.

He lifted my chin delicately with his fingers in a manner that made my stomach twist. His eyes locked on mine with such force it felt like the wind was picking up for a storm.

And my eyes, in return, roamed over every fleck in his, mooring myself to every perfect detail. "God, you're beautiful," he said, taking me all in. His pure green eyes were searching over every salty imperfection of my visage, his words burning me and his stare leaving no atom of my skin unturned. And I knew, at that moment, he intended to finish what we had started earlier, and I wanted nothing more than what he was about to provide. I wanted all that care, affection, and passion in his eyes.

And as soon as he recognized my want–without a second to lose–his face moved toward mine, and my body instinctively reacted to invite him in. My face lifted upward, my lips parting slightly to make room for him. Those soft lips of his were making their way closer, and my heart paced rapidly as they did. And just like that, his lips landed with hungry intent on mine. My senses were met with the woodsy scent of him that I had inhaled all morning long as he cradled me while I was ill. The scent of a man who had done nothing but take care of me since I'd met him.

His hands grabbed my waist to bring me closer and then slid up my back to caress my neck and fully embrace me. There was a gentleness in his passion, a care in his hunger. Something that burned for me and made me feel like a woman again. An eagerness when he tasted me that set my heart alive and restored a new life. A renewed rhythm that I'd been searching for when I came here. Darby seemed to accept all of me and like me just as I was. I hoped I would be able to do the same for him. And I wondered if he was going to give me that chance.

NINETEEN
Darby

I'd seen an opportunity and taken it. When life hands you something like that, you grab hold of it, no questions asked. When I saw her beauty shining through that incredible amount of pain, I couldn't resist the urge to kiss her any longer. Maybe it was wrong. Perhaps it was the most poorly timed romantic impulse. I probably needed my wiring checked. I was pretty positive that other men's impulses wouldn't have been to kiss a woman for the first time while tears were streaming down her face. But there was something so raw and intimate about the moment. She'd trusted me with the most intimate details of her life, so all logic, or thoughts of what would be best or "normal" in this situation, left my head completely. There was only her and this moment, perfectly crafted for us. And I took it alright, probably a little too passionately.

Why she expected that her situation would scare me, or make me not want her, was beyond me. It only made me want her more. But then again, I was damaged. Her pain was raw and beautiful because of the way she channeled it and connected with people, but mine certainly was not. Mine was the type of pain people ran away from screaming. The type that helped someone immediately know it was not a good idea to get involved with that person. That was my type of pain. A vicious *Happy Death Day* time loop. And Eyre was the only thing that made it feel like the pause button had been hit. Allowing me to breathe for the first time. And the air with her scent in it was so sweet. A taste of what life could be like, and I didn't want to let it go.

I parted from her enough to look deep into those hazel eyes that were constantly shifting color, keeping me on my toes. Nothing in life had ever kept me this alert. I had been sleepwalking through my life to try and dull the pain. But now she was waking me from my slumbers. There was an exquisite beauty to it–to her. And I was feeling; I was feeling it all. The numbness was wearing off. And I just wanted her.

"Darby, I–" she breathed, but all I could focus on were those soft, full lips. This was so inappropriate. But for some reason I felt I needed to shut us both up. Silence those hurtful inner voices clawing at us, trying to destroy us.

I just wanted to kiss her again, but instead, I said, "I'm not sure I want to have kids, Eyre. I'd probably be a terrible father. Maybe if you were their mother, I'd change my mind." I looked at her intently. I had not intended to tell her any of this. What was I saying? She was literally staying in Ireland for a week or two. She wanted to tell me she couldn't have kids. Nowhere in that equation did I, nor should I, factor in. *How was this even remotely helpful, Darby?* Answer: it wasn't.

"I'm sorry," I apologized. "I shouldn't have kissed you

just now. It was probably really inappropriate. You are just so beautiful, and it shines through your pain. You have this strength about you, and I just felt connected to you . . . The fact that you let me in like that . . . It felt so raw and special. Like a moment I'd never have again. Like this perfect moment with you that I never wanted to forget. And now I'm really struggling because all I want to do is kiss ya all over again."

"Why?" Her arms started tightening around me. "Who's saying what's wrong and right, Darby? What do you feel? Please, with me, always go with how you feel."

"I'm scared that's going to end up going very badly. I have horrible instincts." She shook her head at me. "I literally could taste your tears."

Her voice was soft, but firm. "If something is wrong, then I'll tell you, Darby. But nothing has been. Well, except for your sarcasm and cynicism." She laughed. "But I have to admit I am attracted to both of those as well. I'm very attracted to your instincts."

"I'm hearing the word 'attractive' a lot. Does that mean . . ."

"Darby, go with your instincts," she replied breathily.

"Eyre, you would be a wonderful mother. I really hope you find a way to have children or another way to use your love."

A few tears made their way slowly down her cheek.

I didn't get to follow my instincts before she pulled me back into a tighter embrace, asking for more. Her lips raised up to meet mine. And in that instant, I knew that, for the first time, my instincts were going to be right with someone. *I was going to be right with someone.*

TWENTY
Darby

When I pulled back, I kept her in my arms, allowing us to watch the waves crash on the rocky pebbles, their beautiful surfaces worn smooth from the rough, repetitive beating of the waves. I felt like our souls could have easily been those pebbles. They looked so smooth and shiny on the outside, beautiful even, but no one realized the rough wear that they weathered every day. It was invisible.

Over the roar of the waves and the sea breeze, I asked close to her ear, "I know Sinead was talking about the festivities at the pub on the weekend, but maybe it's best to just rest tonight. They have dancing and live music on Sunday night as well. How about a night in? I've got just the thing to keep you busy." She looked at me quizzically, unsure of what I might have in mind. "Puzzles and tea by the fire, Eyre." I laughed. "You do like puzzles, don't you? You seemed to perk up at the mention of them last time." I felt the biggest grin spread across my face. It felt glorious to smile this wide again.

"Yes, but that was mostly because of the idea of *you* working puzzles. But I do. I am most definitely ready to see what a "night in" with you looks like." My eyebrows raised. "Puzzles, Darby, we're talking puzzles." Her voice was firm. "And I was promised a raging fire. I want nothing else."

"Oh, you'll get a raging fire." She shook her head at me, and I continued, "Let's walk back up to the picnic spot before Mak comes and drags me back with his walking cane or asks to borrow someone's leash. You don't understand, once that man gets something in his thick head . . ." I looked at her with warning. "Don't you even say anything about the leash. I don't want any quips from you."

"Ohhh, but I think you do, or you wouldn't have brought it up. You're secretly dying for that leash. You know I'll have to bring it up to Mak now." I rolled my eyes playfully in frustration. Being infuriated and bested by this woman was easily becoming the best part of my day. Her dry wit matched my sarcasm, and I loved it. A wit that came from true struggle and heartbreak in life. I was convinced that the funnier the person, the more heartbreak they'd survived. They didn't want you to feel any of the things they'd been forced to feel in their lives, so they made you laugh instead. The greatest entertainers made you cry, too, but they always made you laugh more, so you never felt the pain. I got the sense that Eyre fell into this category. That she'd always want to try and protect me from the pain.

I slipped my hand into hers as we walked back over to the picnic blanket, letting her guide me more than I did her. I had a feeling that was going to be happening a lot. And surprisingly, I was okay with that.

Mak looked up from talking with Sinead. They'd both been looking out at the ocean. Although I think he was enjoying the view of Sinead more than the one the deep blue seas provided. A devilish expression was on his face, and I knew from the look of it that I was in for trouble. "We were trying to enjoy the view, but it was pretty difficult when you were marring it with your sparking," Mak said bluntly.

"Sparking? Really, Mak? Is it 1940?" I asked, but he just ignored me.

"Darce, a first kiss is supposed to be gentle. It shows a woman what your relationship and potential future holds. So you best be showing her that you're gentle, kind, patient, and will be there for her whenever she needs ya. That you're a safe place for her to land. No matter the day or time. That your heart is going to be available. She's going to be a priority." He looked at me, but his eyes darted to Sinead every so often. "What I saw you saying is that I take what I want and I'm here when times are good. You might want to rethink things."

"Do you want me to be alone forever?" I asked. I couldn't believe he'd just said all that in front of Eyre. But Sinead was looking at him with such tenderness that it was almost worth whatever fallout happened for me.

"No, that's why I'm trying to help you out before it's too late." I could only laugh under my breath at him. He *really* was unbelievable.

"Ok, Mak. Why don't you open your 'Dating School for Dummies' sometime when Eyre isn't around. You can critique me all you want then," I joked, relenting. Eyre just started laughing.

"Don't I get a say?" Eyre said unexpectedly. Mak and I both looked at her in surprise. We were so used to it being just the two of us bickering that we hadn't expected a third party to throw their hat into the ring. We both nodded slowly, with grave hesitation. "I don't think you can teach something like that." She nodded down to the beach, referring to our kiss.

"I sure hope not," Mak said emphatically.

"No, it was perfect. Maybe teach him to believe in himself more, but don't mess with anything else, please," Eyre requested adamantly.

Mak started shaking his head in utter disbelief. "You're lucky, Darce. I mean, really *jammy*. You better keep this one. Find a way to keep her passport so she can't leave the country. You're not going to find another one as good as this one."

I looked at Eyre, whose eyes hadn't left mine since she'd spoken those last words. I cleared my throat and finally said, "Ok, Mak. I'm taking Eyre away from you before you completely ruin everything for me. There's a high chance that between you and me, one of us will *make a bags of* it. We're good at messing things up." I laughed to lighten the mood. "I'm going to show Eyre a little more of the area and then we're going to have a quiet night at home." I turned to Sinead. "Is it ok if we take a rain check on the pub for tomorrow night? You're still going to have music and dancing on Sunday?"

"Of course, Darby. You know I will. I think that's a lovely plan," Sinead responded.

"Mak, be good to her," I said, nodding to Sinead. "I mean

it." Mak started muttering things under his breath as we thanked Sinead for lunch and headed back to our bike. I gently placed Eyre in the sidecar. Although this time, I tried to give her a little more warning. I needed to start thinking about things like that. Earlier, I had been consumed with my concern about not hurting her incision. I never once thought about startling her. I was going to have a lot of things to work on in the future.

As I pedaled the bike, I thought about what our kiss had meant. And I began to realize I was allowing myself to think I could have a relationship with Eyre. Probably because my stupid brain thought that since she was going back to America, it would be okay, but really it wasn't alright for anyone to get involved with me even for a short amount of time. Especially not Eyre. I cared about her way too much for that. I was going to have to put that space back between us again, and I really didn't know how to do that. I needed to somehow let her know she shouldn't become involved with me. *But maybe for a week or two, it was fine?* My thoughts yo-yoed back and forth. No, I wouldn't do that to her. Yet, I still wanted to spend time with her. I just needed to make our relationship platonic. Which was going to be extremely hard to do since, number one, I'd kissed her, and number two, I didn't want to stay away, and number three, I wanted to kiss her again.

As I steered the bike toward Doonagore, these thoughts consumed me. The thirteen-minute bike ride turned into a torturous expedition with my destructive thoughts spiraling along with us. When the ruins of the castle came into view, I was a little mesmerized by them. I'd been to this castle so often, passed by here so many times over the years–but it didn't even look or feel like the same place. I was seeing through the eyes of someone else, all the beauty Ireland had to offer. It was like seeing everything for the first time.

I'd taken the beauty of so many things for granted. For instance, I'd never stopped to notice how the shoreline stretched out to meet the sea on the horizon. Or how the tall grass swayed in front of the castle. I'd never even paid attention to the colors of the ocean before. Not really. It was just always *there*. And I'd certainly never really looked at the castle. I'd never taken notice of the one tower that was left standing with the base of the walls that flanked it. The outline of the castle's foundation served as a reminder of what was and could have been. Why had I never taken the time to really look at and appreciate this place? After all, it was one of the most photographed castles in Ireland. It was just one of many things that I was starting to take notice of in my life now that Eyre had entered it. I finally gave enough of a farthing to start questioning things again. Because life without curiosity was dull and meaningless. It meant you'd lost the spark and interest to live. Eyre was making me care again.

I parked our bike beside the road, and I could see the joy in her as she looked at the castle. I couldn't help but feel a sense of pride and happiness that she appreciated this place I called home. I looked up at the castle with her, our eyes silently scanning the weathered stone structure. The castle's battered ruins made it hauntingly beautiful. I couldn't believe this place existed only a short distance from where I lived.

"This is Doonagore Castle. The one I was telling you

about last night. In the distance is Doolin pier, where we just came from." I pointed off into the horizon.

"Darby, it's . . . it's gorgeous."

I smiled at her words. "I'm glad you're enjoying Ireland." I started walking toward the castle, motioning her to follow me. I fought the urge to take her hand, remembering that it was better for her if we kept a little distance from one another. The last thing I needed to do was touch her, because I was pretty sure I knew where that was going to lead at this romantic castle on the hill. To something a little more than just friendly.

"This is not typically on my tour guide route, but I'll *give it a go*," I said, and she grinned at me.

"Please do, I don't have anything to evaluate you on yet and Mak *is* expecting a full report," she teased.

I couldn't help but laugh. "Well, I don't want to ruin the beauty of this place, but it has kind of a sad story to it. Do you still want to hear it?" I glanced over at her as we continued walking toward the tall sandstone structure, which now looked dreadfully lonely. She nodded resolutely. "There was a ship that belonged to the Spanish Armada that crashed close to the Doolin pier in 1588, and the crew sought refuge here. They thought they would be saved from being shipwrecked without any means of survival, instead since they were enemies of the British crown, they were all hung."

Eyre's mouth fell open a little. "Darby, that's not just a little sad. Ok, maybe I didn't want to know that. How can a place this beautiful have such a tragic history?"

"Looks can be very deceiving," I replied and held her gaze. I stopped walking abruptly, and she looked at me with a befuddled expression. "The castle is now privately owned, so we can't go inside. This is probably as far as we should go."

"What? Are they going to hang us too?" She said in outrage. "I really hope they're not still doing that. I still can't believe people could be that cold-hearted and cruel."

"I ruined it for you, didn't I?" I laughed a little.

"Well, it certainly doesn't look quite the same now. All I can see are their hopes of refuge and relief at being saved, and then . . . I can't imagine."

"You're not going to be able to get past this, are you?"

"And you are?" she asked in disbelief.

"Well, I guess it's something I grew up with. It was just one of those tragic facts that has always been part of the history of this area," I said, thinking about it more now.

"I'm at least going around the wall," she said defiantly.

"Eyre, it's private property," I hissed as she made her way closer. "I don't think you're going to enjoy Irish jail. Now, you're just trying to have a bad experience here."

"No, I just don't think this place belongs to anyone after something like that happened here. You can't own pain like that."

I was totally confused as to what was happening, but I did know that I didn't want Eyre dragged off of private property. And possibly worse, put in jail for trespassing. "Eyre," I hissed even louder. But it wasn't going to do any good. I hurried up to her, trying to decide what to do. She had increased her speed and was rounding the corner of the wall to the backside. Obviously, she didn't want me to catch up and stop her. I rolled my eyes in disbelief. She was going to be worse to keep tabs on than those sly, older women. I had not expected this from her. She was supposed to *love* following the rules.

I found her nonchalantly leaning against the wall, taking in the view when I finally rounded the corner. "Eyre, what do you think you're doing?" I asked through gritted teeth.

"Enjoying a place as it was intended," she said briskly.

"Right," I said sarcastically. "You're breaking the rules in an act of rebellion for those people that died here. That's not helping anyone. Especially if you get arrested." She grimaced at my words. I sighed heavily. "But fine, I like it. Just don't blame me if we get arrested. Mak won't bail us out. Well, maybe you, but not me."

She laughed at this as I sat down against the wall. She slowly lowered herself to the ground and joined me. She let out a little murmur of pain as she did so. Hearing her discomfort, I asked. "Can I do anything to help? Is there something I can get you for the pain on our way home? There's a grocery store–a supermarket–in one of the surrounding towns."

"No, I don't know of anything to help. Sloane gave me some extra bandages. I told him I had run out. But he didn't have any other medication that could help."

"I'd suggest another bath, but we saw how well that went. Maybe if we bandage it up well enough with waterproof wrapping."

"Yes, I don't think I want any more visits from Sloane than absolutely necessary." She laughed. I loved the melodic sound and when I looked down, I realized that my hand had found hers again. *Of course it had.* I couldn't stay away. Well, as long as I just kept it at hand holding, then maybe that was okay. But no more kissing.

She stared down at my hand in hers, and it was at that

moment I could tell how much it meant to her—and how much it meant to me. And my mouth couldn't stop itself, "Well, I'm really glad I'm the one who gets to be here with you."

"Yes, I am too." And I knew with those words and sincerity in her eyes that I'd never had anything to worry about with Sloane. She continued, "I had given up on having a connection with anyone. My conditions make me feel pretty unlovable. I was beginning to think I was going to be just like Austen. And look how well that turned out."

I could see the pain the word "unlovable" had brought her, even as much as she tried to joke. "Yeah, she's still remembered and loved by everyone," I quipped. "That doesn't sound so bad. She's loved around the world over a hundred years later."

"No, I mean destined to be alone. I didn't think I'd ever find my Mr–" But I cut her off right away.

"Oh, Eyre, you better not finish that sentence," I warned, in mock sternness, trying to get a laugh out of her.

"Bingley. I was totally going to say Bingley," she emphasized.

"Sure you were," I rolled my eyes playfully. "You know I was forced to read that book with everyone calling me Darcy's name."

"And?" she prodded.

"Not bad," I mused and watched her eyes widen.

"Oh, one of the greatest pieces of literature ever written is just "not bad." Yes . . . I think you're lying," she said with a deadpan stare. That glimmer in her eyes said she knew I was most definitely lying and that there indeed was a romantic guy hiding in me after all. Something no one else had seen.

And it only made me want to kiss her more . . . which couldn't happen.

So I let my lips keep themselves busy doing something else. I had so many questions that I could use to preoccupy them. "So . . . What happens with the one percent?"

"Huh?" she asked, confused.

I was nervous to ask her personal questions. She'd been really open at the picnic, but earlier this morning she'd been so closed off. Maybe I shouldn't push it. Maybe I should let her tell me in her own time and in her own way. But our time together was so limited, and now that I had gotten a taste of caring again, I couldn't stop. It was like I'd gone so long without breathing that all I wanted to do now was drink in the sweet air.

So while every nerve buzzed with anticipatory rejection, I asked, "Your Crohn's . . . You said you were in the one percent. I just wondered why and what happens when you're there."

"Well, you don't win any prizes," she said sardonically. I looked over at her, begging her to look back.

I sat patiently and continued to look at her. I wasn't going to take it back. I really wanted to know, and maybe I hadn't earned the right, but it was the first time in forever that I cared enough to ask. I wasn't going to back out now. I wasn't going to give her an out. If she said she didn't want to talk about it, then that was fine, I wouldn't push. But I was going to let it hang there until she decided. So I waited.

Finally, she looked at me. "I already told you way too much at the picnic. I think I freaked everyone out. That's probably more than enough personal information for today."

Probably. "Not for me, it isn't, but if it is for you, then that's ok," I said bluntly.

She continued to look at me and said, "When I was first diagnosed, I didn't sugarcoat what I shared with people. Then I quickly learned that was a mistake. People weren't ready for the truth. So, I started to wager with whom I could use 'semi-sugar coat,' 'fully sugarcoat,' or unvarnished versions of the truth. I learned quickly that no one fell into the latter. What I shared needed to be 'semi-sugar' or 'full on' sugar. No one gets the raw truth."

"That sounds incredibly lonely." I looked at her with such empathy. I'd never felt such a connection to someone before. Then I added, "I'm pretty sure you still sugar-coated some with me earlier. Give me raw."

"Ohhh, no." She half laughed, half sighed in refusal. "You don't want that. No one really wants that. You think you do, but you don't. And honestly, that's probably the least sugar-coated version I've given to anyone other than my immediate family. And when I say immediate, I mean my parents. Otherwise, I try to gently allude to the truth. Kind of like putting broccoli in brownies. I totally disguise it."

"All these candy references are making me really hungry," I said in jest, and she laughed. "*Give me raw.*" My eyes were strong and hungry for the truth.

"Uhhh. Ok," she said with skepticism. As if she didn't really believe I knew what I was asking for. "I told you most of everything, though. I guess it's just how much I told you . . . esophageal Crohn's means you get ulcers in your esophagus. They continue to reappear every so often. They can last weeks to months, and they can be so painful that you can't eat. A lot of people have to go on feeding tubes. One of the doctors' fears is that the ulcers will go so deep that you'll get a hole in your esophagus. And as I've been told so bluntly before, I'll have twenty-four hours to live if that happens and they're not able to repair it or insert a tube. There's only so many times it can be fixed. And most people also end up needing a colostomy bag because their G.I. tract issues aren't usually isolated to just their esophagus, because the condition can also affect the whole G.I. tract.

"So, when I was first diagnosed and the treatments didn't work, I figured I had five to ten years to live. My doctors hadn't had many patients that lived very long with this disorder—what few patients they had treated with this condition. And I couldn't find anyone with my condition to even talk to about it. My body pain got so severe that I couldn't continue with my part-time job. Even without the pain, I was too sick anyway. I couldn't pay my medical bills, I had to stop going to school, I had student loans that I was never going to be able to pay back, and I had to move back home with my parents. I couldn't even drive to my doctor's appointments. I was too dizzy and weak from lack of nutrients, and frankly, I was in too much pain to drive. Everything in my life changed drastically in a very short time period. And even without the financial obstacles, the symptoms and pain made it impossible to continue pursuing my dreams.

"If it wasn't for my family support and my diet, I don't think I'd be alive today. I'm also very well aware that not everyone has the means to try everything I did. And I wish I could change that. I wish that diet could become part of healthcare. I wish there was coverage for holistic treatments, therapies, diet plans, and medications. Treatment should also encompass the mind, body, and spirit."

With pained eyes, she continued, "I was finally able to start working again. I live right down the street from my parents because I can't be too far from help. I never know from day to day what is going to happen with my health. I was happy I was able to teach and share with others what I had learned in my program. That was the silver lining." She looked at me, saying nothing. Her eyes went blank as if she didn't dare hope to want anything from me. "There's raw," she finally ventured.

I stared at her. I was in total disbelief that she'd shared so much of her painful journey with me. I hadn't believed she would actually give me the raw truth, and I admired her for it. Finally, I found some words to respond to her. "Raw looks beautiful on you. It's too bad that so many people are afraid to hear it. That's their loss." The words came out before I'd had time to think about them and I just hoped they weren't too Darby-like. Translation: accidentally insensitive.

Her eyes closed and she took a deep breath. I squeezed her hand tighter to let her know I was still here and that I would continue to be. Without opening her eyes, she said to me, "Where did you come from, Darby? I wish I'd met you ten years ago, before my disorders. I wish you could have known me then." There was a break in her voice. "I wish I could have had someone like you with me while I was going through it all. I wish–" But she was unable to finish.

"I feel like I was always supposed to know you, Eyre. Like I've just been waiting here for you to find me–to wake me up and help me start living my life. I wish I'd met you years ago, too. I wish I'd known you from the beginning, because I know my life would have been different. I've been sleepwalking through my existence, dulled to everything.

I've been missing something that made my senses work. I already know that no amount of time is going to be enough with you."

We let the silence cleanse us as we looked at one another. Our nerves were raw and frayed, along with our exposed feelings and emotions. She came over to me and rested her head on my shoulder, and I wrapped my arm around her to try and protect her from the world. And then we just stared out at the gorgeous expanse of coastline and sea that had been a witness to such tragedy all those years ago. How much sorrow the ocean must have seen throughout its lifetime, yet its beauty was never failing. It made me tighten my hold on this special woman in my arms. A realization of how lucky I really was and hoped to continue to be.

Finally, I broke the sweet reverie. "Come on, we better go before we really do get in trouble. Let me take you home."

And the smile that formed on her face when I said those words made me feel things I'd never felt before.

TWENTY-ONE

Eyre

Darby seemed pleasantly surprised that Mak wasn't home when we arrived back at the cottage. I really enjoyed Mak's running commentary and good-natured fun at Darby's expense, but I could tell it made Darby anxious in my presence. But I was honestly a little nervous about being alone with Darby. I had to remind myself that while I should be cautious, I also needed to pay attention to how Darby had treated me so far. He was completely unexpected. A little Darby enigma that continued to reveal another layer every time I pulled a new one back.

As soon as Darby closed the front door, I felt my nerves hit a new high. He looked at me with a furrowed brow as if he had a sixth sense that could read my mind. He began speaking to break the ice. "It's probably too early for dinner, but I can make us a little something. Or we can wait to eat until later and I can make some tea for now. Why don't you choose a puzzle for us to work on together. I'll show you where they are," he said, eying me with hesitancy and giving me déja vu of how he had stared at me the first time he'd introduced himself and asked for my name. I guess I kept leaving him hanging in new territory. Something I told him I wouldn't do.

"Sounds perfect," I breathed. And he finally let out a held breath. It was still light out, but the cottage didn't let in much daylight, so he started turning on lamps. I noticed he didn't turn on the harsh overhead lights, though. I still stood in the entryway, which was actually part of the living room, unsure of myself. It was already such a cozy and intimate atmosphere, and everything Darby was doing was just adding to it.

He chuckled. "Are you coming, or are you afraid I'm better at puzzles than you? I mean, I would be afraid if I were you, so it's fine if you are." That dry charm had me laughing. I was being ridiculous. This was *Darby*. The man who wanted to play puzzles and board games and have a "night in" with me. The man who'd cradled me while I vomited and kissed me through my salty tears.

My feet were now moving. They couldn't wait to reach him. My smile, meeting his first. He was standing in front of the sofa between the coffee table and the fireplace. His smile warmed me so much that I thought the raging fire he'd promised was already going. Wisps of his auburn hair floated in front of his eyes as he bent down to look at me. Slowly, he reached out and brought me to him.

"Hi," he said softly. All I could do was look up at him. His arms were on mine, sending pulses of heat through me.

"Hi," I said back, my voice not sounding nearly as sexy as his. His smile intensified.

"Do you want that raging fire I promised you?" he asked. "It can get pretty cold at night."

I swallowed, unsure of my answer. I still couldn't figure out exactly what we were talking about.

"So I could preemptively make one while you look through the selection of puzzles," he continued. "There's a pretty good selection to choose from under the coffee table. Mak and I are fairly boring, and we often have a lot of free time. So we've gathered quite the collection."

Air escaped my lungs in a rush without my permission. He looked at me quizzically. *Ahhh, I felt so stupid.* "Yes, I would love a fire. I stay pretty cold with my conditions. I usually have to stay glued to my heating pad or hot water bottle. It helps with the pain. I know that it's pretty sad that I even named them," I said with a laugh. That ought to kill the over-abundance of sexiness he was providing that I couldn't handle. "And I do want the full cozy, Irish 'night in' experience." *Wrong thing to say.* "I want to know what a typical Mak and Darby night looks like." *There. Fixed it.*

He pulled me in tighter. "Well, I can definitely help with warming you up. Hopefully I'll be a good replacement for ... whatever their names are. One of them isn't named" —he looked at me with a raised eyebrow— "Darcy, is it?"

"Of course not," I exclaimed, looking away. He looked at me with a smile that completely saw through my words.

"Well, maybe if I do a good enough job, you'll rename one Darby." He laughed at his joke and slowly released me, then went over to start tending to the fire. Seeing him put real chopped wood on the stone hearth and tend to the growing flames was more than I could handle. He turned his head to me as he knelt, eye level with the fire, his forearm resting on his upper thigh in a nonchalant and irresistible way. "Don't you have something you need to be doing?" He eyed me and pointed at the pile of puzzles under the coffee table. His face contorted into an expression of pure pleasure.

"Uh . . . um, yes," I said, directing my attention to the large collection. Truthfully, I was actually jealous of that fire and all the attention it was getting. Those were words I never thought I'd think. *Who in their right mind gets jealous of a fireplace?*

I started shuffling through the pile of puzzles when I felt his strong hands on me. They were resting on my shoulders, the contact making me a little weak. And then he started massaging my shoulders, which only increased his attractiveness. My shoulders relaxed immediately and dropped down to relieve their stress. I let out little sighs of happiness. I could feel him lower his body to the ground behind me. It felt so good. Not only what he was doing but to have him so close to me.

I leaned back into him, wanting to be as close as possible, needing a physical connection. He lowered his hands and started to wrap his arms around me, pausing with indecision. I placed them for him so he didn't have to guess how best to avoid my incision. His thoughtfulness just added to the whole package that was Darby.

I leaned back to rest my head on his shoulder and allowed myself to relax into him as he supported me. I could feel the firmness of his chest and shoulders for the first time. He felt like someone who worked out *a lot*. And it really made me think about how his whole façade was so hard and stony. Not just physically but emotionally too. I could be wrong, but it seemed like he was hiding or running from something. And he hadn't shared anything really personal with me. Sinead's words kept ringing in my ears. I wasn't anywhere near the vicinity of the room with his heart, so I certainly didn't have a prayer of finding the key. Not that I needed to be worried about that now, but I at least wanted to know it was a possibility. That he was willing to share something of himself with me, especially after *all* I'd shared with him. But as his arms cradled me so tightly and his head nestled into me so tenderly, these thoughts seemed to vanish. And all that was left was this tender moment.

"What do you want with your tea?" Darby said, breaking the serene silence between us. The roar of the raging fire he'd promised providing the score for the evening. Definitely a Chopin Nocturne kind of night.

"You," I responded quickly. "Oh no. *No, no, no.*" I put my hand over my face. "That's not what I meant."

He laughed with an Irish lilt. "Kind of sounds like it is. That can be arranged."

"No, Darby. It's *definitely* not." My face flamed hotter than the fireplace.

"Ow. Ok, please don't be so emphatic about it." He chuckled lightly again. "Eyre," he said slowly. "What would you like *in* your tea?"

I couldn't help but laugh now. "Whatever you're having."

"And I'm guessing my answer can't be you?'" I shook my head. "Ok, how about some chamomile, honey, and lemon? I think that's good for the stomach."

"Perfect. Thank you." I let out a breath.

"I'm not letting you off easy. Keep looking." He got up slowly, disentangling himself from me.

I honestly couldn't decide if I'd rather see Darby work a puzzle with puppies pictured on it or play a board game like Candy Land or Banana-grams. This I had to see. I grabbed the game of Life as well, just for good measure, and put the Candy Land game on top.

Darby came back with two cups of tea and he burst out laughing. "No, Eyre. That's for Sinead's granddaughter. We are not playing Candy Land," he said emphatically.

"You were just saying today how badly you wanted something sweet. Well, here it is," I said with a sweeping gesture. "And I thought you and Mak probably played this one all the time." I started chuckling.

He responded, "No, we don't sit around playing Candy Land. That really makes us sound like a bunch of old 'pervs,' Eyre. Like some real *gombeens*. I sincerely hope you think better of us and you don't think we're that dodgy."

"Well, I would think pretty highly of you if you played it with me."

"There's no way," he said decidedly. But I gave him a pathetic pout that I could tell was beginning to melt his resolve. "Not unless you find a grown-up version." He raised his eyebrows. I looked at him sternly before he could say anything else along those lines. "Fine, because apparently, I have some sort of gigantic weakness for you. But *no one* ever finds out," he relented.

I gave him a massive grin as he handed me my cup of tea. I could not wait to see Darby play this game. Somehow I just couldn't imagine this man and a game involving pink candy being able to co-exist together. As I took my first sips of the tea Darby had brought me, I quickly found out that I had never truly tasted tea before. This man could make some liquid sunshine in a cup. And the second thing I discovered was that he was as competitive as I was when it came to playing games. Candy Land definitely turned into the adult version. And it got cutthroat fast.

We huddled on the floor, sharing a blanket with our cups of tea and our backs pressed against the sofa. Both of us looked onto the board that lay on the coffee table and out onto the fireplace. It was magical. A whole lifetime of evenings like this would never be enough. And it seemed with every turn we took, we each inched a little closer to each other.

Candy Land had gone from sweet to steamy. I was calling him on a dice technicality when our hands touched over the board. The bantering and hand gestures ended abruptly with the connection of our touch. The electric shock stopped us both in our tracks.

His vibrant green eyes landed softly on me, and my body pulsed with anxious energy. Tenderly he raised his other hand up to my neck, caressing my jaw, not wanting to disturb our hands that touched. Afraid, I could tell, of breaking any contact. I'd never been looked at in this way. I was sure now I'd never seen true desire. And everything that I'd suppressed came roaring back with a vengeance. Every ounce of me that I'd pushed aside because I didn't think I could find love or be lovable again surfaced like a buoy that had been pushed down to the deepest depths and boomeranged back to the surface. All my emotions resurfaced at the same time and knocked the wind out of me.

There wasn't any hesitancy on his part, just a slowness in his movements to savor the moment as his face came closer and his lips found their way to meet mine with a reassuring sense that this was where they were always supposed to be, where they belonged. The softness in them contradicted everything you would have assumed about him—his strength and passion undermined any theory that he was full of apathy. This man was more alive than any man I knew. And certainly he was the most caring one I'd ever kissed.

I was getting absorbed by him—by the sounds and warmth of the fire—and the evening was swallowing me whole. I had to remind myself to come back to Earth, to my logical thoughts, because unlike before, there was no stopping this kiss. And all of a sudden, things were moving really fast. The kiss was deepening in ways I didn't think would happen with Darby. And then his hands were moving. And they were going faster than his lips. My cardigan lay limply on the floor, and his hands were roaming carefully over my back.

I broke away from our connection somehow. "Darby."

His eyes snapped open.

"Yes, what's wrong? Did I hurt you?" He reflexively looked down at my abdomen, inspecting me with care. I half expected him to lift up my cami to look again. I bit my lip at his question, overwhelmed by his care.

"No..."

"What is it?" he asked with such sweet concern.

"I can't... Can we just slow down? *Please*."

"Yes, of course," he responded, rubbing my arms. But I could hear all the confusion in his tone. "Is it painful to... Are you not supposed to..." That blush was back. The one I loved to see on him. My kryptonite. It made me want to say "forget it all" for the first time in my life.

"Well, I'm sure it would be, and I'm sure I'm probably

not. I really wouldn't know. I'm not exactly an expert in this area, quite the exact opposite . . ." Darby looked shocked as much as he was trying to hide it. I think he got what I was trying to subtly tell him. And I couldn't be more in over my head with the man in front of me. "I didn't date much in college, Darby. I was never that healthy and I had to focus on my studies. What little free time I had, I spend with friends or family. And after I withdrew from college, I was too sick to think about dating. And when I started to get my life somewhat back together and began working again, I really only dated the one guy. And well . . . nothing ever felt right with him." Darby's disbelief was getting harder to hide. "But, Darby, I don't know anything about you. I've completely spilled my soul today and I haven't gotten a glimpse of yours. You seem to keep it pretty well tucked away." His hands stopped on my arms abruptly, and he inhaled sharply.

"I wasn't supposed to get involved with you. It's not fair to you." His words came out rushed. He began to get up, but I tugged him down. His eyes sprung wide open.

"Don't do that. Please don't do that." A plea I hated, seeped into my broken voice. "Talk to me."

"Eyre, I don't deserve to talk to you. This was a mistake. I'm really sorry," he said, detachment in his voice.

"No," I said emphatically as I pulled him to look at me.

"Yes, Eyre. I can't give you what you want. I'm never going to be able to give you that. Let's just drop it. I can give you Candy Land and that's about it." He grunted out a sigh. "I can give you earlier today–sharing time together and learning more about you. I mean . . . connecting with you is easy, but it's not something I ever do. That was special. Me saying all this to you now is . . ."

"Special?" I filled in, and truly I did believe him. But there was so much more. I looked at him, holding him accountable. He wasn't giving me anything. Not really.

"Eyre, this is hard for me."

"It's hard for everyone, Darby, but at some point, you have to choose to let someone in. If they're worth it."

"No, Eyre. It's different for me," he replied a little more firmly.

"Ok," I replied softly as I backed off. I leaned in and rested my head gently on his shoulder, letting him know it was truly okay. "Either way, I need to go slow." I could feel him nod. I raised back up and went to kiss him gently again to show him that we really could move on, but *he* broke it off this time.

"Eyre." He looked at me. "I'm messed up. Really messed up."

Lucky had found himself a place on one of the armchairs near the fireplace and raised his head at Darby's words. I guess he could sense his distress. I felt as caught off guard as Lucky. I didn't know how to respond. Darby and I both looked at each other, our gazes locked. When nothing was said for a while, Lucky let out a sigh and lowered his head back down, guessing the excitement was over.

"Darby, you are the most considerate and kindest man I've ever met. What you've shown me is the furthest thing from messed up."

"That's just because it's you. But I couldn't even bloody tell you anything about myself before I tried to . . . It's a defense mechanism. I try to avoid anything emotional. I don't want to talk about myself or anything related to feelings. Even other people's. That's why *you* are such an anomaly. That's why Sinead and Mak have been saying all these things around you. Maybe even to you."

"Oh," I replied.

"No, I promise it's a good thing. Please take it as a compliment. It's not your fault I'm so messed up. But that's why you deserve better. I've been trying my best to stay away, but Eyre, it's about bloody near impossible to stay away from you."

"Oh," I said, more than a little flustered. He took my arms in his hands, rubbing them again as he had earlier.

"Eyre, you're really special. If you can get someone as messed up as me to share things with you, to enjoy life with you, and to start thinking about wanting more, then you really deserve someone who can give you the world. I hope that's what this experience has shown ya. You should go back home from Ireland with that much at least." He blushed. *Was he talking about the future?*

My heart fell with his last words. I didn't want to go back with that. I realized I didn't want to go back at all. But I at least wanted to go back having had a real experience with him. He was having an impact on me in ways that he couldn't possibly see or understand. I didn't want him to be just some stepping stone to the next guy or the next opportunity in life. I wanted him to be the landing place. Or at the very least, to have the potential to be the landing place. When I was with him, I didn't want to be anywhere else.

I was just about to try to find the courage and the words to tell him as much. "Darby, I don't—"

"Eyre, you can't have a future with someone like me. I'm a fling at best. Slow is fine as long as you know it's not headed anywhere. Don't get your hopes up with me, I'll only disappoint you. I've been disappointing everyone, including myself, my whole life. So it's best I just tell you now. And I'm not damaged in a good 'bad boy' kind of way, like those women in the village think. Or at least that's what Sinead keeps telling me is the bloody allure. Isn't that fantastic? My pain is an allure. My darkest, messiest parts are appealing. Apparently, that's all I have to offer, and I'm sure not offering that to anyone." He looked at me with such hurt and finality. I didn't know if I should say something or keep silent. I looked over to Lucky for some help. His puppy dog eyes were filled with concern as he took in every bit of his surroundings. But there was nothing to guide me. I couldn't believe I'd resorted to Lucky for guidance. That's how far out of my element I was.

I looked back at Darby, soaking in his words. "I don't want to fix you, Darby. That's not your appeal to me. It never will be. Just as I hope my brokenness isn't for you. There are some men who find that appealing too. That way, they think I have to rely on them more. And they see all my other baggage as a challenge. What a 'man' it'll make them if they can find a way to take care of me, if they can have kids with me, if they can overcome any of the zillion obstacles I face. But guess what? I don't need to overcome any of it to be happy. I have nothing to prove. Neither do you. And it seems you're trying to prove a lot to this village, and it's only holding you back. Your apathy makes as much of a statement as caring would. Don't think it doesn't, Darby. Probably an even bigger one."

Darby's eyes widened and his face started changing shape on me. It looked like I'd struck him when I talked about my own pain. I'd definitely hit a nerve. But more than anything, I could tell he couldn't believe I'd called him out. I took that as permission to continue. "Darby, you're not any more messed up than the rest of us. You're just human. You can decide if you want to face these fears or continue to hide in your apathy. You can keep being scared and push everyone away, or you can take a chance."

Darby interrupted me. "I know you've shown me a lot of your pain since we met, but I'm attracted to you as a person, Eyre, not your 'brokenness,' as you call it."

"I know," I responded with a soft firmness.

Darby continued, "But you're the least broken person I know. Wounded, maybe, but for good reason. But *not* broken." Darby's grip tightened on me. "I'm just extremely attracted to you." I laughed at his words. "No, you're a beautiful person, Eyre. *All of you.* Everything you've let me see. And I hope you'll let me see more–that for some reason, you'll think I deserve to see more." His firm grip on me let me know something was about to shift between us. His eyes held mine tightly. "Ok, Eyre. I'm open to seeing where something, *anything*, with you leads. Let's go slow." *Chink.*

I looked at him with happiness. "Good, because I'd never want you just to be an experience that led to the next. You are the only experience I want. When you said that earlier it–"

But I didn't get to finish. He was kissing me again, tenderly, softly. I could tell he needed this physical contact and that this part of our connection had never been merely a distraction for him. Not with me. He'd been telling the truth. Maybe his moving fast tonight had been a default for him, but in the other moments with me, he had been seeking something else–maybe for the first time. As for me, I finally felt seen and truly wanted, because no one before Darby had ever really known me. They couldn't possibly have known those parts of me, nor would they have wanted to take the time to understand them. They would never understand my hurt, or the differences between brokenness and wounds, like Darby understood.

"Ok, ok . . . Sorry." He pulled back as he got carried away again. I was starting to worry we were going to need to have the same conversation again. "But just so you know, it's not about a defense mechanism with you."

When did the words "defense mechanism" make me go weak in the knees?

Just then, Mak burst through the door. We both peeked our heads up over the sofa slowly. His eyes landed on the fire first, then us. He turned around quickly, then back to face us again. "Oh, never mind. *Thank the Lord* she has clothes on. I tried to close the shop as soon as I could. I even canceled the last tour. I didn't trust Teagan after the disasters of this morning, and I figured you needed a chaperone. I didn't know if Darce would behave himself or give Irishmen a bad name."

I started laughing uncontrollably. "Well, he's mostly been the perfect gentleman."

"Oye, mostly. I didn't get here soon enough." His eyes scanned over the room. "Candy Land, seriously, Darce? You're stooping really low now. What, do you give out prizes, too?" Mak rolled his eyes. "*Please* don't answer that question."

TWENTY-TWO
Darby

I could tell my face was changing to all different shades of red that even the fire couldn't compete with. Eyre looked like she actually felt bad for me. Well, not really. She was rather enjoying herself. She seemed completely taken in by Mak's charm. I, however, was not. I was very well aware that my time with Eyre was limited, and I could actually feel it slipping away. She wouldn't be here for much longer, and I wanted as much time with her as possible.

But at this rate, with Mak's little quips, she'd probably end up staying in another village just to get away from me. I'm not sure what he and Sinead had told her, but I had a very good idea since she seemed to think I was emotionally unavailable and used that to my advantage as some type of move. I just didn't deal with my emotions because I hadn't found a way that I could. Worst of all, I could feel Eyre getting too close tonight. I could feel her wanting to delve into my emotions–to learn more about me–which was completely normal, but nothing about me was normal. I hadn't lied to her about anything. I just hadn't shared any of my baggage with her. Getting to know her and connecting with her was a breakthrough for me. But when she wanted that in return . . . when I could sense that's what she needed, I'd reverted back to my methods of "distraction." And I hated myself for it. *What must she think of me?* And now Mak was coming in here making it so much worse. Acting like I had some kind of track record with women and was some kind of a delinquent that needed chaperoning. I might as well start calling hotels for her and preparing a goodbye speech.

"Mak, can I see ya in the kitchen?" I managed to get out through gritted teeth.

"Well, if you think ya can pry yourself away from Eyre, ok," he said with amusement. His blue eyes were twinkling. He was absolutely loving this.

I turned to Eyre in apology. "I'll be back in a minute. I'm going to see what we have to make for dinner. Can you figure out where we were in the board game? *And no cheating.* I'll know if you try to pull anything," I said with a smile. She laughed and looked at the board as if she had forgotten it was there.

I grabbed Mak by the arm and pulled him into the kitchen so quickly he barely could make use of his walking cane, I stopped us in front of the stove. I now really hated that this kitchen didn't have doors. This was one conversation I didn't want Eyre to hear.

I spoke to Mak in a low voice. "What are you thinking? You're supposed to be at the shop! Not sabotaging my date with Eyre."

"Darce is on an actual date?" His eyebrows raised as his voice sang out in a loud, mocking tone.

"Shhh," I shushed him, and he looked like he was going to whack me with his cane. "Mak, I promise if you keep this up..."

"At least you'll finally be putting energy into something. Glad to see ya caring again." His words came out in complete amusement. It felt like steam was coming out of my ears. There was no reasoning with him. Mak continued, "What exactly did I walk in on, Darce? You should be thanking me. Eyre is special."

"And why is that?" I challenged.

He rolled his eyes. "Oh, come on, Darce. I know you're a gentleman, but women do seem to think that you're relationship potential, and well, you're not. You make sure of that, don't ya?"

"What happened is my heart is permanently closed for business. It needed to be shut down. It's for everyone's good."

"Rubbish. Absolute rubbish. Don't be *thick* between the ears, Darce. I haven't seen you be like this in a *donkey's year*. It's been forever... Actually, *never*. You're not going to *bunk off* on her, are ya? Please tell me you won't leave her hanging." He looked at me, assessing. "Darce," he said emphatically. I turned to leave the kitchen. *How had this turned on me?* I had only pulled him in here to stop him from making me look *so unappealing* in front of Eyre, not to have him do a deep dive into my soul. I didn't have the energy for that. I especially wasn't going to do that with Eyre in the very next room.

Before I could get more than two feet, I heard a thwack. Before I could register where the sharp sound had come from, Mak's cane was splayed across the counter in front of me, effectively blocking the narrow aisle way. *How annoying could one man be with a fashion accessory?* This move took the cake. I rolled my eyes at him, and he grinned.

"Grand. Now that I have your attention, we can *crack on*." His voice rose in volume. My eyes widened. "Oh, I'm sorry, were we supposed to be discreet? You lost that privilege as soon as you walked away from our conversation."

"Mak, now is not the time."

"Well, ya pulled me in here like a bull bucking at a rodeo. So I'd say there was a rush and that you were very eager to discuss something with me. I don't exactly like being manhandled, Darce. It better be for a good reason." His face twisted into this absurd battle of amusement and seriousness only he could pull off.

"Fine, Mak. Will ya *please* cut it out?"

"Why?" he asked slyly. "Do ya like her?" He assessed my face. "Do ya like her a lot, Darce? Just tell me and we can *crack on*. She is under my roof, so I think I should know your intentions. I feel a need to protect her."

I lifted my head in complete exasperation. "You're impossible. There's no talking to ya. One minute you're dying or us to be together; the next you're warding her off of me."

"No one is warding anyone away. Just making sure you don't muck it up."

"Yeah. Well, if you'd stop *earwigging* we wouldn't have this problem. You just can't help yourself when it comes to eavesdropping." He looked at me sternly. I let out the most perturbed sigh of my life. "Fine, Mak, I really like her. Ok? *Happy*? I don't know what to do. I've never been in this position. Now will you stop making things harder for me and actually *help me?*"

The grin on his face instantly made me regret my words. I'd never seen such a glow from Mak—well, except when he was with Sinead—but this was different. It was like thirty years had fallen off of him, the sparkle in his eyes making him look so youthful and full of life.

"Yes, Darce. Since you asked *so nicely*, I will help ya." He eyed me and then puffed out his chest like a rooster, saying sagely, "*Stop making advances.*"

"What? How do you—"

But he interrupted me and whacked the cane on the counter again. My head immediately spun toward the living room. There was no way Eyre couldn't hear that, but she seemed to still be content by the fire. I think she'd started setting up a puzzle, apparently assuming we were going to take a while and being kind enough to give us some privacy. *How much of this was she hearing?*

"Darby, look at me." He used two of his fingers and pointed them to his eyes emphatically.

I widened my eyes with an annoyed sigh. I must really, *really* like this woman. Well, obviously I did if I was now taking advice from Mak. I'd hit the lowest rung on the dating ladder.

He snapped his fingers. I eyed the walking stick and held up my hands in surrender as Mak continued, "I'm not daft, ok? You think I'm senile? Show her you care. Listen. *Open up to her.*" I began to open my mouth, but he shushed me. Literally *shushed* me. "Yeah, you can do it. It's not gonna kill ya." I began to speak again, but he wouldn't let me. "We'll have a nice funeral for ya if it does." I couldn't believe him.

"Mak, there are things I can't–"

"Darby." I'd never seen Mak like this. I was actually a little scared of what he was going to say. "Either she's worth it, or she's not. Either you let her in, or you lose her. I would know. Don't be an *eejit*. *Real men* let women in. Real bravery comes from being vulnerable and letting someone see your hurt. I don't care how ugly you think your scars are. If she's the right person, she will hold those things with love and care. Wouldn't you like to know what that feels like? Wouldn't you like to know true love and acceptance? This is how you get there. Intimacy. *True intimacy*. Not the kind you've been playing at."

"Mak–" I began in disbelief.

"Darby, I was *never* honest with the woman I loved. And it's cost me years of unhappiness. You need to speak truthfully, and that means offering up what's on your heart. Not when you're asked, but when you feel it. Don't leave her to wonder. That's all people do with you. Don't make Eyre be one of them. There's a real masculinity in being honest, in laying your heart and mind out for a woman. I'm asking you to be more of a man than I could be. And I know it's not easy." He peered out and glanced at Eyre. "But something in the way you look at her tells me you can do it. *Now* is your time."

"It's not too late for you, Mak. It's never been too late. Why have you never told Sinead the truth? Why have you never laid *your* heart out?"

"Maybe I'm even more damaged than you. Or maybe I'm just too scared," Mak replied flatly.

"I see the way you look at her . . . The way Sinead looks at–"

"Darce, I think you better get back to Eyre now. She's gonna wonder what happened in here. Don't you think it's just a little weird for two grown men to be whisper-shouting in their tiny hovel of a kitchen? We both know neither of us can cook."

I let out a laugh. Obviously, that was as much as I was going to be able to say to him about the matter.

"Go on, I'll make myself scarce," he said, lifting his cane.

I slowly made my way out to Eyre, glancing back at Mak every so often. I felt like a man ready to walk the plank. Kind of like Captain Jack Sparrow, except I'm pretty sure I didn't have his fancy footwork. But when I saw Eyre in front of the fire with her face scrunched up in contemplation over a puppy puzzle, I couldn't help but relax. Maybe she would be able to handle my unique mess. Maybe she'd hold it with the love and care Mak thought she would instead of the judgment I so feared and probably deserved.

I knelt down on the floor beside her. There was something so serene and idyllic about the moment, especially the instant she felt my presence and looked up at me. A smile spread across her concentrated features. My eyes searched over her features as if she were a crystal ball, trying to find anything that told me I shouldn't proceed, looking for any warning that told my heart it needed to hide. But all I saw was her.

I slowly leaned forward and brushed my lips to hers. Allowing us to feel all the textures, the warmth of them, and our breaths intermingling. And this time, when I kissed her, it was gentle and sweet. Not rushed or needy. Not going anywhere or needing to lead to something. I lived in those lips, in that moment, with her. It was all I needed. She let out a small sigh that just about stopped my heart. I'd never kissed someone like that. It was the most gentle kiss of my life. I wrapped an arm around her as I settled myself at her side. She just continued to look at me, amazed and befuddled.

"Are we on to a puzzle now?" I asked quizzically. "Too afraid of the outcome of Candy Land?" She laughed in response, but I could tell she hadn't come back to the world yet. "Mak," I yelled, knowing he was sure to be close by and most definitely *earwigging* again. "Would you come help us with this puzzle?"

Eyre's eyes widened with surprise, then a slow grin overtook her. This was officially unlike any date I'd ever had or attempted. And she knew it now. This wasn't me making a move; this was me letting her into my world.

Mak hobbled into the room with extra dramatics, his actions accentuating his disbelief. There was so much incredulity on his face that I almost sent him away, but I was learning to be vulnerable. *Baby steps.* Okay, maybe more like a crawl, but what did people want from me? It was a start.

"Decided I wouldn't show ya up too badly?" Mak said with a devilish gleam. "Or maybe he just really needed expert help," he said to Eyre. Mak dragged a chair over to the coffee table so he could see.

I tightened my arm around Eyre and those large, inviting eyes stared back at me as if they were trying to tell me everything would all be alright. Maybe even thanking me. Mak looked at the hold I had on her, his eyebrows raised, and I only stared back, not lessening my hold or removing my arm. A smile quirked his mouth as he said, "Let's see what you've got."

After about an hour of intense puzzle playing, I left Mak

and Eyre to go make something for dinner. Eyre had insisted on helping, but I wouldn't hear of it. I told her omelets weren't going to take much culinary skill to achieve, thankfully. We huddled around the tiny kitchen table when it was ready, drinking more chamomile tea and eating our omelets with cooked vegetables and cheese. Eyre complimented my cooking multiple times, but it really felt like she was complimenting something else, especially since there was nothing special about them. She seemed to be looking at me differently. And I loved it. I wanted more of it–I was starting to crave it.

I could honestly say it was the best dinner of my life. Even though we kept bumping into each other above and below the table in our cramped space. Let's just say Mak and I didn't usually have company. But the laughter never stopped, and the wit continued throughout. Eyre's laugh was infectious. I think Mak and I were in competition to see who could make her laugh more. Both of us raised an eyebrow at each other to claim a point in our favor each time we did, like a heated game of air hockey. Lucky had especially enjoyed the evening, following us from one activity to the next. Always looking for any possible table scraps. Unfortunately, he also counted puzzle pieces as table scraps, too. If any pieces fell, he would either gobble them up or chew them up and spit them back out as a present for us.

When we'd completed the puzzle, we all decided to turn in for the night. Eyre's head had already fallen on my shoulder for much of the last part of the puzzle, and I could tell the day had worn her out.

"Come on, let's get you upstairs. You look especially knackered." She agreed, and we said goodnight to Mak.

Lucky bounded up the stairs after us. "I guess no bath tonight," I said with a laugh as Lucky sat at my feet.

"No, Sloane told me no more of those. Apparently, I didn't remember or listen to his instructions very well. I'm just lucky my incision hasn't gotten infected so far."

"Well, maybe you can ask him about waterproof bandages tomorrow. Are you in a lot of pain? I noticed you're kind of limping."

"You noticed, huh? Well, my joints are still stiff and swollen from eating the wrong food. And I'm still pretty exhausted and uncomfortable from my flare."

"So that's a yes. Please always tell me if something is too much for you. We didn't have to go out today. I want you to see Ireland, but not at a cost to your well-being and comfort."

She said nothing in reply. Instead she rocked back and forth a little, maybe to try and ease the pain or maybe because she was nervous. Lucky now sat more alert and was looking from one of us to the other, his head cocking from one side to the next, waiting to see what we were going to do next.

I finally broke the silence, "I'll see you in the mornin', Eyre."

"Night, Darby," she said. But neither one of us moved toward our rooms. We just stood there. Our eyes searching each other, minds racing.

Finally, she moved toward her room, and I echoed her steps in the direction of mine. Lucky sat in place, playing the same game of tennis, with his head bouncing between each of us. We continued to look at each other as we moved further away from each other and closer to our separate rooms. Eyre pressed her lips together, then opened her mouth, closing it again and pressing harder.

Finally, she said, "Night, Darby," for a second time and closed the door quickly.

"Goodnight, Eyre," I said as the door shut. I called Lucky over to me, but he had raced to Eyre's room. Apparently the little traitor had made his choice, adding insult to injury. He pawed at her door, his scratches growing louder. I felt like doing the same thing. I was utterly pathetic. I went over to collect him, bending down to pick him up, knowing he'd never come when called now. He knew what he wanted. *So did I.* I'd never been in this position before, never been this guy before. I wanted to be in that bed with her. I wanted to hold her and wrap my body around hers, especially when she wore those boxers and–

Her door opened abruptly, and her face was a lovely shade of pink. Only her head poked out, but she quickly scanned down to find me kneeling at her door. *How humiliating.* Her eyes averted mine.

"Uh, Lucky wants in, but don't worry, I was just about to collect him." This had to be the most humiliating situation ever. I looked down at Lucky with exasperation.

"Oh." She looked into my eyes, then at Lucky. Apparently he looked more pathetic because she said, "He can stay with me if that's ok . . . I'd love the company."

My eyebrows raised at him, and I swear that dog smirked at me. I released my hold and he bounded out of my arms and up on her bed. "I hope you realize that means he'll be in your bed. He *doesn't* sleep on the floor. He won't lay on you, though, so he shouldn't bother your stitches, but if you think–" I made a move toward her door.

"Oh, no," she said, moving forward. "He'll be fine. Really, I want some company."

I nodded my head slowly and looked at Lucky, who had already made himself *so* incredibly comfy. Right, just not my company. I stared at Lucky. I couldn't believe I was jealous of a dog. *Absolutely jealous of my dog.*

"Right, well, let me know if I need to come get him. Night, Eyre."

"Darby . . ." There was such a wave of hope that flooded through me. *Oh no, that lip bite of hers was back all of a sudden.* Then hurriedly, she said, "Night, Darby," for a third time and closed the door. She'd changed her mind, which I knew in my head was a very good thing because nights were a war zone for me and I didn't want her left to defend herself in the crossfire alone without me. But my heart said something very different. It's the first time it ever had. And as hesitant as I was about ever letting someone experience this part of me, my heart was winning when it came to Eyre every time.

"Night," I said quietly as I headed back to my room, hoping more than I'd hoped in a very long time that she'd change her mind yet again.

TWENTY-THREE
Eyre

I lay awake thinking of him. After I went to the bathroom and got ready for bed, I'd come back to see Lucky lying in the same spot. He was eagerly awaiting my return.

"Looks like it's just me and you, boy," I said quietly to him as I slid under the covers. Their coolness was a welcome respite for my tired body. I began to pet Lucky's silky fur. He snuggled closer to me, his cool blue and warm brown heterochromia eyes peering up at me with such heart and soul. I felt myself melting into them. I really didn't know how I was going to leave him. I was becoming so attached, well . . . I was definitely attached to more than just one Irish male.

As I snuggled with Darby's dog–wearing his tee and boxers–it was no wonder I could only think of him. Honestly, all I'd wanted to do was invite him into my room. I had wanted to be held by him–to know what it felt like to have his whole body protectively wrapped around mine. I'd gotten a little taste of that tonight, and now I wanted more.

His arms around me felt so right. Better than anything I'd ever experienced. My ex-boyfriend's arms had always felt possessive, like they were claiming me. It wasn't a loving or protective gesture. Instead, I felt like I was being used as a prop. A life piece that needed to fall into its proper place. First, he needed a girlfriend, then a wife, and finally a mother so he could take the necessary steps to complete his life plan. And when he put his arms around me, it only felt like he was securing his future and robbing me of mine.

When one of those three pieces threatened to break away, he just pushed harder to make sure that his life plan would work, never thinking about me or asking what I might want or need. But it wasn't really *me* he needed; what *he* needed was to *not* go back five steps in his life plan, especially when he was so close to securing everything he felt he had so carefully put in place.

Once I realized I was not much more than a piece of a puzzle to my ex-boyfriend, I was so happy to break free. I felt like a bird let out of its cage or a butterfly that had just discovered its wings. However, I now realized that I was blessed to have experienced some bad dating choices in my life so that I could truly appreciate when someone as special as Darby came unexpectedly into my life. And truthfully, now all I really wanted was to have him near me.

I looked down at Lucky, contemplating. His eyes stared back up at me, lost. I was ready to take myself and Lucky to Darby's room–more than ready to knock on his door–but the problem was that I didn't think knocking on Darby's door would mean the same thing to him as it did to me. But so much of me wanted to believe that Darby was capable of a different type of intimacy because he and Mak had not been as stealthy and quiet as they thought they were when they were talking in the kitchen. I had definitely heard bits and pieces of their conversation. Although, I was still terribly confused as to what caused those loud whacking sounds. But Darby had come back to me a changed man. And while I wasn't ranking kisses with him—because they were all the best ones of my life and each one had been incredible in its own way—that last one might have been my favorite so far. It felt like I was finally getting to experience an unguarded Darby.

These thoughts and a raging debate in my head quickly wore me out. They swiftly guided me into a deep sleep with Lucky curled next to me, protecting me from everything bad in the world.

I woke to a knocking sound and Darby's voice calling to me. I thought it was a continuation of the dreams I'd been having. Or maybe he'd decided to do what I'd been too hesitant and skeptical to do, and he had come back to my room.

Groggily, I trudged to the door. Lucky did not move a muscle, apparently still quite comfy. I peeked out to see Darby's tired face. He was obviously not a morning person, either.

"Um, Sloane is here," he said with a little perturbed edge, which seemed to make his features wake up.

"Oh? Ohhh. To check on my stitches. Right. This early?" I asked.

"Well, I guess you don't get to the top of your veterinary class by being the last one up in the morning. I bet he embodied the phrase the 'early bird gets the worm.'"

I started laughing. But I could see his wheels turning. I was pretty sure he'd wanted to say "girl" in place of "worm." Sloane was obviously very caring since he was here this early on a Sunday morning. I felt kind of bad for laughing.

I halted my laughter and said, "I'll be down in just a minute. I'm really sorry he woke you and Mak. I didn't think to ask him what time he would be coming today. I assumed he'd come in the afternoon–"

"Don't worry about it. Mak gets up early, and I'm just happy Sloane's checking on you. Although there might have been some motivation for his early morning arrival. Maybe he wanted to see if he could spend the day with you," Darby said astutely.

Even though I thought he might be right–only because of his offers yesterday–I said, "Darby, I think he just wants to get his house call out of the way."

But he looked at me with a raised brow.

I hurried to get ready after Darby left. My hair was an absolute wreck, and it dawned on me that Darby had seen me this way. I had washed my hair last night, but I never seemed to have the energy to dry it anymore. Pain and fatigue had taken that luxury away a while ago. Plus, I was sure these two men didn't have a hair dryer in their house. I had long ago perfected a rolled updo with a skinny headband that I slept in at night while my hair air-dried. For many people, it would have been a Greek goddess look, but I was pretty sure I couldn't pull that off, not by any means. By the time I woke up in the mornings, after rolling around the bed all night in my attempt to get some decent sleep, I certainly didn't look like Aphrodite. No, probably more like Medusa.

I considered myself lucky that I had a few headbands and a brush. I was really lucky that my hospital overnight bag had these basics. After a few surgeries and hospital stays, you get this down to a science. And you start to think about the little things. I was especially glad since I had nothing else to use to style my hair. At least this left me with some soft curls.

I finished getting ready. Very much aware that I was going to need to buy clothes today or be stuck doing daily laundry. *The only attire I thought I'd needed was a hospital gown. The lack of planning and preparation was really, really stupid, Eyre.*

I took the staircase steps with caution, not only because my joints were still raging a war with me but also because I was reluctant to start this day. I saw Lucky in the kitchen chowing down on his food. He'd followed Darby from my room immediately. I didn't blame him. My stomach rumbled as well.

Sloane stood as soon as I entered the living room, rising swiftly to his feet from the sofa. "Eyre, it's so good to see you again," he said as he moved toward me. The lilt of his Irish accent seemed especially spry this morning, but perhaps it was my non-morning personality taking over. I could really use some coffee. Too bad my Crohn's hated it. But when he began speaking again in his chipper manner, I thought I was going to have to make an exception. Don't get me wrong, I was glad he loved this beautiful morning, but I was not ready to partake in his excitement. It was like someone opening the blinds with the sun on full blast, right in your eyes, when you had the worst migraine of your life. *Ok, that was a little dramatic.* Maybe I was more tired and in more pain than I thought.

"Are you ready to go? I've got the car out front and I'm ready to escort you to the office," Sloane said sweetly. He really was a kind man, and he was dressed so nicely in a light blue polo shirt and slacks.

"Yes, of course. Thank you," I replied.

"I think Eyre could use a minute and something to eat," Darby interrupted, coming in from the kitchen. Ahh, my knight in green shamrock armor. He was looking extra good today. Those words made him so attractive, especially in his jogger sweats and torn tee. What a stark contrast between him and Sloane. Mussed hair versus gel shellacked into place. Bare feet versus loafers. These two were definitely at odds. But Darby most certainly spoke my language, and I preferred how good he looked doing it. *So much more.* That was the Sunday morning I wanted. Give me the funny papers with hot tea, a man in a torn shirt, and noon instead of early morning, *any time.*

"Yes, please. I'm actually really hungry," I said with relief.

"Well, I would offer you a boiled egg, but you're going to think that's all we can cook for you." Darby laughed. "Um, what else can I make you? I think everything else is going to have gluten in it, but we do have oats."

I responded, "Usually oats have come into contact with gluten, unless they're marked. The egg sounds great, but I'll just grab something quickly so Sloane doesn't have to wait. Do you have some cheese and fruit?"

"Of course," he said, looking at me with that warm Darby smile. The skin around his eyes crinkled with goodwill. "Sloane, would you like something?"

Sloane looked at me, then at Darby. "No thank you, I ate hours ago."

I went into the kitchen with Darby, and he helped me find some things to take with me, even making me a to-go tea. As he fixed it, I couldn't help but think of him packing lunches for kids. Despite what he said yesterday, I think he'd be an incredible dad. The thought of him missing out on having children tore at me and I could feel the pain in my abdomen worsen with that thought.

Darby turned to me. "What is it?" His face crinkled with concern. I smiled back at him and shook my head. I was honestly worried about going to the clinic without him, but it didn't seem like he would be invited to go on our little field trip. He moved closer and whispered, "Just so you know, our Sunday morning together would not look like this. Believe me, this is not what I had in mind." I smiled even bigger. "Go on, get *cracking*, so you can come back sooner." He leaned down, kissed my forehead, and then handed me the tea.

I heard Sloane's movements in the entryway of the kitchen. "Eyre?" Sloane called impatiently.

"Oh, yes, sorry, I'm coming," I replied. I faced Darby before leaving and said, "I'll be back soon. I hope my tour guide has something good planned."

He chuckled at my teasing remark.

Sloane escorted me to his car, guiding me with his hand on my back and taking the tea from me. These Irish men were certainly considerate. I think I was going to be forever ruined after all this fine Emerald Island attention.

When we reached the car, he handed me the tea before opening my door. I looked at the tea and my packed breakfast. I couldn't help but think I was forgetting something. My brain fog was seriously getting the better of me. "Oh, I'm sorry, I forgot something," I said, turning to Sloane, "I'll be right back."

"Sure thing. I'll just warm up the car."

I quickly entered the house to see Darby and Mak looking out the kitchen window like a couple of old biddies. They were whispering to one another.

Lucky cocked his head and looked up at me, and then looked over at Mak. "No, Lucky, it's just Eyre. You do not need to announce her presence," Mak said with exasperation. Lucky cocked his head further at Mak and then impishly looked at the wall by the front door where the musical instruments were hanging. Bouzoukis—a variation of the lute that originated from Turkey—and mandolins lined the wall. I assumed they were Mak's. I sure didn't see Darby playing them. Lucky's mischievous eyes seemed to glow brighter as he took aim at the instruments and started barking. All three of us covered our ears and ducked our heads as Lucky's barking reverberated through the holes of the instruments, which only served to loudly amplify his barks. Lucky, quite proud of himself and his "welcome alarm" that had produced such a loud, raucous noise, started prancing and dancing around the living room furniture at a high-spirited speed, the white tip of his tail sailing proudly in the air. I looked at Mak and Darby, checking if it was okay to uncover my ears. I definitely was looking to their lead on this one. I don't know that I'd ever heard such loud barking in my whole entire life.

I cleared my throat, uncovering my ears as they did. "Sorry, I forgot my purse. Mornings really aren't my best hours."

Darby started walking over to me. It was fairly obvious that Mak and Darby were both embarrassed to have been caught gawking at Sloane and me through the kitchen window. Although Lucky's little show had distracted me from some of their nosiness, they still looked like little boys who had gotten caught with their hands in the cookie jar.

"Sorry about that, Eyre," Mak said quickly. "Lucky has this habit of sounding the alarm. He's realized very quickly that he can amplify his bark by projecting it into my instruments. It's been a very loud and alarming discovery." He glanced over to Darby with an eye roll.

"Oh, it's fine–" I started just as Sloane's car backfired, and I jumped. I noticed Darby stopped mid-motion and he seemed more than startled. He'd gone chalk white. Mak glanced at Darby as he quickly raced over and grabbed my purse off the kitchen table. But my eyes went back over to Darby who was now starting to sweat and looked filled with a hollow panic. Like he wasn't here with us anymore.

"Hear ya go, Eyre. It's best not to keep Sloane waiting, he's a very important man. Off ya go. *Go on*," Mak said, rushing me out.

I looked back at Darby again, and he looked so pale. Hopefully, he was going to be alright. He didn't look like he was feeling okay. But Mak didn't give me a chance to ask any questions before helping me out the door.

THE IRISH FALL

It took less than five minutes to get to the vet clinic, which looked like something out of a Nora Ephron movie. A little cottage had been converted into a clinic and sat by itself on a hill. I seriously was having an *All Creatures Great and Small* moment. Someone needed to alert the BBC about this location.

After Sloane helped me from the car and into the clinic, he directed me to a "patient" room. I was very well aware that this was a vet clinic, and I felt oddly uncomfortable about the whole situation. I sat in a chair instead of the examining table and pulled out my breakfast from my bag. I'd been too scared to eat in his car, afraid I might drop some crumbs in his meticulous vehicle.

Sloane sat in the chair beside me, scooting it closer. Now he seemed to be in no hurry and was more than happy to keep me company while I ate my food. "Sorry for the rush over here. I just wanted to make sure I could make it to church on time. Hope you understand. Would you like to accompany me?" Sloane asked somewhat shyly, which surprised me.

"Oh, um . . . Well, I should probably check with Mak and Darby about their Sunday plans. I'll accompany them if they're planning on attending a service. Does everyone in the village attend the same church? I've only seen one and it looked damaged."

"Darcy won't be going to church," Sloane said rather bluntly. "And the church you've seen is under renovation. It was damaged by a fire. We've converted one of our stores for church services for now until the renovations are completed. And some people drive to a church in another village."

I looked at him cautiously. *Why the remark about Darby?* "Oh, is Darby not religious?"

"Oh, you could say that. I don't think you really know what you've gotten yourself into there."

I really didn't care for what he said about Darby. I decided to change the topic of conversation. I didn't like discussing Darby with him. "When did the church fire happen?"

"About fifteen years ago. Really tragic," he said. "It was a beautiful, historic church from the 1800s. But enough about that. I want to hear more about you. Enough about Darcy."

The way he said his name really irritated me. It was so condescending and belittling. *"Darby,"* I corrected, "is a really wonderful man. He's been taking great care of me."

"I don't see him taking care of your wound," he said in a matter-of-fact tone. As he looked at me, he scanned his eyes from the top of my head down to my abdomen as if he could see right through me with his X-ray vision, hoping to uncover my secrets and lay bare my soul.

Since we seemed to have finished our conversation, he instructed me, with very few words, to hop onto the examining table. I was hoping the table was strong enough to support my human weight, and without preamble, he started to examine me. He undressed my wound in uncharacteristic silence. And when he broke the quiet, I certainly wasn't ready for what was coming. "I think you need a real man. One that can take care of you. Why don't you let me show you around for the day."

THE IRISH FALL

There was another tense, long pause. I certainly hadn't expected such remarks from Sloane. He was definitely letting his ego take the lead.

I replied tersely, "I really appreciate you taking this time so early on a Sunday morning to check on my wound, but I think I need to get back home."

His icy blue eyes looked startled, as if he wasn't used to being rebuffed. He tried to brush it off, but I could tell he'd not expected this outcome. He took a slight pause before he told me that my incision was looking good and that there was no sign of infection. Then he gave me some antibacterial cream to use on my surgical areas and more dressings. I couldn't believe this cream for pets was also going to work for me, but I was extremely grateful. He also gave me some materials I could use for waterproofing but advised against a bath until it was a full week after my surgical procedure.

The drive on the way back home was awkward. At least it was short—less than five minutes—but it was an excruciatingly uncomfortable five minutes. When we pulled up to the cozy cottage, I reached for the door handle and was about to thank him when he coolly said, "I don't think you know what you're getting into. When you figure it out, I'd really like to get to know you better. My office door is always open. Please be careful."

"Goodbye, Sloane," I replied, unhappiness clouding my features. "Thank you for taking care of my wound." I made sure to be extremely specific. Not *thank you for the offer*. Not *thank you for the warning against Darby*. And certainly not a thank you for the extra dose of his ego this morning.

I exited and quickly closed the car door. I hated that he had made me so curious about Darby's situation. I wondered what mess Sloane was referring to. *What was it that he thought I was getting into? And why was Sloane so adamant that Darby wouldn't be found in a church? Was he just not religious or was there something more?* I guess I hadn't really thought about it before now. I was more consumed with what my limited time here would mean and trying to figure out so many other things about him. And now Sloane had just thrown so many more ingredients into that ever-expanding mystery dish. I couldn't figure any of it out. And there was something really weird about the way he said all of it.

I certainly could understand being a mess when it came to one's faith and even questioning it at times. I'd been struggling with my own faith, battling to keep a grip on it and to not become angry about what was happening in my life. At times, things felt too difficult to overcome. The higher the mountain of tribulations, the deeper the chasm in my faith, and the more my faith seemed to be slipping from my grasp. Until it started to feel much harder to believe. Until it was getting harder and harder to pray.

I tried to shake these thoughts from my mind as I stood outside the cottage, staring at the door. As soon as I entered the room, I saw Darby waiting in the living room for me. He sat in the armchair with a book in his hands, but he didn't look like he'd actually been reading. Evidence: the book was upside down.

His expression was sweet and tender when he saw me. "How did it go?" he asked, not bothering to hide the anxiousness in his tone.

"Oh, I don't think I want to see Sloane again."

"What did he do?" Darby asked.

"Nothing. He was very nice and checked over my incision. But I don't want to see him again. Can we please not call him again?"

Darby's smile lit up at my words. "Of course, I'd honestly like nothing more. But that means we have to make sure you heal completely."

I went over to him and wrapped my arms around his firm torso, relaxing into the hug I so desperately needed. I could tell my reaction made Darby happy as his arms tightened around me.

Sensing that I needed my spirits lifted, he said, "I promised to take you to find some new clothes today. Are you still up for it? And Sinead has live music at the pub tonight, if you'd like to go. I'm not sure what to do in between, but I have a few sights in mind. Maybe something will appeal to you. Whatever you're up for. I didn't slack on my tour guide duties—I even did some research while you were away. Just don't tell Mak I actually got out a guidebook." I laughed in response to his humor. "Tomorrow we can go to a grocery store in Dublin, unless there's something you need today. Or we can even take one of the walking trails to the Cliffs of Moher if you're up for it tomorrow."

"I think I've already been on that walking trail."

"No, that wasn't the scenic coastal one. The one by the coast takes about three hours—four if we go up to Hags Head."

I looked up at him with wide eyes and he chuckled. "Ok, well, that better not be on the schedule for today."

He laughed at my reply. "No, I'm taking it easy on you. Did you get enough to eat? Or should I ask, did you actually *get* to eat?"

I nodded, loving the concern he showed.

Then he spoke with an eagerness in his tone that he couldn't hide, "Ok, well, if you're ready to go, then I will take you for a once in a lifetime Darby shopping experience. And you should know, I don't usually go clothes shopping." I laughed, the mental image alone enough to send me over the edge. "You're going to make me reconsider," he said, looking at me and pointing at my obnoxiously large smile.

"Me? I would never–" I started playfully.

"Oh, Eyre, you *are* on very fine ice here." Laughter exploded out of me as he quickly turned away from me. I grabbed his arm but couldn't control my fit of hysteria. My laughter was probably due to the stress built up from my encounter with Sloane that so desperately needed to be dispelled.

"I'm sorry, Darby," I managed between chuckles. "I'll behave. Please take me shopping. Really, I'm all out of clothes."

"Said every woman ever." Darby's jest only added to my fit.

"Ok, I'm fine now. Promise."

He leaned down and softly said, "I really like you, but don't expect me to try anything on."

I lifted my face up to him with a challenge in my eye. "Oh, we'll see about that."

TWENTY-FOUR
Eyre

Darby and I walked to Fisher Street. He offered to let me ride in the sidecar again, but I was up for a fifteen-minute walk. The Irish air and countryside made me want to go everywhere on foot. How could you pass up that experience when it felt like you were walking through a scene of *P.S. I Love You* at any given moment, especially with Darby at your side? Plus, I much preferred my hand in his while meandering down the side of the road, compared to his sidecar, which didn't offer me that option. I also couldn't easily turn to see him from the sidecar, and I wanted a visual of this man for as much time as I had left in this country.

Excitement bubbled over in me when the village's colorful shops came into view. I hadn't really gotten to appreciate them on my first day here. After Darby's long guided trek back to the village that day, I hadn't exactly been in a state of mind to appreciate anything. Now as we made our way to the first set of shops, he stopped us and turned me toward him, guiding me with his strong hands on my arms. He was looking at me with regret already. I guess he could see the wild excitement in my eyes. "Eyre, privileges will be taken away. Please remember, I do live here, and I have to continue to do so."

"Oh, so make this extra good, huh? You shouldn't have said anything. I'm dialing the embarrassment level up to eleven."

"Did you just make a *Spinal Tap* reference?" he questioned.

"I don't know, Darby. Maybe you'll get really lucky and that number will be eleven out of one hundred, and not ten." I smirked wickedly, and he groaned in response. I continued on toward the shop, leaving him behind as he debated whether he was going to follow. But I slowly felt a hand slide back into mine, and I grinned with reckless abandon.

We came to a clothing shop that featured handknit apparel and handcrafted artisan items. I could see the store was empty except for a shop owner or clerk who was staring absentmindedly into space. I opened the door for Darby. "After you. Enter at your own discretion."

He just shook his head at me.

I glanced around as we stood in the doorway, and then said loudly, "Aww, snookums, this is perfect—exactly what I wanted. You know me so well." I reached up and kissed Darby's cheek. The man behind the counter coughed to hide his laughter.

"I'm gonna get you," he gritted out, but there was amusement in his tone—the *I-can't-believe-you-had-the-gall-to-pull-this-kind-of stunt* amusement.

"Yes, we can totally get matching sweaters, and beanies,

too, honey bear. What a fantastic idea," I cooed. Darby turned toward the door, but I just broke out in laughter. "I'll behave. I've gotten it out of my system now."

He eyed me sharply and raised his eyebrows quickly in that signature Darby move. "Right, sure. I definitely believe that now. Well, are you going to try on something or not? You thinking about actually supporting a local business? Any day now . . ." he said with a teasing edge.

"Yes, but I do think the matching sweaters are a brilliant idea."

Darby rolled his eyes at my comment.

I wandered through the store, taking in the talent of the local artisans. There were so many gorgeous creations. I picked up a sweater wrap to try on over my clothes. It looked like an oversized infinity scarf to the untrained eye, but I'd seen the tag description on the shelf. I handed it over to Darby. "Can you demonstrate this for me? I don't have the Irish knowledge that you do," I said helplessly.

He quickly grabbed it from me. "Yeah, of course," he said nonchalantly. After what must have felt like ten minutes of torture for him—but, in reality, was more like ten seconds of entertainment for me—I took mercy on Darby. He'd tangled himself up in the contraption and twisted his arms in several awkward maneuvers long enough.

"Oh, heavens, it's just a sweater wrap. I think it just crosses in the front over your chest like this."

"Yeah, and how is that supposed to keep you warm? Your whole abdomen and some of your sides would be exposed. Not that I'm complaining," he stated.

"Well, I think you put it over a tee or maybe just save it as a top for parties," I suggested.

Darby scoffed, but the owner called out, "She's right, Darcy. Wish I had some cameras in here, though. I'd replay that little sequence of events I just witnessed, for our paying customers, all day long. It would make a great addition to the display."

Daggers shot from Darby's eyes at me.

"Eleven, baby. I promised," I said in total amusement.

"I will get ya back," he said confidently.

"Oh, I'm counting on it," I replied.

I tried on some more sweaters in the back and decided on a few purchases. Then I came out to meet Darby.

"Um . . . this is really embarrassing, but do you know if one of these shops is going to have . . . underwear?" I asked, the last word in a minuscule whisper.

"Underwear?" he said loudly. "Did you lose all your undergarments over here already?" His voice grew louder with disbelief. My eyeballs raised toward the ceiling and stayed there. He continued, "Really, you shouldn't be leaving your underwear all over the place. They're scattered around like lucky charms all over this country. We can't afford to keep buying more." Okay, now my eyes *were* never going to come back down from the ceiling.

I ignored him and walked over to the man at the counter. "Like an idiot, I forgot to pack underwear. Is there a shop around here that has some?" I queried. It took a while for him to stop laughing. I think Darby and I were the best entertainment he'd had in the store that day. Perhaps all month.

"Well, we have some lingerie that is handmade silk, but it's like a specialty thing. There's another clothing store down the road that might have some funny, gag gift ones.

They probably have 'Kiss Me, I'm Irish' written across the bum."

"Oh no." I let out a loud sigh.

"We'll take it all," Darby joked. I stared at him with a look that said *no*. But I did indeed have to buy something. I made him wait at the counter, though, as my red face and I looked through the small selection.

The man rang up my purchases, and we left the shop. We stopped at the other clothing store and, to my utter dismay, the man had been spot-on with his description of the underwear. I selected some to buy and Darby had a field day with his comments because *Kiss Me, I'm Irish* wasn't the *only* saying across the bum.

They also had an assortment of pants and sweatshirts to commemorate Ireland, as well as some gorgeous knit sweaters, beanies, and ponchos in an Irish style. I had the best time showing clothing to Darby that I liked and wanted to try on–and ones I jokingly wanted him to try on–and he was a surprisingly good sport about it all. Although he did draw the line at my buying us matching beanies and ponchos. Too bad, we would have been so cute together. And I would have loved to hear the comments from Mak.

After the clothing store, Darby took me over to a deli to see if there was anything I needed. There wasn't much I could buy since everything was pre-packaged, but I did find a few things. I even managed to find something to eat for lunch in their café–a delicious homemade quiche. I just had to avoid the crust, so we were able to enjoy a quick meal. Even this tiny deli was adorable in Doolin, with its bright mustard-colored exterior and vibrant neon-colored outdoor seating.

When we were done, I eyed the bookstore. It was a little hole in the wall, and I just had to check it out. I grabbed Darby's hand and pulled him along, his eyes widening before his mind caught up, and then he smiled. We stepped through the front door, and I was immediately met with the wonderful smell of ink and paper. I breathed deeply, letting the bibliosmia drive me wild. Darby chuckled under his breath.

"Hey, Darby. Ya gonna introduce me?" a curvy woman called from behind the counter.

"Of course, Rosie," he replied.

I looked at Darby quizzically. This was not a place I would have expected him to visit very often. He looked at me with a satisfied smile. "What? . . . *I do* read. Quite often, actually," he said.

He brought me up to the bookstore counter and made introductions. Then Rosie told us about the shop's latest additions. The place was filled with odds and ends. It was like a sea of misfit toys, and I absolutely loved it. It wasn't like a normal commercial bookstore. This was like a treasure hunt that made the adventure of starting a new book all the sweeter.

"Go on, find your latest, Darby," Rosie said jovially. "I'll be anxiously waiting to see what you find. You always keep me guessing. And you're both welcome to leave your bags up here while you look."

We thanked her and started making our way through the store. The place was stacked high with books. It was like going through a gigantic maze. It allowed you privacy while shopping, but also gave you the ability to get sucked into another world, just like the promise of a good book.

There was a curved area at the back of the shop with a narrow walkway. We meandered over to it and started exploring, our eyes daring to look at each other, meeting briefly then looking away like schoolyard crushes. Finally, during one of our brief eye contacts, he stopped me in the aisle and turned me to face him, backing me up with his gaze. My breath seemed to get caught in the air and my feet edged back until I hit the bookshelf with a louder thud than I'd anticipated, causing both our heads to snap toward the front of the bookstore. I pictured mounds of precariously stacked books falling on us and burying us in an avalanche of ink and paper. But that thought was quite fleeting with Darby's green eyes on me, their depths drawing me in and his breath warming my skin.

I swallowed hard, trying to push all those butterflies back down. My breathing hitched and his eyes scanned down to my neck, right where my veins were thrumming hard to contain themselves. He smiled and slowly lowered his lips down to meet that exact spot. Like he knew. Like he had some type of adrenaline sonar. I arched my neck backward, inviting him closer. His warm breath washed over my skin, causing goosebumps to ripple through me. He began kissing me gently, and I was thankful he hadn't started with my lips. I didn't think I could handle that yet. But slowly, he was making his way up my neck, and I was trying to prepare myself for his lips to finally meet mine.

A noise escaped me, and he put his hand gently over my mouth, obviously not wanting Rosie to hear us. It was so quiet in the store that you could hear a fly buzz. I didn't know how she could not have heard me. But I wasn't exactly in control of myself to do anything about it. He paused, pulling his lips away for a moment. I pulled him tighter as if in response to his unspoken question. When he began gently moving again, another sound escaped me without my permission. It didn't phase him, though; he kept moving. I was going to have to pull myself together, or Rosie was going to think we were having an *Atonement* moment back here.

He went to pull back his hand that still covered my mouth, his eyes dancing with more than just desire. There was something else in them that I hadn't seen before. Something more like a deep affection. He lifted his fingers one by one from my mouth in a cheeky manner, and I shook my head at him in silence, but I was just met by a proud grin.

"Ahem ahem...mmm, ahem...mmm," a throat cleared madly. Our heads darted wildly in unison toward the noise. I was afraid we would bump heads together with how fast they moved in reaction to the startling sound. There stood Rosie, hands on her hips, staring at us. And there we stood, with Darby plastered to me, pinning me to the bookshelf.

"How many book sales is it going to take to make this go away for you?" Darby asked hesitantly.

"To remove this mental image, Darby? Probably the whole store." She laughed. "Why don't you buy your new 'friend' at least nine or ten, but probably best not to make them romance."

"And if I would like two more minutes so I could finish what I started? I mean–finish the kiss. That's all. *I promise.*" Darby's words rushed out with heat flooding his face. I could not be more embarrassed. I cannot believe he thought it needed clarification.

"I should hope so . . . Well, *you are* blocking the path to the exit and the handicap bathroom, Darby." Rosie rolled her eyes. "Ten books, Darby. Good thing we're having a sale. And ya better come back to see me often. Don't let this embarrass you so much that you don't show your face again in here, ya hear?" There was a twinkle in her eyes as she walked away.

Darby turned to meet me with a blush that only made me go weaker. "Now, where was I?" he asked as he proceeded to finish what he'd started.

We exited the bookstore with a mound of paperback books, and I was honestly worried how we were going to carry them all home, but Darby carried them like precious trophies. He'd even refused the box Rosie had offered, instead opting to hold them close to his side in a bag.

"How about some ice cream? My treat," I asked as I spotted the white and vibrant yellow-painted ice cream shop. "You've been so wonderful to show me around the village today and you were a really good sport, too."

"I'm pretty sure the bookstore was my reward. I'll take another one of those if you're doling out prizes. Those are my kinds of sweets."

"Oh, such a bad pun Darby." I laughed, but I couldn't help smiling at how sweet it was. With our book haul and other bags, we decided to get one scoop to share. Mostly because we didn't have more than one hand to spare between the two of us, but it was also really sweet to share a scoop together. It reminded me of the scene from *The Notebook*. I almost said as much, but I was pretty certain that was something Darby would not have watched.

We made our way outside to find a spot to sit and enjoy, taking turns passing the cup back and forth. We could see the pier and the water from our little spot of paradise. Gazing out over the water, I said, "The islands look amazing. Can we take the ferry out to them? Is there enough time before we go to the pub tonight?"

But Darby looked at me with such intense concentration, as if he hadn't heard a word I'd said. "Eyre–" There was such a conflicted look on his face.

"Yes, Darby?" I responded with concern. There was a painful uncertainty clouding his features.

He shook his head quickly, dismissing his previous thoughts. "Of course we can. That would be grand. I'll ask Rosie if she can watch our bags. Taking the ferry tour around the Cliffs of Moher or to Inis Oírr are my favorite routes on the water. Loads to do at Inis Oírr. We can take one ferry tour today and then take the other one another day if you'd like."

I looked at him, unsure if I should let the previous moment pass, but he seemed to have changed his mind and was ready to move on from what he was going to say, so I thought it best to do the same. "I wouldn't even know how to choose."

"Yeah, I can tell you want to do both of them." He chuckled. I guess he saw the sparkle in my eye. "Well, there's a lot to explore on the island, so maybe the tour of the cliffs would be better for today. And that way, maybe you'll be able to save some energy and have a better chance of feeling like going out to hear the music at the pub tonight. What do you say?"

"Sounds like you know me well, Darby," I replied, looking into his eyes and admiring him as his hair danced wildly in the breeze.

TWENTY-FIVE
Eyre

As we waited for the ferry, I could feel a shift in Darby. There was something clouding his mood. He seemed to have been enveloped in a storm of worry and darkness ever since he'd almost told me something earlier today. I was more than a little concerned as to what it could be. *Was it me? Did I do something? Was it something he didn't want to share with me?*

My mind was going faster than a spinning top and making me just as disoriented. Possibilities were filling my head like an overflowing cup, spilling out every which way.

Darby curved his lips up at one side, his handsome face straining to read me. He pulled me to him, wrapping his arms around me as we both faced out toward the water.

"Hey, are you going to be ok to go back to the cliffs?" he asked with kind concern.

"Yes, of course. They're gorgeous." I turned my head upward to look at him. Then I paused and said, "You know you can always talk to me, right?" He nodded slowly. Seeing that he acknowledged my words, I continued, "You can always tell me what's going on inside your mind. Whatever you want to tell me, it isn't going to change how I see you."

I felt his muscles tense more with each word I spoke. Just then, an older man in a bright red shirt shouted a call to board the ferry. We took our tickets and readied ourselves to board. It was quiet at this time of day. Maybe because it was one of the last ferries for the day. Darby guided me to the bow. It was a double-decker with an enclosed area and an upper deck that housed the captain's tower.

The sun had mostly gone away, tucking itself behind the clouds. It seemed the sun was rather timid in Ireland, but the overcast hues gave everything a silky glow on the Emerald Isle. Especially since it made the water deeper shades of blues and greens while also making the cliffs appear even more stoic. The guide was talking over the PA system about what we could expect to see on our tour today—an array of wildlife ranging from puffins, basking sharks, dolphins, and seals. The ferry would take us to the furthest point of the cliffs, Hags Head, which was also the highest point at seven hundred feet. There we would see O'Brian's tower. We would also see a large bird sanctuary and a cave that had been used for the filming of *Harry Potter*, as well as several islands along the way.

"There's nothing like seeing the cliffs at sea level," Darby explained as he held on to me. His voice came from behind me as we looked out together over the water. "It's really amazing. The people on the cliffs look like little specks. I've never seen anything that compares to it."

I looked out, already amazed at the beauty of the sparkling water. I was having a hard time getting my brain to process what was in front of me. As we started moving, and the large rock formations rose up ahead of us in the distance, it was hard to fathom this was reality. Our ferry came close to a standing rock formation, and its sheer size beside us was enough to blow my mind. It looked like something out of *Jurassic Park*. None of this seemed like it could possibly exist. To make things even more surreal, I couldn't believe that this man was here to enjoy it with me.

"Eyre," Darby said again as the big rock formation loomed beside us. I tried to turn, but he had me solidly planted between him and the ferry railing in front of me. Somehow he'd managed to make it impossible for me to turn my head to look at him. *Oh no.* He'd brought me to the most beautiful place in the world to deliver terrible news. Did he not know how to ask me to leave his house or something? That would be awkward. Or was it even worse: Was he sick? He was acting like it was something of great importance, and my stomach bottomed out at the thought.

I'd so badly wanted for him to open up to me, and now that the time was here, I was more nervous than I'd ever thought possible. I felt like I was going to get sick. And it made me realize what an attachment I'd already formed to this man. How deep my feelings were for him. Much deeper than I'd ever thought possible. I struggled again to face him, but he just held me tighter.

"Eyre... You know how I said I was messed up?"
"Darby–"
"Eyre, please." His tone had a rough edge. It was urgent.
"Darby, at least let me see you," I begged.

He sighed heavily and slowly turned me around to face him. I felt the cold bar of the ferry railing against my back, where the jacket he'd given me had blown up above it. I searched his face. "Eyre, I am very messed up. And I have . . ." His eyes wandered away. "I have these attacks from it. And they've never gotten any better, and it seems likely that it's never going to get better. They're not that occasional either."

His green eyes were a bottomless pit that I could search forever and never find answers in them. But it also meant he was finally letting me in. And I refused to believe there wasn't a way for him to get some help. And I refused to let this have any effect on how I saw him. It broke my heart that he thought it would.

"Darby, this doesn't change–"

"No, Eyre, you're not hearing me. I'm not a good person. I deserve this horrific curse, but nobody else does. And they sure don't deserve to carry the burden with me. I can't get close to anyone. I could accidentally hurt someone. I've hurt myself before. I wanted so badly to ask you if I could sleep in the same bed with you, just so I could be near you. But I can't predict what will happen. I've never let anyone sleep beside me."

"Darby, there's no way you deserve–"

"I deserve it," he said with finality.

"No one deserves that, Darby," I repeated more firmly. I couldn't imagine what demons he was tackling and what it felt like to go through the pain of relieving them so vividly. My whole body ached for him. "Hey, look at me. *Please*, Darby. I'm still here. I'm not going anywhere."

"Yeah, well, we're in the middle of an ocean." His biting

wit had more snap than I'd ever heard. I looked around at the cliffs and felt like we were in a prehistoric world. I felt so completely out of place and out of my element. Everything had turned eerily foreign, like an alien world. I felt like I couldn't possibly know what to predict in this new universe, and I was worried I was going to say the wrong thing.

I looked at him, hoping I might be able to provide some reassurance with my words. "I've had some training with panic and anxiety attacks, and if you tell me what helps, I will be there for you in the darkness of the night. I want to be there for you when you wake up. Darby, please give me a chance. Open up to me. If you do, I promise I'll do everything in my power to be there for you. I'll try to help you in whatever manner you think is best." He shook his head, shame soaking in. "Darby, you once kissed me through my tears. Let me do the same for you."

I could see his hands visibly shaking, and I noticed his face was chalky white and covered with perspiration. He seemed to be slowly slipping away from me, like he wasn't there any longer. He was a shell of a being, his demons becoming his placeholder.

"Don't follow me," he said so firmly that I felt glued in place. Before I knew it, he had disappeared. I stared out, trying to focus on the mysterious water and coastline while I listened to the guide. After a while, I decided I had no intention of listening to Darby's request, and I went to find him.

I thought he had gone to get some air up top, but to my surprise, he was inside the enclosed area, bent over, head in his hands. It looked like he might have been praying, except I was pretty sure he didn't do that.

I went to say his name and then stopped myself. Instead,

I sat in a chair one seat away from him so as not to startle him. And waited. He finally looked over minutes later, head still bent and murmured, "I told you not to follow me, you're gonna miss everything. It's beautiful out there." But now, there was that teasing tone back in his voice. Humor to deflect and shield himself.

"It's not so great. Is that really the best you have to offer?" I teased back.

His head slowly lifted up toward me. I could see the emotional drain on it. I scooted over a chair and slowly took his hand in mine, testing it out to see if it was okay. He smiled faintly. "Sorry," he said quickly.

"Don't apologize, Darby."

"No, I shouldn't have talked to you like that. I hate . . . There's just so much about myself that I hate, Eyre."

"Darby–"

"It's the gasoline in the air. It's a trigger. So is riding in cars and even just hearing them run or backfire . . . Even that does it sometimes. The smell of gasoline, especially with the ocean air, is a Holy Grail of triggers. Other times it can be the wind if it howls just right, especially if I'm in a bad emotional place. Seems like it depends on how bad the day is as to what's going to get me. Sometimes I can make it past so many things that are unavoidable in everyday life, but then one just hits me out of nowhere. There are days when I can't even go with Mak to the pub because I just can't face any more possible triggers. I just want the quiet of the cottage. It's gotten brutal. There are things that can't be avoided. They're everywhere. And I just never know when it will happen."

I now realized why they didn't own a car. Why Darby

opted to walk places. Even on that first day when we met at the cliffs, he'd probably not wanted to take the chance of being triggered around me. A passing car seemed like a smaller risk than riding in one. And I had thought it most peculiar that an Irishman didn't drink at all. After all, drinking seemed to be a part of their culture. When we'd visited the local pub together, I thought it odd he'd not even glanced at the alcohol.

"Let's just stay here." I went to lay my head on his shoulder.

"No, I'll be fine. The episodes usually don't come close together, even with that strong of a trigger. I want to enjoy the ferry ride with you. I finally want to enjoy life and appreciate it with someone. Let's just not talk about my attacks anymore," he said with total defeat.

He stood and helped me up, guiding me outside. He held onto me at the rail. I noticed his hold was even tighter now. I couldn't help but think how strong he was. I would be a shell of a person if I had to endlessly undergo that battle without a moment's warning. There was something so strong and beautiful about him. Where all he could see was his damage, all I saw was his strength. And somehow, he seemed to be able to enjoy the rest of the ferry ride with me. The fact that it meant so much to him to be able to enjoy this experience with me, even after what he'd just undergone and could possibly undergo again, made me appreciate him even more.

We arrived back on land and collected our things from Rosie, slowly making our way back home. I think we were both drained from the day. And our bags now seemed to weigh triple their actual amount. When we reached the cottage, we both sighed with relief. Darby took most of our bags upstairs, despite my protest. He'd already carried most of the load. My body ached all over from the activities of the day. I felt pathetic that just a day of shopping and a ferry ride could do this to me, but my conditions were no laughing matter. They were quite painful, and when they decided they wanted to act up, they didn't do anything halfway. They put on a whole Broadway production.

I plopped down on the couch, sinking into the cushions and letting them bear the weight of my body, so the pain could ease. Darby came back downstairs and sat beside me. "Do you want to skip the pub? Or we can go for dinner and just sit—no dancing. I could always beat you some more at Candy Land." He winked.

Who would have thought he'd be so incredibly sweet? But I wasn't going to pass up this opportunity with him if I could help it. I took off my shoes, which took some effort with my swollen feet, and stretched out on the couch, laying my head on his lap. "Can I have a nap first?" I asked quietly, already drifting off.

He chuckled softly. "Of course, Eyre." He reached to pull one of the books from the coffee table that he'd brought down from the selection he'd purchased today and started reading out loud. I almost burst out laughing when I realized right away that it was a romance novel. Rosie had him under strict orders not to buy any. I should have known that would make it a surefire guarantee that he would. Smiling at the bookstore memories, I let the lyrical rhythm of his voice sway me to sleep.

When I awoke, Darby's head was laid back on the sofa. He'd fallen asleep, too, and his book was resting open on the curve of the couch. I slowly went to get up so as not to disturb him, but he was already stirring, rubbing his eyes and pinching the bridge of his nose. "Maybe we are too tired, after all," he said groggily.

"No way. I can't wait to dance with you. I'm sure you can get 'jiggy' with it." A large groan escaped him. "I'm going to change clothes and I'll see you back here in a few minutes. Remember, I'm expecting a full-on *Lord of the Dance* experience."

Darby's eyebrows raised quickly, his nose flaring with disbelief. "You're unbelievable. But I'll see what I can do. But there's no way I'm shaking my lucky charms. Sorry to break it to you, but I'm a terrible dancer. We should have got you some steel-toe shoes today."

"You're Irish, how is that even possible, Darby?" I joked.

"Go get dressed before you make me change my mind about this whole 'jiggy' thing," he said in mock warning.

I went up to my room, looking for a decent sweater or shirt. Maybe that wrap with cut-outs would be good. I just needed something where I looked *somewhat* appealing. I wanted to look good for Darby. As I dug through my clothes, I stumbled across an emerald green satin dress. Apparently, lingerie hadn't been the only satin in the store. I hadn't bought this, though. I wondered if the shop owner had put the dress in my bag by mistake. I wouldn't buy something like this for myself. The sleek satin was way too sexy for me to think I could ever look good in it. I was just thinking about having *some basic clothes* and underwear when we were shopping. It never entered my mind . . . *Darby. So that's why he didn't complain when I took my sweet time trying on sweaters in the dressing room.*

I couldn't believe it. This man continued to surprise me. I pulled the dress out of the bag and laid it on the bed while I tried to tame my hair by pulling it into a clip, thankful I'd found it in one of the stores today. I looked at the dress, trying to decide if I was really going to let him have his way on this one. Leave it to Darby to find the sexiest thing in the store that could actually be worn out in public. It was quite stunning, though; the craftsmanship was beautiful and tasteful. I couldn't let this dress go unworn, and well, it was possibly the sweetest thing a man had ever done for me. Well, besides the other wonderful things Darby had already done for me. I was really becoming attached to this man. *How did this happen?* I never saw him coming. I never saw *any* of this coming.

I slipped into the dress, feeling raw and exposed but beautiful in a new way. The smooth and silky texture glided under my hands as I moved them down the length of the dress. This must have been what Marilyn Monroe felt like in her iconic dress. It was a similar style too. No beading, just a solid, light color and fabric. It was classic. No frills or fuss. Sleek and very sexy. It was exactly what I would imagine Darby picking out, and it made me even more nervous. I felt like my body was blushing all over just from thinking about him picking out this dress. Or maybe it was my temperature fluctuating from my conditions. No, it was from thinking about him seeing me in this dress, for sure.

I let out a sigh. *How am I supposed to go downstairs like this?* Maybe I could pretend I didn't see the dress. But knowing it was from him, something he picked out and bought for me, made me reconsider.

TWENTY-SIX
Darby

Every part of me felt raw: my nerves, my heart, my emotions, and my body. The episode on the ferry had come out of nowhere. Well, actually, I never knew when to expect them. I was always trying to predict them. Even on the weeks I didn't have any, I was looking over my shoulder like a kid expecting their neighborhood bully to appear around the corner at any moment. I'd started to lay my emotions out to Eyre when I smelled the gasoline. That was certainly poor timing, especially considering my experiences with attacks in the past. That's what I called them—"attacks." I didn't bloody know what they were, and I didn't bloody care to know. I thought maybe after my late teenage years, I'd grow out of them. But I didn't. It seemed like I never would.

And now I'd had to share one with the woman who I was beginning to have strong feelings for. The one person, other than Mak, who didn't think I was a lost cause. Because even though Eyre would be leaving soon, I hoped she'd carry something of me with her. And I just hoped it wouldn't be the memory of what happened to me on the ferry today. Because it mattered greatly to me what memories and thoughts of me she carried back home with her. *She* mattered greatly to me.

My thoughts were battling each other in *Gladiator* style when I saw a glimpse of her on the stairs. I froze and then shook myself back to the present moment and immediately stood. feeling like that's what a man was supposed to do when he was greeted by such a beauty. I couldn't think of anything else but Eyre as she walked over closer to me. For the first time, I was sweating from something other than a stupid attack. I was sweating from something good happening to me, actually very good, *finally*. I wore those tiny sweat beads proudly. Well, maybe not proudly, but at least happily.

The green satin fabric of Eyre's dress was the perfect color for her skin tone; it brought out the tinged flecks of green in her eyes. I couldn't believe how well the dress fit her since I had only guessed at her size in the store and had hoped for the best. And the dress turned out to be a knockout on her. I was speechless when I saw her coming down the stairs. As I stood there, unable to form one coherent thought, I was glad Mak wasn't here to see me like this. He'd be rushing over to the pub to tell Sinead all about it. I'd turned into a total sap in Eyre's presence, and I'd never hear the end of it.

I'd never seen her with her hair up, either, and she was stunning, Her neck was just begging for round two from our earlier encounter today. I was going to have a difficult time remembering she wanted to go slow, something that I'd never been good at doing. Most likely because I hadn't had any real relationships. But tonight, there were completely different thoughts behind my desires. I really wanted to tell her she looked beautiful and make her believe it, but nothing was coming out.

"That bad, huh?" she said playfully. My eyes widened, and I shook my head, but my words were inaudible. I couldn't have seemed any more like a muttering moron.

"Eyre–" I tried.

"Yes?" she questioned nervously, playfulness leaving her tone. But that's all I could manage. I was frozen. There was no way I could be expected to make a complete fool of myself on the dance floor with someone who looked like this. *No way.*

She began talking while I just stood there. "I'm assuming you are the one who bought me the dress. I really love it. Thank you." She came over, so she was standing only inches from me, but I still couldn't move. I was frozen like an ice sculpture at an '80s wedding. "Are you going to escort me down to the pub, or did I get all dressed up for nothing?" She chuckled as she *slagged* me.

I just nodded, words still dry in my mouth, like they were stranded in a desert. My hand managed to find the small of her back as we left the house, and her face blushed with happiness. *So this is what I'd been missing out on all these years.* I really was an idiot. But maybe this only existed with Eyre.

My mind seemed to be conducting its own symphony,

and I floated along like I was walking on air. It was an out-of-body moment for me. Maybe all those Disney movies finally made sense—how being with the right person could feel so . . . magical.

Before I knew it, we were walking into the pub, and I was holding the door open for Eyre. I don't remember how we got here. I just hoped I'd managed some decent conversation along the way. *Was this what it was like to go on a date with someone you really liked?* It was absolutely unreal. All sense of time or place seemed to escape, turning into a looking-glass illusion. It was so nerve-racking, yet absolutely worth every minute of it. I didn't have to steal glances at her anymore. I could just take her in as much as I wanted, which was probably too much since it was obviously hindering conversation. But she didn't seem to mind. She seemed to be having some difficulty herself. I'd never seen her so flustered. She usually seemed more self-confident and ready with a comeback at a moment's notice. Now she seemed really nervous, vulnerable, and unsure of herself. Well, I would make certain she felt secure, because there was no way anyone lookin the way she did should feel anything else.

That thought was just what I needed to finally snap myself out of my dating stupor. "You look gorgeous," I said, and I could feel the heat in my eyes as I met hers. Finally, I managed to say something coherently. Only twenty minutes late at the very least. Better late than never, or at least I was sure hoping so.

Eyre smiled at me and returned the compliment. I'd selected the furthest corner of the bartop so that we could still chat with Sinead but so I could also have some privacy with Eyre. Mak, of course, was up front and center at the bar, doing his usual little dance with the pub's owner.

"So what do you think the real story is?" Eyre asked, interrupting my thoughts. I was utterly confused until she nodded at Sinead.

"Oh," I said, raising my eyebrows. "You're really intrigued with them, aren't you?" She nodded quickly. I let out a sigh because I really didn't know the answer to her question. "I think Mak missed his opening and really regrets it. Every so often he talks about it. From what I can gather, he's been in love with her from the very beginning."

"I knew it!" she exclaimed. People nearby were looking at us. A grin spread over my face. I loved being able to make her this happy. I leaned toward her in the dim corner of the pub.

"Well, he finally outgrew his teasing phase and started complimenting her—I think he even told you that. But one night, when he was really *ossified*—drunk—he told me that his best friend had asked him if it would be okay if he asked her out. Apparently, it was right before Sinead got up the courage to ask Mak to go to the dance with her." I could see her eyes waltz over to look at the two of them. "And, well, Mak said this guy was like a brother to him. And I guess the guy didn't think Mak really had feelings for Sinead because he'd never made a move. Who knows. But from what I gather, Mak used it as an excuse to turn her down because he was scared, and Sinead has never forgotten he turned her down.

"Eventually, Sinead got married— it wasn't to Mak's friend—and then divorced. I don't know what happened to Mak's friend, but he's no longer around. And well, Mak has had a few of his own romantic liaisons, obviously, since he has a daughter, but he never married. He never committed to anyone. I often wonder, did he ever try to tell Sinead how he felt about her? Did he ever try to explain before she got married? I don't know the answers. I'm hoping Mak will get *langers* again and tell me. And now, Sinead seems to want to just be friends. You heard what she said about their friendship."

Eyre responded, "But in the kitchen, Mak said—" My face flamed like Hades itself. So she did hear. "Sorry, Darby, I did hear some things. I thought everything I heard was sweet. It only made me like you more." She looked at me, assessing if she should continue. "I did hear him say to you not to make the same mistakes—to open your heart and let her in. Yet it doesn't sound like he's ever tried to do the same with Sinead. Can you encourage him to talk to her? They seem like they belong together."

I laughed. "You do fit in well here, Eyre. Three days and you're already playing *Babhdóir*. Fixing everyone's problems. Being an Irish matchmaker would be perfect for you."

"Well, good thing for you that a nosy matchmaker and a smirky leprechaun seem to go so well together." I shot her a look as she continued. "And by the way, I did love that movie, *Matchmaker*. It's one of the few Irish movies I've seen. It might have been a little part of the inspiration that helped me choose my destination for this trip."

I couldn't help but laugh. I should have known. That sounded perfect for her. She really should have come for the matchmaking festival. I thought she might like to know more about it. "There's actually a huge matchmaking festival in County Clare that you would love. It's in Lisdoonvarna, just a town over. Around forty thousand people flock to it every year. It's held in September. You need to go there sometime . . . but *not* to participate."

She laughed at my serious tone. I laughed at myself too. "No, seriously," I went on, "I've heard the music and dancing are wonderful, and the pubs are excellent, too. The town was made popular because of its mineral water and mineral baths in the mid-nineteenth century. People came from all over to get help with their ailments, especially rheumatism. The sulfur in the water was able to help people with that condition. So many people came to the town that it became popular for special events and holidays. And with so many people coming from all over, the matchmaking festival was born. It's the perfect event for a destined-to-be-matchmaker like yourself. I think this means you definitely need to come back and experience it."

Eyre responded, "Yes, I do see another visit in my future for sure. I'm sure Lisdoonvarna has some pretty amazing matchmaking skills, but I know for certain I won't be needing their services." Her face blushed a little at her bluntness. "But, Darby, I think it's time for Doolin's matchmaking services to give a little help to Sinead and Mak."

I gathered my thoughts, having trouble after the statement she'd just made, and continued, "I guess you didn't hear the part where I tried to tell Mak it wasn't too late, but he just wasn't receptive. It seems he's accepted his fate to be alone."

"Darby, no, that can't be it."

"Well, you've met him. Try doing anything with that man. It's like trying to keep your feet dry without wellies. *Impossible.*" She looked at me, slightly confused but also possibly charmed. I was glad she liked my "Irishness" so much. At least something was working in my favor.

Eyre suggested, "What if we set up a re-enactment dance for them? We could have the same theme they had at their high school dance, and we could send them both an invitation, of sorts, to the dance. It could be in the form of a letter. Each of their letters would ask the other to meet them at a designated place. Do you know where their high school dance was supposed to be held?"

"Yeah, the school. Probably in one of the larger classrooms or the library. That's where they always hold things like that."

"That's going to be hard. Maybe–" she said, pondering.

"We are not doing this," I interjected.

"Well, we could. It seems like it might be the only way to get them to reconnect with their romantic feelings for one another," she said firmly.

"No, they'd both kill me. And I finally have something, or *someone*, I want to live for."

She smiled at me. "Well, at least think about it." Her smile made me forget all logic. *How* had I turned into this kind of guy? In an attempt to change the subject and get her mind off of it, I stood up and extended my hand to her. "Eyre, I don't know how to dance, but would you like to show me how? I'm sure I'm going to be terrible at it. But maybe I'm worth a good laugh . . . That is, if you feel up to it."

"What?" she asked. I felt a nervous lump in my throat. The thought of rejection from her was making me start to sweat. It actually might break me–might finish me off. I didn't realize how fragile I was until that instant when it came to my feelings for her. I hadn't known how frail the human condition could truly be. Not until her.

She must have noticed the look on my face, because she immediately replied, "Of course, Darby." Grabbing my hand, she said, "I just meant, I couldn't believe you didn't know how to dance."

"No, I don't think I've ever danced before," I replied. "I never went to the school dances, and I haven't made it a habit of taking anyone dancing, either." Hearing it said out loud, I sarcastically thought about what a *great* date I sounded like. Yet again, I was hoping she wasn't going to change her mind about me. But a warm glow just spread over her face.

"I'd love to be your first." Her willowy body was already swaying as she led me out onto the makeshift dance floor of the pub. I loved the way she looked like she was dancing when she walked. Like she was painting colors with her movements, creating a beautiful picture with just her body. I heard the fiddles strumming a melodic rhythm with a melancholy undertone that was hauntingly beautiful. Only in Ireland could this kind of sorrow be so beautiful. We were known for it. I had purposely picked a slow song because it seemed as if her body pain was getting the better of her today. I had thought about not even asking her to dance because I knew she'd say yes, even with her pain. I was hoping that her eagerness to dance was because she didn't want to pass up the opportunity and not just because she wanted to be polite.

There were a few other couples on the dance floor. And we quickly found a spot amongst them that we could make our own. I didn't even know where to put my hands. Great, I was off to a fantastic start. I was regretting this already.

"Darby," she said softly, "just look at me. You'll be fine." I grabbed onto her hips and pulled her close—probably too close if I didn't want to step on her feet. I could feel the heat of her skin through the thin satin material, and it was driving me mad. I could smell the scent that I'd grown to recognize as distinctly Eyre. I now understood the appeal of dancing.

Although, I'm not sure that's what this could be called. I swayed–maybe–from side to side and she smiled up at me. She looked so angelic and completely at home. *Could Ireland be home to her?* I could only hope. I was daring to hope again. And my heart filled with a swelling desire for her to stay here. *Could I be enough for her to do so?* It was such an absurd thought.

It would have been nice if I'd had any moves to try, but honestly, I didn't know where to begin. I was terrified to try anything I'd seen in a film. And considering my dance film repertoire was limited to what Mak watched–Gene Kelly and Fred Astaire–I didn't see movies like *Singin' in the Rain* or *Easter Parade* helping me much. Although *You Were Never Lovelier* did seem to embody Eyre. But there were absolutely no moves in that movie I was willing to even think of attempting. You didn't venture an Astaire move . . . *But a turn couldn't be hard, right?* Just then, Eyre spoke, and it was like she was reading my mind.

"Do you want to try something like a turn? Or maybe a rollout?" she asked softly. "I promise I'll be gentle." I laughed as she positioned our hands, and I stood still, letting her do the work. "Just twirl me, I'll do the rest."

And she spun so effortlessly. It was beautiful. Spinning not just once but multiple times with a grace in her movements that looked honed and skilled. "Now for a variation . .

.," she began, explaining as she wrapped herself in my arms and faced away from me, arranging our hands. I allowed myself time to breathe and enjoy her essence. "... then just throw me out. Pause, so I can do something pretty, and when I look back at you, you'll know I'm finished and you can bring me back in." What I wasn't expecting was the footwork she did while she was away from me.

"What was that?" I asked. "You never told me how good a dancer you are. You never let on–" I looked at her, putting the pieces together. Her build, the way she moved, not being able to continue to pursue her dream anymore due to her arthritis and pain. "Are you . . . ?"

"A dancer? . . . Yes, well, I wanted to be a professional dancer. I was pursuing a career in dancing, but now I teach dance. I was getting a Bachelor of Arts with a minor in dance. I had no idea what I was going to do with it, especially since my true love was ballroom dancing. It's not like there are a lot of career opportunities for those types of professional dancers. I guess I thought I'd open a dance studio or maybe join a dance company–if I was so lucky. I saw *Tango Fire,* a dance company from Argentina, and fell in love with ballroom dance on the stage. I always dreamed of touring with a company like that. Now I'm lucky enough to teach dance. I have students ranging from lower school to high school age, as well as adult students. I guess they've become my children in a way. Maybe that's what life always had in store for me. Maybe I will get to love and teach dance to many children instead of having my own."

My mouth literally fell open and I stopped dead in my tracks. The music seemed to mute itself as well. "Are you serious? You let me dance with you when . . . How could you let me continue to dance with you when . . . I've never danced in my life, and you let me dance with a professional?"

She started laughing uncontrollably and I was beyond scarlet. *Why are all my most embarrassing moments happening with this woman?* She was able to finally get out, "Well, I do teach now if it makes you feel any better. And I was never a professional–just a dreamer. Plus, who better to give you your first dance lesson?" She smiled coyly.

I started pivoting to walk away, but she grabbed my shirt. My eyes landed on her. There was a sweetness in her tone as she said, "This is the best dance I've ever had."

"Uh huh," I replied sarcastically. "I'm just going to go find a place to disappear now and maybe bury myself under the pile of books we bought today."

"No, really," she insisted.

"I'm pretty sure what I'm doing cannot count as dancing, so maybe it's the best sway you've ever had. And secondly, I've stepped on your feet at least twice, which is a pretty big accomplishment for just s*waying*–"

But the look in her eyes told me I had it all wrong. Her hands wrapped around my neck so quickly I was a little confused as to what was happening. Next thing I knew, her face was inches from mine, and her lips were shutting me up, for which I was so very grateful. All of a sudden, I heard someone shout, "Darcy's finally living up to his name." The proclamation was followed by a few steins hitting the bar and table tops in rhythmic unison. Then a few more people joined in on the fun and started shouting out similar sentiments. And Eyre, well, Eyre just continued to show them that they had been wrong about me all along.

I pulled away, gazing with gratitude at her as we got lost in all the noise around us. "I'd prefer to find a dark corner to continue," I said mischievously. "Something more like the bookstore experience."

"Well, I don't think we're getting any privacy here after that display. So if you want to kiss me, then you might as well do it here."

I held up my hands in defeat at their raucous noise. They all quieted, staring at me, shocked I was going to address them. "It just took the right person for Darcy. Haven't any of you ever read a book?"

With that, I leaned down and kissed Eyre passionately. The pub broke out into a boisterous roar. I broke it off quickly, not wanting to give them any more than I had to. I looked into Eyre's eyes and hoped she realized there would be more later . . . but just for her. There was so much life in those hazel pools I didn't think I could stand it. Without breaking my gaze from her, I took aim at the grinning onlookers with my words. I was too entranced to look away. "Alright, enough, you *eejits*," I said loudly and took Eyre in my arms to start another attempt at dancing again. The fiddle players abruptly resumed playing as they kindly tried to keep up with me. Although they couldn't decide what tempo or style of music I was attempting to try and dance. I didn't know, either. And frankly, I didn't care because I had her.

Eyre seemed thoroughly exhausted after a couple of more dances. I guided her over to a secluded table, where we ordered some food. She wanted to go for a second round of dancing, but I could tell the pain was weighing on her. I'd give anything if I could carry the pain for her. Even just half of it. *Any* amount. I'd make a deal right here and now. I just wanted to relieve her.

So we sat in the dark corner booth and talked—for what seemed like hours. About nothing and about everything, it seemed. Well, except for my attacks. Eyre was extremely kind not to go there. Talking about our interests—mostly hers—and our pet peeves—mostly mine. We even discussed our favorite colors, and I *never* thought I'd be that guy. But yes, I was dying to know hers. And the discussion led to the places I could take her for the rest of her stay. Our eyes locked deeply at the end of that discussion. There were so many unasked questions. So many unanswered thoughts. *What happened when her time was up here?*

I helped her out of the booth. She seemed to be having more difficulty moving after sitting for a while, explaining that while the rest was nice, her joints stiffened the longer she sat still, making it difficult to stand up. I offered her a piggyback ride, but in that satin dress . . . it wasn't going to happen. I was disappointed in myself for not bringing her on the bike—for not owning a car.

We quickly said goodbye to Mak and Sinead on our way out of the pub. I wasn't really sure it even registered with Mak, who only had eyes for Sinead. Who knew when he'd be home. Eyre thanked Sinead for a lovely night, and we were off, stepping out into the Irish moonlit night. Out of all the nights I'd been here—which was my entire life—I don't think I'd ever really stopped to look at the moon. I'd like to think it was something special here. I couldn't imagine that it looked this beautiful everywhere.

The countryside glowed with its reflection from the moon and the road was bathed in its beauty as it guided us home. I looked at Eyre and we both smiled, enjoying the sound of the crickets that would provide the soundtrack for our journey. And as I took her hand slowly into mine, something came over me. A feeling so strong I knew I'd have to heed it. I needed to do whatever I could to keep this woman in my life.

TWENTY-SEVEN
Eyre

As we walked down the road with the sounds of the nocturnal animals–such as tawny owls, bush-crickets, nightjars, nightingales, toads, and badgers–escorting us, I couldn't help but continue to steal glances at Darby. The man who was so full of contradictions. Darby—the man who couldn't dance, yet somehow gave me the best dance of my life. Darby—the man who didn't date yet was the only man I ever wanted to go out with again. Darby—the man who didn't get emotionally involved yet had proclaimed his attachment to me in front of everyone. Darby—the man who lived in Ireland. . . so very, *very* far away. Darby—the man I'd fallen for in a matter of days.

I was beginning to see I was in serious trouble. And I didn't have the faintest idea what to do about it. We walked in silence back to the house, not needing any words. Taking our time and letting our weary bones and bruised souls journey together. The slow pace was a welcomed relief after the day's events. With the moonlight bathing his features, I could safely say that Darby was definitely the most handsome man I'd ever met.

The sky seemed to darken more as we walked, and I looked over at Darby with concern. He smiled back to reassure me. But the clouds grew heavier, and they were soon releasing their burdens. The soft Irish rain was coming down, and neither of us had any energy left to walk any faster. I think it was indicative of our lives. So we strengthened our grip on each other, our hands clasped tightly together. And we continued to walk as if it wasn't raining. It didn't seem to affect the beauty of the night or the moment for us.

By the time we reached the cottage, we were soaked, and my skin was covered in goosebumps. We ventured into the tiny cottage together, darkness covering every inch except where the moon managed to seep in. Lucky met us at the door, wagging his tail fiercely. I bent down to pet him. I would miss all the men of this house, Lucky included. When I straightened back up, Darby was there to greet me. His arms were ready for me, a warmth radiating off of him that I wanted to soak up so I could keep it forever. He was like a large rock the sun shone upon in those Irish streams. One you couldn't pass up and had no choice but to go rest your weary bones on it. I wanted to lay on that stone and soak up its warmth and let it provide firm ground for once in my life.

"So what do you want to do for the rest of the evening?" he asked in a tone that was so attractive. "Do you want me to read to you while we sit by the fire?" That was not at all what I had thought he was going to suggest. "Or do you want to take a bath? I think a hot bath would help your joints. I can tell you're in pain." I really didn't expect this. "Or more

Candy Land?" Wow, none of these were the suggestions that had popped into my head.

The lights were still out, and I felt completely exposed in his arms while wearing this thin piece of satin. It felt more like lingerie at this point, especially since it was clinging to me now. And now my goosebumps weren't just from being caught in the weather.

"Darby." My voice barely managed to say his name.

"Uh huh? Oh . . ." he said as he released me. He immediately went over to the fireplace, not turning on any lights, and started to position some logs. I wandered over to him, and he said to me, "I know you're tired. Why don't you sit on the sofa? It'll be warm soon, and I'll make you some tea. You must be cold; I could feel you had goosebumps."

The rain picked up on the roof, and I was certain its rhythmic melody could easily become one of my favorite sounds. We were lucky we'd gotten home when we did. "It's really *bucketing down* now," he said, looking at me as he got the fire going. It was soon a warm, raging blaze with plenty of pops and crackles. I sighed with relief as the fire lit up the room. Darby grabbed a blanket and laid it over me on his way to the kitchen.

He came back with peppermint tea and asked, "So what do you think you'd like to do?"

"Oh, uh . . . Maybe some more of the book while we warm up, if you don't mind. You have a wonderful voice."

He smiled and picked up the book. Looking over at me, he wrapped an arm around my shoulders gently and pulled me in. Before he began reading, he said, "Eyre, I could really get used to this." And before I had a chance to respond, he picked up reading where he had last left off.

THE IRISH FALL

It was absolutely the most perfect night. Everything I'd ever dreamed of–with a man I could have never dreamed of but was so grateful existed. We made our way upstairs with Lucky, and I stopped at the bathroom to get ready for the night.

"Why don't you soak for a while—I left the salts in there for you from last time. I'll keep Lucky company until you're ready for bed. He and I have a pile of books to read."

"Really?" I asked, touched by his sweetness.

"Yeah, I think it's a good idea. You could at least get some relief for your legs."

I walked over and hugged him. He bent and rested his forehead against mine. I didn't think he was ever going to let me go. With great reluctance to leave him, I disappeared into the bathroom.

Darby was right about my joints. My bones immediately sighed with relief in the salty water. It was a little chilly keeping my torso with the incision out of the hot water, but I wore a shirt that I'd grabbed from my room. Even with the waterproof bandaging, I wasn't ready to take any chances. Suddenly, I heard a knock.

"Eyre, um, sorry, but it's . . . the storm has . . . taking a bath . . ."

"What?" I called out. I couldn't hear him over the hot running water that I was adding to the tub. I liked to keep my bath water pretty hot to ease the pain in my joints.

He cracked the door that I hadn't even bothered to lock at this point. "I said it's not safe to be running the water or taking a bath with lightning in the area. I'm going to get you some new pajamas too. I'll leave them outside the door."

I stopped the water, but before I knew it, the door swung

wide open, making that banging sound again. And I saw that same black and white flash, just like the last time I tried to take a bath. Only this time Lucky had bounded into the tub and was standing in the water, staring at me, an intense gaze in his eyes.

I obviously was in his territory. I had forgotten this was his storm shelter. "Darby!" I called in a panic. "He jumped in the tub with me!"

Darby came running, and within a second, he was there. "*Oye!* Not again. Oh *oye, oye, oye.*" I heard him slap his face, probably covering his eyes again. "I didn't see anything. Don't worry, Lucky and the side of the tub are blocking everything. I thought I had shut the door. I only cracked it to call to you about the storm."

Lucky was hovering in the tub, staring me down, most disgruntled that his bomb shelter had been turned into a spa. "Ok, ok, I'll get out," I said, relenting.

"No, that wasn't what I meant," Darby said quickly.

"No, I'm talking to Lucky, Darby, but I know I need to get out of the water anyway because of the lightning," I said laughing. "He's soaking wet now. He's decided to sit down in the water and claim his spot. He's really mad that I'm in his special place."

"Oh, uh . . . I can come and get him." Darby started to walk forward and ran into the doorframe. "*Oye.*" *Oh, that one sounded like it hurt.*

"Darby, stop," I said with a mixture of amusement and sympathy. "I'll drain the tub, and then we can dry him off and let him be. He's definitely outmaneuvered me. He can have his tub. Just . . . Just don't move. You're only going to keep hurting yourself. Throw me some clothes, please." He threw them, but they landed in the middle of the bathroom.

"Right . . . the clothes only made it to the middle of the bathroom floor, Darby."

"Well, how am I supposed to know, I'm trying not to look. If they'd landed right in front of you, then you would need to be worried."

I started laughing and reached for the towel, wrapping it around me. I breezed past him to the other side of the bathroom.

"Oye, are you going past me right now without wearing any clothes?"

"No, Darby, I have on a towel," I said with an eye roll.

"Well, why didn't you tell me? *Please* feel free to continue walking around as freely as you like," he said playfully.

"Yeah, sure," I said sarcastically. "Ok, you can open your eyes. I'm going to show you how to really close a bathroom door. Apparently you don't know how to do that in Ireland . . . Then I'm going to drain the tub and change." He stepped out of the doorway so that I could proceed.

After we got Lucky dried, we headed to our rooms for the night, completely exhausted now.

Darby looked at me and said, "Well, I don't know when he'll get out of the tub . . . maybe when the storm stops, but you can crack your door if you want him to keep you company. Although the wet dog smell might not be too appealing. I can crack mine instead."

"Let's crack both our doors so he has a choice." I had a feeling every day with this man would be an adventure, and I loved it.

"Ok." He grinned, stopping at his door and shifting his weight from one foot to the other as he said, "Night, Eyre."

"Night, Darby," I said hesitantly.

Darby had seemed reluctant to say goodnight. As if he'd wanted me to stay with him. Something he'd always been too afraid to do with anyone because of his attacks, but I wanted to be there for him. Yet, for some reason, I wasn't ready to invite him to stay with me. I didn't know why. I guess I just couldn't muster up the courage. I didn't know what a nighttime attack was like for him, and I didn't know if he was ready for me to be present if one did happen. But I felt so close to him. He had shared a huge part of himself today. Even though Mak had talked to him about sharing his feelings and thoughts, I never thought he'd actually do it. *It meant he had feelings for me, didn't it? Serious feelings. Was it possible that he'd fallen for me too?*

And as I continued to look up at the ceiling, I couldn't stand it any longer. I let the pounding of the rain set the pace for the movement of my feet. I reached his door with my heart hammering in my chest. My whole body was coursing with nerves. I pushed the crack of the door open wider.

"Darby?"

"Oh! I thought you were Lucky," he said with a laugh.

"Eyre, are you ok?"

"Yes, it's just that—well, I was wondering . . ." *I can't do this.* "Darby, could I stay with you? You know . . . because of the storm and all. Lucky isn't the only one that needs shelter from the storm." I let out a tiny laugh.

"I thought you'd never ask." His Irish lilt had taken on the sweetest tone. I opened the door all the way and saw him sitting up in his bed, looking so devastatingly handsome in his torn tee. "Come on, I've got plenty of room."

I made my way through his room, bypassing all his wooden carved boxes and bookshelves. I took his extended hand and let him pull me to him, then lower us down gently and kiss me with equal care.

"Thank you. I was hoping you'd ask," he said, and I smiled back at him. I couldn't help but feel somehow even more connected to him. He looked into my eyes. "Also, I don't know what I'm doing here . . . this is all new territory for me. But I'm pretty sure I'd like to spoon with you. That's what the Americans call it, right?" I burst out laughing at his question. "Oye, what?" he asked defensively.

"Oh my goodness, Darby. You do know that's cuddling, right?"

"I'm trying to be sweet here." He looked at me sternly.

I pressed my lips together. But as soon as I went to open my mouth, the laughter flooded out. "I'm sorry, I'm sorry," I said, pulling him back. "Yes, that is what it's called, and I would love nothing more. As a spoonie, I think it's in my DNA."

"What's a spoonie? Is that a different cuddling position?" His eyebrows raised in curiosity. Just then, Lucky came bounding up on the bed. "Of course he wants to come to my room now. Hope you enjoy the smell of wet dog."

Lucky curled up at our feet at the end of the bed. "It's absolutely perfect, Darby. And how do you manage to make a chronic illness term sound *so* enticing?" I looked at him, and in the moonlight, I could see a red scarlet color fan across his face. I let him off easy as I continued, "A spoonie is someone who has a chronic illness condition. It refers to *spoonfuls* of energy. So something gentle like spooning is perfect for me. I always have energy for that kind of activity."

"Good," he said and then eyed Lucky, "as long as nothing is going to run you off." I shook my head and turned away from Darby. He complained, "Wait, I don't think I like this. I like being able to see your face."

"So you asked to do something that you have no clue what it really entails?" I asked in disbelief.

"Well, spooning sounded pretty sweet. I thought I'd just go with it. I don't think there's much I wouldn't do with you. You could ask me to wear matching footie pajamas, and I'd just say, 'Where do we buy them?'"

I just laughed at him. "Only you, Darby,"

I grabbed his arm so I could show him a good area to place it away from my injury. "Ah, I'm liking this more now." He kissed my exposed neck.

"I can't believe you've never cuddled."

"Well, I will now." I could feel his warmth wrap around me, and it helped me start to drift off to sleep.

"Eyre," he said.

"Yes?"

"If I wake you up . . . If I have an . . ." There was a long pause. "Just leave," he said with stern care. "I mean it. *Leave*. Go to your room, ok? Since I had an attack today, I don't think it will happen again . . . but it was an emotional day."

"Darby—" I began to protest.

"*Leave*."

"Ok," I finally relented.

He pulled me tighter to him. And I could feel how much it frightened him that he might not be able to protect me. That I might need protection from him.

I awoke to see Darby sitting straight up in the bed, shaking. I could feel his tremors ripple through the mattress. I sat up, quickly assessing. Trying to determine what I could do to help him. He looked terrified and sickly from what little I could see of him in the near darkness.

"Darby," I breathed out as I neared a little closer. "Listen to my voice, Darby. Think about what it sounds like." He seemed to be responding. He nodded slowly. "Good . . . ok, tell me what it sounds like. Describe it for me." There was no response. "*Please,* Darby."

Slowly he started to name adjectives off. His words were a little slurred and difficult to understand, but they were there.

"That's good, Darby. Now name five things you can see. What do you see, Darby?" He shook his head. "Please tell me." Nothing. "Darby, five things," I soothed.

Slowly he named five things he could see in the room. I worked my way through all five of his senses until he started to turn toward me. The look in his eyes was glassy and dull. Like he was spent. "I told you to leave, Eyre."

I wrapped my arms around him, and after a while, he

slowly wrapped his arms around me as well. Gradually, he began to tighten his grip, hanging onto me more firmly. I could feel perspiration all over his skin. "Thank you," he whispered softly in my ear. And a cacophony of *chinks* rang out in my head as if I could hear the rubble falling all around me.

TWENTY-EIGHT
Darby

The unfiltered reality of my attacks was laid bare before her. The demons had fallen at her feet. Now I was going to see if someone could accept me. If someone could actually accept my hurt. I was going to see what it was like to be loved completely or rejected. I was about to either experience the best feeling I'd ever felt or face the worst pain. It felt like a gut punch to the soul as I waited. Knowing after this moment, nothing would ever be the same.

But what she did next completely surprised me. As I held her in my arms, covered in perspiration and reeking of fear, she said clearly, "Darby, I've fallen for you."

I pulled back, too astonished for words. Her eyes moved back and forth, searching mine. "Darby, I've really fallen for you. Not just a little, but a lot. A whole lot." She swallowed audibly. "And I had given up on that idea some time ago. I had closed that chapter of my life. Determined I was unlovable and didn't have enough to offer. So I shut that part of me down. Accepted it as my fate as best I could because I didn't know what else to do. But you woke it all back up. And I've fallen so deeply for you."

I just sat there, not even blinking. Now I must be hallucinating. Wow, this had certainly never happened before. Although I usually didn't get much sleep because of my horrible nightmares, I'd never before experienced a hallucination from sleep deprivation, but maybe I wanted Eyre to want me so badly that I was actually experiencing some demented trickery of my mind.

There was no way she could have just talked me through an attack and was now telling me that she *what*? She'd fallen for me. *Me*? It wasn't possible. This had to be my mind playing tricks on me.

"Darby?" Her voice sounded so small and unsure. Like I'd left her stranded on an island to fend for herself and the natives were coming for her. They must symbolize my insecurities in this trippy dreamland.

But she felt so real in my arms. I felt the fabric of my tee she was wearing and looked down at her boxer shorts, reaching out to feel them too.

"What are you doing?" she asked in disbelief.

"There's no way this is real. I must be dreaming. I've never hallucinated after a nightmare before, but I have to be dreaming."

"Darby," she said incredulously. Then her voice took on a new tone and she brought her hand up to my face. "I've *fallen* for you."

And there was so much soul in each word that it made me wake up. I stammered, "You are real, aren't you?" She nodded her head. "But all of this . . ."

"Darby." There was a plea in her tone.

It was enough to encourage me to say the words I'd been feeling so deeply today. "I've fallen madly for you, Eyre. I think I did as soon as I first met you. Probably as soon as I first saw you. I just didn't know what I was feeling."

Eyre smiled at my words and let them sink deep into her soul. She brought her head down to meet my shoulder and sought comfort there, tethered by the strength of our connection. She nestled against my salty, cooling skin and seemed to find a home. I closed my eyes and finally allowed myself to relax–to enjoy this moment and having her so close to me tonight.

It was difficult to feel like much of a man when there were so many things out of your control. When you felt so helpless. When you were sitting covered in fear and wearing your panic all over your skin. But somehow, Eyre managed to make me feel like one. In a situation where I didn't think anyone could seek comfort or security from me, she was defying all the odds. In one of my darkest moments, when I believed everyone needed protecting from me, here she was, buried into me.

I lowered us back down on the mattress slowly and let her rest on top of me. "Now, I believe in all the Irish gibberish. Maybe you were right. Maybe four-leaf clovers and pots of gold do exist here," I said with disbelief at the words coming out of my mouth.

She laughed. "You've never found a four-leaf clover before?"

"Never, Eyre," I said seriously.

"Oh, we've got to fix that," she mused with humor.

"Oh, we already did." I tightened my hold on her.

"Well, I'm not sure the pot of gold will be as easy to find." She laughed.

I looked at her with certainty. "I've found that too, Goldie. I think you're my—"

"Do not say lucky charm, Darby." She laughed, and the sound was magical. I loved to hear it. "I can't believe it. Who would have ever thought words like these would come out of Darby's mouth. But if I'm going to be 'Goldie,' then you better be prepared for some leprechaun nicknames."

"I really don't care anymore, Eyre. As long as you're the one calling me them, then I'm fine with it. Call me whatever you want."

She looked surprised at my words, but I knew I was so in love with her that it wouldn't matter what she called me. And I honestly couldn't believe it. "Oh, you have no idea what you have unleashed."

And I actually loved the thought of that.

With her head resting peacefully on my chest, I thought now would be a good time to venture into some of the questions that had been scraping at me. My words came out faintly, "So . . . did you have to give up dancing because of the pain? You didn't say much about it tonight at the pub."

"Well, I was a little busy trying to teach someone how to dance. He was a very demanding student." I laughed at her good-natured teasing, and she continued, "Yes, the arthritis I developed from my Crohn's, along with the joint pain and swelling, made everything difficult. Then the pain from the endometriosis just got so bad that I didn't want to dance. Although I tried to dance through the pain, it got to the point where I just couldn't bear it anymore. The endometrial lining can grow in all parts of your body, not just your abdomen, and mine sure did."

"Could you ever go back to school and get a performing arts or business degree for your studio—if your pain were to become more manageable? I'm sorry if this is hard to talk about. We don't have to."

"Don't apologize, Darby; the fact that you care means everything. Most people don't stick around for the bad times. I found that out when I got sick. Most people just want to be there for your successes or breakthroughs. They don't want to hear about the everyday struggles or the bad times, which is when you need someone the most." She looked at me with steadfastness. "You're different. You've already been there for the good and the bad. And it doesn't seem to make a difference to you which one it is—you just want to be there. It's really beautiful, Darby. I don't think you understand how rare you are. How wonderful you are."

I fell silent, definitely not feeling deserving of anything she said. I was about to speak when she said, "I don't think I'd want to go back to school—even if my prayers were answered tomorrow and all the pain went away. I've changed. And I like myself better now. I wouldn't want to go back to the performing arts anyway; I have a new dream or maybe an adaptation of a dream. A better version. My dance students have become like family to me. And I feel like I have the potential to make a difference in someone's life. To help them grow and reach *their* dreams. Or at least help them on their life's journey—help prepare them for what they're meant to do. We learn so much from creating art. We learn so much about ourselves."

The beauty that shone through her words was overwhelming. And I couldn't believe she was choosing to spend her time with me. She could be anywhere in Ireland, and yet she was here. That she saw something in me was . . . beyond my ability to grasp.

"Eyre." I gazed into those hazel eyes. I knew what I was about to ask was not going to be comfortable, and I was having second thoughts about asking it as soon as the words left my mouth. "What were you doing at the cliffs the day we met?"

Her body went rigid. Her breathing seemed to stop. There was a long silence, and I was worried that maybe I'd gone too far. Finally, with a loud intake of breath, she said. "I don't know. Debating, I guess."

Now all the breath left my lungs and didn't return. We lay there and let the air continue to leave the room, creating a vacuum. I felt some relief when her soft voice returned and said, "It felt like my disorders had taken everything from me. First, my schooling and dreams, then finding out you didn't just get 'better with these disorder'–that this change was permanent, and everyday life would alter dramatically too, and then . . ." She couldn't bring herself to say it. I just continued to search deeper into those eyes, trying to give her what she needed to continue. "Then I was met with that conversation after my surgery . . . So when I was staring out from those cliffs, it just seemed like such a peaceful and easy choice. Immediate relief to all sorts of pain–not just physical. And while I've had these fleeting thoughts before when my pain has been unbearable–that's all it was, just fleeting. But it felt different this time because the loss felt too great, and there was nothing to bring me back from the edge. This time it wasn't just a fleeting thought. It's insane we have about seventy thousand thoughts a day, but one like that can destroy you. One like that can take it all away. If it takes root and holds firmly enough, it can change the trajectory of your life–it can change everything. That's the power of our thoughts and words..."

It took me a long time to speak. I was shocked and humbled she was opening up to me in this way. And I wanted nothing more than to respond right away. To be able to say exactly the right thing and not leave her out there alone by herself, but I couldn't find any words. So I just held her like a useless idiot.

Finally, my inept mouth spoke. "Were you glad I came along that day? Do you think–"

I was surprised at how quickly she began to reply. "I was actually irritated at first. Well, I did appreciate your handsome good looks, but I think they irritated me even more. It was like this huge reminder of everything I couldn't have. But then you started talking to me with that dry humor and biting charm of yours, and it jolted me out of that moment– you made me pay attention to something else, something outside of that dark portal. I knew you didn't pity or judge me. Actually, your challenge brought me around, instilled a little life–a little fight–into my blood. You were a shot of something I desperately needed. And I was so extremely curious about you. More than anything, you lured me away from those cliffs. You made me forget. And then you made me remember what I had to live for. And it's so much. So very much."

She looked at me, and I could see a glassy look taking shape in her eyes as she said, "I can't imagine that moment going differently. I can't imagine the alternative . . . if you hadn't come along and showed me the heart of Ireland . . . showed me how much heart I had left in myself . . . I'm not sure what would have happened. But I do know that I don't regret that day—*any* of it—because it led me to you."

I gulped hard, thinking about the alternative too. Thinking about a world without Eyre, a world where we didn't exist together. Thinking about what my miserable existence would have continued to be. We had saved each other.

I gently tucked a strand of hair behind her ear and said, "There's an Irish proverb: 'Your feet will lead you where your heart is . . .' I think you were supposed to get on that plane, Eyre. I'm just really sorry you had to go through so much to get here."

"Yes, I think you're my heart, Darby," she whispered as her eyes floated over to mine.

TWENTY-NINE
Darby

Those words had held me in a way I never knew could exist, making peaceful sleep possible for the first time. I'd never felt so loved or understood. So cared for. Her soft words had floated between us and then continued to levitate through my mind. Like it was impossible that they were out in the atmosphere instead of just living in my imagination.

I hazily remember being conscious of her in my arms throughout the night and of having a new feeling. One of being able to protect something finally. Of being able to protect someone I loved. And I was looking forward to the morning when I could hold her in a conscious state again. But the jabbing in my arm was telling me that wasn't going to happen.

The intruding jabs started out light and then grew more aggressive. I thought I was dreaming, but my dreams had been surprisingly peaceful. It wasn't until I cracked open my eyes and looked through the slits that I saw Mak, peering down at me—poking me. Now, I really couldn't believe him. This had better be an emergency. He better need the hospital.

"Darce!" he whisper-shouted. "Darce!"

I cracked my eyes open a little wider. Eyre seemed to be immune to the voice of this crazed little imp. She wasn't stirring. Maybe this was the first decent sleep she'd gotten too. "Mak," I said as quietly as possible while still showing my displeasure. "There is a door for a reason. I didn't know I had to lock it. This *better* be an emergency—"

"Ya have a woman in your room and ya didn't lock the door? Not very gentlemanly. Seems like ya should make sure ya have privacy—" Mak's mouth was taking on that special shape it got when he teased me—an impish grin that signaled he was up to no good.

"Very funny, you know I was a gentleman, so I didn't need to lock the door. Plus, Eyre was the last one through it. It wasn't like I dragged her in here. Even if that is the only way you think she'd be in my room."

Mak smiled even bigger then. "*Good on you*, Darby." Then he shook his head like a *Tweety Bird* cartoon. "Darby, you're supposed to be volunteering at the church today. Did ya forget? Why don't ya take Eyre with ya? You're going to be late."

I stared at him in total disbelief. Did he seriously think I was going to take Eyre there? *No way.* I had already made it clear I didn't want to do that at the pub the other night. "No, Mak, I'm not going to the church to volunteer. Father Kelly will just have to understand. I'm sure he'll figure it out when I don't show up."

I was just debating if I could possibly roll us both over to the other side to get away from Mak when he started jabbing me again. He really was like an annoying little leprechaun who was cranky without his pot of gold. "Darby, I think it would be good for Eyre as well."

"No, Mak. *No way* . . ." My voice had risen, and Eyre was moving in my arms as if she might awaken. The idea of her hearing this conversation was even worse than her waking up with Mak looming over us.

Mak stared at me sternly. "Darby," he said, raising his voice even higher this time.

Eyre's eyes started fluttering. "What's going on?" she murmured, thankfully with her eyes still closed. Mak could not be in this room when she woke up. That was just beyond creepy.

"Fine, just leave. *Now*." He looked at me with raised eyebrows, trying to ascertain if I was telling the truth. "I'll do it, ok? Please, just leave. We'll just be a little late, so Eyre can rest a little longer."

Mak literally did a little jig as he walked out of the room. I started to shake my head and roll my eyes at him, but Eyre nestled into me, distracting me from his shenanigans. I didn't understand why it was so important to Mak that Eyre go with me today. I also didn't understand why missing one day was such a big deal. I never missed my "volunteer" work.

I gazed down at the beauty that was in my arms, the beauty that was molding itself further into me and seeking comfort. More than anything, I didn't know how I was going to explain my "volunteering" to Eyre, and I was afraid of what might be said to her about it. I wasn't ready for her to know. I wanted this to last a little while longer. No, I was pretty sure I wanted this to last forever.

Little noises fluttered up to meet my ears, landing with happy notes. In all of Ireland, with its gorgeous melodies, I don't think I'd heard a better sound. Well, except for her laugh. Then Eyre's eyes did actually open, and she was looking at me differently. There was a new softness in those swirls of color and a new respect. Her smile made the morning worthwhile, and when she had me mesmerized by her mouth, she said, "Was I dreaming, or was Mak in here?"

Grand. So I wasn't going to avoid the creepiness. At least he wasn't looming over her when she woke up. I tried to offer up some type of explanation. "Yeah, I was hoping you wouldn't remember that little bit." I chuckled nervously. "He was worried I'd *bunk off* on going to the church today for . . . *volunteering.*"

She looked at me in surprise. *I know, volunteering and church aren't words that seem to go in the same breath with me. How am I going to explain this?* "Mak gives me Mondays and Thursdays off from tours and I spend those days working on the historic church in the village," I explained. "It burned a while back and we've been trying to repair it. The village people thought my carpentry knowledge would be useful. I still think they should have called a professional contractor, but this small village doesn't really have the funds for that type of project—it's been hard enough to get the materials. And, well, they wanted me to do it . . ." I trailed off not wanting to say anymore.

"Why?" she probed.

"Well, there are a lot of reasons. It's really important to Mak . . . and this village. It's a beautiful, historic place. And it's really tragic what happened." That was all I was going to say. I was hoping it was enough. She nodded, and I let out a pent-up breath. "So, would you like to go with me?"

I could tell she didn't like leaving the subject, that she wanted to dig deeper. I could see there was so much more she wanted to know and uncover. But she relented, saying, "Yes, of course, Darby. You already know the answer."

I grinned at her words, loving that "Darby" and "of course" seemed to naturally belong in the same sentence where she was concerned.

We reached the church with Eyre situated securely in my sidecar. A sight I loved to see. The church stood in its perpetual state of limbo. The front entrance was still standing, while the back had been completely destroyed by the fire. Wood columns stood like lonely pillars, making a frame for what was to come. The white wooden framed door at the front of the church was still charred and marred with soot at the edges. It always provided some relief to see the historic stone arches and mammoth wooden doorway still standing intact, but the sight of the rest of the church was gut-wrenching. The entrance was nothing more than a front wall and a small overhanging. A mockery of a shelter at best. The overhang probably couldn't even keep you dry in a strong rainstorm. It was really heartbreaking.

Father Kelly came down the steps from the front entrance upon seeing our bicycle approach. He was a younger man in his forties. He'd taken over for Father O'Brian a while back. Maybe the burning of the church had devastated Father O'Brian too much or possibly what happened that evening of the fire. Or maybe Father O'Brian thought the church needed a new start as he was nearing retirement age.

A warm smile greeted us from Father Kelly. He was dressed in his Parish clothes, and he had a welcoming cup of tea in his hand. He was tall with oddly tanned skin for the Irish countryside and dark brown hair. "I would have brought more tea if I'd known you were bringing company," he said with a surprised look on his face that not even he could manage to hide.

Since Father Kelly didn't know to whom he should hand the cup of tea, I stepped in and said, "We'll be more than happy to share." I thanked him as I looked at his increasingly befuddled face. Wiping the shock off his countenance, he quickly introduced himself to Eyre and offered to show her around the church—or what was left of it.

As he toured her around what I had nicknamed "the Irish ruins," I couldn't help but feel incredibly awkward. Father Kelly seemed to sense my discomfort and talked even more than usual. His ease of interpersonal skills was always overflowing. He returned with Eyre from their tour and said to me, "So, Darby, what are we working on today? I'm here to help in any way." He turned to Eyre. "He doesn't let me help much, but occasionally he has to relent. Can't do everything yourself," he said softly.

"Um, I'm just going to keep working on cutting those beams. Maybe you can keep Eyre company for a while," I offered.

"I'd like to help," Eyre offered. I nodded, a little surprised, especially by her enthusiasm. As I guided her over to a tarp, I couldn't help but feel a sense of warmth that she wanted to be a part of my world. It was oddly attractive that she wanted to help with my carpentry. I had thought this would be an uncomfortable experience, but it was turning out to be quite a nice one. Or maybe I was a lost cause, and everything led me to be even more attracted to her.

We uncovered a pile of wood from the tarp and started gathering pieces to measure. I offered to let her try her hand at cutting some small pieces on the bandsaw, giving her protective glasses to shield her eyes. I instructed her on the best way to slide the wood through and demonstrated the movement several times. I stepped over to let her *have a go* with the machine. I made sure to assist her and guide her hands, but she was determined to do it herself. So I stepped back, making sure to stay close to her side, ready to step in at a moment's notice. When the wood popped up on her, she jumped backward, completely unnerved. I tried to help, but she was determined to handle it on her own. And I can't deny that it was extremely attractive seeing her determination around the powerful machinery. But I could also see how visibly shaken she was. I don't think this was particularly Eyre's favorite activity. But it made my heart melt at how important it was to her that she tried something that she thought was of importance to me. I could see the reluctance–and a little fear–on her face as I cut off the machine.

"I'm just going to go gather some more wood and supplies. I'll be back," she said a little sheepishly. I smiled and nodded, knowing she wanted to be as far away from this machine as possible. Which, I had to say, saddened me a little because I was enjoying the view and her company. However, I understood. I somehow didn't think Eyre and power tools mixed well. *And why would they?* She had this gentle strength and calm warmth that made you feel comfortable in her presence. This machinery was strong in a full-on, in-your-face kind of way.

 I continued working, shrouded in the haze of my thoughts of Eyre, not thinking about the possibility of her speaking with Father Kelly. But I *definitely* should have been thinking that way.

THIRTY

Eyre

It was difficult to focus on anything else besides Darby working with his hands. I had no idea that seeing him in his element and watching his masterful carpentry was going to affect me in this way. But it sure did. He looked so sexy, commanding that machinery so effortlessly. However, it was the machinery that I didn't like. Or rather, it didn't like me. Either way, I needed to get away from it before I hurt myself. I was a dancer and had no business being around power tools. The last thing I wanted to do was lose a finger.

I was more than satisfied to watch Darby work from afar for now. Maybe once the heavy machinery went off, then I'd find a way to help him. I really loved being able to work on a project with him. There was an element of intimacy that seemed to bring us ever closer together. I was finding all kinds of intimacy existed with Darby, and I loved discovering each new facet with him. It made my nervous butterflies come alive in the best possible way. I had always thought of

Darby as an island, never thinking he'd let me come ashore. But I loved the symbiotic archipelago that seemed to be forming between us while we worked together to form something beautiful.

I slowly made my way over to Father Kelly, a little reluctant and embarrassed since I was afraid he might be able to see how interested I was in Darby and his measured movements. However, the man was such a comforting soul. He seemed like a character straight out of Mayberry, R.F.D. A real *Andy Griffith* regular.

I glanced over at him and tried my hand at some idle chit-chat, which, thankfully, he made extremely easy. It wasn't until I asked more about Darby that I noticed him tense up for the first time. It seemed completely unnatural for him, and he seemed momentarily surprised by his own response.

"So why won't Darby let you help him? Seems like things would go faster," I asked a little timidly, testing the waters.

Father Kelly sighed, his handsome face actually taking on a stormy concern. I could see now that it was indeed weathered from all the burdens and worry he must have to carry. "Well . . . I guess he just feels he should do it all himself. It's some type of personal repayment." He looked at me, and there was reluctance in his eyes. It was as if he was hoping I wouldn't ask any more questions. All it did was spur me on. I now knew there was so much more I needed to ask. And this man of the cloth was the only person I trusted to give me the unbiased, truthful version.

"What kind of personal repayment? It seems he has undergone a lot of trauma," I began.

'Eyre, I don't think—"

"Please, Father Kelly. Sinead and Mak seemed to really want me to come volunteer here today with Darby. They even mentioned it on my first night here and they've continued to mention it to me every so often. There must be a reason. Sinead and Mak have been alluding to something, and it's been hard to decipher what they are trying to tell me. I can tell they're worried about me hurting Darby, that they think he's fragile—"

Father Kelly sighed. "Darby's not so much fragile as avoiding everyone and everything." He looked at me, assessing my reaction. "Eyre, this is really, *really* not my place," he added with emphasis.

"Please, tell me. I'm not sure anyone else is going to. Sloane only implied some things to me. I knew he'd probably tell me if I asked, but I didn't want to ask *him*," I explained.

"Well, Sloane is a good guy for not saying more about the situation. He probably could have used it to get a date with you." *Wow, news travels fast around here.* He looked at me as if debating if he should continue. "Ok, but I wouldn't talk about it with Darby if I were you, and it would be best if he didn't know you heard it from me. Alright?"

It was hard to hear Father Kelly over the noise from the power tools, but with him standing so close and his voice raised, I managed. I was going to make sure I didn't miss anything he said. I didn't want to be left to figure out everyone's cryptic clues on my own anymore. At least I knew there was no way Darby could possibly hear us.

Father Kelly looked at me like he was already regretting what he was about to tell me. "Well, when Darby was a young teenager, he was supposed to be watching his friend, who was younger than him, while we held a village meeting. Well, I guess boys being boys, they decided to come down to the church and set off some firecrackers that they had left over from one of the summer celebrations. One of the matches didn't go out completely, and it started a fire. The church went up in flames pretty quickly because they weren't able to put it out. They were afraid they were going to get in trouble, so they took off in Mak's car. He must have left his keys in the ignition. Mak was always doing stuff like that. We're a safe town so it never really mattered, but tonight was different. Darby wasn't even old enough to be driving. It wasn't until the fire was really raging, and glowing so brightly, that we saw it from where the council meeting was being held—"

"But he was just a kid," I interrupted, looking at him. "It doesn't seem like the whole village should—"

Father Kelly held up a hand and sighed painfully. "Mak was in the council meeting with us. He had no idea they'd taken his car. Darby took off quickly down the road, only thinking about not getting in trouble, I imagine. He probably thought the car was their fastest escape option. And, well, he wasn't an experienced driver. Far from it. There was someone passing through from the next village, and Darby didn't exactly handle the car well on the curve, and . . ." He paused, sorrow devouring his eyes. "Well, the cars collided, sending Mak's car off the side of the road. The way I've heard the story told was that Darby was knocked unconscious, and when he woke up, the car was teetering on the edge of a cliff. He panicked and tried to get out of the car as quickly as possible. And when he did, there was a shift in weight. Well, there was no way he could have reached Brock in time. He was still buckled in."

Father Kelly's last words slipped out just as the machine cut off right when he said them. My face fell, and the pit of my stomach felt like it was going to revolt. Slowly we turned our heads to look at Darby, like an excavation team afraid to see what they had unearthed. What I saw completely obliterated me. The wooden beam he held fell out of his hands, looking as violently dejected as he did. And without another word, he walked out. The look on his face said it all—a look of hatred for himself.

And the man that walked out of the church looked completely broken, shattered beyond repair.

THIRTY-ONE
Eyre

I followed Darby out of the church, knowing full well that it was a horrible idea, but unable to stop my feet. We had grown so close in these last couple of days—so connected—that I felt like I had to hear it from him. That I at least needed to know the truth and to hear the words from his perspective. We had a closeness that could afford the truth and survive it, *right?*

But when his eyes looked up from the bike so he could start pedaling and they met mine, I realized that everything in our relationship stopped here. There had been a line drawn. I hadn't known I was up against one.

"Eyre, just don't," Darby began. "There's nothing that can make this better or make it ok. I told you I was a terrible person—that I was messed up. I told you not to get involved with me. I should have listened to myself. I warned you because I was worried I wasn't going to be able to stay away from you. That's what bad people do. They only think about what they want and not about the other person. And I was right. I'm *not* a good person." His words were firm and unflinching.

"Darby." My voice fractured into a million pieces as it came out, seeming to shatter in the air.

"It's bad enough that I'm trapped in this purgatory, but now this . . . that you have to know. I didn't want you to know. Not yet. I was going to find a way to tell you. I just didn't know how or when. I was waiting to see what happened with us. But it was never Father Kelly's place to tell you. I just wanted . . . I just wanted this time with you, I guess. I was greedy. Maybe I wanted this time with you before you went back, so you could remember me in a certain way. To never have to tell you my awful truth if you didn't need to know. So you could go back home with good memories and never have to be burdened or touched by this. I wanted to give you that—this good mental image of me that you could always keep. To have at least one person who didn't view me as—" His voice broke off.

"It's not Father Kelly's fault, Darby," I said as gently as possible. "I didn't think you could tell me. And it was obvious that Sinead and Mak wanted me to come here for a reason. They've been dropping cryptic hints. I just wanted to know what was going on. And I thought Father Kelly would be the most unbiased person to ask."

"Well, now you know," he said painfully.

"And this place doesn't have to be purgatory, Darby. It could be a place of healing and forgiveness. I've been struggling with that—with my faith. I know it feels like we couldn't possibly deserve something like that, but—"

Darby's face angered, and he cut me off immediately. "If there's a God, Eyre, then that's even worse. Because that means He *let* Brock die. But if there's nothing, then I can live with that. I can at least get up every day and face my fate with that. I can live in that nothingness, but I can't live with false hope."

I swallowed hard, feeling pain claw at me. His words had torn open wounds I'd been trying to hide. Ones I'd been trying to hide beneath so I had an excuse not to address my faith or my lacking relationship with it. I'd used the pain from my wounds as a shield to avoid facing my questions–questions that threatened to crack my foundation beyond repair. Darby's words split open my insecurities and doubts about my own faith. But the bitter man standing before me made me want to cling to it. As I opened my mouth to speak, all I could see was his hardened expression, as if carved of stone. And I knew, at that moment, it was best just to let him go.

I sat with Father Kelly on one of the few intact pews, having just watched Darby ride away. The pews at the back of the church near the entrance were weather worn and in bad condition, having been left exposed to the elements, but they were still functional. I felt a kindred spirit in these pews. And I wondered if I was still capable of serving a purpose.

There was a silence between us that wasn't deafening or uncomfortable. Rather I sat in it for respite, and he allowed me to seek refuge in it. Never once trying to speak. He just sat with me.

I looked over at him and searched his face, which looked so tired and weary at the moment. I hadn't noticed it before, except when I had asked him about Darby. His smile and cheerful expression had completely covered it. Obliterated all traces of discomfort. His soft brown eyes looked kind and nonjudgmental, asking you to take a chance on him.

"Father Kelly . . ." I trailed off. I didn't know where to begin and I felt even more hopeless.

"Eyre." He looked at me gently. "Eyre, sometimes things happen to us in life and we can't find a way to work them for good. And I think we get so lost in that defeat that we can't find a way out of it. So we start to question ourselves, our faith, and what we've done to deserve it. I don't know what you're going through, but you don't deserve it."

He looked at me pointedly, and I was shocked. I thought we had been talking about Darby. It never entered my mind that we weren't. How could he possibly . . .

"Eyre, you can't control what happens to you, but you can control how you react to it. You can't control how fair life is to you or what it gives you, but you can choose to believe–in yourself and in your faith. Believe enough in yourself to know it didn't happen because you deserved it and that you can find a way to work this for good. Believe enough in your faith that you'll be guided by it. I truly believe we all have a 'Job moment' coming our way. Maybe this is yours."

I looked at him, confused. He laughed lightly. "No one ever understands when I use that term. Job lost everything and still kept his faith. And what was returned to him was even greater because of it. And I'm not saying that necessarily means possessions—it can be peace within yourself or love. It can be an intangible quality that can never be taken away from you . . . So I think you can choose what you want to do here. *Especially* with Darby."

Was he saying I should abandon Darby? That he wasn't a good influence on my faith?

"Darby needs someone. He's lost, and I think you understand that feeling all too well," he said, looking straight into my eyes. "So are you going to work it for good or are you going to hide? Do you let your fears overshadow you, or do you stand against them and tell them you're enough? That you're going to fight for yourself and your faith . . . and for Darby. Because he obviously needs someone to fight for him."

Father Kelly's words shocked me. I hadn't been prepared for him to advocate for Darby. I hadn't given this man nearly enough credit. I thought he was the village parishioner that put on a smile and made everyone feel good. That he was there when times were good and offered empty platitudes when life was hard. I was so wrong.

"Thank you," was all I could possibly say through my constricting throat.

He simply nodded at me like he hadn't just given me one of the biggest gifts of my life. As if it was nothing. As if he and this moment weren't something I would carry with me every day for the rest of my life.

"Father Kelly?" I asked softly.

"Yes, Eyre?"

But I just let myself feel the tears. Allowed myself to embrace the cold, wet trail they made down my face. Little icy travelers that escaped my soul. He reached over and put his hand on my shoulder while allowing me to cry on his.

"You don't deserve it, Eyre," he repeated softly as he let me shelter myself from the world in his caring presence, knowing my heart's greatest fear and exactly what I needed to hear.

THIRTY-TWO
Eyre

It was in this position—crying on Father Kelly's shoulder—that Sinead found me. I was startled when she'd shown up in the church and her deep, sultry voice had spoken its first words.

"*Oye*," she'd said. I'd immediately looked up from Father Kelly's shoulder to see her carrying her same lovely picnic basket. "Mak said you and Darby had come to the church today. That he'd finally convinced Darby to bring you. Mak asked if I could have lunch with you since he was busy at the shop . . . Ok, that's a lie, he asked if I could find an excuse to come check on you," she said, raising the picnic basket in the air with a shrug of her shoulder like that was the best she could come up with on short notice.

Father Kelly looked over at me and said, "I'm just going to give you some privacy. I'll let you have some time together. I'm going to go back to my office. If you need me, you know where I'll be."

"Thank you, Father Kelly, you have no idea what

you've—" I began as he started to get up, but he waved his hand.

"Eyre, it was a privilege to get to talk with you today. Sinead will tell you where my office is located. It's a bit unusual right now since we've been getting the church sorted out, but I like it." He looked at me. "Don't ever second guess coming to see me. You promise you'll come see me if you need to talk. Please."

"Yes, thank you, I could never repay—" I started, but he stopped me.

"We don't work on payment plans here," Father Kelly said as he looked at Sinead, and she nodded with a slight laugh. "We do things because we want to help, and we don't expect anything in return. That's the best way to live. And I have really enjoyed our time together."

He nodded at me to see if I would follow through with what I had told him and I nodded back in agreement. This was such a novel concept to me. I was used to people wanting something in return. Everything had always come with strings attached, especially in my romantic relationships. It was hard to believe this other selfless type of exchange existed. I guess I had just been hard-wired to expect some type of payment in return. I was really hoping these people could reset me.

As Father Kelly exited the church through its vast open space and headed down the road, I realized he hadn't come in a car either. Perhaps his office was a short walk or bike ride away, but more likely, he knew about Darby's triggers. He certainly was the type of man who would take that into account. And this type of care and consideration seemed to be prevalent in this country. With every person I got to know here, I fell more in love with Ireland. Father Kelly was certainly no exception.

Sinead came to take his spot beside me. She kept looking away and then back at me as if she was trying to figure out where to begin. The worry on her beautiful face seemed so out of place.

"It's ok," I said to relieve her mind. "It was best I found out somehow, especially if Darby couldn't tell me himself. And who better to tell me than someone like Father Kelly . . . He explained everything to me while Darby was working." My voice could barely raise above a whisper, especially when I got to his name, my words getting lost in the expanse of this place.

"Oye," she said again. "Eyre, I'm sorry. I thought Darby would tell you himself. I thought–*we* thought–that working here would prompt him to tell you. Give him the little nudge he needed to open up. We thought it was only fair you know and only a matter of time before you found out in a village like ours. But I'm truly sorry. He really seemed like he would open up with you."

She looked over at me, evaluating the damage, and continued, "I told Mak he should just tell you himself. That he should take you aside one night when Darby wasn't around and tell you. Of course, he made jokes about Darby being glued to you like an Irishman to his ale." She laughed, though the tension was still visible in her body. "But you know it's still very difficult for Mak to talk about. And he thought it would have been so much harder for you to hear from him. He's forgiven Darby. It's Darby that hasn't forgiven himself. But nothing can bring back a grandchild. His only grandchild. Nothing's gonna—"

My head snapped up like I'd been electrocuted. My eyes went wide with shock. "His grandchild?" Heartbreak and disbelief swirled together in an unpleasant manner in my tone.

"Oye." Sinead plopped back against the pew with a thud. It sounded kind of painful. "Oh . . . Father Kelly didn't tell you?" I shook my head wildly. "I should never have brought this stupid picnic basket. I'm never making one again."

Pain seemed to wash over her face, and she looked like she didn't want to be here. As if she didn't want to be the one to have to tell me this news. She let out the longest breath, and I wasn't sure she would be able to speak again. Finally, she looked back at me and slowly said, "Brock was Mak's grandson, Eyre."

Hearing the words from her suddenly allowed everything to fit into place. The room at the end of the hall that was never used and no one was allowed to enter. The way they talked about Mak having "had" a grandson—as if he had moved away for college and then for a job. The way Mak had taken Darby in like a grandson and treated him like he was one. The way Darby had adopted him as his grandfather. The fact that they lived together because they were the only two people that could possibly understand . . .

My head swam with a very discomforting feeling—quite a horrific one actually. Sinead looked at me. "Eyre, you ok? You look really pale."

"Yes, I just didn't . . . It's one thing to find out . . . But Mak has taken Darby in . . . He's like a grandson to him. He's even given him a job. I don't . . ." I couldn't finish. My thoughts were swirling faster than I could keep up with them, creating a twister in my mind.

Sinead looked at me with kind sympathy. She softly said, "He forgave Darby a long time ago, Eyre. But it doesn't make the loss any easier on Mak. He knows what happened was an accident. A devastating one, where boys were being irresponsible and immature. But that's all Darby was–just a thirteen-year-old boy who was immature and made a bad decision. We all have things we've done in our lives that could have led to a horrendous outcome. One we could have had to live with every day for the rest of our lives. What makes any one of us any different? It just happened to Darby. What if that car hadn't been coming? What if their car hadn't gone so close to the edge? It would have been such a different outcome. Brock would still be here, and it would be a stupid tale they were telling to this very day, but it's not. I think we pass judgment on people so easily and we forget that if things had gone just a little differently for us in our worst moments–in those times we made our worst decisions–we would be the people being judged. It would be the other way around."

She looked strongly at me to ascertain if her words were reaching me and continued, "There's really not many degrees of separation between people. We forget that. We see homeless people on the street, and we dismiss them, thinking they are so different from us and we could never be them. But just a few changes in our lives and we could be them. And the homeless person's life may have looked a lot like yours not too long ago. Something could have happened suddenly to put them in that position. We like to say *we would never do that* or *we could never be like that*, but there's never much separating us. Just a few twists of fate. Maybe just a few things going differently in our lives. We forget how quickly our lives can change, but I think you know that with your conditions. That's one reason why I thought you would understand Darby." She eyed me. "We forget our blessings, how lucky we are. And we like to think we know what we would do in someone else's position, but we can never truly know until we're in it. That's why we should never judge."

I looked at her in silence, shocked at the words coming out of her mouth and in awe of her wisdom. But most of all, hoping she would continue. I felt so lost. Her voice, beginning again, comforted me. "I know you're not one of those judgmental people, Eyre. I knew it as soon as I met you. You'd never need to use judgment or discrimination to make yourself feel better or gain some false sense of power or control. I could tell—it's one of the perks of being a bartender." She smiled at me, trying to lighten the mood and then spoke solemnly again. "I also knew there was a good chance you'd be able to understand him. It's one reason that I wanted to push Darby to tell you himself. But the village . . . well, not everyone here is like that. And we lost one of our own . . . and the church with it. It's been hard for people not to judge–to be able to forgive. There's some of them that never will. They've never treated him the same. Whether that's judging, blaming him, being uncomfortable in his presence, or walking on eggshells around him. Some of them do it subconsciously, some of them not. Sometimes I think the 'Darcy' jabs aren't all good natured fun. Not for everyone."

She looked at me solemnly and continued, "The burned church sat untouched for the longest time. The village didn't have the funds to do anything about it. And once the people of the church relocated, it just continued to sit vacant. The church restoration was put on a to-do list that never happened. When Darby became such a good carpenter, a few of us thought it would be good for him to start restoring it. A way to try to heal. A way he could feel like he was physically repairing things. Making amends by fixing the church. So we pushed to have Darby rehabilitate the church. But it took a lot of convincing–both the village and then Darby. Ultimately, it took Mak asking Darby. And as soon as he did, Darby agreed without hesitation, and he's been here every week since without fail. Nothing could keep him away. I've tried to pull him away from here when he's had the flu or it's *lashing* like mad, but he won't budge. It doesn't matter how he's feeling, if it's his day to be here, he's here. But I didn't expect this work to turn into some kind of harsh penitence. He's taken this work the last couple of years and turned it into some sort of retribution, branding himself with it. As if it's the final mark, sealing that he's a terrible person. And it's only driven him to work harder. I'm not sure the volunteering has done what we thought it would do. Maybe when the work is completed . . . but even then, I'm not sure. I just thought if he could physically see his amends . . . but I'm worried that all it's done is push him further away from his faith, searing together the connection of the church and the accident that night."

When it was clear I wasn't going to be able to speak or collect myself, Sinead continued to explain, "Mak thought he could help Darby forgive himself. Others of us did too. But he can't seem to forgive himself–and we can't make him. He has to do that for himself. I think Mak has finally come to that realization too. And it's hard because Darby has always been like a second grandchild. He was like Brock's older brother. They were always close. And Darby took good care of Brock. I know it's hard for the village to remember that side of Darby, but Mak remembers. And that's when Mak took Darby into his home and gave him a job. As soon as Darby was old enough to get his hands on alcohol, he did. He tried to drown everything and everyone out, even himself. It was horrible to watch. He went numb. And even when Mak helped him through it, I think Darby clung to that numbness. The drink had taught him how to do it. He doesn't even like to look at alcohol now. It just reminds him of that time–of all of it. I know it's hard for him to even visit me at the pub. It's not that he has a hard time staying away from alcohol, it's the reminder for him. But I also think drinking was a way to deal with his attacks." She looked at me questionably as if to ask if I knew about them.

I was finally able to push some words out. Solemnly, I said, "I experienced an attack with him last night. And I saw the aftermath of another one."

Sinead nodded and allowed me some time to gather myself. Then she spoke compassionately, "Well, you can imagine how someone would need or want something to dull those terrifying attacks; it's just that Darby numbed everything else in the process. So Mak helped him through that period, and they became even closer. He took Darby in under his roof, and the drinking lessened until it finally stopped. And Mak was able to get Darby to work–to show up for a job. He dislikes the job, but he needs it. Darby needs to have something to keep him busy. And Mak teases him relentlessly because that's their relationship, but also because I think it helps Darby feel normal. It helps to remind him that Mak has forgiven him. And honestly, I don't know what Mak would do without Darby. He's his grandson now. Mak has Darby to protect and look after. And I can tell that Mak loves it and I know he loves him."

Sinead smiled at me and explained, "It's really unfortunate Mak never married because he didn't get to have a close relationship with his daughter. The mother moved away from our village when his daughter was quite young. I know he would have liked to have had the opportunity to be there for a child every day. It tore at him that he didn't get to have that with his daughter. Both Darby and Mak have missed so many opportunities in life. They've let them pass by intentionally. Darby is an incredible woodworker, yet he won't pursue it. I feel like he wants to continue his job as a tour guide as some kind of misguided punishment. And maybe he secretly does really enjoy working with Mak, but I also know he has a passion in life and that's not it. We used to try to encourage him to pursue woodworking, but he got so angry with us. We've had to let it go."

"I saw all the wood boxes in his room. They're beautifully carved. I wondered if they might be his creations," I replied hesitantly.

"Yes, he's really talented. I think it's become his therapy. But, Eyre, the carved boxes don't hold a candle to what he can really do. You should see the shed out back. He won't bring any of his larger carved pieces out. I'm surprised he even puts the boxes in his room. Mak lets me go in there sometimes when Darby isn't around and see what he's been working on. He'd kill us if he knew, but I think we're entitled to some grandparent privileges. His work is amazing. He makes these carved rocking chairs that are just exquisite—

calla lily leaves carved on the backrest and vines wrapping around the legs of the chairs. All sorts of gorgeous other pieces with carvings of yarrow, fairy thimbles, and marigold."

Rocking chairs? Darby? My face fell in total disbelief. "I know," Sinead said. "Not what you expect from Darby. He has so many layers, Eyre. You just have to penetrate his numb exterior shell to see all the layers that lay beneath it. And so far, you've gotten further than anyone. *Please* don't give up on him. I really hope this doesn't change how you feel about him."

I glanced down at the floor that had once been beautifully polished wood and was now so warped it would have to be replaced, along with everything else in the church. I didn't need to think about it. I'd known the story of Darby's past didn't change how I felt about him as soon as I'd heard it. But not hearing about it from him was the difficult part. If he never opened up about it to me, I wasn't sure I could get past that. As a friend, I knew I could, but not as something more. And my heart ached at that realization because I wasn't sure if Darby would ever fully open up to me. Something I'd been worried about from the start and something I'd continued to overlook because I'd fallen so completely for him. But he'd opened up to me a little, so maybe in time, he could let me in entirely.

"It doesn't change my feelings for him," I breathed, and Sinead let out a huge sigh of relief.

"I wouldn't blame or judge you, Eyre, if it did. But I'd just like you to really think about it. If he does open up to you—well, I don't think he could withstand it if you didn't want him any longer. Not if it was for this reason."

I looked at her light green eyes that tiptoed over me,

trying to read me like tarot cards. I nodded. "I understand, I wouldn't want that either. I want nothing more than for him to let me in." She nodded back to me and then a smile made its appearance on her rosy lips. However, I couldn't help but ask her, "Do you think he'll ever forgive himself? The way he was talking about God earlier, there was so much hate. It seemed like he had as much hate for God as he had for himself."

"Oye, he didn't?" Sinead asked rhetorically and rolled her eyes up toward the sky. "In a church nonetheless. That's Darby for you . . . with Father Kelly here. He's the nicest man." Sinead looked embarrassed, just like a true grandmother. "I'm assuming you're religious? Are you very offended? I don't know what all he said, but I know it can be a lot. I've heard it."

"Well, I was . . . I am . . . I'm trying to be." She looked at me with a questioning brow. "It's just really difficult to have faith still . . . after everything." She grabbed my hand instinctively like she was my grandmother now, too, and I smiled, feeling her warmth. It helped me to continue. "What Father Kelly said really helped and well . . . seeing Darby made me want to try as hard as possible to keep my faith. It made me want to fight for it even harder. But that's what I know I'll have to do. I'll have to fight."

Sinead nodded empathetically. "We can't have faith and not struggle; we have to fight for it. It's not easy. You can't just decide and never have doubts, bad days, or struggles. You're not alone. Don't ever think that. And don't ever think that makes you less worthy as a person of faith for going through those struggles. And I'm always here if you ever need to talk. I've lost my faith on more than one occasion." I looked at her, surprised she was sharing this with me. "Not every pregnancy was easy or successful, Eyre. And I didn't have faith through all of them. I will understand. I will never judge."

She squeezed my hand tighter, and we just sat there, not knowing what to do with ourselves. Two women who very much needed the silent presence of the other, the understanding and comfort it provided. And it was in that silence that we grieved each other's losses and felt them as our own.

Finally, she broke through the thick ether. "I don't know if he can forgive himself, Eyre, but I have to hope. Just like I have to hope that we can forgive ourselves for every mistake we've made and for all the things we've done that have ever made us question our faith or even want to lose it."

THIRTY-THREE
Darby

I came home to a mostly desolate house. Relief washed over me as soon as I saw Lucky waiting patiently at the door when I arrived. I bent down to pet him as my thoughts swarmed around in my mind and ambushed me. The entire ride back had been sheer torture as they tried to suffocate me. I couldn't believe Eyre now knew about my terrible past, but worse than that, I couldn't believe that I hadn't been the one to tell her about it. What a horrendous thing to find out from someone else. I was beyond ashamed, not only of my past but also of my lack of trust and openness with Eyre.

I went over and sat on the sofa, letting it absorb all of my weight. I wished I could unload all of my burdens on it, but I knew nothing was capable of withstanding those. Lucky rushed over and hopped up beside me, curling into a ball next to me. He could always sense when I was sick or emotionally distressed. Lucky was the best therapist. Lucky looked at me pointedly with those sad eyes as if encouraging me to tell him all about it. His look really said it all. It always did. Somehow he always knew.

"Yeah, I messed up . . . *again*. I was really trying hard not to do that with her." His soulful eyes raised up to me slightly. I swear he could understand what I was saying to him. He didn't want to lose Eyre either. If he could speak, he'd tell me to fix it, but those big sad eyes were even more effective. I started petting his head, one of the only motions that truly calmed me. "Yeah, I know. I don't know if I can fix it. I'm sorry, boy," I said earnestly.

My therapy session with Lucky continued on for a while until I heard the door open with an ominous creak. It was one of two people coming through that door, and I wasn't prepared for either of them. I didn't even turn around. I expected someone to speak, but the room remained silent, the door closing more softly than this house was used to hearing. I kept focusing on Lucky, my port in the storm. He sat up beside me to take in the new presence that had entered the house. The one that was sitting in the armchair to the left of me.

The silence continued for a while, and finally, my eyes edged over enough to see the tip of a walking stick. Of course someone had called Mak. This was probably as fast as he could leave the shop and make it back home this afternoon. I wondered how Teagan was holding up. Probably cursing my name already.

Mak went to venture a word and then swallowed it. This was completely unlike him. I must have royally messed up. *Like really, royally messed up.*

But I could never have been prepared for the words he spoke: "You know you aren't just like a grandson to me, right? Although you are my grandson in every sense of the word, there are some things that can be thicker than blood. Tar, for one, that's probably the thickest of them all. And we're both as stubborn as it is, so that's probably what runs in both of our veins." Mak gave a little laugh, trying to get a smile out of me, but I didn't possess one right now. My soul had gone dark. "Darby, *when* are you going to forgive yourself?"

The question hung there in the air like Norman Bate's knife in *Psycho*. Ready to slash through me at any moment. It wasn't a matter of *if* but *when*. Then it hit–all the pain and guilt. A flood knocking out every other emotion in its path. An all-consuming natural disaster. My head drooped even lower.

Mak inhaled sharply. "Darby, you aren't going to be able to have what you deserve in life without your own forgiveness. I thought I could give it to you, but I can't. I'd do anything to be able to give you that. You're never going to be able to have someone like Eyre until you do. You're never going to be able to pursue your dreams or the life you want until you can face those demons. You've got to make peace with them because only then will they become angels. And maybe this needs to be said . . . and you know I'm not good at doin' this. I've just tried to imply it because this is not something I'm good at saying. And I'm sorry, son. I'm really sorry because, Darby . . . I forgive you."

There was hot liquid burning in my eyes, and I really hated it. He couldn't just come in here and say this to me. I wasn't ready for it. I'd never be ready for it because I didn't deserve it. I'd never deserve his kindness. And then the liquid intruders slowly started to burn fiery paths down my face. This day couldn't get any more difficult. I didn't know what to do with it, with *any* of it.

Mak gently took his walking stick and extended it to rest on my knee. This was as close to affection as we were ever going to get. It was a movement that made me completely lose it. Mak's voice had the most compassion I'd ever heard in it. "Darby, I'm asking you to forgive yourself. If not for yourself, then for me . . . *for Brock.*" I could feel his gaze pierce me in a place that no one had ever been capable of reaching. Somehow that place had come unguarded without my permission. "It's time, Darby, it's time."

I grabbed hold of his walking stick tightly with one hand. It was all I could manage as a reply. I'd never felt so connected to another human being in all my life. Mak was my lifeline. There were some things that were thicker than blood. We were tar, foraged through the most rigorous heat and stress. He was right. He seemed to nod gently, but I honestly couldn't be sure. My vision was blurry, and all I could focus on was our connection, that point of contact.

He allowed us to stay like that for some time, speaking only once again. "Darby, forgiving yourself is the hardest thing you're ever going to have to do in this life. It's the most difficult to accomplish. And it's ok to fail at it as long as you keep trying. But I believe in you, Darby. I'm always going to believe in you."

All I could do was grab on tighter, closing my eyes to block out all other sensory intrusions, because I couldn't handle anything more than the emotions that were flooding through me. After a long while, Mak got up slowly, leaving the walking cane in my hand. He went over to the coffee table and pulled out a puzzle and started to spread it out for us. Just like this was any other day. Just like I wasn't sitting completely wrecked on this sofa.

I watched him pick up the pieces, gathering them carefully in his hands, and start to fit them together. I saw him start to build something beautiful from something so completely broken. Individual pieces that made no sense alone. But as he started to put the pieces together, it would begin to make sense. I knew it would. Everything would be alright. And I was no longer thinking about the puzzle.

I laid the cane beside the sofa and patted Lucky before making my way over to the coffee table. Mak had set two cushions down in front of the hearth and was sitting on one as he worked the puzzle. The other cushion was open and waiting for me. I cautiously sat down beside him.

My hands were shaking slightly as I reached for the first piece. I looked over at Mak, but he just busied himself with the pieces. "Thank you," my strangled voice managed to say. A completely gutted and vulnerable tone of voice came out of me that didn't seem like my own.

"You know I love you, Darby, right?" he replied.

I nodded slowly, taking in a shaky breath. "I'm so lucky you do." It took everything in me to speak. "I love you too, Mak."

THIRTY-FOUR
Darby

I kept waiting for Eyre to walk through the door, wondering how I was going to explain how I came to be pleasantly sitting here with Mak as we worked a puzzle together. We looked like something out of a Norman Rockwell painting when only just a while ago, she'd seen me looking like something from Picasso's worst nightmares. A real *Guernica*–a bloody, wounded mess. This scene was a stark contrast to the earlier one at the church and one I didn't even know how to begin explaining.

After completing the border of the puzzle, I think Mak could tell I was getting anxious. I got up to make us some tea and sandwiches. We spent the rest of the afternoon like that, and Mak provided the perfect escape for me. Never pushing and allowing the silence to envelope me in comforting arms. And I kept waiting–watching the door–without a plan, nonetheless. I should have been using this time to figure out what I would do if she walked through that door. But I guess I knew that was already a losing battle. One I didn't have the energy or the equipment to try to attempt.

Halfway through the puzzle, Mak spoke up. It seemed clear at this point that someone was keeping Eyre preoccupied. I just hoped it wasn't that *clown*, Sloane. Mr. Adonis probably had some type of sixth sense for these things. An old Grecian love sonar (*or a modern tracking device*) innately tuned to siren cries.

Mak cleared his throat. "I asked Sinead to go check on you all. She found Eyre at the church after you left. That's how I knew to come check on you. Father Kelly said he left the two of them to chat. He said Sinead had brought a picnic basket, so they probably were going to be there for a while. He also suggested that if I brought you back to the church and we all had the picnic lunch together, maybe we could sort it out. But I didn't think that was such a grand idea, though."

I just looked at him blankly, not really sure what I should be feeling. It was difficult, to say the very least, to have everyone know your darkest secrets and your biggest flaws. How I hated that Eyre had to be one of those people, too. Thoughts of what Sinead must be telling her sickened me. All truths . . . but that didn't make it any easier.

"It's ok, Darby, I trust Sinead to talk with her, don't you?" Mak said calmly. "And it will make it easier for you when she does come back. She'll know the whole story and you won't have to go through it."

"But I should have been the one to tell her." I hung my head low. "I just wanted–"

"Darby, she'll understand. You just have to worry about what you'll say to her next. Just open up to her and you'll be fine. It won't matter that you weren't the one to tell her. She'll understand. This is Eyre. We've gotten to know her pretty well, and I think we can give her the benefit of the doubt on this one," Mak said confidently.

"What does it matter? She'll be leaving soon anyway," I said defeatedly.

"Don't do that," Mak said with an ache in his tone. "You're going to push her away, aren't ya? Believe me, you're always going to regret it if ya do."

We continued on and fell into a solemn silence, finishing the puzzle. We even began another one. But I couldn't take it any longer. It was getting more dangerous to be down here, where she could come through the door at any minute, and I couldn't handle it. So I went up to my room to read, leaving Mak alone. And as I did, he heaved out a heavy sigh on my departure.

I read for the rest of the night, but my mind couldn't fully escape, like it normally did, into the world of books. I kept reading the first fifty pages of a book and then going on to the next, completely uncaptivated. My mind felt like an amusement ride that was never going to stop. Like the creepy carousel scene from *Strangers on a Train*. Ominously whirling, with no end in sight, as everything morphed into something sinister.

I'm not sure what time she got home. I guess she had wanted to give me some space, which was extremely kind of her, or maybe she didn't want to face me, either. I wondered if she would knock on my door. I'd already gone to bed, depression sinking in. *I wouldn't knock at my door.* But a little flicker of hope dared to burn in my soul. One that burned brighter than the dark shadows cast by fear. Fear of what I'd say to her. Fear of what she'd been told. Fear of how she now felt about me.

But she didn't knock. And I laid there awake for the rest of the evening, staring at the crack in the ceiling, begging myself to get up the courage to go knock on her door. Instead, I let the thoughts consume me. Devouring me in a painful way. The glow-in-the-dark star on the ceiling that Brock and I had stuck there so long ago was taunting me, as it so often did. I had wanted to take it down, knowing it was a trigger, but I couldn't bring myself to do it. The star was a piece of him I didn't want to lose. But when I looked at the star now, I saw it a little differently. I was hearing Mak's words now. Words saying that Brock would want me to forgive myself and to live—to live for him.

As light finally dared to stream its first tendrils of the morning into my room, I began to think about this new day. I began to think of this as a new beginning, an opportunity. Eyre wouldn't be in Ireland much longer. *So why did we need to go through all of this? For what end? So it would taint her time in Ireland?* It seemed pointless to ruin her time here. I was supposed to be her tour guide, and this was way more than she'd ever bargained for. So that's what I would be. A great tour guide. I could play to my strength. Give her the only thing I really had to offer.

I'd just let the rest of the stuff roll off my back. Everyone in the village knew my story and I'd survived this long. I could do this with Eyre too. It would just be a couple more days and she deserved to have a good rest of her trip. And I'd be the best tour guide she'd ever had to get her mind off of things. No reason for her to have to deal with this on her trip, especially on her short stay here. She probably didn't understand why everyone was making such a fuss when she'd be gone soon.

So I'd make it up to her with the best day of sightseeing in Dublin. That's what I was going to do. I may not be much in life, and I may not have much to offer, but I could offer her this... Because at least I'd heard I was a great tour guide.

THIRTY-FIVE
Eyre

The sound of clanking pots in the kitchen woke me early the next morning. Maybe Mak was trying to entice Darby out of his room. I thought if I spent the day yesterday with Sinead and let Darby have his own space, it might give him the time he needed to think, and maybe he'd be ready to at least talk to me when I got back. But no, I was very wrong. I came home to Mak sitting by the fire, reading. There were puzzles started all over the place and one even finished to boot. He'd obviously been keeping Darby busy.

Mak wouldn't really tell me anything, insisting that I speak with Darby myself. That was kind of hard to do with Darby squirreled away in his room and obviously not planning on coming out. I hadn't even thought about knocking on his door that evening. It was obvious he didn't want anything to do with me.

But when I'd come down to the kitchen expecting Mak and saw Darby dressed in the most ridiculous-looking apron, humming a tune while making pancakes, I was more than a little taken off guard. His disposition was as happy as his brightly colored apron. This situation was like a Trojan horse. And I was seriously waiting for it to attack. I now knew how those Trojans must have felt. How could you see such an attractive gift before you and not want to accept it?

"Darby?" I said, with a flood of questions in my tone and total disbelief.

"Hey, I was hoping you might get up early. I wanted to make a good breakfast so we could go see Dublin . . . it's a perfect day for it."

Okay, seriously . . . *What is with "Mr. Bright-And-Shiny," and what happened to my Darby?* I really loved that adorable, snarky grouch in the mornings. And he didn't even have on his sexy tattered tee. He was already dressed. His jeans and button-up shirt fit him so nicely, but they looked extremely out of place.

"Darby, are you ok? Do you want to–"

"I know you can't have pancakes because we don't have any gluten-free flour, so I made you some eggs and bacon, if that's ok? If only I could get some coconut or almond flour . . . I was just researching that this morning."

Darby knows about coconut and almond flour? Okay, it was time to call those X-file people. We had a case of the *Invasion of the Body Snatchers* on our hands. Like seriously. I was actually concerned now. But he obviously didn't want to talk about it. Actually, he'd gone to a lot of trouble so he didn't have to talk about it. And if he was going to go to these extremes, then I guessed I should leave him alone.

But I didn't know how I felt about going sightseeing with him, especially all the way to Dublin since it was so far away. Not after yesterday, and especially since he wouldn't talk to me about any of it. And now this . . . What were we going to do in Dublin? Pretend we were on some trippy alternative reality tour with "Elle Woods" Darby? No, this was too weird. Seriously, I think he could give Elle a run for her *chipper* money right now. He probably had a pink-scented paper itinerary with a list of all the things we were going to do today. I was just waiting for it. Chipper didn't even begin to cover his mood. It shouldn't be allowed in the range of vocabulary when it came to Darby.

"Darby, are you sure you're—" I tried again.

But he just cut me off *again*. "You can't go home without seeing Dublin. It would be unfair to keep you in our little village the whole time," he continued as he set the eggs and bacon down in front of me. I half expected it to be in the shape of a smiley face. Before, I would have been giving him a hard time about the frilly apron he was wearing that must belong to Sinead. But now, I was too concerned about him to even make that joke.

Just then, Mak came hobbling into the kitchen. Probably sitting on the floor yesterday for all that intense puzzling had gotten to his joints. He stood beside me, glancing at my wide-open mouth and then letting his eyes travel to Darby. He leaned down to my ear slowly, like he might disturb the wildlife in front of us.

"What's going on here? Is June Cleaver for real? I've tried to get him to clean his dishes right after he uses them for the last five years. Doesn't matter how *manky* it gets here. It can be so dirty and it doesn't even begin to phase him. . . . This is—"

"Strange," I finished, and he nodded vigorously. Darby turned and looked at us. We froze mid-motion.

"Mak, sit. I made pancakes," Darby said brightly. Mak's eyes bugged out of his head. Mak tried to move toward him, looking like he was ready to pull him off to the side to talk to him. But Darby cut him off at the pass and walked him back to a kitchen chair and sat him down.

"We're going to Dublin today. Eyre hasn't been anywhere outside of our little village. Don't you think she'll enjoy it?" Darby asked rhetorically and Mak huffed out his reply.

"And how do you plan to get there, Darce? You can't bike there, and I don't think hijacking a tour bus is going to be too much *craic*. Not my idea of fun anyway."

Darby replied, "That's a great idea. A tour bus will give Eyre the true Irish tour experience."

"Ok, Darce. You've completely lost it . . . But I'm sure Sinead will let you take her car. I'll give her a call," Mak said in a confused voice.

Mak began to rise from his chair slowly. I could tell his arthritis smarted just as much as mine did in the morning. "Wait, Mak, what about your pancakes?" Darby asked with such seriousness that I almost burst out laughing.

"They'll be just as weird when I get back." Mak eyed me as he left.

I motioned for Darby to sit down beside me, but he just ignored the gesture and continued puttering around the kitchen, making himself busy with nothingness. "I wonder if we can get some gluten-free flour while we're in Dublin. Surely they have a place to get some *messages*. I wish there was a closer place for groceries here," he muttered under his breath. Okay, so he wasn't going to talk about anything of real substance. He was going to keep himself as busy as possible and make sure I had no way to talk about anything important with him. I never expected this from him. It was like he'd completely snapped.

My eyes wandered over to Mak, searching for a shred of normalcy in this wormhole I seemed to have fallen into today. I saw him pacing back and forth in the hallway as much as his bones would allow, not having yet warmed up for the day. He had turned into that lovesick teenager again. He'd obviously managed to ring Sinead. And then it dawned on me. If Darby wanted a distraction, then maybe he'd help me with my plan to bring them together. Maybe this alternative version of Darby would be good for something. He could channel all that perky perfection into something productive. Maybe now he'd actually agree to the idea. I was pretty sure as long as we weren't talking about him, he'd agree to anything right now.

I smiled at him for the first time today, and he looked back at me nervously, running a hand along the back of his hair as his head shifted back and forth, assessing me. Then Darby returned to his tasks in the kitchen. A few minutes later, Mak returned and quietly slipped into his chair as if he was trying to avoid waking a colicky infant. He turned to me and began quietly talking while Darby busied himself.

"I think an alternative to Dublin would be good. It's at least three hours away, Eyre," Mak said with concern.

"Three hours?" I exclaimed.

Darby turned around and looked at me, startled. He looked like a librarian who had just heard someone disrupting the peaceful silence. I raised my eyebrow in

THE IRISH FALL

response. Mak and I didn't make another move or sound until he turned back around. "Three hours?" I mouthed a whisper back to Mak.

"Yeah, that's a long time if something . . . goes wrong," he said, looking at Darby. "Hey, Darce . . . Sinead said she was happy to let you borrow her car for the day. How about taking Eyre to Galway? I think she'd enjoy that even more. You know everyone goes to Dublin. What's so great about it anyway? But *now* Galway . . . That's special. A place not everyone goes. It would be really *grand* for Eyre. Much more original for her."

Darby seemed to ponder this and then looked at me. "What do ya think, Eyre?" Darby asked me patiently.

"How far away is it?" I asked hurriedly. Mak kicked me under the table. *Right.* "Yes, I'd prefer that."

Darby just looked at us strangely. "It's much closer. Just about an hour and twenty minutes away. Maybe a little more with traffic . . ." He trailed off, looking suspiciously at us.

"Great, it's settled," Mak said adamantly.

Yay. Just me and R2D2 Darby. What could possibly go wrong?

I quickly learned a lot could go wrong, especially since this was going to be almost an hour and a half drive. I was thanking Mak for suggesting an alternative to Dublin, which would have been three painful hours trapped in a car filled with robotic tension. However, to my surprise, as soon as we got in the car, Darby found a music channel and filled the car with soul-warming Celtic sounds. I let their fiddles relax me and ease some of the tension with each swipe of their bows.

"What, no 'Galway Girl?'" I asked, pointing to the radio. He just laughed in response. I countered, "It's my favorite Ed Sheeran song."

"Well, good thing that Mak suggested Galway then. You should have said something. You'd make a perfect Galway girl." There was a heat that rose in his cheeks that I had already grown to miss, and then he quickly snapped his focus ahead as if reprimanding himself. *So that was it, was it?* He was going to completely retreat. Not only was he not going to talk about it, he was also not going to allow himself to have any attachment to me. My heart spasmed in grief.

I reached my hand over and slid it on his thigh. I wasn't testing out the waters, I was daring them to fight against me. Because truthfully, that blush and seeing him behind the wheel of Sinead's tiny, bright yellow, vintage Volkswagen Beetle were too much for me to handle. And I realized at that moment that he was still Darby. The Darby whom I'd fallen for so deeply. My thumb started rubbing tiny circles as if forcing him to call attention to its presence on him.

"Eyre." I couldn't help but notice his speed had picked up as he began to speak. Maybe this wasn't such a safe activity for us in our emotional limbo. But that was it. All he said. So I just left my hand there. He was going to have to push me away completely to get rid of me. I was shocked at this realization. I couldn't believe that I was willing to continue to put myself out there when he wasn't able to open up any further. But there was just something about him that let me do so without pause.

This was going to be a very long car ride if we didn't have anything to talk about. I allowed my hand to continue drawing a pattern at a steady rhythm. Finally, I said, "So what are we going to see today?" Darby seemed to let out this massive breath. Some of that intense tension left him, and the corded muscles in his forearms that had been clenching the steering wheel so tightly loosened. I breathed a sigh of relief too. We were able to talk for the rest of the car ride after that, slipping into companionable silences along the way when our conversation lulled.

Conversation had never been difficult for us; it had always flowed so easily. I guess I took that for granted. I sure was glad to have it back. But I noticed he never rested his hand on mine. Something Darby definitely would have done before. At least we were talking again. And even normally.

It had been a beautiful drive across the peaceful countryside. Darby had been right; there wasn't a bad place to walk, well, in our case, drive in Ireland. Darby parked the car and quickly came to my door, helping me out. The touch between us seemed to confuse my body—as if it didn't know whether to be sad or send up celebratory flares for his touch that it so greatly savored. Darby seemed to sense my confusion, but there wasn't a thing he could do about it. He was clearly lost. I wasn't even going to pretend to have a clue as to what was going on in his mind.

He started leading us toward a cathedral. On the drive, he'd gone over some of the places we could see and this one had stood out to me. It was definitely beautiful with its green copper dome and light gray stony exterior. We walked across a matching stone bridge toward the massive structure. I went to reach for Darby's hand but then pulled away as I took in his standoffish exterior. He looked at me quickly, and there was a flash of sadness on his face. I could tell he didn't really want to partake in any avoidance or withdrawal techniques, but I guess he couldn't handle the alternative.

As beautiful as the cathedral was inside—and believe me, it was stunning with its stained glass windows and high vaulted ceilings—I couldn't enjoy it. Darby seemed to take note of this, as well. And it made me disheartened that the magnificent interior of this church was being lost on me. I looked up to see angel mosaics surrounding the stained glass rotunda in the ceiling. Having been built in 1958, there was a new and contemporary feel to this gorgeous cathedral, even though it had been built in a medieval and Gothic-Roman style.

I was just looking up even more intently at the gorgeous sight, determined to will my brain to take in this extraordinary beauty, when I felt a hand take mine and slowly curl around it. I looked over to find Darby. He was staring up at the rotunda as well. I wasn't going to question his movement or what it meant. I was just going to be happy with this moment. That might be all I got from him now. I squeezed his hand back. As hurt as I was, I would not allow it to take him away from me. I would be his port in the storm if he allowed me.

I thought back to all he had done for me—especially in his response to my pain and the shared pieces of my soul. I surely could do this for him. If this was what he needed, then I could do that. It really was asking so very little. If he needed to not talk about it, then I could do that. I realized at that moment that whatever he needed me to be, I wanted to be for him. If I could provide him any relief, then it was worth it.

And that smile, the crooked, weak one, that shone back at me made it so worth it. His smile started to shine brighter the tighter I held on to our connection. He was starting to slowly return to me.

Darby stopped me on the bridge when we exited, pulling me to face him. "Thank you," he said quietly. His words barely reached me. I nodded as if to say "any time," but I was too scared to use words. I didn't want to break this spell. "No, really, Eyre, thank you," he said more loudly.

There seemed to be a serene understanding between us as we stood on the bridge over the waterway. He slid his hands down, resting them gently on my hips as our gaze locked on one another. It seemed we had reached a mutual understanding. He knew I wouldn't push any further and I knew I shouldn't. And we would leave it there. The rest we could explore as long as that was tucked safely away.

He seemed more surprised than relieved, but the long-held breath he let out made me realize I'd underestimated that. His shoulders let go of this massive stress, relaxing him so much that he seemed to lose a few inches in height. And I nestled into his chest, burying my head there while placing my ear right over his heart. His heartbeat was a sound I didn't think I'd get to hear again. I'd really thought I'd lost him. I thought I was securely on the outside of his fortress again and nothing terrified me more. I was so happy and relieved to have made it this far inside that impenetrable structure again. This was enough. I didn't need to push anymore. *I loved him,* and this was more than enough.

He held me tighter, as if he couldn't believe my decision and didn't want me to change my mind. "Come on, let's go see Galway the right way. I've got so much planned for you, my little Galway girl. And I'm not going to let anything ruin the day."

I knew, in fact, by "anything," he actually meant "anyone." And by "anyone," he meant himself.

His breath was warm by my ear, his accent soothing to my soul while slowing my mind's furious rhythm of thoughts. I looked up at him slowly and said, "I would love nothing more." And with more surprise than I'd ever seen cross his face, I kissed him passionately, letting that bridge and the beauty before us sweep me away.

THIRTY-SIX

Eyre

There was a spark of life back in Darby's eyes. One that was full of mischief, humor, and happiness that I had come to love as uniquely his. And it was like he was pulling a reverse *Ghost* on me. Patrick Swayze fading back into life instead of out of it. Darby reached over and took my hand with decreased hesitancy, and that alone made me grin.

"There's something I want to show you that I didn't mention in the car. It's kind of a surprise. It's just a short walk—about ten minutes away if you're up for it. We can get some take-away first if you're hungry."

I looked at him curiously, wondering what he could possibly have up those perfectly rolled sleeves. He seemed to guess as much.

"I promise, it's good. Actually, it's more of a sign that this was always where you were supposed to travel," he said, with more seriousness than I expected from him today.

Ok, now I have to know. "That sounds amazing, Darby," I replied.

As we walked through Galway, I took in the sights of the city. There was plenty of greenery and nature. I was falling in love with this Irish city, as well as my decision to open my heart back up to Darby. The world was better with an open heart, especially when it could invite a man such as him inside it. I smiled over at him as I took in the sounds of the city, the cool Irish breeze playing on the leaves of the trees as they caressed the grays on the stone buildings.

We came to a shiny black storefront with bright red lanterns. I looked at Darby with confusion as to what this was doing in a place like Galway.

"I know," he said as he looked at my skeptical face. "But they have really incredible sushi, and I was wracking my brain last night to think of something you could eat, and I figured–"

"Yes, sushi is one of the safest things for me to eat. I never order anything raw, but the rice is super easy to eat." He smiled at my words, proud he'd been able to figure out something like this for me.

"Ok, take-away it is, and then we'll go to your place," he said mysteriously.

"My place?" I asked.

"Oh, you'll see," he replied.

And I sure did. As we stood in front of Eyre Square, it became very clear what he had meant. I looked over at him and rolled my eyes with the biggest grin on my face. I couldn't even pull off feigned annoyance at him being so spot on.

We walked deeper into the square with our takeaway.

Eyre Square was a nature park designed to break up the concrete jungle of the city. There was plenty of seating built into the design of the park, creating scenic places for rest and relaxation. The whole area beckoned you to breathe and forget your worries for a while. It was the perfect escape.

At the entrance to the park, we were greeted by a free-standing stone entryway at the front of the square. I looked over at Darby, asking him for an explanation.

"It's the 'Browne Doorway.' They were a large trading family in the Renaissance. The doorway from their home was moved here. They dominated the trade in Galway," he said effortlessly. I really loved it when he spoke history to me.

Hungry for more, we moved over to a huge metal contemporary sculpture in the middle of a splash pad that stood close by. Its large, rust-colored metal sails loomed over us.

"It's the 'Hooker' sculpture," Darby said. "I kind of love that there's a sculpture like that in your park." He laughed his iconic melodic tune, provoking my eye roll, followed by a smile that he elicited way too often from me. "Don't worry, it's named after a ship," he teased. "Ok, so where should we eat? In front of the Hooker?"

I shook my head, knowing it was futile. I wandered further through the park, enjoying the greenery, gently pulling Darby along with me. I already missed the Irish countryside, so the surrounding greenery of the park was helping me to breathe easier. And I was also breathing easier now that I had my connection back with Darby. He'd imprinted himself on me in a way that could never be undone.

I found a seating area in the shaded shelter of a tree near

the end of the park. Darby sat down and laid our food bag on the stone wall, then reached out for me. "Hey," he said as his hands found my hips. It surprised me. Such a blatant contrast to how our morning had started. "I didn't get to start this morning off properly," he said as he pulled me to him.

"Oh really, it seemed like you started off this morning pretty well, Ms. Betty Crocker. Or do you prefer Paula Deen or Julia Childs?"

He cleared his throat. "Hmm, I deserved that," he said with a laugh. "Although, I do think those are some very smart, talented women."

"Well, Paula would have had the pancakes in the form of smiley faces, so I don't think you're quite there yet, sorry," I teased.

He laughed deeply. "Fair." His firm hands pulled me even closer to him. "But I really only need one thing for a good morning."

I looked at him. He was unbelievable. "Darby, you've already had that today," I said in disbelief.

"Yeah, well, we're starting our day over," he rationalized.

"Oh, are we?"

"Yeah," he said firmly. And there was something about him that gave me such hope that it sent a jolt of electricity right to my core. I took in his hopelessly handsome face and the quirky smile that was asking for a fresh start. I couldn't help but agree.

My heart started beating rapidly as I leaned down to him. With him sitting there, I realized I was in complete control; he was letting me come to him. He was just waiting on me, allowing me to decide if I wanted this. If I truly wanted to continue with what he had to offer. And, of course, I did. I was gone the moment he said "hey" and those calloused hands found my hips.

As I continued to bridge the gap, he stayed completely still, just looking at me with his head raised. It was doing things to me. I swallowed hard, taking in those emerald crystals that held so much promise, scanning down to his lips that could not be more inviting. I sighed, and his hands grabbed tighter onto me, as if I was torturing him. But still, he stayed motionless. I was shocked. I didn't think he had it in him.

But when I continued to hover above his lips, I could tell his willpower was gone. As soon as I began to kiss him, he pulled me down onto his lap, caressing and supporting my back. Showing me how he intended to start each and every one of his days with me.

"Hey," he said, so sweetly in greeting when I pulled back. Oh, this man undid me. I let out a sigh because words were going to be unavailable to me for a while.

When I didn't or couldn't say anything, he started to go back for more. I pushed him back slightly.

"Darby," I said breathlessly.

"Hmm?" he replied dazedly like he wasn't really thinking.

"Food . . . Galway . . . sightseeing," I managed.

"Hmmm?" he said, even more distractedly. I looked at him. "Fine," he replied. "But I don't see why this has to be an either-or situation."

I started laughing at the seriousness of his words. "While I have you here . . ."

"Yes?" he said coyly.

"Have you thought any more about the dance plan for Sinead and Mak?" I asked hopefully.

"Oye," he groaned. "You really picked your timing on that one. You could have anything you wanted right now. You know that, right? That's really what you want?"

I laughed. "Well, you're not a genie, and I don't think you're going to fix world hunger, so I'm going to go with that. I was always going to ask you today, I just thought while I had you pinned here . . . Plus, I'm sure there will be plenty of other *opportunities.*" I laughed, knowing he understood that I was just joking. I would never give affection in hopes of getting something in return.

I started to get up. "Oh no," he said, keeping me on his lap, "if we're going to discuss this, you're staying here."

I laughed at his words.

"Ok, fine," I said as he rubbed my back. "Have you thought any more about how to get Sinead and Mak together? Like the dance? Do you think it's possible?"

"I've been pretty preoccupied lately thinking about one dancer in particular," he replied.

"Darby . . ." I said seriously.

He groaned. "I just don't think it's going to work, Eyre. It's been over sixty years. I haven't even been able to talk to Mak about the situation. How are you going to get them to reconnect after all that time has passed?"

"I still think if I write a letter to each one of them expressing interest in a renewed connection, that could work. If you help me put in certain details, then maybe they'll buy it. We can come up with what we think they'd want to say to the other . . . enough to get them to think the other is finally willing to admit their romantic feelings. Get them to both drop their shields. Then the nostalgia of the dance should do the rest of the work for us," I finished.

"If I say yes, do I get a reward?" he asked.

"You're impossible." But he just continued to look at me coyly with raised brows. "Yes . . . it's called sushi," I remarked dryly.

But we both knew I couldn't resist him or those soft Irish lips that did things to me not only when they spoke but also when they were quietly expressing themselves.

THIRTY-SEVEN
Eyre

Sushi in Eyre Square couldn't have been more perfect. That is, once I finally convinced Darby to eat. I think he was so relieved to have a fresh start that he was having a little trouble believing we had actually gotten one.

We walked out of Eyre Square and wandered across the street. I stopped abruptly and halted Darby as I pointed in exuberance. "Look!" I said a little too enthusiastically.

He groaned deeply. "No, no, *no*. I forgot *that* pub was here."

"And you said Darcy was a British name. Obviously, you were wrong."

"Says the American against the Irishman," he said exasperatedly as he peered at the Darcy Bar sign staring at us from across the street. "I'm not wrong, it's obviously a tourist trap. And apparently, it works. Thought you were smarter than that. Like a moth to the flame, this one," he snickered, looking at me.

"Yes, and you better be glad that's true," I said and raised my eyebrows as I ran my eyes over his face. A smile spread across my face like kindling hit by a spark. I started heading over to the bar, but he grabbed my arm.

"No, we have way too much on the schedule. And be glad I don't drink anymore because you wouldn't have wanted to see what I'm like when I drink. *I promise.* Park Darby is nothing compared to *locked* Darby. You'd have a very hard time reining drunk me in."

"Oh, we would be a pair then. Inebriated Eyre laughs at everything," I said in embarrassment.

"Well, at least you'd have liked all my cheesy pickup lines. And I would have tried them *all* on you."

I couldn't help but laugh. "Oh, please go ahead and try them. Don't feel like you need alcohol for that."

"For you, I'll see what I can do." He winked, and I laughed. I could only imagine how truly awful they would be. I really liked that he didn't drink anymore since I couldn't drink with my health, either. Alcohol was an immediate trigger for exasperating my conditions.

I kept staring at the Victorian-looking Darcy's Bar and Hostel across the street from us. The exterior looked like something straight out of a Charles Dickens novel. *A Christmas Carol* had come to life. Darby, seeing my enthusiasm, relented and said we could walk down Forester Street. He said we could go to the main shopping area in Galway, which surprised me. I didn't think he would have any shopping left in him after our time together on Fischer Street in Doolin. However, I think he enjoyed it more than he let me know.

It was mostly pubs on the street, but I just enjoyed seeing the outside of the buildings, especially the ones with the bright cherry red façades. Darby led us to another area, getting a little lost on the way but never saying as much. However, I could tell we had taken a few unnecessary detours, but it just gave me more to see.

We reached High Street and I looked at Darby with eager excitement. The street was filled with people, charming shops, bustling activity, and colorful banners crisscrossed overhead between the stores.

"I don't know why I'm asking for round two of this," Darby joked. "The last shopping experience was embarrassing enough. Maybe I don't think you can do much more damage." He looked at me, then said, "Okay, maybe I don't think you can do too much here. I don't know anyone. *Give it a go*—take your best shot."

All I could do was chuckle at his words, but after yesterday, I knew I'd be taking it easy on him. He'd probably hate it if he knew my thoughts, but I felt that as much as he enjoyed our teasing banter, what he needed more right now was affection. Even if he was claiming otherwise.

"So you'll try something on?" I teased.

"No," he said quickly. "But I'd be more than happy to assist you."

I shoved him playfully. *Ah, there he was..* He was coming back in full force now. All the pixels were shining brightly into view. They'd fallen into place in the park, and now, standing here, I could see them all so clearly.

"Right," he started. "So this is the Latin Quarter. It's medieval in feel. The most well-known streets are High, Cross, and Quay Street. If you're good, I'll take you to all of them. And there's a really cool monument, the Spanish

Arch, near the end of the Quarter that I think you'd enjoy seeing."

"Oh, I'd like to see all of it," I replied.

"Yeah, I thought you would. This is the best way to get a sense of Galway. The street performers are almost always out. It reminds me of *Once*. And for some reason I always envision Ed Sheeran singing his 'Galway Girl' song on one of the street corners when I come here. It's just got such a great feel to the place. And the shops are really unique. High Street has a lot of knits and pottery, while Cross Street is filled with gift shops. I thought you might want to find something to take home to your friends and family. And Quay Street is the most iconic of them all. It has quirky, unique shops, which are iconically Irish. There are toy shops, vintage lace shops, print shops, and loads more. You'll absolutely love it."

"So, I guess I don't really understand it," I said as I looked around. "I mean, why 'Latin Quarter,' and why is it so medieval?"

"Galway is actually known as the 'City of Tribes' and was once a fishing village. It was conquered by the Anglo-Normans in the twelfth century, and they built defensive walls here in the thirteenth century to protect themselves from raids by the Irish clans. You can still see a lot of the original walls, including the Spanish Arch. That's why Galway has such a medieval feeling to it. The ruling class in Dublin once said there were more Spaniards than Irish in Galway. There was also a lot of trading with the Spaniards, and their ships docked close to the archway, so they called it the Spanish Arch."

As I listened to his words, I could hardly contain my

excitement as I looked at all the historic character and vibrant life surrounding us.

"Ok, enough history," Darby said, seeing my features, "let's go explore."

And I have to admit that this area was quickly becoming one of my favorite places in Ireland. The people were so kind, and the festive atmosphere was infectious. Darby was right: there were street performers scattered throughout, as well as artists set up amid the streets, painting and displaying their work for sale on easels. He said there would be even more performers later in the evening. I enjoyed the authentic Irish music so much; I couldn't wait to hear more. Most of all, I was glad that today was a "good" pain day and that my incision was finally feeling better, especially since there was quite a bit of walking involved. I was still relieved for the rest breaks in the stores, and if there was a bench nearby, Darby and I took a few moments to sit on one.

But when Darby stopped in front of a few fiddle players whose music particularly moved me, there was no way I was going to say no to his offer of a dance. His gesture surprised me to no end. When he'd turned to me and pulled me close with a questioning look on his face, I just looked up and nodded vigorously. A silent chuckle broke out on his handsome Irish face. I couldn't believe that he was willing to go for a second round after our first dance at the pub, but I was beyond ecstatic that he was willing to try. I also didn't really know what he was going to do since this was an up-tempo song and he wasn't even comfortable dancing to slow-tempo ones. But I was confident he would figure something out if his self-doubt didn't get in the way of him believing he could.

However, Darby was so happy today that he had no

problem keeping up with the fiddles and their quick, lively tempos, swaying and even effortlessly turning and twirling me. He hadn't forgotten anything he'd learned. And his Irish genes must be coming out naturally now because he was really good at it. Or maybe I was just extremely biased. As he pulled me back into him and held me tightly against his chest, I knew I had made the right decision earlier today. Darby was the perfect fit for me. All my curves and edges were meant to be resting against him, matched perfectly, just like all my wounds were innately understood by him. We didn't need to talk about them. I could feel our deep connection, how we understood one another and held each other in unmatched empathy.

When we finally made it to Quay Street, there was one shop in particular that stood out to me. It was brightly painted in strong red and black colors. The sign out front read, "Thomas Dillon Claddagh Gold, Est. 1750, Original Makers of the Claddagh Ring." Necklaces, rings, and other types of jewelry were displayed in the shop's window, and I was dying to see more inside the shop. I'd always been enamored with the Claddagh and wanted to learn more about it.

To my surprise, there was no reluctance from Darby. There was no hesitation from him today. He was happy to go into any store with me. I studied the different jewelry styles on the shelves and cases, awestruck by their beauty. The curves and lines of the Claddagh really touched my heart when I saw them. I gravitated toward the sterling silver necklaces, knowing they would make wonderful presents to take home. I was trying to decide on styles for each person when Darby said, "Do you know the story of the Claddagh?"

"I think so . . ." I responded.

He smiled and grabbed a sterling silver ring from the shelf and gently pulled it out of the box as if he was picking up someone's heart. It might as well have been mine, the way my heart reacted to him touching the Claddagh symbol. "Well . . ." he said as he looked at it. "There's a legend that a sailor named Richard Joyce set sail for the West Indies in the seventeenth century and was kidnapped by pirates and then sold into slavery. He was bought by a goldsmith. While working for his master, he slowly collected bits of gold specks to keep for himself, hoping to one day save enough to make a ring for his true love back home. He hoped if he could save enough gold pieces, maybe one day he would have a chance to propose to her. He could have been severely punished for collecting the gold specks for himself, but thankfully he didn't get caught. His master was so impressed by his duty and devotion to his craft that he offered the sailor half of his wealth and his daughter's hand in marriage. However, all the sailor wanted to do was to go home to his one true love, which the master finally allowed him to do."

I looked at Darby and then at the ring, unable to take my eyes off of it. I finally looked back at Darby, and he continued, "So if your heart is open, you wear the heart outward, and if it's taken, you wear it toward yourself so people know you've found true love."

He glanced back down at the ring and very slowly took my right hand. He slid the ring onto my fourth finger, facing it toward me as he held onto the ring box, saying as he did so, "The hands holding the heart mean friendship, the heart itself represents love, and the crown on top of the heart represents loyalty. Everything you want and need in a good relationship." His eyes penetrated me, and I froze. For some reason, Darby doing something like this—giving me a tangible symbol of our connection—made me freeze. All I could do was look at the ring on my finger. He was being so incredibly sweet, and I just stood there. *How ironic.* I guess the tables had turned.

The salesclerk, dapperly dressed in a dark gray suit, came over to help us. Maybe he saw this kind of thing happen a lot. The older gentleman began chattering away, but Darby just kept staring at me intensely. That was the thing about Darby—he was all heart and passion. There weren't half looks or stares from him. And as much as I loved him for it, right now, it was forcing me to feel—something I was afraid to do. Because I wasn't sure I was ready to leave my heart here. But the feelings inside me said they already knew that decision had been made a while ago.

"So just be careful," the older man concluded. "If you put the ring on your left hand, it means you're married. And if it faces outward, it means you're engaged. But the grand thing about having it on your right hand is that you can always move it over to your left hand when the time is right. A lot of people think the right hand means married in Europe, but that's only in some of the countries, not here in Ireland," he prattled on. "I'm sure the young man knows which hand he needs to put it on."

I almost laughed at his last statement, but that wasn't the problem. This gesture was huge for Darby. I'm sure the man had no idea how big of a deal this was for Darby. He probably was worried that I thought Darby was proposing to me from the way I was standing there and thought he needed to clearly explain between the ring being put on your right hand or left.

Darby spoke up. "Yes, I'd make sure she knew if I was doing that. And we'd need to come back for a much *grander* ring."

He turned toward the man and handed him the ring box, as if saying he'd take it. Darby and I both glanced down at the ring on my finger, and our eyes traveled along the same path up toward one another. I knew there was no way I could ever take this ring off. What was I going to do when I got back home? This was permanent. He was permanent. And it scared me. Trying to be with anyone else or find anyone else horrified me. The thought of living far away from him, or without him, absolutely devastated me, and this just solidified it.

"I love it. Thank you," I said, getting lost in those endless emerald hills.

"Ahhh." The clerk let out a loud sigh of relief. We both turned our heads to him, and he blushed, then began to busy himself. Darby just smiled, though.

I turned back to him and said, "Really, I would have been fine with a necklace."

"I wouldn't have," he returned. "It's all about the meaning here in Ireland. Now I'll always be with you."

THIRTY-EIGHT
Eyre

I somehow managed to pick myself off the floor after Darby's sweet gesture. We exited the shop and I decided that we definitely had done enough shopping for the day. We meandered through the rest of the streets and over to the edge of the Latin Quarter, finding the Spanish Arch. It was a massive archway in a medieval stone wall along the waterway. Much bigger than I had expected.

After exploring along it, we continued walking past the arch, and I looked out at the sparkling water of the harbor bay. A line of buildings came into view around the corner of the arch. They were tightly linked together, painted in bold primary colors with an assortment of paler, complementary hues. It was breathtakingly beautiful. But my conditions were telling me they'd had enough walking and excitement for one day. Out of nowhere, I breathed in sharply as a strong pain hit deeply inside my abdomen. My conditions were screaming for a break. And my incision, which had felt so much better this morning, was also yelling at me, telling me to stop.

I crumpled slightly and grabbed onto Darby. He reflexively went to support me, worry etched on his face. "I saw some steps going into the water by the Spanish Arch," he said quickly. "I bet we could sit on the sea wall there. I think I saw some other people sitting there."

I nodded to him gingerly. "This wave has to pass first, though," I said as I grabbed onto him tighter. He nodded, looking me over, and I could tell he was trying to figure out what he could do to help. There wasn't anything that could be done, though. Another wave shot through me. The Crohn's and endometriosis were playing off of one another, trying to see which one could outdo the other. Like two siblings fighting for their mother's attention.

I crumbled over, and for the first time, I leaned into someone and let them fully support me. My hands clenched tightly into fists while I tried to manage my breathing. When the pain got this bad, it was hard to breathe. It knocked the breath out of you each time a wave came.

"Eyre, tell me what to do."

"Purse . . . there's a Vera Bradley pill box . . . I need my Fioricet. It's a type of pain reliever and relaxer mixture. I can't have pain pills with the naltrexone or NSAIDs with my Crohn's so it's good that the migraine medicine helps for this as well."

"Ok, I didn't get any of those words. I don't even know what a 'Vera Bradley' is." He scrambled through my purse and found the tiny blue-patterned pill box. "All of these capsules look the same, Eyre," he said frantically.

"It's because they're compounded medications, Darby.

Look for the largest one. And while you're in my purse, can you get . . ." A wave ambushed me like pygmies coming after Gulliver, all spearing me at the same time in the weakest spots. "Can you get a heat relief patch too? It heats up when you pull it out of the packaging—the charcoal is heat activated in the air. It's like an on-the-go heating pad."

"Dear God, why do I feel like I'm most definitely going to screw this up and make you worse?" Worry colored his voice.

"Can't make me worse." I laughed through tears as I held onto him. He put the box in front of me and held up one pill in comparison to the others, and I nodded. He placed the pill in my mouth, and I swallowed it dry. Something that was extremely hard to do with my dry mouth–another gift from my conditions and not especially easy with my esophageal Crohn's, but one I could manage. I continued to cling to him. "But, Darby, you're going to have to get the pad out of the wrapping and take the sticker off, and if you could . . . stick it inside my pants . . . that would just be great. Just inside the top of my pants so it's against my abdomen. *Not my underwear.*"

"Right, I've never had a woman ask me to get inside her pants for that before," he said, trying to get me to laugh a little, which I did, but it only increased the pain.

"Ow, Darby. Hurry. Please just do it."

"Now, that I've heard before," he teased. I was laughing in full force. "Ok," he said after he had carefully placed the pad on the inside of my jeans, cautious not to go near anything else. I was so thankful for his care and the fact that I could trust him. "How long does this medicine take? And what was it exactly?" he questioned.

"Usually, it will start easing the pain in about fifteen minutes. And it's a mixture of medications: a relaxer, caffeine, and acetaminophen. It relaxes my gut and helps with the pain and inflammation. I take it to manage my migraines as well. I used to have antispasmodics, but they're like drinking water. I also have some Tummy Drops. They're sweet ginger drops that help with nausea and cramping."

"Right. I can get those as well . . ." He started digging back through my purse. "Should we go–"

"I can't move yet, Darby," I cut him off. "I won't be able to move until it starts working, sorry."

"Don't apologize. I just thought sitting down might help."

"Yes, it would, but I really can't moooooove–" The last word rang out as another pain tore through me like Jack Torrance's ax in *The Shining*.

"Ok, right," he said as he swiftly picked me up and began to carry me over to the steps by the Spanish Arch. He sat us both down gently on a step by the sea wall, facing us to look out. I remained in his lap as he held me with such tender care that it could only have come from Darby. The harbor breeze and Darby caressing me dulled the pain. I focused on the sparkling light dancing along the rippling waves of the bay. My eyes found the boats moored on the other side of the water, pictured against the uniform home fronts. Their sail posts stood bravely in the distance. The scenic beauty, as well as Darby's presence, calmed me while I waited for the medicine to take effect. I was incredibly thankful for the scenic distraction and the shelter this man's arms provided.

As the cramping and pain started to subside, I could enjoy my surroundings a little more. The glistening water really soothed my soul. We stayed like that for a while–two beings finally finding their safe harbor in one another. Two wounded beings moored in each other's arms and souls, molded into each other's curves and edges in perfect harmony. Our pain and vulnerability blended together on that sea wall as he held on to me like he was afraid to let go.

After a while, I fell asleep on his shoulder. When I woke up, he was still in the same position. Just studying me and the harbor like he didn't know how much longer he would have that opportunity. My lips curved upward on their own accord at the first sight of him. "Thank you, I feel much better," I said with a sleepy smile. "The medicine has a lot of caffeine in it for the migraines and to help the acetaminophen absorb better, but sometimes I'm so sick that the relaxer part knocks me out. I should be ok to do a few more things now."

Darby smiled weakly, hating the pain he'd just witnessed. "I'm glad, but we don't need to do anything else. We've had a great day. I can go get the car and pick you up here."

"No, I'm ok, really," I said. "If I stopped for the rest of the day every time something like this happened, then I'd never do anything. Sometimes that's what I have to do, but while the medicine is working, we can do a few more things. Then we should probably get home."

"If you're sure." He eyed me skeptically as he saw me eyeing the harbor. "We can come back to the harbor tonight– if you're up for it. We can look around a little and sit on a bench. It's really gorgeous at night with the harbor lighting." He paused, looking at me. "Um . . . I think I found a place you can eat when I did my research this morning, but we can skip it." He looked at his watch. "I wasn't going to say anything, but I did make reservations. It's the only thing I had planned today. I didn't want to take a chance on you not being able to eat anywhere. It's got a gluten-free menu. I thought reservations would be a good idea. But, like I said, we can skip it if you don't feel up to eating. I'll just give them a call."

"You googled gluten-free places?"

"I googled gluten-free places," he said with a smile.

"Darby–" I said, overcome by his sweetness, but he just took my hand. "Yes, I would love that," I finished and let him gather me up, which he had been doing since the day he had met me.

He led the way to the cutest little sidewalk cafe I've ever seen. Royal blue shutters and doors popped their colors against the light stone accompanied by the brightest, happy yellow accents. Darby asked if I preferred indoor or outdoor seating, and of course, I wanted to be outside to soak up as much atmosphere as possible. I couldn't get enough of Galway. I couldn't believe all the amazing places that were located so close to Darby's home. I knew we had only just begun to scratch the surface of all the wonderful sights around him. He seemed to sense as much too.

As we waited for our food–I was pleasantly surprised with the gluten-free menu–he began to entice me with future outings. "You know, there's so many other places to explore, plus there's so much more to do in Galway. I could have planned a whole week just seeing the sights here. I would have loved to take you to Dog Island or Kylemore Abbey. Those are great day trips. But you know there are so many coastal villages like Doolin that all have their own personality . . . and then there's Dublin, too. You need to come back. You haven't even begun to truly explore Ireland. Maybe you need to come back for a week at a time and pick a new spot to explore each trip. Or you could extend your stay . . ."

The problem was that I wanted to extend my stay indefinitely. I looked at the twinkle in his eyes. "Well, as long as I'm able to book the same tour guide, I may be enticed to do so . . . I think that could be an extremely attractive package. One I couldn't pass up." His smile melted every piece of me. There was no way I could collect myself to go anywhere. I was leaving parts of myself all over this country. A hologram of myself would be arriving back to the United States in a few days. Everything else was going to be staying here. I knew I had to get back, but as many times as I'd tried, I hadn't been able to book a return flight yet.

The most beautiful plate arrived at our table with the fish special, sweet potatoes, and vegetables. Even the food was decorated with character and creativity here. I just stared at the plate of food in disbelief. It was too pretty to eat.

"What? Is something wrong?" Darby asked.

"No, it's just all too perfect." And all I could do was look at him.

After we finished, Darby took us back to the harbor as promised since I was still feeling better. The sun was starting to set over the harbor. And my heart wasn't prepared for the burst of Irish color that was about to greet my eyes as the sun started dropping down on the horizon. I couldn't handle one more perfect thing about this day. My heart was already tugging on me, telling me it was time to press the eject button before I asked to switch this ring to the other hand

and stay with this man forever. *That wouldn't be needy, right?*

Darby walked us over to the catwalk on the opposite side of the Spanish Arch. We strolled down it, looking at the bold home fronts on the other side. It was an eclectic coastal grouping framed by the orange glow of the sunset coming alive in the sky. Darby wrapped his arm around my shoulders and pulled me toward him as we stopped, stunned by the beauty before us. I curled into him and rested my head on his shoulder as I watched the colors unfurl and explode in the sky. The lights in the harbor slowly turned on to meet the eventual darkness of the evening that was soon to come.

"Looks like it's putting on a show just for you, *Goldie*," Darby said. "I don't know how everywhere we go seems to get even better than the last with you. Guess that's just the beauty of being with you."

The colors started to expand with his words as if they were in agreement, bringing forth new ones for added emphasis. Everyone should have this. Everyone should have their Darby.

"I'm pretty sure the show is for *us*," I said, turning further toward him. "And I happen to think the charm is you, not me."

He squeezed me tighter, and we both knew the magic was very much the two of us together—and that was something you didn't throw away. That was something you stayed and fought for. That was something you didn't walk away from. Now the question was, what were we going to do about it?

THIRTY-NINE
Darby

This was a bad idea. I couldn't believe I'd let Eyre talk me into planning a "reunion" dance for Sinead and Mak. But our time together in Galway had been so precious, and she'd been so kind to me that I couldn't disappoint her. She hadn't expected anything from me. She'd just continued to stand by me and offer her heart to me unselfishly. There weren't any strings attached.

Eyre hadn't pried or asked me to share anything about Brock. So when she talked about her idea for getting Mak and Sinead together, I couldn't help but relent. I really would do anything for her. But I didn't know she'd been so determined to see the dance plan through. By the next day, she had Father Kelly and the whole village involved in planning the dance. And by the second day, the whole plan was set in motion. Now that was a small, close-knit community for you–it seemed everyone had a job to do and was more than willing to help. Yet, I'd never seen a group of people in Ireland motivated to move so quickly. These hopeless romantics really wanted it to happen. Usually, when you wanted something done here, it was slower than molasses dripping off a spoon. But when you hoped the village people would take it slow and easy . . . just blink, and it was done. The nosy *craics* were going to make sure it happened as quickly as possible. The Irish gossips were really showing off.

So now I found myself and Mak strolling down to the schoolhouse. He had a letter grasped tightly in his hand, and it reminded me of Jack hanging so tightly onto that door in *Titanic*. Jack's iconic words echoed through my head . . . "Never let go." Although, unlike Rose, I knew Mak wouldn't be letting go, and I was one hundred percent certain Sinead would be finding room for him on that bloody door. I also knew that was the scene that made me unable to watch romance movies anymore. I looked down; the letter in Mak's hand was getting obliterated in the wake of his nerves and sweaty palms. Eyre had decided to go with the hand-written letter in the form of a "quasi" invitation. She had deliberated over writing those letters for hours. I should know. She'd written them in my room while I much preferred to be doing other things . . . spoon-shaped activities. And while I tried to be of use with the way Sinead and Mak talked to one another and the expressions they used, I don't think I was much help on the romance front. But that was where Eyre excelled, and she had written two really beautiful letters. I guess we made a pretty good team after all.

The idea was to give each of them a letter that they would think the other one had sent, with a request at the end. A request to meet one another at the schoolhouse where they had first met all those years ago. And hopefully, they'd let each of us accompany them after we delivered the letter, so we could take them to the scene of that fateful dance years ago.

It wouldn't take them long to figure out what we had done once they arrived, but it would be long enough to get them to see that they had finally shown up for each other. That they both still had feelings for each other over fifty years later. And because Eyre was Eyre, the large classroom would be decorated with the original dance theme, which we managed to find out was "Fire and Ice." It couldn't be more fitting for Sinead and Mak. It described them perfectly. They were complete opposites, and their relationship seemed to fit the theme perfectly. I was just glad it wasn't star-crossed lovers. Otherwise, I think we really would have been doomed.

I was tasked with the job of getting Mak to the school and making sure he didn't back out while Eyre was supposed to bring Sinead. I never thought we'd get them both there, and I told her as much. We were dealing with two of the most stubborn people in the whole of Ireland. And that was saying something. I was trying to prepare Eyre for possible disappointment if her plan didn't work out.

However, what I wasn't prepared for was Eyre's plan to work out, but it was indeed pure magic. The entire village had banded together to create an enchantingly beautiful space for the unlucky lovers. Everyone involved in the plan truly loved Sinead and Mak, and I think they all wanted them together just as badly as we did. The village's homespun decorations perfectly recaptured the atmosphere of their dance from so many years ago. The kids in the village had even helped. I'm not sure what the original dance looked like, but this one felt absolutely perfect. And I'll never forget the moment when Eyre and Sinead turned toward us from the middle of the large classroom floor. The blue lighting the village people had hung from the ceiling in the center of the dark room created a kind of spotlight, bathing Sinead in an ethereal glow. She was the fire, and Mak was the ice, and there was something so palpable between them that it made you take a step back.

Mak's cool blue eyes slowly drifted over and found mine. His awestruck movements looked like stop-motion animation. It was one of the only times I'd seen fear in his eyes, and I believe one of the only times they had asked for my help. He was actually looking to me for guidance. Well, obviously, I was the last place anyone should look. But I loved Mak with all my heart, and I would do anything for him—would be whoever he needed me to be in this moment. Even if I had no idea how to be that person, I could at least try. I went with my heart for once and hoped it wasn't going to lead us both astray.

"You can do this, Mak." I looked at him firmly as I spoke. "You've always been able to do this, but for some reason, the timing wasn't supposed to be until now. But as you said to me the other day . . . The time is now."

He just looked at me blankly as if he wasn't mentally capable of processing my words. I grabbed his shoulder, looking at him as I spoke. "You love her. You've always loved her and only her. I know you've made yourself miserable all these years without her, and I don't know why. It's none of my business, nor anyone else's. That's between you and yourself . . . and Sinead. I don't know. What I do know is those demons aren't in this school. This whole village has fought them off for you tonight, so you could have this

THE IRISH FALL

moment with her. Everyone is here to support you and make sure you have a chance to get it right this time."

The stormy skies were starting to clear and give way to blue skies in his eyes. I was beginning to think we might have a chance now. "Darby . . ." he said with so much fear and hesitation–like he was going to back out now. *Oh no.*

"Mak . . ." I grabbed a hold of his shoulder and looked him straight in the eyes. "In your own words, grow a pair." And with that, I gave him a little shove.

I was fully aware that this was not the approach you would take with most people, but this was the type of relationship Mak and I had with each other. I knew from past experience that this was how Mak had shown me he cared about what was happening to me. As my little push forced him to take a few steps out onto the dance floor, I saw him look back at me and smile that wicked little smile of his. Some people needed a little push, and Mak needed a literal one. It was how he knew someone really cared about him and believed in him.

I widened my eyes at him as if asking, "Well? Any time now." Then his grin got even wider. He turned to face Sinead and never looked back again. Sinead's eyes never left his as he made his way over to her. He might as well have been climbing to the top of Mount Everest instead of half the length of a large classroom in the schoolhouse. When Mak finally reached Sinead, my eyes found Eyre. I wasn't going to wait over here in this desolate "no man's land" any longer. I wanted to be near Eyre and hear everything that was going to be said. I guess I wasn't any better than the other villagers. But if things went as I was hoping they would go, then this would be one of the biggest moments of our lives, and Mak's life would be forever changed.

I found Eyre and quietly wrapped an arm around her waist. She nestled into me and looked up at me with hopeful, eager eyes. I felt the exact same way. I think we were both actually holding our breaths. Because the look in Sinead and Mak's eyes as they stood on the dance floor was filled with such longing and hopeless love. Seriously, I thought they might steal a few of the Oscars away from *Titanic*. Those looks could have sunk them all. Even I, Mr. Numb Feelings, couldn't handle this. What was everyone else going to do if *I* felt this way? I even had goosebumps from their shared looks of love.

"I got your letter," Mak finally spoke as his eyes continued to permeate every inch of Sinead's being.

"I got yours–" Sinead said in a tiny voice. And they both looked over at Eyre, obviously knowing who sent them. *It was a really good guess.* Their gazes traveled back to one another slowly, meeting again.

"Ya showed," Mak said in disbelief.

"Of course I showed, Mak. There was never a time in my life when I wouldn't have come when asked," Sinead replied with strength in her voice. Shock registered on his face. Yet another emotion I wasn't used to seeing in this man. I was getting a colorful array of the emotional spectrum that was Mak today. One I'd never witnessed before. But I guess that was true love. You felt it all.

I saw Mak swallow hard, his blue eyes battling themselves and getting lost in their own raging seas. I could tell he was just trying to survive them, trying to survive the overwhelming war taking place inside himself. It seemed he couldn't decide what words to pick next. "Sinead . . . Rory was a truly terrible best friend to ask what he did of me. And I should have ignored him, but . . . I was scared. I've always been scared. I used it as an excuse. Of course, his family had been really kind to me and took me in like their own, providing me with a home. You know I didn't really have much of a family growing up. I didn't come from much. And if it wasn't for his family's kindness, then I'm not sure what my life would have been like during those years. There were plenty of nights I would have been home alone and hungry. And I probably would have been completely uneducated too. There were so many nights his ma worked with me when I couldn't learn what they were teaching in school because of my dyslexia. I couldn't even learn to read. So I did owe him a great debt. But my love . . ."

He looked at her, the words scaring him as they left his mouth. The look on her face sent a shock wave of adrenaline to my gut. It was a mixture of utter disbelief and pure unadulterated happiness as he continued, "Well, my love for you should have made me selfish enough to say he was on his own and to bloody throw it all aside and go for it whether it was right or not. All I wanted was you. All I had wanted was you for so long. But the fear . . . Now that was what reached up and strangled me. I did come from nothing, and I didn't think I was good enough for you. Not only because of that, but for so many other reasons. And I didn't even give those words—the ones that told you to ask Rory—permission to leave my mouth before they were out. And I knew by the look on your face how much I'd hurt ya and that I wasn't coming back from it. And I couldn't undo it. I was just frozen."

Sinead's face was soft and covered in shock. I, on the other hand, was having trouble remembering to breathe as I waited for her to speak. I think Eyre was as well. We probably should have been giving them their privacy—the whole village should have been, too—but I don't think the pair noticed anyone else. Finally . . . *finally* she spoke. It probably wasn't that long, but for a man in Mak's position, I'm sure it felt like a bloody century. "You loved me, Mak?" she asked breathlessly.

The question seriously gutted me. I can only imagine what it did to Mak.

"Yeah, Sinead, I loved ya," he said emphatically. "I loved ya then, every day after, every day in between, every day since, and today, standing before ya."

A tear rolled down her beautiful cheek, and he moved closer to her and gently wiped it away with his thumb, softly saying, "Please don't cry. I know I'm not exactly who anyone would particularly want to fall in love with 'em, but it ain't so bad—" he said with what humor he could manage.

"Mak . . ." she said hopelessly. "I thought . . . I thought all these years you just felt bad for me. That you'd been giving me those compliments because you felt sorry for me. That when I went to ask you to the dance, that was your way of politely declining and then . . . you never asked for anything after that. It seemed like you liked me, but you never did anything about it. So I told myself you obviously couldn't like me that much. And I decided you thought I just needed the self-esteem boost. Maybe you just always felt bad for me in that regard. I'd never had much self-esteem in that area. Actually, none at all. We excelled in our teasing relationship and banter, so that's what I thought we should continue.

Even as much as it hurt me to think... that we should just stay friends. Because I couldn't figure it out. And if you did like me, it didn't seem like I was worth putting yourself out there for and taking the risk. And my low self-esteem fed off of that."

She paused, looked at him, and began again, "Well... you know how well all my relationships have gone. You've always had my heart, Mak. I couldn't give it away to anyone else because it wasn't there to give. And they all knew it."

Mak looked at her deeply with those crystal blue eyes, his lips contorting upward. He closed any space between them and stood inches away from her. Their eyes locked completely. His lips parted, "I'm sorry."

"Why are you apologizing to me?" Sinead said.

"Because I've wasted over sixty years, Sinead."

"None of them have been wasted, Mak. And it's both our faults." She looked at him with the deepest desire.

"They have been wasted because I've just been waiting for you, Sinead, so I can finally start my life. It's been so empty without you."

"I've been right here, you fool," she said helplessly.

"But not in the way I've so desperately wanted," he returned with hopelessness.

"Then do something about it," Sinead said with a passionate demand.

He swallowed even harder. "Sinead O'Shea, I've loved you ever since the day I first saw you hit that cricket ball so horribly on the pitch. I've loved you ever since you made that first wickedly funny remark at my expense. I've loved you since you traded my pudding out for mud. I've loved you more every day since. Let me love you for real. *Please be with me.*"

More quiet tears were falling from her face. Mak spoke with more lightness now, "You're going to have to stop crying. It's making my worst fears come true." He said it in a teasing tone, but I could also tell he was worried.

"You're so daft, Mak. I'm completely in love with you. Those tears should be telling you that. I've been holding my love for you inside for so long that it's spilling out." She wiped tears away from her eyes. "But there is something I've wanted from you for a very long time. Ever since that first cricket match, if we're being honest. Even if I didn't really understand what I'd have been asking for at the time." She laughed.

He put his hands at her hips and pulled her into him. Her smile lit up every part of her being. "Oh, don't worry, I intend to give it to ya. I've imagined it every day since," Mak replied with a rough edge to his tone. She let out a little giggle as his hands moved to her neck, molding into her skin —the way they were always meant to be—and brought her face inches from his. But he stopped to look into her eyes. There seemed to be an understanding–almost a moment of reflection–as they took their time to fully savor the shift that was about to take place.

Then he brushed his lips against hers gently and began to kiss her. A languid flow to his movements as he took her, and their bodies moved with one another. The interplay between the two was so in sync you would never have known this was their first kiss.

I was surprised at how gentle Mak was with her. After sixty years, you would have thought he would have gone for it. That there would have been such an intense hunger it wouldn't have been appropriate for the onlookers in the gym to witness. But the gentleness in his touch even melted my Grinch-sized heart. I think it filled everyone's heart in the large classroom that night. Both of them did. Their love seemed so limitless. It had defied all the odds. And as they swayed to the music under the blue lighting, surrounded by all their pent-up emotions from nearly sixty years ago, they looked absolutely stunning. They were the stuff of romantic legends. Something to rival the Guinevere and Lancelot lovers of the world.

FORTY
Darby

Two souls who had been lost for so long had finally found the courage to reach out to each other, was what I had witnessed last night. Souls that had known they were always meant for each other but were too scared to admit it. They were too afraid of losing whatever part they had of the other, so they settled. They took what they could get and stayed quiet, burying a part of themselves for over fifty years. Perhaps letting the fear of rejection fester until there was not a shred of boldness left. Two beings that had lost their daring, their courage . . . their shine. Because without their other half, they'd drifted aimlessly through life.

I didn't want to be like that. I saw that clearly last night when Mak and Sinead had looked at each other, both holding a letter in their hand, with realization slowly dawning on each of them. I'd come to this revelation when they'd met on that makeshift dance floor. The one Father Kelly and Eyre, with the help of the villagers, had somehow managed to pull off, so they could unite these two lost souls.

THE IRISH FALL

And, in that moment, I saw what it was like when two soulmates found and accepted each other. I witnessed the beauty that came from being able to admit their love to one another, as well as to everyone else. That moment shined so brightly, especially because, for a lot of us, we couldn't even begin to attempt to relate to it. We didn't have any frame of reference. We'd never been so lucky. And there were no guarantees we ever would be.

But as I had allowed my eyes to wander over to Eyre, looking so beautiful in her satin green dress that I'd nervously bought and given to her, I realized that I was actually that lucky. I'd been given a special gift. And while most of the people in this room would kill for something like that, I was willing to squander it. Eyre had been brave and continued to share herself in Galway. She'd been affectionate and patient. She hadn't pushed at all while we'd been on our trip. Not once.

It was clear she was willing to accept me and take me just the way I was, warts and all. That she was willing to love whatever part of me I was willing to give her. And that she wasn't going to be greedy or resentful about it because that was true love. The purest form of love from the purest heart. But I didn't want her to settle for that. It angered me that she should have to. I was going to make sure that didn't happen. Because a soulmate meant giving your whole being, not just part of it. It wasn't called a part-mate, or a sometimes-mate, or half-mate. No, it was called a soulmate for a reason. You didn't get there by being afraid and not laying it all out there. *And who better to do that for than Eyre? Who better to trust than this woman whom I love? Yes, I love her. So deeply.*

And maybe there was a chance she would find a way to

stay, but I wasn't doing it for that reason. I knew that if she was going to remain here, she would stay for what we had right now. Giving her access to all parts of me wouldn't make the difference in her decision or increase the odds. I was doing this because she didn't deserve anything less. And if last night had taught me anything, I didn't want us to settle for less. Not when we'd been given something so incredibly rare.

I had decided to take Eyre back to the ferry boat today, as promised. After Father Kelly told her about my past, I had thought that I would avoid potential triggers even more stringently, but now I didn't want to worry about that. I was exhausted, and my weary heart was crying out to trust her–to finally take that plunge with someone. I wanted to give her the opportunity to continue to hold my heart with the care and love she had already given it every day since I'd met her. I was ready to take a risk with it, although with Eyre, it didn't feel like a risk at all.

I came down the stairs to a whole new sight and one that I couldn't have loved more. Perhaps this was my Grinch moment, and the kitchen my "Whoville," because this sight would make anyone's heart explode. Sinead and Mak were eating breakfast together at the kitchen table, sharing a newspaper, the comics tossed to the side, and a crossword laid out before them. Their heads were close to one another so they could whisper their thoughts about potential answers and be close to one another. Their handmade pottery mugs sat abandoned to the side as they sat lost in one another.

And I couldn't have been happier for them. I started to remember the words Mak spoke to me last night. Words that had already helped me to amass some more courage today.

He'd graciously taken time away from Sinead to talk with me on one of the most special nights of his life. But that was Mak. He truly had a heart of gold, just like Eyre, and I couldn't be more thankful for him. And it was then that I'd realized I'd had so many Irish blessings, those elusive pots of gold, all around me and I'd been too blind to see them.

Mak had pulled me aside and talked with me, checking in to see how things were going with Eyre. I think he wanted me to be as happy as he was now. Now that he knew he could do it, he wanted me to be able to do it, too. Maybe he hadn't thought it truly possible until that moment. One thing in particular stood out to me. He'd said, "It's worth it, Darby. I don't know why we've been so afraid. I'm not sure why we let fear conquer and take so much away from us for so long. Once you're on the other side, nothing will be able to take it away from you again. You just have to get there. Trust her heart and let it change your life. Let her in, Darby."

I stood there dazed as they both looked up at me in unison, apparently already so in sync. They must have felt my eyes on them. I hurried over to grab something from the refrigerator, so I could leave quickly and give them their privacy. I'd wait somewhere else until Eyre was ready. But Mak pulled out a chair beside him and insisted I sit down. I thought it was so generous at first, until I saw the look on their faces. *Uh-oh,* maybe them being together was going to work against me. The adorable grandparent factor had multiplied, and there was no way I would be fighting it. I was at their mercy, and they seemed to know it. Mak's fluffy eyebrows were moving upward like he knew they had me.

"Darce, Eyre seemed hesitant last night about where she might stand with you. And you're a lucky sod because it seems like she knows exactly how deep her feelings are for you." Mak's eyes bore into me.

"Yeah, I know I'm going–"

There was a creak on the stairs, and we all snapped our heads up toward it. Eyre must have woken and was coming downstairs. When she came into the kitchen, we were all quiet. I stood up as soon as she got close and pulled out a chair for her. She eyed me with a cock of her head, Lucky trailing behind her. The little rascal had totally thrown me over for greener pastures. Or, in this case, more beautiful ones. *Who can blame him?* Dogs were only colorblind, after all; they could still see everything else. But I had a feeling it was her disposition and personality that sold it for him.

I stiffly stood behind the chair I offered to Eyre, with both of my "grandparents" beaming at me, even if it was with a little disbelief at my gentlemanly manners. Okay, with a lot of disbelief. This really did feel like a *Darcy* thing to do. Maybe I should watch the bloody movie. But I preferred to read it, and that I had done–all last night. I hadn't slept again. Looking for any pearls of wisdom I may have missed because my heart definitely wasn't in it the first time. There was no way my wired thoughts would allow me enough calmness or serenity to even attempt sleep.

Eyre came over and kissed my cheek. "Thank you, Darby." I was almost startled at the name. For once in my life, I'd actually expected a "Darcy," but I loved that I was always going to be Darby to her, even if everyone was thinking something else.

After I made breakfast, we headed out for the ferry. Eyre had tried to get Sinead and Mak to go with us, but there was no way Mak was going to let that happen. He'd even quickly grabbed Sinead's hand when it seemed like she might be thinking about giving into Eyre's persistent invitations. Apparently, after last night, Eyre wanted a buffer with us. I wondered why. Maybe she saw in them what she never was going to get with me. Like looking into a crystal ball . . . or maybe she just wanted to see more of the couple. I honestly couldn't tell. But it started to make me nervous, nonetheless. Mak nodded at me as we went out the door and it helped to calm the sea of nerves raging inside of me.

Without many words, I lifted Eyre into the sidecar, and she gasped as if we hadn't done it so many times before. I just chuckled and enjoyed the vision of her seated there. This bike was going to be useless when she was gone. I wouldn't be able to use it without thinking of her, and I knew that meant I'd probably avoid it. I knew I was headed for heartbreak soon, like a rudder stuck on a ship with the fateful destination of a rocky shore.

Thankfully, I did a better job of steering than that analogy, and we arrived in one piece and boarded the ferry. Her excitement to be on the open Irish Sea was just as apparent as before. I was so proud of my homeland every time I saw it through her eyes. I loved the lens of her mind's eye. Loved to see the world through her viewfinder.

Inis Oírr island was only a short distance away—about fifteen minutes by ferry. As we leaned over the railing, I took it as my chance to also lean into Mak's words. I took in the smell of the gasoline on the sea breeze and my body's chilly and feverish response to it as extra encouragement that this was the right time.

I wrapped an arm gently around her, and pulled her closer to me as she angled her head upward. Wisps of hair had wrangled loose from her clip and flew around her soft complexion, the cerulean blue waters framing her against their background. My heart hoped more than anything that she would continue to be part of this scene and stay forever. She fit so perfectly.

"I'm so happy we're doing this, Darby." She smiled through her words. "The first ferry boat ride was wonderful. Thank you for taking me on another one."

My heart seriously spasmed at her words, each one tugging on it. "Eyre . . ." She looked at me with concern. I could tell she was worried I was going to have another attack. It gave me the encouragement I needed to speak next. "Eyre, could you show me those techniques you talked about?"

My throat tightened with worry, fully splaying my heart and vulnerabilities wide open before her. Just a hopeless man, standing beside the woman of his dreams, asking her to hold him with a care and love that there was no way he deserved. But there it was, finally. My heart was open for her to see. I was going to allow it to continue to stay open for her today, and hopefully every day she'd allow it to be.

The look that spread across her face was one I'll never forget. The most beautiful look I'd seen on her yet. "Of course, Darby. Nothing would make me happier." There was such love, comfort, and compassion mixed in those features, each a block with its own equal space on a cubism painting. One that would have made Pablo Picasso proud.

"Thank you," I managed to say as I pulled her a little tighter and felt her muscles relax. I hadn't known they'd been so rigid and stressed with worry, but now I knew the truth. Her body wasn't good at hiding secrets. I did really like that about her. For someone like me who was terrible at reading women, it was a crucial gift. And it was also a miracle that Eyre would open up to me and guide me with her words, so I wouldn't have to wander helplessly.

"I think 'Lazer Tapping' might be really helpful," she said with gentle care.

"Now, where am I going to find something like that in Doolin, Eyre?" I asked with mock seriousness, really hoping that what she was talking about did not actually involve a laser. She couldn't help but laugh at my question, and I smiled at the beautiful sound, even if I was starting to worry about this whole laser thing.

Eyre began to tell me all about "Lazer Tapping," a technique that focused on pressure points. She'd taken a seminar on it to help her dance students calm their nerves before performances. Apparently, you tapped a pressure point on your body until you started to feel an increased sense of calm, and then you moved on to the next one. She said it was good to have a list ready in your mind with the order of points you would go through so you didn't have to think about it before or during an attack.

Her hands fluttered gently over me as she talked about the technique, and then her warm fingers started tapping on different pressure points. It felt oddly good, but what felt even better was this level of intimacy—a level I'd never known. One I didn't think actually existed. I thought they made it up for the silver screen, only existing if two people were acting. But now, as we practiced together, I felt something stir in my heart. No, not stir, more like swell. As if the layers that had been shrouding my heart had all just been completely ripped away and Eyre had done it in the best way possible.

And I could tell as we stepped off the ferry that this is what she had needed from me. What she wanted so desperately from me, and nothing made me happier than the fact that I could give it to her. We took our first steps on Inis Oírr as new people; everything had shifted. It gave me courage that I could continue to let those layers fall away as she patiently waited to collect them and to be there for me when they revealed what lay beneath. I was so happy that someone thought I was worth the fight.

The island of Inis Oírr was truly breathtaking. I'd forgotten how much so. I hadn't been here since I was a lad when Mak had taken us here one summer day. And just like the memory of that glorious time from so long ago, the sun was out in full force, as was the wind. It felt like a holiday. Like a day at the beach. And truthfully, I think we were taking a holiday from ourselves, perhaps permanently, because we were leaving those shrouded versions of ourselves behind. That skin had been shed on the ferry floor.

There were a couple of ways to get around on the island: walking, biking, and even a donkey carriage. We decided on bikes, so we could cover more ground and it would be less strenuous for Eyre. The sun reflecting off the royal blue water all around us and lighting up the bright green grass made this an even more remarkable day. Eyre was mesmerized by the short stone walls that lined all the makeshift roads. I could tell she was completely lost in their charm. I could happily live here with her. For that matter, I could live anywhere with her.

The biggest attraction on the island was the Plassey shipwreck and that's where we headed first. I let Eyre take the lead and followed behind, feeling set free. This was the lightest I'd ever felt since childhood. I felt like a kid again and exploring this island with her really added to the wonderment; it felt like one of those experiences that you only got to live once when you were growing up.

We left our bikes against the rubble wall, and I reached for her hand. Her face was lit with wonder. I could tell she loved this.

Eyre laughed and said, "When I was little, I wanted to be a marine biologist or a deep-sea diver. Maybe in another life. I love the ocean. Being here is incredible." Her eyes soared with amazement as she took in a rusted-out ship that started to loom heavier and taller over us as we grew closer.

As I took in her wonderment, I explained, "This was actually used in *Father Ted*. It's a really popular Irish television show. We'll have to watch it together now." And she smiled at the future plans we made as if we had all the time in the world. Our heads instinctively trailed up to look at the battered side of the ship, hardly able to take in all that stood before us. "Do you want to go inside it?" I asked eagerly, but she was already nodding vigorously before I could even finish, and I couldn't help but laugh.

The ship was more like a rusted shell, and it felt like we were walking inside its rib cage. It was oddly nurturing. And all I could do was look at Eyre and know this feeling was not coming from this place. Eyre had created a home for me in herself. She'd created a safe place for me to be free and begin the work of accepting myself. And for the first time, I was going to allow myself the opportunity to explore that—to have that with her—because I trusted her. And then I leaned even further into Mak's words.

"Brock was so funny, Eyre. He was the goofiest kid. I was always having to get him out of some sort of mess, but I loved it. He made life so entertaining. He never really fit in, but I always appreciated that about him. He was different, and I loved it. I loved him. He really was like my little brother. You would have loved him, Eyre." My voice came out strangled at the end. The cool shade of the metal overhanging made me shiver. And at the mention of his name, I could see the ghosts of the past dancing amongst the ship carcass. Two little boys playing tag around the shipwreck, exploring every inch and pretending like they were pirates. Their souls danced around me like an old projector illuminating the film right in front of me.

Eyre's eyes widened with shock. I could tell she'd never expected this, and she wasn't prepared for it. What I'd said to her on the ferry was what she was hoping for. That I'd open up again with her. But strangely, her silence and look didn't scare me.

"When we lost Brock, I lost a large piece of myself. And then the guilt and anger made me lose the rest. It ravaged everything else. And there wasn't room for anything except punishment and a lot of self-hate. And then the flashbacks and the nightmares began at an unrelenting pace. And I couldn't let anyone in. I definitely couldn't let anyone help me—not even my parents. They even tried to get me to talk with someone, but I refused. I didn't think I deserved anyone's time or help. I didn't want to pull anyone into the mess that I'd made and rightly earned. People definitely didn't need to waste their time on me. Especially not Mak... but he's the only one that's ever gotten through–until you."

Her face twisted with so much empathy it gutted me. "I understand some parts of you, Eyre, because I've experienced those emotions, and I can empathize with the other parts because I've felt a wide range of terrible feelings. So much so that apathy was the only way to go. It was the only survival option. And that begs the question you asked me at the church: Do I have faith? But I think after all this, you can see why I don't. Whether it's right or wrong, I think you can see why. I'm really sorry about my response the other day, though. I never got a chance to apologize for walking away like that."

She began to open her mouth, but I started again. "Something changed for me when I met you. Miracles felt like they could happen. More than anything, a second chance seemed possible, which is a miracle in and of itself. And I know standing here that Brock would want me to take it. But that's as far as I've gotten. Because something had to bring you to me, and I can't fathom that it was the same force that ripped Brock away from me."

She looked at me with tears in her eyes that matched mine and opened her mouth several times to speak, only to quickly close her mouth. Eventually, some words wafted from her lips and onto the sea air. "I'm sure I would have loved him, Darby. He sounds amazing. And he would want you to take any opportunity that came your way. I didn't know him, but from what I've heard, I feel confident of that. I feel confident that he loved you. So very much." She looked at me with pain in her eyes. "As for the rest, I lost my faith,

Darby; I couldn't hang on to it. I'm not sure I'm the right person to . . . Losing my faith was the best thing that ever happened..."

My eyes opened so wide in surprise at her words that I couldn't contain them. She looked at me seriously now. "Because I hit my rock bottom and saw what a life without faith looks like. I'm pretty sure you got to see what that life looked like for me from that day at the cliffs too. But it brought me to you. And I got to glimpse what a life without faith has looked like for you as well. And Darby, I don't want to live that way anymore. I don't want either of us to have to live that way.

"I don't want to keep punishing myself by staying away from faith. I don't want to continue saying I'm not good enough, so I can't believe. That I'm not deserving of God's love. I think that we are guided through our faith, but I also believe we make our own choices. And that means there's suffering and bad things that happen in this world. And that means so many things are out of our control. But I do know, through faith, we can try to choose to work it for good—to do something with the fallout—so that the pain and suffering aren't for naught. Don't let Brock's life be for nothing. You living like this and punishing yourself is doing just that. And he would hate it. He would hate to see you living your life this way. I would know. I'm allowing my conditions to do the same thing to me."

I pulled her into me, anchoring myself to her port in the storm. "So, what do you suggest?" I questioned.

She looked up at me, searching. I couldn't believe she was looking at me—that she was still seeking shelter here. And there was a shift in those hazel eyes that I loved. I could see I'd done what she'd needed me to do all along. That our relationship was never going to be strong—never going to truly work—without me opening up to her in this way. And I trusted her. I trusted her with all of it.

Her lips parted and I eagerly waited for her words. "I suggest we rely on each other for strength and see if we can find the courage to believe again. Because I prayed last night, for the first time in a very long time, and today so many prayers were finally answered." And she looked at me as if I was one of them.

FORTY-ONE
Eyre

Chink chink. Slowly the sounds rang out in my mind and then they cascaded, all at once, like echoes of an avalanche. Somehow his walls had all crumbled faster than an unguarded medieval castle. It was a *Princess Bride* moment. This was it. An "as you wish" type of exchange. A moment you shared only with your true love. He'd completely let me in and handed his heart over– every part of him laying bare, with no conditions or status quo attached. No need to give anything in return; it was just a beautiful gesture all on its own.

And we'd stood there absorbing it, absorbing each other. Basking in the warmth and comfort of the arms of one another. There'd never been a place like this for me, and I immediately knew there never would be again. I'd never expected it, and I'd never imagined he'd let me in like this. I never would have thought he'd offer his whole heart–his raw soul–up to me in one swift, fragile gesture such as this. Under the exposed ribs of this ship, a carcass of security and comfort, I ironically felt the safest I'd ever been. Because I just received something I never thought I'd get from a man—let alone Darby. And it came exquisitely packaged. Zero strings. Zero expectations. Only pure intentions.

There was such a sorrowful beauty in the fact that we didn't know how much longer I had here, yet we clung to each other like we'd stay this way forever. And the exchange that had just occurred existed within the same sentiment. One built between two people that thought they belonged to each other.

The look in his mossy green eyes was almost pleading, and I'm sure mine echoed them in return. Our souls had overridden everything else, and they were asking to stay together. But neither of us uttered a word. Instead, our pragmatic brains took back over, allowing us not nearly enough time to savor that perfect moment. And suddenly, we spoke quietly at the same time about moving on to the next sight.

We both looked out and saw the lighthouse in the distance. It seemed to rest hesitantly at the next finger that jutted out into the ocean in the distance. We seemed reluctant to move from this spot, almost as if we left this moment, we wouldn't be able to access it again or the emotional progress we'd made. With grave hesitancy, we left the safety of the ship's interior and headed for our bikes.

We slowly pedaled to the lighthouse and enjoyed the views along the coast, but not quite in the same way as before. We seemed to have come out of that shipwreck somehow changed. We were different people now. When we came upon the navy blue and white lighthouse, we quickly realized it wasn't open to the public. While beautiful, it didn't have nearly the same effect as the shipwrecked ruins. *But how can anything after that experience?*

Darby turned to me quickly and I could see an idea taking shape as a new expression spread across his features. "I have an idea. Are you wearing the swimsuit we bought at the tourist shop underneath your clothes?"

"Yes, but I don't . . . I still don't know why you had me buy that—"

"Just follow me," Darby insisted, grinning mischievously.

He led us down the road a little ways before stopping in front of a grassy area where we left the bikes. I was very confused. But when we walked down a long trail that had been cut through the grass, and it became sandier as we went, I quickly realized that it led to a beach and the gorgeous aquamarine sea. It was exquisite.

The salty air whipped around me in tantalizing gusts, bringing back all the memories of the times I'd been to the beach throughout my life. The salty smell and the feel of the wind conjured up its own feelings as all my past memories of beach escapades rushed in. I felt at peace, and immediately my soul tethered itself to the calm of the sea. I closed my eyes instinctively to enjoy the feeling.

Darby's soft voice gently brought me back from the salty ether. "Ahh, so you do really love the sea. I can see that. Good to know. I didn't know if you enjoyed the beach or not, especially since you weren't crazy about my mention of a swimsuit this morning."

I slowly opened my eyes and let the nautical beauty greet me. "Well, I'm just not a fan of the cold, and I didn't see how we could possibly use our swimsuits here. I'm also

THE IRISH FALL

not a fan of you seeing me in this bright green swimsuit that was so obviously marketed to tourists."

He laughed with a deep sound that made my stomach flutter madly. He was laughing because the underwear pieces at the tourist shop weren't the only garments with sentiments written across the bum. No, of course my swimsuit bottoms had to say "Don't Touch My Lucky Charms," and there were shamrocks on the tiny bikini top to add to the whole aesthetic. I was seriously never traveling without luggage ever again. I'm pretty sure this was supposed to be a great gag gift that you brought back to someone at home, not an actual wear-out-to-the-Irish-beach and wear-in-the-freezing-water attire. I looked at Darby with a perturbed gaze, and he only laughed harder.

"I'm dying to see this . . . and you are a tourist, so it's perfect," he said with a quick raise of his eyebrows. "I may have even picked today's activities just so I had that opportunity." Then his face fell into seriousness. "But, Eyre, I know I love to *cod you*, but I really do think you're beautiful. I hope even though I like to joke around with you, that I've always been clear about that. There's no way you should be concerned about wearing a swimsuit around me." Then he returned to his usual joking manner. "I mean, I've been wracking my brain trying to figure out an activity that you might enjoy that required one. So *please* don't be concerned about that. It's the last thing I want you to worry about . . ." He trailed off. "Wait, is your incision going to be ok? I'm such a *dope* not to have thought about that."

I looked at him with burning cheeks. "Well, it's almost been a week, so I think it'll be fine, especially since I'm going to keep it covered. I used those waterproof bandages this morning." He eyed me, assessing the validity of my words. I reaffirmed, "Really, I will be."

He nodded and began removing his clothing to uncover his swimsuit. I was so lost in him that I hadn't even begun to take off any of my clothing. After seeing what was in front of me, I didn't think I wanted to start undressing, either. He was more than a little intimidating. The muscles that I knew must be hiding under all that clothing were no longer left to my imagination. The cool Irish weather meant that bulkier clothing, such as sweaters, were a requirement here. It also meant that I really didn't know quite how fit Darby truly was. *Nuh-huh. This was not going to happen.* My dancer's physique went out the window a while ago when I started teaching due to my pain and physical limitations. And now I had a wonderful scar on top of my sometimes swollen "endo belly" or bloated "Crohn's belly." It was probably the closest I was going to get to being pregnant or at least looking pregnant. But instead of babies, I was either giving birth to fibroids or throwing a party in my intestines. *Not quite the same.* And when they decided to flare at the same time, I seriously looked like I was having twins. Thank goodness today was not one of those days.

"Are you going to swim in your clothes?" He looked at me and laughed in a teasing manner. I continued to stare at him. *There's absolutely no way I'm ready for him to see all of these things. He's already seen too much.* His tone was even more joking as he said, "What, do you need me to help you out of them?" I just looked at him and shook my head with an eye roll, but he kept speaking. "What's going on? Clue me in on those thoughts."

"I'd rather not," I replied.

"Well, you just leave me to make an *eejit* of myself when you don't," he said quickly and continued speaking before I could respond, sensing my nervousness. "I'm sure the water will be cold at first, but it will be worth it. We don't get many days that are this sunny. I'm going to take our bags over to the sports rental hut and see if we can leave them there so we don't have to watch them. Then I'll get in first. I'll even turn my back until you get in if you'd prefer," Darby said most sincerely.

He began to turn to get the bags and something about the way he always put my comfort above everything else made my heart speed up. It made all those unkind thoughts in my head quiet down like a conductor issuing a command for silence. When I began taking all my layers off, he froze in mid-motion. There was a quick hesitation, like he wondered if he was supposed to turn around and walk off to give me my privacy, but then he just stayed in place with his eyes fixed on me, those greens creating a look that would forever take up residence in my memory.

He turned to get the bags after I'd finished and straightened. This thing was way too skimpy, especially when I was used to one-piece swimsuits. I reached out a hand to add my clothing to the bag he held. "That's not what I was looking at," he began as his eyes dismissed my outstretched hand of clothing, "I've never seen tourist merchandise look so good. I'm regretting all those times I've bashed it. We obviously need more," he said seriously.

"For the bag, Darby. Thank you," I said with a shake of my head. But he still didn't reach for them. Finally, he took my clothing and headed over to the small hut. When he returned, I had self-consciously folded my arms over my abdomen. He swiftly reached over to me and very gently took my arms from my stomach so that all of me was on display. He shook his head slowly at me, and my stomach twisted in anticipatory knots.

Gone was the overwhelming hesitancy he'd had before when he touched me. I could tell it was still difficult for him to take the initiative, but his desire won out. He continued to shake his head, and I could tell he wanted to speak, but it didn't matter—I knew what he was telling me without saying the words. He was saying I didn't need to do that. I didn't need to hide myself. The look in his eyes was telling me I was beautiful. And when he did actually utter the words, I didn't think I could handle them.

He took my hand and guided me to the water, all the while continuing to look at me instead of out at the ocean. As we slipped into the water, he had been right about one thing: it was really chilly. I certainly didn't adjust to the cold water as he did, so I really appreciated him allowing me to steal some of his body heat as he wrapped his arms around me in the cool ocean currents.

And the buoyancy of the salt water was especially nice as I floated in his arms and he kissed me softly. And his words, "I'm right here, I'm not going anywhere," that gently floated on the breeze weren't lost on me. Between the chilly kisses from the wind and the warm kisses from him, I thought I might never leave the sea again. Except for the small fact that it was really, *really* cold.

We finally left the water and found some large rocks to sit on at the end of the beach, not having thought to bring towels, and dried off our wet, goosebump-covered bodies in the sun. I was so glad for the sun's heat rays that warmed my chilly flesh. Although Darby's stares were still heating me up as well, really working up that blush of mine. It felt like we were about to have our own *From Here to Eternity* moment. I tried looking out to the sea as the sun sparkled across the rippling patterns of the waves when it got to be too much for me. But I could feel the presence of his gaze as intently as the sun, and honestly, it was just as enjoyable and welcomed, even if I didn't know what to do with it.

"So," Darby's voice broke through the serenity of the Irish waves, "there's a few options left for the rest of our time on the island."

"Ok, I'm listening," I said coyly. "My tour guide has yet to disappoint."

"Oh, I'm sure that's not true, but I appreciate you throwing me a bone." He laughed. "There is a spa–"

"What?! A spa . . . on the island? Really? What's it like? And what kind of services do they offer? Are there like special Irish techniques–"

"Somehow, I knew you were going to be this excited about it. I called this mornin' and talked with them, and they're not too busy today. The owner was nice and said she was sure she could fit you in. They do seaweed baths, hot stone massages, and even acupuncture. She said it's good for food intolerances, too, as well as different types of conditions–"

"Oh, Darby," I cut him off. "I have heard the spill before. I have tried pretty much everything. And I've heard it all. I actually have tried acupuncture for the migraines and terrible headaches I get with my condition. And actually, it was an extremely weird experience. They just kept sticking more needles into me to try and get it to work. I felt like a pincushion. I must have had at least a hundred needles in me and then my migraine started bouncing around like a ping-pong ball in my head. They removed the needles quickly and said that had never happened with anyone before. They didn't tell me to come back either," I said with a little laugh. Darby looked at me with wide eyes. "Yes, being a complicated case is super fun. But it may be different here. Ireland does seem to have a healing touch. I'd probably be willing to try it again here, sometime . . . maybe in the future."

His mouth widened in a smile at my word choice. "Ok, so maybe a seaweed bath for you or just skip it entirely?" he questioned.

"Oh no, you have to participate," I responded.

"No, I'm not a spa person. Do I seem like a spa person? You know me well enough to know that I don't belong there, right?"

"Seaweed wrap it is. We're already in our swimsuits," I said triumphantly. "Maybe even a hot stone massage too," I added. He groaned, knowing he wasn't going to win.

To my surprise, Darby really enjoyed the spa. He actually didn't take too much persuading. Although, I was beginning to think he'd do pretty much anything where I was concerned. I wasn't used to having this effect on a man. It was a strange feeling.

We stood outside the spa feeling relaxed and not only from our time there but from the whole day in general. The emotions we had unloaded, the trust we'd placed in one another, and the time we'd spent together in the comfort of the sea had eased our souls. I looked at Darby and then out to the island's shoreline where it met the sea. I didn't want to leave this place ... and he seemed to feel the same way.

"Let's not leave," he said slowly.

"But the last ferry is going to be leaving soon, isn't it?"

"Yeah, but there are places to stay here. There's a special one I hear people really like about five minutes from the ferry." He looked at me. "I think they stay busy during the high tourist season, but we could get lucky. What do you say? Want to miss the ferry with me?"

He was so adorable in the way he asked. And especially because it took everything in him to do so. I could tell he wasn't used to asking something like this and being spontaneously romantic was new to him–even if he was extremely good at it.

"Of course I do. And if they don't have room, then we're right at the ferry." The wild grin that came over his face was worth my response.

But Darby was going to make sure they had a room. He talked to the man at the front desk and poured on the friendly Darby charm. The man was more than happy to find a spot for a local to enjoy. And while he was confused by Darby's request for a twin room so that we could have two beds, he did find one. I guess the way we looked at each other didn't really convince the guy we knew what type of sleeping situation we were asking for. I thought it was really sweet and considerate of Darby, though.

I was surprised at how modern the inside of the hotel was. While there were light brown woods like Mak's house, there was a much more modern flare to the furniture and the overall feel of the hotel. The man led us to our room and left us to unpack. What we were supposed to unpack, I didn't know. Good thing basically everything I had brought with me to Ireland was pretty much already in my bag. I hadn't left much at the house except my heating pad, which I hoped I wouldn't miss too much. But when Darby showed me the heated blanket that he had eyed on the list of complimentary hotel amenities, I couldn't have loved this place any more. Ireland was too perfect for me, as was this man beside me.

Darby suggested dinner at the hotel after reading the restaurant's menu provided on our room's information pamphlet, which I was very happy about since I was surprisingly starving. He'd read they were famous for seafood, cheese, and fudge, and that was all it took to send my hunger over the edge. This island was seriously a haven and now this hotel seemed like a dream.

Good thing we'd packed a change of clothes since we'd worn our swimsuits and coverups here directly from the beach. And we'd made use of the showers at the spa and already changed. So we made our way down to the hotel's restaurant and bar. It was filled with as much color and character as the rest of Ireland. Different flags covered the ceiling and two-tone tiles accented the floor. The space was decorated with license plates from all over the world. It created a laid-back feel, and I was looking forward to just relaxing with Darby, who seemed to be equally enjoying this whole experience. It appeared he was relishing our time alone and not having to worry about any interruptions. I had to agree that it was nice, but I did miss Mak and his antics. I'd grown extremely fond of him.

The food was even more delicious than promised. I had the fresh fish–some of the best I'd ever tasted, which said a lot since I ate a tremendous amount of it on my special diet–and Darby, to my surprise, had the pizza. Yes, out of everything on the menu, this man had pizza. He had the palate of a child and somehow it made him more endearing to me. But I definitely ate healthy enough for the both of us, so I was glad someone else could eat that way. And somehow, the pizza made me feel more relaxed at this intimate dinner in our little seaside oasis. And I was most thankful for that fact.

As I stared at Darby across the table, I was beginning to realize why staying here on the island had been so important to him. It was like he wanted me to see how things could be. As if he wanted me to see what life with just him–without distractions such as Mak–could be like. Almost as if he wanted me to see what life could be like if I stayed. I tried to clear my head quickly, shaking it like trying to erase an etch-a-sketch. *No, there's no way . . . that couldn't possibly be right.* But the more I looked at him, the deeper I fell into those emerald green seas, the more it felt like that sentiment must be right. Because the look in them seemed to be unmistakable. It didn't just look like passion anymore, it looked like care . . . Like he really loved me.

There was no way that this man had truly fallen for me. It wasn't possible that he wanted me to stay, to build a life together. It just couldn't be true that he was secretly hoping for that outcome–that he was trying to show me what life could be like. And most of all, there was no way he was in love with me . . . in love with me enough to ask me to stay.

It had been hard enough for me to believe a man could want me in my state of health, with the damage that had been done and would continue to be done to my body. *But to have one love me enough to want a life with me? That just seemed like an impossibility.* And not just any man, but one that fully understood all the wreckage that was me.

My eyes scanned up to meet his eyes, the ones that had never faltered looking at me. There was something about that stare of Darby's. He was so uncertain in so many aspects of his life, but never in the way he looked at me, not from the moment I'd met him. And it anchored me. And those eyes–the look in them had always been wonderful, but the look in them now was unmistakable. Even I couldn't deny it.

Words were not exactly Darby's forté. The ones he said were really beautiful, but he didn't say many. It was like he was too scared of messing them up and maybe not brave enough to float them out into the world. So we walked back to our room in silence after dinner. I got ready for bed as best I could with what I had brought.

When I came out of the bathroom, he was at the window, staring out. He turned to me with a soft smile and said, "Which bed would you like?"

I loved how he never assumed anything and had insisted on two separate beds at the front desk, to make me more comfortable–to show me there wasn't any pressure or assumptions. Even though I didn't think Darby had ever been a separate bed kind of man in his life. But the longer I stared at Darby, the more I realized I really didn't have any intention of staying in that other bed away from him.

"Whichever bed you're in," I said without hesitation. The reaction on his face was probably the best one I'd seen yet.

"Oh, thank you," he breathed out a held breath. "It was

going to kill me to have you sleep in the other bed." I laughed at his words. "Get over here," he said in firm mock demand, and I happily complied. I allowed myself to be wrapped in his arms and the moonlight as we stood at the window looking out, rooting myself to his firm chest. I peered up into his eyes which looked like they were going to explode with happiness, such a stark contrast to the way they had looked when we first met.

His lips parted to speak, "This is why I love you so much."

My eyes widened in shock. I knew I had seen this emotion at dinner. I knew I'd witnessed this emotion so fully in his eyes that it didn't seem like it could be contained, but I didn't expect it to spill over. And if I was being honest, I'd seen it for a while now. And I'd even felt those words at the boat wreckage today. It was like I'd heard him speak them, because they were so clear in his eyes, in his being. But actually hearing them said, from this man who never uttered sentiments out loud, well, that was a whole other experience. One I wasn't sure I could handle. And maybe if it was just "I love you," that would be one thing, but he had to tack on "so much." Such an un-Darby-like thing to do. My heart was swelling against my ribcage as my stomach danced with nervous flutterings that were growing into a stampede.

I think my mouth had fallen open as I stood there in shock, but I wasn't the only one. Darby's eyes were probably wider than mine. He hadn't meant to say it. That much was obvious. The words just couldn't be quarantined. That was apparently how much he loved me. And now the stampede had taken off and trampled me. I couldn't keep up with the emotions I was feeling. I was never going to get my heart back from him now. I had just lost it. The organ I had thought was so useless to me was going to be staying with him forever, here in Ireland. Good thing I'd already come to the conclusion I didn't need it any longer.

It took a few minutes for the shock to turn into something else on his face: worry. Because I was just standing there, eyes still wide and throat still frozen, except for the occasional gulp. Our eyes were locked tighter than they'd ever been. I honestly thought with Darby that he'd never utter the words. That there would just be an unspoken understanding. I wasn't prepared for this.

"Uhhh . . ." he said quietly as his eyes searched mine, shifting back and forth rapidly. "Obviously, I couldn't keep that in any longer. Let's just go to bed and you can forget those words slipped out."

I bit my lip and shook my head. A little moan escaped me as I replied to the sweetness of his words. "No, I just need a minute."

"It's been more than a few minutes," he said with a laugh.

"Darby," I said with a look of incredulity. "I never thought you'd say those words to me. I just . . ." But that was all that was coming out as my heart raced away into the night. But he just stood there patiently with me, giving me what I needed. It took a brave man to do that. One that obviously loved me a lot. A whole lot. "Darby, I love you. You have no idea how much I love you." There was a desperation and a need for him to understand as I let go of everything for him.

He grinned like his face had been waiting to do this his

whole life. "Well, that would have been nice like ten minutes ago."

I made a mock annoyed sound. "Don't ruin it." Then I looked at him and kissed him with everything I had.

I awoke in Darby's arms—arms that had cuddled me as I drifted off to sleep. Ones that provided a loving, safe haven and the first ones that I honestly believed truly loved me. They provided the security only a true love could.

We had a wonderful breakfast in the hotel's sunroom, and then we took the ferry back to the mainland. It was difficult leaving the magical world of the island, but it was even more difficult leaving behind the fantasy of Darby and Eyre that existed there. The fantasy where those two souls could stay together for eternity. Because reality was starting to creep back slowly for me.

When we returned back to the cottage, we were met with the sight of Sinead and Mak on the sofa in front of the fireplace. Sinead's granddaughter was at the coffee table looking through the puzzle options, obviously bored. Perhaps they had run out of ways to entertain her already.

We were also met with an infuriated Mak. He popped up from the sofa like a jack-in-the-box, and his thickened Irish brogue flew at us. "Darce, have you never heard of a phone? Where in Hades have you been?"

I looked over at Darby, thoroughly confused because I had assumed he'd called Mak, but the look in his eyes said he'd clearly forgotten. There was a very large blush overtaking his face that told me he had been consumed with other thoughts that had totally overshadowed any logical thinking. Apparently, "I love you" had completely fried his brain.

"Mak, I am a grown man," Darby said in a perturbed tone.

"Yeah, well, you're something alright, that's for sure," Mak remarked.

"What does that mean?"

"You're important to me," Mak grumbled. "Did ya miss the ferry or what? Why am I asking ya? Of course ya missed the ferry. It's you." He rolled his eyes.

"No, I didn't miss the ferry. I asked Eyre to stay the night with me there." Mak's eyes widened at Darby. "If Eyre wasn't here, you wouldn't care if I called or not." Darby rolled his eyes.

"Now ya know that isn't true," Mak returned. "Well, as long as you didn't kidnap her or something."

"Really, you just have so much faith in me," Darby bantered back. But before they could continue their display of affection, Sinead's granddaughter, Saoirse, ran over to Darby.

"Darby! Darby!" she yelled and grabbed onto his leg. "Thank goodness you're here. They're so boring. They've been making googly eyes at each other all mornin'. I liked it better when they were fighting. Will you come play with me? You're the best at puzzles anyway. And will you make the voices for the puzzle pieces, *please*?"

What? There are puzzle piece voices? This I had to hear.

"I didn't get to hear any puzzle piece voices," I said to Darby and raised my eyebrows in a joking manner. His face looked at me sternly with a full-blown crimson taking over as if saying, *don't even start*. But he couldn't pull off that same mock firmness with me anymore. He'd gone completely soft on me. There was too much love in his eyes. And while I never wanted to lose that banter with him, I did love seeing this other side of him. It absolutely melted me. I knew he'd even do the puzzle piece voices for me since I'd asked. I could see it in his eyes.

Saoirse beamed. "Oh, yeah, you've got to hear 'em," she said as she dragged me over to the coffee table. Darby groaned, but his heart wasn't in it. He was way too happy to even pretend to be disgruntled. We sat on either side of Saoirse, giving each other looks over the top of her tiny head, and I have to say the puzzle piece voices did not disappoint. And the other thing that didn't disappoint was how incredible Darby was with kids. I would never have expected it, but I loved it. And as Sinead and Mak joined in on the fun and the banter, this eclectic family filled a void deep within me that I assumed would always be hollow. Their warm laughter filled me with so much love that I felt like I was brimming over with joy and happiness.

I saw so much brightness in the future when I looked at this man. He was going to do so many wonderful things in his life. The future seemed endless when it came to him. I really wished it looked the same for me. But as I sat there with him, he made me believe it could be for me as well.

FORTY-TWO
Darby

I could feel my time with Eyre dwindling further out of my control. A cruel little game fate was playing with me. And I hated it. Every day with her was better than the last; every day my heart opened up a little further as we grew even more connected, feeling tethered to her in ways that couldn't be undone.

It seemed Mak could sense it too. He could see this war raging inside me. One side fought to allow her completely in, while the other side was fearful of how much it was going to hurt when I lost her. I knew that she'd always be a part of me and that this time would always be imprinted on my heart, but having her leave was going to break me in a way I'd never imagined, and I was already gearing up for the anticipated impact. I didn't think calling and talking with her in America was going to be anywhere near enough, and while I wanted to keep our connection, I also didn't want to set myself up for failure. I would still want to know about every part of her day, but I knew that wouldn't be possible. It

THE IRISH FALL

couldn't be the same. And I didn't know if we should end communication and leave what we had as this beautiful and rare anomaly or if we should try to continue speaking. Maybe we could have a once-a-week recap. That way we wouldn't put any more pressure or expectations on ourselves.

It was going to be hard when she found someone else though–devastating. It was going to be excruciating to have to move into that "friend" territory, which would be the natural progression–or rather regression. And I didn't know if I could do it. Maybe I should just talk with her, but I didn't know how I could possibly ask her to stay and leave her whole life in America. I didn't know if it could ever be right to ask that of her. I would do whatever was best for her, but I was ready to fight for her if there was any possibility she wanted to be with me.

I had gotten up in the middle of the night to make some tea, and I guess Mak heard me. He'd scared the ever-living daylights out of me when he walked into the kitchen. And his outfit alarmed me even more. I'd never get over his bright red onesie pajamas and walking stick combination. You'd think he was the *Daidí na Nollag* in this "get up." Mak could very easily pass as retro Santa Claus. It even had some sort of butt flap thing on the back. *Seriously, where did he find his clothes?* I think he needed a new style other than "endearing old man" or maybe a new definition of "endearing."

"Mak, do you get pleasure out of giving me a heart attack?" I asked as I spilled hot water all over myself.

"It is fun." He shrugged nonchalantly and sat down at the kitchen table. "What's got you up having tea time at midnight? Couldn't you sleep?"

"I've not been sleeping at all lately." I sighed, getting out another cup for Mak and bringing the tea over.

"Eyre, huh?" But that was all Mak said. He'd been acting extra squirrelly recently when it came to her, even for him. There was suspicious activity going on.

"Mak, what is going on? There's something you're not telling me. Are you up to something?" I asked with a suspicious tone.

"Me?" Mak asked innocently. "No . . . I would never. I always mind my own business. Nothing's worse than an old busybody." He acted like he was most offended and crossed his arms.

I sat hunched over my tea at the table, staring at him.

He rolled his eyes. "Fine." He held up his hands, his cane in one. "It'll be best if I just show ya."

I looked at him, my eyes narrowing with suspicion, not liking where this was going. "It's the middle of the night, what could you possibly be showing me?"

"Just come on, you *goon*," he said as he got up from the table.

I didn't especially want to leave Eyre all alone in the house to wonder where we'd gone, but hopefully she was sound asleep. When Mak's bike stopped in front of his shop, I was actually stupefied and super annoyed. "Mak, have you gotten me down here to work? Just because I can't sleep doesn't mean I want to work so that I can–"

"No, Darce, this is not my rendition of counting sheep," he said sarcastically. "Just come on. I swear, why do you have to make everything so difficult."

"I get it from you," I said as I went inside the door that he held open so graciously. When he cut on the lights in the shop, they blinded my eyes. I still didn't understand what he could possibly want me to see. "Yeah, ok, Mak, I'm still seeing a lot of sheep to count."

"Darce, just give me a minute. I'm going to show ya. Seriously, you'd think *you* were the crotchety old man. Sometimes I wonder what Eyre sees in ya." I rolled my eyes. He whizzed past me, making extra good use of that cane. He made a beeline for the stairs in the back, and I followed him. I was really confused now.

"Ok, Mak, this isn't cute. What are you–" I started.

"Darce, can't you have any faith in me at all? I've been coming here every night while you've been asleep. I've been trying to do something nice and you're ruining it, ok? Now shut up."

Well, ok then. We reached the top of the stairs, and I was anxious to see what Mak could possibly have been doing here every night. I'd never been up here before. I'd just assumed it was storage, probably where he stored the humiliating work outfits and paraphernalia. But what I saw was a mostly cleared space. He'd obviously been cleaning it and making room for something.

"It was a huge mess," Mak began to explain. "I'd just junked everything up here. I've been trying to go through everything and clear it out. Then I've been trying to push what I needed to keep over to the side."

"Ok . . . So you've been itching for some spring cleaning. Who are you now, Martha Stewart?"

"Darce, you really are so daft. I want you to ask Eyre to stay," Mak said emphatically.

"You want her to live here? I think it would be weird for her to live at the shop, but maybe . . ."

"I'm going to stop claiming you as my own pretty soon," Mak said exasperatedly. "Darce, I want you to ask Eyre to stay and to offer this space to her as a dance studio. Give her a reason to stay. Paint her a picture of what her life could look like here. Ever since you told me about her job I've been thinking of ways she could use it here. I think there's plenty of people in the village and the surrounding areas that would love to take dance lessons–and their kids too. I don't know of any dance lessons offered anywhere in the area. It would be a wonderful addition to our village. There's nothing like it here. And I wanted her to be able to visualize what it could look like. But I'm obviously not in as good of shape as I thought because I've been having a hard time getting it cleared out. And I want it to be nice for her. She deserves the best." He looked at me sternly. "Darby, *you* deserve the best. Do you want her to stay?"

I stared at him in utter disbelief. I couldn't believe he'd done this for . . . for Eyre . . . and for me. Mak was an incredible human being, but this was . . . this was the nicest thing anyone had ever done for me. And I didn't deserve it. I had completely lost sight of his question.

"Darby?" he asked impatiently.

"Yes," I said emphatically. "I've never wanted anything more. I've never wanted anyone more. I was never going to ask her to stay, though. I didn't see how I could. I thought it was too selfish–"

"Darby, she's in love with you. Quite clearly. And it seems like she's also in love with this village. I think if you give her a reason to stay, it wouldn't be selfish, it would be romantic. Maybe exactly what she wants, what she needs. You should at least give her the option. If you don't ask someone, you take away their right to decide. Don't decide for her. She's a strong woman—she should be able to choose. I'm just worried about you if she decides not to stay. Only do it if you can handle her saying no, although I don't see that happening. I wouldn't have put all this work into it if I thought there was a good possibility of that. But, Darby, I don't want it to destroy you if she says no, because it is a big ask."

"I can't ask her to give up her whole life and move across an ocean to be with a man she's known for two weeks. To give up what traction she's worked so hard to gain in her career back home so she can maybe open up a business here that *might* make it. That's not just a big ask. That's an impossible ask. I'll look like a total jerk."

"Darby. Love asks big things. And I think you're going to find that the answer is yes, and not out of obligation or pressure, but out of a true want and desire." He paused to look at me. "That Irish saying that I'm always telling you— 'Your feet will take you where your heart is'—don't you believe it now? Don't you think this could be what was meant for Eyre? What she needed so desperately that day at the cliffs? Perhaps what was designed? Now the question is, where are your feet taking you?"

There was no question . . . to her. It would always be to her. I was going to ask big. And if I got my heart broken, then it was always destined to be that way because watching her leave was going to destroy me anyway.

"Ok, Mak, what do you need me to do? I've got the rest of the night before she wakes up. Whatever it takes, just tell me what to do."

FORTY-THREE
Eyre

Darby had been strangely off all day, but then again, I had been somewhat quiet myself. I knew I had to go back home soon. I had gone online this morning to find plane tickets and a piece of my soul died just looking at the flights. And as I sat there, I even thought about purchasing two tickets, but what would Darby do in America? There was absolutely nothing there for him. But my family and my students had become my whole world back home and it would be impossible to leave them. As far as other areas of my life, there really wasn't anything else there for me. My life had pretty much crumbled in the last couple of years.

Darby had taken me to see a few more sights today. He was continuing to be the best Irish host, but everything lacked that sheen of the last few days. The glorious Irish countryside that had engulfed me with its luscious hues and soft nature sounds couldn't comfort me today. The blanket of pastoral care didn't feel quite the same wrapped around me.

Something just felt off. Darby seemed anxious and out of sorts, and I was too preoccupied in my own head to figure out the cause.

We'd had a quiet dinner at the pub, basking in the affection that radiated between Sinead and Mak. There was a tender love blooming between them and it was intoxicating to watch. In their stage of life, to see something so new develop and take them both by surprise was truly a wonder to see. They both seemed swept up in it and determined to nurture this gift they'd been given. I could tell by the sweet yet heated stares that they weren't going to take it for granted and that neither wanted to mess it up this time.

I was more than content to rest and watch this love unfold, but Darby seemed quite anxious. His leg kept tapping incessantly under the bar top in the far corner where we sat. We'd claimed the most secluded part of the counter as "our spot." Every time I turned to him and looked down, he stopped; but as soon as my gaze left, the nervous tick came right back. Maybe Mak noticed his distress, or maybe he just needed Darby's help, because he came over from the center of the bar. I was surprised he could break himself away from Sinead's fiery attraction.

"Darce," he said, extending a key in his hand. "Will you go and make sure that shipment came in alright at the shop today? I don't trust Teagan." Darby just stared at the key and Mak's outstretched arm. "Darce?" No reply. "Darce, I really would like to stay with Sinead."

I quickly grabbed the key from Mak, looking at Darby strangely. "Of course, Mak, please stay with her," I said. "We'd be more than happy to check on it."

"Thanks, Eyre," he said to me and then glared at Darby.

I couldn't figure out what was going on, but it seemed like it was more than just this key. "Darce, I really need ya to go now," Mak said sternly. But Darby just sat still, like those unmoving cliffs outside. Mak rolled his eyes and walked away.

"Come on, Darby. Let's go, so we can relieve Mak's mind." But as I said the words, I noticed how pale he looked. I was worried he was about to have an attack, but none of the other signs were there. I stood up from my stool and was just about to get seriously concerned about him when he stood up too. He grabbed the key from me and swiftly led me out the door, a determination in his step now. I guess he was upset that Mak had asked us to do this. It all seemed really odd to me.

When we reached the shop, Darby turned on the lights and stood staring at me from the doorway. I couldn't help but remember the first time I'd been in the shop. The way he'd looked at me so curiously and affectionately too. The way he'd protected me and hung on to me, even though he knew nothing about me. And a smile washed through me.

His expression now was just as unreadable, and it really drove me mad. I also didn't know how long he was going to stand there and stare at me like this. "Darby? What's going on? Are you going to check the shipment, or what?"

He slowly made his way over to me, not answering my question or saying a word. That slow walk with the little Irish lilt made me feel everything, just like the first day I'd met him. His muscular body moved in such a determined way toward me as his shoulders swayed from his steadfast movement.

He met me with that "Darby" passion that I hadn't

believed existed until I met him. That passion I'd resigned was made up in fairy tales to keep women, like me, from giving up completely on love. His hand wrapped around the back of my neck, making my stomach dance with shockwaves of nerves. And my body immediately lifted up to him so that he had total access to me. His lips came crashing down on mine with such a fierce desire and tenderness all wrapped into one. I was feeling too many emotions all at once, and it made me a little dizzy. *This is it isn't it? This is an "I'll be seeing you, kid" kind of kiss, isn't it?* He was preparing for me to leave. He must have realized I was looking up flights today. There was so much unspoken want in his kiss that couldn't be fulfilled, and it made me open up to him even more.

There was no way this could be goodbye. It literally felt like our souls were intertwining in this moment. Telling us that they were going to stay together from here on out, with or without our permission. Whether we liked it or not, we had just lost them together here.

He pulled back, cradling my head and angling it up to him. I guess he could see the glassy sheen in my eyes because he said, "I want to show you something." As if he knew I needed a break and couldn't handle any more. I just nodded slightly, as much as my overworked body would allow. He carefully guided me to a door in the back that I hadn't known existed. And he took my hand to start climbing up the stairs. I just stared at him. My feet were not moving. My stomach felt like it was at the top of a very large building, about to plummet into a free fall to its demise. I didn't know if I was prepared for what was coming next. *What if this is some sort of special way to say goodbye?* I couldn't do it. I wasn't ready.

He had looked so horrified at the pub. Maybe he couldn't do it, either.

He nodded to me gently, and the sparks ignited in my belly. I willed my feet forward, latching on tighter to his hand. When we reached the top of the stairs, all I saw was this huge empty space. I honestly hadn't even realized that this was a two-story building. That's how observant I was or how distracting Darby could be. It wasn't what I expected at all. I thought Mak would have had the place completely cluttered, but it was spotless. The wood floors practically gleamed, and the bay of windows streamed moonlight, creating a gossamer glow. Darby hadn't cut on any lights, allowing the nighttime light to create a hypnotic world.

But I could see clearly in the moonlight, especially the only thing that was in the center of the desolate floor: a Candy Land game. *Oh, this truly is goodbye.* He was going to let us have one really nice night together so we could find a way to part. Maybe he knew how hard a time I was having with the thought of going back to the States, and he was trying to make it easier on me. Today had been kind of awkward after all, like we both knew it was coming. Maybe this was why. I closed my eyes, but when I opened them, he had turned on a small lamp. And all I could do was try to swallow back the monumental anxiety in my throat.

"What do you think?" he asked me, looking around. That was not the question I had expected.

"I think I don't see any shipments here. You're going to have to tell Mak."

He laughed his soul-shaking laugh and my nerves kicked up, spinning like a twister running through me. "No, there's not any shipment, Eyre," he confessed. "What do you think about this space?"

"Oh, it's really nice. I didn't expect Mak to have such a nice space up here. I expected him to be a bit of a hoarder." I laughed shamelessly, expelling what nervous energy I could. I looked around the dimly lit space that was now cast in the warm glow of lamplight mixed with moonlight, and it seemed magical. Leave it to Ireland to have storage spaces that seemed enchanting.

Darby kept his distance from me, staring at me again. He was shifting his weight back and forth from each foot, like he did so often when he was nervous. A flash of anxiety, so undeniable, shot through me with such forceful demand that I thought I was going to have to sit down. "Well, it was pretty horrible," he began again. "I don't think pack rats would have even lived here, but he's been spending nights going through it, and I helped him finish and clean it."

"Oh, well that was nice of you. I'm sure he can find something nice to–"

But Darby was coming toward me again, his pace picking up. He stopped short of me, only inches away. "Eyre," he breathed. "Don't you think this could be a nice studio? I mean, it's got all this space. All this potential." He started looking around again as if he could see it. "I know your dreams could never have included someone like me, but I'm hoping they could now. And this space–"

"Darby, what kind of studio?" I asked barely above a whisper. Now I was the one to gulp. I was so thoroughly confused that I was hardly able to meet his green eyes. The same ones that made the emerald isles lose every time. Nothing could compete with them. There was such a sincere want in them. A hope that burned hotter than anything I'd ever seen before. "What kind of studio?" I repeated, needing to know now more than ever.

"Eyre, I love you, I–" He closed his eyes, barely able to get the words out. "Will you please just open the Candy Land box?"

My heart started galloping so wildly, I didn't think I was going to be able to move. I just looked at him.

"Eyre . . ." he repeated, a desperation in his voice. I silently made my way over to the box, looking back at Darby every so often. I slowly bent down to the floor, my eyes never breaking from his, and reached out for the lid of the box. When I broke eye contact with Darby, I noticed my hands were shaking. I slowly lifted the lid off the box and saw a key lying on top of the board game. The key that Sinead had said no one could possibly find was lying right there in front of me. Because while I was assuming it was a key to this studio, to me it was a key to so much more. No one had ever been given access to this part of Darby. No one had ever seen him this vulnerable before, and he certainly had never put himself out there like this for anyone. And here it was, the key she'd talked about. Both literally and figuratively lying at my feet. And there was a note attached to it that read, "Will you stay with me?"

Epilogue

2 MONTHS LATER | DARBY

"If you folks will turn your attention to your right now, you'll see that we're getting closer to those beautiful Cliffs of Moher. I forget . . . how many feet tall are those gorgeous beauties?" I turned to face my stunning co-guide and also the beautiful woman who had become part of my soul. My smile was so large I almost felt it reflect back to me off of her bright green uniform. I loved taking in the sight of her every day, and I have to say, the company apparel had never looked so good. She had finally gotten her wish of matching uniforms. Although, I knew for sure she'd been joking because as soon as Mak had mentioned it, her eyes had bugged out of her head. Now she knew how I felt.

Mak was monetizing our love the best he could, milking it for all it was worth. And I had to admit he was a crafty little bugger because we were the most popular tour around now. Word quickly spread and everyone wanted to take a tour with the couple who had fallen in love on that very same tour route. They wanted the classic Irish romance package with the legends themselves: Darcy and Eyre, or as Mak had coined it, "A Fated Love Tour." It was required that we tell how we met. But much to his chagrin and much to our amusement, we changed it every time. Our story was not for sale. That was just for us.

I had to admit, though, there was something I absolutely loved about Mak's latest ploy. The first was the fact that I got to have her by my side and that PDA was highly encouraged. I was glad because I couldn't keep my hands off of her. Not that it being frowned upon would have stopped me. They were going to get a show one way or the other. It was just to my advantage that they wanted this one.

The second was that I now understood why Eyre had loved my uniform so much. The female leprechaun tee and other matching attire that Mak had customized for Eyre made every day a good day for me, especially due to the fact that she did not want to wear it. But Eyre was a good sport about it all in the end. I think she loved helping Mak as much as I did, and we were both thrilled that the business was doing as well as it was these days. He couldn't keep enough tours open. But as always, he made sure our bus was filled with all the single older ladies in true Darby style. And Eyre absolutely loved it, so who was I to complain? I loved anything that made her happy. And my favorite thing was that she refused to call me Darcy, even when Mak begged, telling her it was just for the fun of the tour. She had always refused, saying I was *her* Mr. Darby. A lot of the women were hard of hearing on my tour anyway, and it was close enough, so it didn't detract. But for me, it meant the world. I was someone's Mr. Darby.

I leaned over and kissed her, and the ladies on the bus broke out into a chorus of *aww*. This was a reaction I never thought I'd get. I'm glad I did, though, because it reminded me to keep my PDA in check. Especially as I hugged her tightly in the bright green shamrock tee I loved to see her wear, and then her leprechaun hat fell off as I dipped her back. She giggled in a low tone that made me sizzle inside as the ridiculous hat landed on the floor.

"Mr. Darby," she said playfully.

I had to take advantage of the time we were together on these tours. It was special. She wasn't always able to come on the tours with me. And I never took for granted the times when she could. There were times when her conditions made it too difficult for her to participate, and then there were days when she was busy with her own business. After that night when I'd shown her the space that could be her dance studio, we'd continued to work on it together. I'd made all the furniture for the space, and she'd been able to design the beams, practice stage area, and seating just as she liked it. Being able to do that for her had healed a part of my heart. One I had never known could possibly be repaired. They say the heart isn't an organ that can rejuvenate or repair itself, but I was starting to think otherwise. Maybe it was just that she was slowly strengthening my heartstrings and allowing my heart to be able to pump more life into itself. Whatever the reason, she had performed a miracle, and working with her on the dance studio had only helped to heal me even more. Because I saw her come more alive as her dream was slowly breathed back to life. It was as if both her body and soul were resuscitated together. And I wasn't someone who easily cried, but it actually brought tears to my eyes.

I'll never forget how nervous she was for the grand opening. She was convinced no one would come, but Mak and I had made sure that wouldn't happen. Sinead's granddaughter was the first one through the door. Watching Eyre sign her up for classes, take her measurements for dancewear, and show her some beginning dance steps to stoke her excitement, made my heart feel like it was going to burst from being so full. I'd never felt that feeling before.

And I knew, at that moment, we were going to be alright. That if this was the family we were meant to have, we would be blessed. We would treat these children as our own and try to make a difference in their lives as much as we could. But I also knew if she wanted to adopt one day, that nothing would make me happier. That seeing her as a mom in either capacity would be exactly how it was intended to be and would give me the greatest happiness. And I would do whatever I needed to do to make that happen. I would be the man she needed me to be and do whatever I needed to do to give her the support she deserved to make that happen. I knew with her conditions that having a child would mean she would need more support, that there would be bad days for her when she physically couldn't do and give what she wanted. And I would be there to make sure she and the child–our child–had the support they needed. In that moment, I knew I wanted nothing more than to be able to give her that stability. It was a realization I never thought I'd have.

And just when I thought life couldn't get better, something happened. Because Eyre, so very loved by her students, started telling them about the furniture I made, they soon began asking to see my work and if they could buy some of the pieces. I was more than reluctant at first and said no. But with some gentle "Eyre persuasion," I finally came around and started opening up the shed in the back of the house. The one that had been closed off for so long. The tomb to my true self that I had so expertly walled off for so long was finally opening itself up to greet the daylight. Pretty soon, most of the furniture pieces were gone. Surrounding towns and tourists had even started coming to the shed to shop.

And that's when Eyre had started looking around Doolin for a shop for my pieces. It was only a matter of time before she found space to rent in a local artisan store, hoping one day we would buy a shop to call our very own. With Eyre, everything now seemed like a possibility. Nothing seemed out of reach to me anymore, and it was such a startling contrast to my previous life which had been marred with nothing but restrictions. And on top of it all, I loved that Mak's shop, her studio, and the artisan store that housed my pieces were all so close together because that meant I got to walk her home every night. And I *never* missed a night. I'd either pick her up and slide my hand into hers as I let the crickets' music carry us home, or she'd ride home on my handlebars. And each night seemed sweeter than the last one because these were nights I never thought I'd have, not with anyone, but especially not with her.

Eyre's parents had even come to visit and help her move over once she'd decided to stay. I was sure they'd wanted to meet me as soon as possible. And nothing had terrified me more. Knowing you weren't good enough for someone's daughter didn't help get a first meeting off to a great start. But they must have known how much she loved me. Eyre's love continued to save me in all ways and I think they could tell how much I loved her too. I hope they knew I would do anything for her. And soon they started to feel like family too. They even seemed to fall in love with Ireland as much as Eyre and I knew they would be visiting as much as possible, which I welcomed, especially since I now knew where Eyre got her humor from. That was once Eyre's very protective father warmed up to me. But in his defense, I had taken the best person I knew a whole ocean away from them. So I'd say it was well deserved.

As for Mak, Eyre had changed his life, too. Not only had she become a granddaughter to him, but she had been the match he'd needed to ignite the kindling and burn his fears. She was the breath of fresh air that we all so desperately needed. A call to wake up from our routinely mundane existences. Ever since that night she'd brought Sinead and Mak together, they'd been inseparable, working on their relationship, making up for lost time. And she was right—that was the hottest flame I'd ever seen. Something couldn't be stoked that long and not burn brightly. They actually were a little annoying. I honestly felt like Mak was just trying to make me look bad sometimes. I had a whole lifetime to catch up on. He knew everything about Sinead and had over sixty years of knowledge to use to his advantage in the romance department. There was no way to compete. I had to give it to him, he'd earned it.

Watching their love unfold and grow was beautiful. I, of course, had turned into a sap and absolutely loved watching every minute of their romance. It was like watching your grandparents fall in love for the first time. And there was something so magical and powerful about it. They were literally the talk of the village, which I rather enjoyed because it afforded Eyre and me our privacy. But with each passing day, I could see an itch growing in Mak, and I knew every time he did a little jig down to Sinead's home that it wouldn't be long until he'd stay down there for good. I imagined he already had a ring picked out. I was pretty sure he'd already envisioned, for most of his lifetime, the ring he would give her. He'd waited over sixty years for her, so I didn't think he was going to let more than a couple of months pass by this time.

And soon, the house would be very empty without him. I was pretty sure he had left the house to me since he'd been dropping hints that he was going to let me have it. Something that I couldn't let him do, but I also knew that once he put his mind to something, there was nothing in the world that was going to change it. So it left me to wonder if a woman named Eyre and a dog named Lucky might want to fill it permanently with me. Lucky had certainly already adopted Eyre as his mom. Whatever the future held, I just knew she had to be in it.

The abrupt halt of the bus snapped me out of my daydreams. Shamus had not gotten any better at driving this thing. I stood up, bringing Eyre with me to stand in front of me, grasping her tightly. I still wasn't able to hold on to her loosely, always worried that she wasn't real. That this was still a dream I was having. I was certainly due for one after all the nightmares.

"Right, make sure you have your cameras ready–" A flash went off in our faces and Eyre looked up at me and started laughing uncontrollably. I whispered down to her, "Did she really just take a picture of us?" She nodded to me in between the uncontrollable giggles. I raised my eyebrows quickly in what Eyre had said was my classic "Darby" look. More flashes were going off. *Great, now they're all confused.* "For the cliffs, ladies," I exclaimed. "Nothing to see here."

But as I looked down at her and was met with those siren eyes, I knew that was so unbelievably not true. She reached up on her tiptoes and kissed me passionately, disproving me once and for all. A round of applause sounded. These women sure loved the tour Eyre put on. I dipped her in the aisle, a real Patrick Swayze move, because, yes, I'd been watching *Dirty Dancing* relentlessly. I was determined to learn how to dance. And I was set on learning the dance at the end of the movie so I could dance it with Eyre. I was going to be a good partner for her even if it killed us both. And that was a very real possibility. I was determined we were going to have at least one good song we could dance to. Mostly, our dance sessions had just provided her endless hours of amusement and brought us closer together than I'd ever thought possible. But I loved being in that little studio "after hours" with her.

When I brought her back up from the dip, her eyes were dazed, and even she was speechless. The humor had all dried up. "Ok, ladies, let's go see the cliffs. Grab your wellies, just in case, and cameras for *the cliffs*," I emphasized. They all laughed.

I helped the ladies off the bus, and we were met with the beauty of those Irish wonders. Eyre slid her fingers carefully in between mine and we walked slowly over to "our" cliffs, really taking our time, which was in glaring contrast to the ladies who had bolted off the bus to see them as fast as their canes and artificial legs could carry them. Some things never changed.

THE IRISH FALL

We took turns looking at each other in the silence, the wind whipping stray hairs wildly around Eyre's face. Our coy smiles met each other, which made me feel like we were Sinead and Mak now. They had taught us so much, and yet we both still had so much to learn, but I was beyond grateful that this woman was the one I'd be doing it with. Eyre was my undoing and my saving grace all in one.

I was just about to say something when I saw one of the women trying to get some ridiculous, artsy photo standing too close to the edge of the cliffs. "Oh bugger," I said and started to head over to her.

"Darby, she's ok," Eyre said as a friend grabbed the woman and scolded her.

"You'd think these tourists would learn . . . I mean, we did tell them how tall these cliffs are. I guess we're going to have to start doing it in something other than your horrible yet oddly sexy Irish accent. It's a liability," I said with dead seriousness, but she just laughed. It broke through my serious thoughts and a smile cracked wide open on my face. "Well . . . I remember there was one tourist that I was more than happy to rescue."

She looked at me, the breeze whipping around us in the coolness of the overcast day. The sun was trying to slightly shine upon us. The cliffs looked completely different from when I'd met her that fateful day. Whereas before, they'd looked so melancholy and desolate, now they looked beautiful and hopeful. Like they were endless and full of possibilities. It was amazing in life how you could revisit the exact same place in the exact same way, and everything looked completely different, showing you how much you'd changed.

And it made me realize that I couldn't thank God

enough for bringing me this woman. Everything in my life had been leading to her and all my hurt molded perfectly into hers. Only she could hold it the right way with her love. It was like she'd been sent to me. And looking at her, I felt like my heart wasn't going to be able to contain its emotions for her any longer. I had been a wide-open canvas, wiped clean with apathy, and she had completely filled it with love.

"Oh really, did you rescue her?" she asked with a cheeky smile.

"No, she rescued me," I answered seriously. And I let the Irish breeze carry our words away as they mingled into one sound over the vast cliffs that had brought her to me. How they were supposed to always be, never again to be parted.

Movie List

In need of ideas for a movie night? Grab some popcorn and relax with the movies/TV discussed or mentioned in this novel. Enjoy :)

Golden Girls
The Quiet Man*
Laws of Attraction*
The Grand Budapest Hotel
The Luck of the Irish (1948)*
Finding You*
Dirty Dancing
Grease
Wild Mountain Thyme*
Psycho (1960)

Splash
The Wizard of Oz
Tristen and Isolde*
Romeo and Juliet (I'd recommend Shakespeare in Love or Rosaline)
Disney's Haunted Mansion
The Breakfast Club
Bad Sisters*
All Creatures Great and Small
P.S. I Love You*
Atonement
The Notebook
Harry Potter
Jurassic Park
Matchmaker*
Singin' In the Rain
Easter Parade
You Were Never Lovelier
The Andy Griffith Show
Strangers on a Train.
The X-Files
Legally Blonde
Leave It To Beaver
Alice and Wonderland
Ghost
A Christmas Carol
Once*
The Shining
Titanic (May I suggest An Affair to Remember or The Lady Eve instead. Kate Winslet did almost drown making it and I almost didn't survive watching it. lol)

THE IRISH FALL

How the Grinch Stole Christmas
King Arthur
Pride and Prejudice
Father Ted*
Princess Bride
From Here to Eternity
Casablanca

*Movies/TV set in Ireland

PF Fish & Chips

GF Fish & Chips

SERVINGS: 2   PREP TIME: 15 MIN   COOKING TIME: 12 MIN

Ingredients

- 1 lb Cod
- 2 Birch Bender Waffles
- 2 Eggs
- 1/2 tsp Salt
- 1 tsp coconut sugar
- 1/8 tsp Garlic
- Squeezed Lemon
- 1 tsp Sweet paprika (if peppers don't bother you)

Directions

1. Mix together wet ingredients in a bowl and dry ingredients in a separate bowl. (Put waffles in food processor). You can add 1/2 cup flour, such as almond or coconut flour, but to me it just made it dry.
2. Cut the fish & coat it in the egg mixture and then dip the fish in the breadcrumb mixture.
3. Put fish in the air fryer & air fry at 400°F for 12 minutes. Flip halfway through. Make sure to check fish! (Use an air fryer liner for easy cleanup!)
4. This is also really good without the breading! Stick fish uncoated in the air fryer for same time. Spray with coconut oil. Sprinkle salt and coconut sugar. Then make a sandwich with cheddar cheese, tartar sauce, and a Birch Benders Paleo waffle!
5. BONUS: Cut up some potatoes (sweet or regular) and put in the air fryer at 375°F for 20 minutes for the chips! Salt & spray with coconut oil. Yum :)

Brookegilbertauthor.com | @enchantingbrookevoiceover

Pf & Df Tartar Sauce

GF & DF Tartar Sauce

SERVINGS: 2   PREP TIME: 5-7 MIN   COOK TIME: 0 MIN

Ingredients
- 3 Tbsp Green Valley Sour Cream
- 1 tsp Dill
- 1/8 Garlic (fresh)
- 1/2 Tbsp Sweet Onion
- 1 tsp Agave
- Squeezed Lemon

Directions
1. Chop onions finely
2. Squeeze lemon
3. Mix all ingredients together
4. Enjoy!!

Brookegilbertauthor.com | @enchantingbrookevoiceover

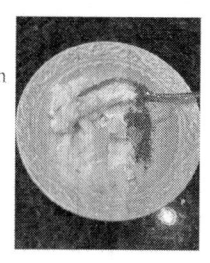

Autoimmune Paleo Diet

This diet was passed down to me by a special couple: Rebekah & Frank. When Frank shared his diet with me and all he learned from his Naturopathic doctor, it changed my life and the trajectory of my conditions. I truly believe diet has helped to save my life. And I would not be writing books without the quality of life that it has afforded me. You are two extraordinary humans with the most beautiful hearts and giving souls!

You can find the diet on my blog at https://www.brookegilbertauthor.com/blog or https://www.brookegilbertauthor.com/blog/categories/spoonie-life. I hope this diet will be of help to you whether you have Crohn's or another autoimmune, inflammatory, or chronic illness. I'd love to talk about diet or exchange nutrition tips with you! Sending you so much love and spoons!

    Brooke :)

Discussion Questions

A few questions to start the discussion at your next book club meeting. If you are choosing *The Irish Fall* for your Book Club meeting, I would love to join your discussion! Send me a message at brookegilbertauthor.com, @enchantingbrookevoiceover on IG, or email me at brookegilbertauthor@gmail.com.

Question 1
- How do you feel about the disability representation in the novel? Can you relate? Did it make you feel more connected to the main characters?
- Was it portrayed differently than in other novels you've read? If so, how?

Question 2
- What is your favorite quality about Darby?
- Did you think he was a good fit for Eyre?
- Did you know his mental health condition was PTSD? Did you guess the cause of his PTSD?

Question 3
- One of the things the author often hears is how relatable Eyre is with her health concerns. Can you relate to Eyre?
- What is your favorite quality about Eyre?
- Eyre really feels unlovable because of all the things she can't give in a relationship due to her conditions. How do you feel about that? Can you relate?
- A major theme of this novel is infertility. What did you think about the passage where Eyre was describing a woman's worth being tied to fertility? Can you relate?

Question 4
- Mak forgave Darby for his grandson's death; would you have been able to?
- How do you feel about his relationship with Darby?
- What did you think about the reason Mak turned Sinead down?

Question 5
- What's your favorite quality about Sinead?
- Do you think Sinead and Mak are a good fit?
- Mak has waited around sixty years to finally be with Sinead. After all this time, if it was you, would Mak have been too late?

Question 6
- Eyre needs a break from reality and jumps on the first appealing flight. Has there been a point in your life where you've been close to doing something like that?
- Eyre has an ex-boyfriend that she left because he didn't understand her conditions or her needs associated with them. Have you been in a relationship like this?
- Darby seems emotionally unavailable and hasn't gotten emotionally involved with anyone. Would you have pursued him? Do you think Eyre was being too risky taking a chance on him?

Question 7
- How do you feel about the mental health representation in the novel? Which character do you feel grew the most in their struggle throughout the novel?
- Was the mental health representation portrayed differently than in other novels you've read? If so, how?
- Suicide is a theme in this novel. Do you think discussing it in literature will help it become more easily discussed in our society?

Question 8
- What do you think about how Darby and Eyre met? Was it a different "meet cute" than you're used to?
- How do you think Eyre changes throughout the book? What growth and changes did you see in her?
- What about Darby?

Question 9
- Eyre doesn't want to tell Darby about her conditions but is

forced to tell him when they show themselves. Darby is forced to do the same. The difference is that Darby can't talk about his condition. How do you feel about these differences? Would you have been able to continue seeing Darby when he didn't open up?
• How would you have felt about Darby when you found out about his past from Father Kelly?

Question 10
• What do you envision for the characters' futures? Sinead and Mak? Eyre and Darby?

Question 11
• What is your favorite scene in the novel?
• If you had to pick one place to visit mentioned in their story, where would it be?
• If you were going to travel with one character from the novel, who would it be?

Author's Note

Thank you for taking this emotional journey with me! I hope you enjoyed Eyre and Darby's story. I have become extremely attached to these characters, and I hope you enjoyed your time with them too! They will always have a special place in my heart.

If you are someone like me who has a chronic illness, I hope this story has encouraged you to continue to pursue your dreams. While our illnesses do not define us, they are a part of us. So that means we have to find ways to live with them in harmony and adapt. My wish is that you will find ways for your dreams to grow and adapt with you, just as Eyre did. I certainly never could have foreseen writing in my future.

Growing up, I always wanted to be a writer, artist, and

actress. What a combination! Lol. But I never believed I was good enough for any of the arts. So I pursued a degree in science. I recently stumbled across an assignment from middle school where we were asked to write what we dreamed we would do with our life. My dream was to write a children's book set in every European country. It's amazing where life can take us and how if we can have the courage to believe in ourselves, our dreams will find a way to adapt with us. Don't give up on your dreams and don't ever let yourself, anyone else, or your disorders tell you that you're not good enough. I truly think believing is most of the battle. As my favorite Bible verse says, *"For I know the plans I have for you,"* declares the Lord, *"plans to prosper you and not to harm you, plans to give you hope and a future* (Jeremiah 29:11). I pray this novel has inspired you to believe you are worthy of your dreams and that you are good enough *because you are.*

The basis for Eyre's infertility came from the fact that I do not know if I can have children with my disorders. This was a topic that was laid on my heart to write as many of us with chronic health issues face this question. While at times painful to write, I felt this was a topic that needed to be discussed. It breaks my heart when I read posts saying a disabled person, or a chronically ill person, was told they shouldn't have children by someone in society. So it was extremely important to me that Darby see Eyre as completely capable of being a mother and someone who would be a wonderful mother. This novel hits close to home in many ways. I have always struggled with hormones relating to migraines, cysts, and other female issues since I was a teenager. After finishing this novel, I was diagnosed with an extremely large hemorrhagic cyst. I had no idea while I was editing this novel what was causing my pain and exhaustion. And I was faced with the same possible dilemma Eyre faces in the book regarding the removal of her ovaries. I have now truly walked in this character's shoes and it's devastating. So devastating in fact, that I almost pulled this novel from publication. I could never have envisioned how real this story was about to become for me. But it is my deepest hope that this story will be of comfort to someone. If you are facing something similar in your life, please know you are not alone. There is a whole community of women to reach out to. And please know that my door is always open as well.

Many of Eyre's medical stories are grounded in truth, as well, and are based on my own health experiences. Eyre's dietary restrictions, symptoms, and medical struggles are ones I battle daily with my autoimmune disorders. The inspiration for her endometriosis came from the journey I have begun with my own female health problems and my mother's early life experience with endometriosis. I was fortunate to be able to speak with my friends and family members who do have this condition. And I have used my own experience with anxiety and panic attacks to help write Darby's struggles. Darby uses coping techniques that I have used in my life as well. I would like to thank the Sensitivity Beta readers for helping me with the chronic health representation in the novel. They have been wonderful! Portraying an accurate depiction of these disorders is extremely important to me.

5% of the net Amazon profits from this book will be donated to Crohn's and endometriosis research. I believe that we must advocate for more time and money to be spent on chronic illness/autoimmune disorder research. The spoonie community tends to get overlooked. I was once told by a medical intern that I was going to need to advocate for myself and never stop. I believe that's what we need to do for ourselves and each other. Together we are stronger.

To make a donation to the Crohn's & Colitis Foundation visit https://www.crohnscolitisfoundation.org/donate

To make a donation to the endometriosis Foundation of America visit https://www.endofound.org/donation

The basis for the suicidal thoughts in this novel is twofold. I lost my cousin, who is mentioned in the dedication, to suicide a few years ago. Suicide prevention is a cause that is extremely close to my heart. 5% of net Amazon sales of this book will be donated to the American Foundation for Suicide Prevention in honor of Chad and other loved ones who have suffered like him. Half of people with endometriosis have suicidal thoughts, and one study has shown as high as 34% of autoimmune patients had suicidal thoughts. I myself have had them, and I wanted to begin a discussion with this book to remove the "taboo" associated with talking about them. When we are at our lowest and these thoughts occur, that is when we should be able to reach out for help, not feel as if we need to hide. Let's help make mental health discussions more acceptable and encouraged in society. And if someone you know is struggling, take this time to reach out, let them know that you're there and you're thinking of them. It could make all the difference in the world. Unfortunately, we usually don't know until it's too late. That's why I believe it's so important for us to start changing how our culture views these topics so it's easier for people to discuss them and ask for help.

To make a donation to the American Foundation of Suicide Prevention visit https://afsp.org/. There is also a helpline readily available there.

If you enjoyed this novel, I would greatly appreciate it if you would consider leaving a review on Goodreads, BookBub, The StoryGraph, LibraryThing, or recommend my book to any family members or friends who you think might enjoy it! Reviews are invaluable for authors and help us be able to continue to do what we love and, hopefully, what you enjoy us doing too. I also love seeing readers post photos with the book on social media! Meeting readers is one of the most exciting parts of this journey :)

Thank you, Brooke

Sign up for the newsletter at www.brookegilbertauthor.com/subscribe and receive a free romance quiz to see what type of man is your perfect match! You'll also be matched with a leading man from one of my current or upcoming novels! There's also a giveaway in every newsletter!

I am constantly writing and hope to release more novels soon. I am currently working on publishing my next one. It's my healthy addiction. I'd love to connect with you whether to discuss writing, literature, pets, hobbies, travel dreams, spoon theory, or everyday life!

Connect with Me:

Amazon Author Central: https://www.amazon.com/author/brookegilbert
Official Website: brookegilbertauthor.com
Email: brookgilbertauthor@gmail.com
Pinterest: www.pinterest.com/brookegilbertauthor
Instagram: @enchantingbrookevoiceover
Facebook: www.facebook.com/enchantingbrookevoiceover
Youtube: https://youtube.com/@brookegilbertauthor
Twitter: https://twitter.com/brookegauthor
TikTok: https://www.tiktok.com/@brookegilbertauthor
Audible

Follow Me on:

Goodreads:https://bit.ly/brookegilbertgoodreads
BookBub: https://bit.ly/brookegilbertbookbub

The StoryGraph: bit.ly/brookegilbertthestorygraph
Library Thing: https://bit.ly/brookegilbertlibrarything
Storyrocket: https://bit.ly/theirishfallstoryrocket
AllAuthor: https://bit.ly/brookegilbertallauthor
Books2Read: https://bit.ly/brookegilbertd2d
https://linktr.ee/brookegilbertauthor

Acknowledgments

I would like to thank every person who takes the time to read this novel. I know there are so many options, and the fact that you decided to read my book truly means the world to me. You truly make this experience so fulfilling and meaningful. I am humbled and honored that you have chosen to take this journey with me. And if, by chance, it resonates with you or provides some escape, you will have made this whole writing journey worthwhile.

I have to take a moment to thank my incredible mother, who has not only been a role model for me my entire life but who also took such great care in editing this book with me. When she suggested that I go ahead with this book, I was scared, to say the least, because it was quite the emotional journey for me, and honestly, not one I knew if I could publish. But in only the way an amazing mom could, she stepped up to the plate and helped me through it, encouraging me every step of the way. This book really feels so raw and vulnerable to me, and I don't think it would have seen the light of day without her reading through it and encouraging me. Mom, thank you for all the late nights we stayed up talking through scenes, all the care you took in making sure I said what I needed to say, and for making sure this book was the best it could be. It means the world to me, and *you*, of course, mean the world to me. "Thank you" would never be enough. The bond built through this experience has only made us closer. And as always, thanks for making sure I never went "a bridge too far." I love you!

Thank you so much to Caitlin Miller, who is an incredible editor! This is my second time working with Caitlin, and I was so excited to be fortunate enough to work with her again! She was so patient and kind throughout the whole process. Her sweet and compassionate nature made the editing process fun and less nerve-racking. I am so lucky to have her insightful comments and meticulous proofreading, which helped make this book the best it could be! I feel so blessed to be able to call her a friend and editor! I'm so grateful that God brought us together to work on these projects, and I can't wait to see what the future has in store!

Thank you to all the Beta readers, ARC readers, and Bookstagrammers who have encouraged me on a daily basis. Becoming a part of this community has been one of the best experiences of my life. I have never met such a welcoming community. I think I lost ten pounds the month my first book was released due to fear and anxiety, but you accepted me as your own, and through your kindness and encouragement, you made me stronger. I will never forget your compassion, kind words, sweet postings, beautiful reviews, and fun book discussions. And I also want to thank the spoonie community, who makes up part of the book community as well. I have found such a wonderful support group with you, and I no longer feel alone with my conditions. Your beauty and strength encourage me every day. And I hope you know my door is always open if you need to talk.

And to my beautiful Beta readers: Abigail, Amber, Brea,

Claire, Chloé, Evelyn, Fedy, Helen, Joelle, Marie, Priya, and Susan. You have always shown me nothing but kindness from day one. On days when bad book reviews came in, when I doubted my abilities, or when I didn't think I could continue, you all were there. Even when I thought about pulling my first book from publication, you were there. Thank you so much for *always* being there! You are such a very special and beautiful group of women :)

I'd be very remiss if I didn't include the authors and voice-over artists I have had the pleasure of meeting along the way. I am always amazed at the encouragement you give one another, and I am so thankful you have accepted me as one of your own. From the first moment, you made me feel like I belonged. Coming from the competitive world of medical sciences, I can say it was an extremely pleasant shock to my system! I have loved learning from you and hope to pay it forward one day! I have been blessed with meeting my "rainy day" author/partner in crime, Tomi Tabb, who is always there to discuss book ideas, book covers, and even boring book logistics. Lol. I have loved getting to know you and truly feel I've found my kindred spirit, especially in loving all things Jane Austen :) I have also been so blessed to have met the beautiful poet Kelly Mac, who has been there to discuss everything from book ideas to spoonie problems to dating scars and future dating endeavors with me. Thanks for being such a rock and being there, even at 3 a.m., when I'm debating St. Paddy's Day speed dating (good call on that one, by the way. Lol). You're a beautiful soul.

To my parents, who have supported every creative dream I have ever imagined, I want to say thank you from the bottom of my heart. I know having a creative daughter who marches to the beat of her own drum has been a handful, but I appreciate all the love you've always shown me. I'm sure you never envisioned having "Mrs. Maisel" as a daughter, but just as her parents did, you have always supported me and fought for me. Thank you to my mother, who always wanted me to be a writer and encouraged me. I never imagined I'd ever become one. It's still surreal to have written a novel. Your love has been a light and a guide, especially in times of trouble. Thank you to my father for shaping my sense of humor and always providing laughter in my life. It is laughter that has made the difficult times bearable. You have helped mold me into the person I am today, and I will be forever grateful. Your continued support has meant the world to me. I love you both very much.

I also would like to take a moment to thank two very special people, Rebekah and Frank. It was fate that I met you both at the rock climbing gym that day. I cannot thank you enough for all the help that the two of you have given me with my conditions. When Frank shared his diet with me and all he learned from his Naturopathic doctor, it changed my life and the trajectory of my conditions. I truly believe diet has helped to save my life. And I would not be writing books without the quality of life that it has afforded me. I vowed that I would find a way to pay it forward. I hope I will be able to continue to do so. You are two extraordinary humans with the most beautiful hearts and giving souls. I hope life continues to bless you with all the joy you deserve!

To all my friends and family who have helped me through my rare autoimmune conditions and reminded me of my self-worth, I cannot express my gratitude. You have been such a blessing in my life. Your love and support have made a wonderful difference in my life. I am so fortunate to know you.

And to Caroline Wolfe Grimm and Devon Meske Herrin. Thank you for including me in the "mom club" and welcoming me as an honorary member. I may have as many wounds as Eyre, but you've never seen or treated me any differently because of them. Thank you for sharing your precious children with me. You'll never know how much it means to me :)

To all the caring doctors, nurses, and healthcare workers who have helped me in my journey, I want to say thank you. Your compassion in the most difficult times of my life has been appreciated more than you could ever know. To all the people that made this experience bearable, I want to say thank you, and I hope to somehow pay it forward.

Most of all, thank you to God for showing me that "all things work together for good for those who believe in the Lord" (Romans 8:28). And for proving that faith can overcome all odds. I am humbled and unbelievably grateful for this Job moment.

About the Author

Brooke Gilbert is a Tennessee native, a microbiology graduate of the University of Tennessee, and a border collie mom. She is, as you may have already guessed, a hopeless romantic and a lover of Jane Austen. When she isn't writing, she works as a jewelry designer, an audiobook narrator, and a graphic designer. Her writing features characters with autoimmune disorders, something she deals with herself. She believes it is important for these types of characters to be seen in modern literature and started writing so she could see someone like herself in literature. She is considered a medical mystery and has several rare autoimmune disorders.

These disorders caused her to withdraw from Physician Assistant School, but she is happy to be pursuing her dreams of designing, creating, and writing. She thanks God for leading her heart on this new path and recites "perhaps this is the moment for which you were created" in times of doubt (Esther 4:14).

She loves watching classic films (thrillers and romantic comedies, too), reading, playing the ukulele, painting, dancing, Pilates, and spending time with her dog, family, and friends. One of her favorite quotes is from Flashdance: "When you give up on your dreams, you die." She believes that if you're waiting to pursue your dreams, stop waiting and start doing. Your time is now. And may you never stop being a hopeless romantic. Contrary to popular belief, it's a very good quality. She's still looking for her Mr. Darcy. Visit brookegilbertauthor.com to connect and stay updated on her latest projects.

Also by Brooke Gilbert

The Paris Soulmate: A Sweet Romance Novel.

Reeling from the reality of turning thirty soon, Christine decides to take a trip that has been on her bucket list for years. She has dreamed of going back to Paris, but since being diagnosed with several rare autoimmune disorders, she never imagined she would get the chance to return. Now, she finds herself on the way to the city of love with an unexpected surprise ... An extremely handsome British stranger seems to have mysteriously fallen onto her path. Is it just a coincidence that they are both traveling to the city of love at the same time? It all seems too good to be true.

Chapter 1

I sat nervously at the boarding gate, seriously doubting my mental functioning capability. I couldn't help but question what I was doing. This was not me. I was not spontaneous, and I was not an adventurer. The most spontaneous thing I had done recently was try a different flavor of dairy-free ice cream. Ms. Big Risk here. So, why did I think I could possibly pull this off? I must have been delusional. I needed to stop making decisions at 2 a.m. So, what was I thinking, imagining I could do this?

Okay, just breathe. Let's think this through. You're not on the plane yet. It's not too late to change your mind. You can go back to being safe and extremely boring. Actually, boring didn't even begin to cover it. They needed to invent a new word for what I'd become with my disorders. I would say I'm as boring as a grandmother, but frankly that's offensive to grandmothers everywhere.

I was going to hyperventilate. I could feel my cheeks flaming. The red lupus rash felt like it was giving itself away and the dizziness of my rare mast cell disorder was flaring. I felt the heat of the butterfly wings race across my cheeks and nose, and I was hoping it appeared like I was blushing under my make-up. Get my rare type of Crohn's to kick in and we'd have hit the trifecta.

The room was starting to spin. I was sure I'd gone chalk white as I grasped desperately for my suitcase in front of me. I leaned over my lap with my hands on the luggage pull and hung my head between my arms. To those around me, hopefully it just looked like I was tired. *Airports are an exhausting place, right?* But I could feel the flight attendants at the front desk looking at me. I'd grown very good at knowing when people were looking at me. A nice side effect of my disorders. I usually stood out somehow. Even though my conditions didn't really have any physical manifestations, they were pretty good at attracting attention. I required a lot of "special attention." I hated being *that* person. You know, that person at the restaurant that changed what they ordered ten different ways. But I didn't do it to be difficult. I did it because I wanted to live. I understood that it was annoying all the same. I despised being that type of customer, and I would have been annoyed by me too.

The flight attendants were very well aware of my conditions and dietary restrictions. It took an act of Congress to allow for an exception to bring all of my liquid medications and enough food with me onto the plane. And I'm sure they were all waiting to see who the mysterious person was that caused all the trouble. They probably had bets going. Well, *I* bet they didn't think it was a woman in her twenties that looked so normal. I felt bad for costing them money on their bets. Actually, I didn't; it's rude to bet on disabilities.

Well, it was no secret now. I'm sure they were tallying up their losses. Maybe they were still debating whether I was "the one." I can tell you I was "the one." Because "the one" was about to pass out. Like, literally pass out. And I hadn't even gotten on the plane yet. I hadn't even left Atlanta and I was already going to have a medical emergency. *How pathetic and embarrassing.* I was going to have to call my best friend and say, "Hey, guess how far I made it?" We'd have a good laugh, but it was not exactly what I had in mind when I booked my plane ticket. I thought I would at least make it onto the plane before disaster struck.

When I booked my ticket, I decided to keep my mind distracted instead of imagining all of the many possible disastrous scenarios that could ensue. I busied myself with calls to my best friend about which outfits to pack and Googling beautiful photos of the places I would be visiting. Believe me, when you have this many disorders, you map out all of the possible disaster scenarios that could happen just by going to and from the doctor's office in town. But I hadn't allowed myself to do that this time. Blame it on the "I have to do something with my life" mindset, the now-or-never carpe diem mentality. If I was a betting person like I imagined the flight attendants to be, I would be losing the bet that I'd make it to Paris in one piece. The plane wasn't even boarding yet. Like I said, it's not cool to bet on disabilities. That was karma for you.

God must have decided to have mercy on my desperate soul at this moment. Suddenly, I felt a gentle tap on my shoulder, and a voice I knew I'd never forget swept over me.

"Are you ok?" a deep baritone voice rasped in my ear. "You look a little pale. Traveling is maddening these days."

He said it softly so as not to alert the small few who hadn't already noticed my impending doom.

I felt grateful for the help as I kept my head lowered. I wasn't sure how to respond. I didn't think anyone but the flight attendants would be aware of how severe the situation could become. And I was pretty sure that everyone else around me had just assumed I was tired. He must be a good Samaritan who just sensed it.

When I didn't reply, he said, "Here, let me get you something cold to put on your neck." How did he know exactly what I needed? And to my delight, I detected a bit of a British accent. My dizziness began to slow itself, but I decided not to raise my head until I felt I could straighten again. Maybe the handsome voice of this kind gentleman was putting me more at ease. I couldn't believe a complete stranger could do that. *How could just the sound of someone make you feel at home like that?* I wanted him to keep talking. His voice was as warming to the soul as looking out a rainy window of a cozy London cafe could be. I was hooked. As the dizziness continued to lessen, I started thinking about how much of an idiot I was being. But, before I could continue with my very well-practiced self-deprecation, I heard that voice again.

"Now I'm getting worried. Can you say something?" His husky tone was enchanting.

"Oh, I ... um ..."

Great. Just flipping fantastic. He's like a warm English fire after being caught in the rain, and I'm like a hillbilly tractor stuck in the mud. This was just perfect. Why was I terrible with men? I hadn't even looked up yet. I didn't even know if he was good-looking or married or anything. I needed to get it together. It was pathetic enough to almost pass out waiting for a plane, but this . . . Well, this just took the proverbial cake.

"I'm sorry," I said shakily, my eyes still staring at my luggage beneath me. "I just started feeling really dizzy, so I grabbed my luggage and, well, it will pass. I'm ok. Thanks for your concern, though."

"It doesn't look like it's just going to pass." There was genuine concern in his voice. Did he know how hard it was to find true concern in a man's voice? I felt like I'd struck gold with this gentle stranger. He had my full attention. No aggravation in his voice, just a genuine want to help. "How about that cold water for your neck? Hold one second."

I was terrified to look up now. He was like my own personal Hugh Grant. I didn't want to ruin it. I wanted to live in this dream for as long as I could. Allowing my mind to be transported to *Nottinghill*. I suppose it's quite sad that a note of genuine concern and an offer of a cold water bottle got me this excited, but it did. My Hugh standards had severely fallen in my twenties after a few terrible relationships. So, if you gave me a sexy baritone with actual concern, I was ready to say, "I do."

A moment later he placed the bottle of water on the back of my neck. Most people I'd known didn't have any idea about putting ice on pressure points like that. I could feel the flight attendants' eyes still on me, but now I knew it was for other reasons. This guy must be attractive. It was time to rip off the band-aid. I knew I couldn't live in this dream forever. It was time to look up.

I took the water bottle off of my neck and started to bring it in front of me so I could drink some of it. I kept my motions slow so I could steal some glances toward my Hugh Grant stranger.

The first thing I noticed, he was dressed nicely. Not lazily like a lot of men dressed at the airport. He had on nice jeans that hugged his very well-defined legs and a blue button-down shirt that I instantly loved. I'd always loved blue button-downs on men. Now if only the eyes . . . Yes. Oh yes, they matched. I again felt like I was going to faint, but for other reasons now. Yes, this was quite a man. Exactly my type. He was more ruggedly handsome than pretty, with blue eyes that had soul and spirit deep within them. Tousled, sandy blond hair only added to the effect on me. And that smile. That was the clincher for me. Yes, this was my type of man.

Chapter 2

From the instant our eyes met there was a spark. I know I'm a hopeless romantic, but there was something almost palpable in the first moment I gazed into his eyes. I had never experienced that feeling before. There was an instantaneous connection, as if we already knew each other. As if he was my safe place.

"Are you feeling any better?" he asked as he broke my trance.

"Oh, yes, much better. Thank you so much." I took a moment to breathe as he sat down in the seat next to me. "Most people wouldn't know what to do in a situation like that. Actually, I don't think most people would have even noticed a situation like that." I was beginning to babble as I usually did. They didn't call me "chattering Christine" for nothing. It was a seriously bad flirting habit. Really the only flirting habit I had. I was sorely out of practice since I had adopted a "no dating rule." What made me think I could ever get back in the dating game? What made me think it was time to get back to dating, much less that I *deserved* to get back into it at all? And why did dating always have to be such a game? I wish it could just be straightforward. Maybe then I could actually win at it some of the time.

Before I could start back down that self-disparaging rabbit hole, I was becoming increasingly aware of his presence beside me. And I couldn't help but notice that his presence was quite tall and muscular. Guys like this didn't usually pay me any attention. I'm 5'11," and it has always been my luck that short, non-muscular guys were attracted to me. Nothing wrong with short guys with gym aversions; it's just that when you're almost six feet tall, you feel pretty unfeminine when you can look down and see the top of your date's head. Not that I thought this good Samaritan man was interested in me in a romantic way. But my mind and my body were acutely aware of him. His knee touched mine, and my face managed to flush an even brighter shade of pink. It might as well have been neon at this point. My body was a pro at betraying me.

"No problem. I'm happy to help," he said, interrupting my train of thought.

"I feel so pathetic," the words slipped out before I could filter myself.

"Really, don't. Traveling gets to the best of us."

If only it was the traveling that had gotten to me. I needed to pull myself together. I wasn't even on the plane yet. I needed to prove to myself that I could do this, and so far, it wasn't looking very good. As a Capricorn, I was extremely determined to make this trip happen.

"So you're taking the non-stop flight to Paris too?" he asked a little skeptically. As if he had already realized that the flight wasn't a good idea for me. I felt like he knew me well already, or at least could read me better than most. But my situation was anything from normal and ordinary; there was no way he could have any clue about the mess he was stepping into. I almost felt bad for him. I wanted to say, "Thanks for the water, but save yourself." Or, "You're too nice. Find a seat somewhere else by a normal woman who will have ordinary answers to your questions." I'm the first to admit that normal is overrated, but my weirdness was more than anyone bargained for.

"Yup," I said quietly. I was still trying to assess the situation. It was like triaging from my medical training all over again: What information was I going to classify into the 'safe to say' pile that wouldn't be an explosive word bomb full of pitfall questions? This was something I had gotten accustomed to on a daily basis, but not with handsome strangers. I couldn't triage with a handsome stranger next to me. My guard was down. My filter was missing. I was already doing something really stupid by going on this trip, but it was important for me to go, nonetheless. There were so many holes in my logic as to how I was going to make this trip a success, I only needed one to be pointed out before I got up and walked out of the airport. Never again to think about this ridiculous plan. But I needed to take this trip, and I didn't want to be talked out of it.

So I deflected. Deflection was my number one strategy in dealing with the battlefield that is socializing.

"What about you? Why Paris?" I asked. He looked at me. His eyes held me accountable, and it annoyed me. He knew I was deflecting. Most people would be thrilled to talk about themselves, but not him. He looked me over as if he was calling me out for the cheap ploy I had just played.

"Business," he finally replied. "So why Paris for you? I bet your reason is much more interesting. Obviously you've gone through a lot to get here."

Wow, he was blunt. Blunt, direct, and most definitely holding me accountable. His interest in my trip to Paris made him even more attractive. People usually let me cop out. *Where did he come from anyway? And why was he suddenly so curious about this distressed woman who almost passed out in the middle of the airport terminal?*

"Um, it's really lame and I don't want to talk about it. If I talk about it then I'll probably end up not even getting on the plane," I said.

His blue eyes widened with curiosity, which only made him look more mysterious. He had this sexy smirk on his face that all at once infuriated me and set all of my senses on fire. He seemed extremely intrigued now. *Fantastic.* I'd said the wrong thing. I had wanted to appear uninteresting and make him go away. *Or did I not want him to leave?*

"Ok," he said with a laugh. "I have to hear this. We've got two hours to kill before the plane starts boarding. Let's get some coffee and you can tell me all about it. I'll make sure we get back on time and that you actually get on the plane. I won't talk you out of it. Everyone needs to see Paris once."

"Oh, I've seen Paris."

His eyes widened with shock. He looked like he truly didn't know what to make of me.

"Well, I'm still not going to talk you out of it," he recomposed himself. "Everyone needs to see Paris as many times as possible. How about that?"

We stood up to start walking toward a small café nearby when he abruptly asked, "Wait, are you some hopeless romantic? Is this some *Sleepless in Seattle* fantasy? Please tell me you haven't received a cryptic message from some stranger on the internet asking you to meet them at the Eiffel Tower with a pile of cash that they need for some life-saving procedure," he laughed. "I can guarantee that's not going to end like the movie."

I was furious. What did I look like to him? So he did think I was pathetic. He was a pathetic sick girl chaser! I'd met enough of *them*. The type of guy who loves to find a sick helpless girl who's all out of options so that he can feel like the hero. Now this guy thinks he's scored really big because he assumes I'm getting catfished at the Eiffel Tower! I was going to agree to get coffee because, well, look at him. Even my "no dating policy" would bend for *this* guy, but now . . .

"I don't drink coffee," I said a little too forcefully. "And I don't do social media. I have an account for my handcrafted jewelry business, but that's it. So, no, I'm not getting catfished under the Eiffel Tower. At least pick a more original landmark." There was a biting edge to my tone.

"Well, I thought the Moulin Rouge would just be crude." Playfulness filled his voice.

"You know what?" I said, feeling my blood pressure rising. "I'm not going anywhere with you and your Mr. Darcy accent." I knew that I needed to calm down. I didn't need to add to my troubles, and with my heart racing so quickly, I knew the dizziness was sure to return. This trip already felt nearly impossible; I didn't need to make it any harder.

"Wow, I've hit a nerve. Mr. Darcy, huh?" he chimed. "So

the hopeless romantic bit is accurate. Let's just back up a little, ok? I didn't mean to offend you. I just thought you needed someone to look out for you. I mean you're not even on the plane and–"

"Oh, so, what are you? The disability police?" I said emphatically. Anger was coloring my words now and making my head swim. "I was doing perfectly fine. *I'm* perfectly fine. I *will* make it to Paris on my own, unchaperoned and without assistance."

"Well, you will need the pilot and the plane. Probably the crew as well," he said nonchalantly.

"Argh. You–you really think you know me, don't you?" My blood was beginning to boil.

"I'm really not sure how this escalated so quickly, but considering you were just about to pass out, I don't think we should be raising your blood pressure so much." I could tell we were beginning to draw an audience from prying eyes.

"We? We?!" I turned from him and started collecting my things. He noticed that I had several rolling luggage cases. Normally passengers get one carry-on. I assumed he was beginning to realize that I was a special exception; that there was a reason I was allowed more. *Great.* He probably thought I had some horrendous issue. Not that I didn't have my share of disorders, but I doubted it was the type that was racing through his mind. I looked like a basket case. Well, to be fair, I was a basket case, but I didn't want him assuming that.

Here I was ready to share with him my reasons for taking this trip and what led me to this moment. I couldn't believe I'd almost opened up to a complete stranger. I knew better than to do that. It had never gone well in the past. Even opening up to people I already knew hardly ever went in my favor. I learned I needed to be very selective with what information I shared and with whom. For the past five years, I had to be guarded and prepared for whatever reaction a person could have to my disorders. But it was getting more difficult to deal with negative reactions. I began to only share my reality with a select few I truly trusted; people whose reactions I knew I could handle, whatever they may be. So, if the information was too vulnerable, I kept it locked deep inside a metaphorical vault. There was a copious amount in that vault. 97% of my life was tucked away in there. Only 3% open to the public. Because that's what it's like to be chronically ill. I was feeling stupid for almost opening up again to someone who hadn't yet earned my trust. Thankfully, I was stopped before I made that mistake again.

"At least tell me why you don't drink coffee," he called to me as I walked away.

Sneak Peek

Coming Soon. *Dear Doris: A Sweet Romantic Comedy Novella.* Please enjoy a sneak peek chapter! This romantic comedy novella features Doris from *The Paris Soulmate*. Add to Goodreads. Learn more at the launch page. Subscribe at brookegilbertauthor.com/subscribe for the author newsletter (a giveaway in each one), updates about new releases, and to receive a free romance quiz!

A diner waitress is about to get swept off her feet with a year of love letters all written on the back of order tickets.

Carey has just stepped foot on American soil and the first thing he plans to do is propose to his girlfriend. As he waits for her in a diner booth, he's starting to realize he might not get the warmest welcome after coming back from the Vietnam War.

Doris is a waitress working hard to pay her medical bills and trying to manage her newly diagnosed diabetes. She can't help but notice the handsome soldier fidgeting with a ring box in one of the diner booths. Being compassionate and somewhat nosy, she can't stop herself from going over and giving him a confidence boost.

When it's clear that Carey's girlfriend has moved on while he was away at war and that a "no" is fast approaching his question, Doris feels an even stronger connection to this man. She leaves a special note on Carey's ticket and pays for his meal. It's the first kindness and feeling of welcome he's gotten so far. And he begins coming into the diner every day to leave her a written message on the back of his ticket in hopes of getting to know her . . . and soon with the hopes of winning her heart.

But Doris has a reason she doesn't get involved with men. Is patient kindness and a gentle heart enough to make a soul believe in love again?

Will Carey be different? And will he be able to win her heart?

This novella features disability representation written by an author who also battles autoimmune disorders herself. Diabetes and mental health is represented in this novella. The author's aunt battles diabetes, and this condition is close to the author's heart. This is a clean novel. Descriptive kissing only. No cursing. Faith conversations included. Trigger warnings: mild medical episodes, harassment, and PTSD.

Dear Doris

CARY | ATLANTA, GEORGIA | 1969

> "*Of all the gin joints in all the towns in all the world, she walks into mine*"-Humphrey Bogart, Casablanca."

I couldn't believe I had set foot on beautiful American soil. I would never take it for granted again. I thought I wanted to travel the world, but after my tour of duty in Vietnam, I was perfectly content to stay in my hometown of Atlanta, Georgia, forever. After grueling years of writing postcard after postcard to the woman I loved, I was finally getting to see her in person. It was surreal, to say the least.

I sat in the tiny booth of the diner she'd recommended, my hands sticking to the thick vinyl seats from the sweat on my palms. The air was as thick and humid here in the South as it had been in Vietnam, but I welcomed it. This type of thickness in the air was home to me. And the sweet smell of good home cooking and pies filled the air in a way I never thought I'd get to inhale again. The smell of pecan pie and peach cobbler that Georgia was known for was so strong that I could practically taste it. But it wasn't the heat making my hands slide against the bright red vinyl booth of this little 50s diner.

I tried to take in my surroundings to calm me. After all, this was what had gotten me through my active duty, the idea of coming home: to her and to the South. And this small little diner, filled with laughter and friendly chatter, embodied it all so well. This place was cozy and hospitable, just like the good ole South, even if it was stuck in the 50s. The sock hop feel was going strong with the black and white checkered floor, red and white vinyl booths and occasional bright aqua pops of color. The only problem was that I didn't seem to belong here any more. I appeared to make people uncomfortable and there was a wide berth around my booth. No one got very close and there were too many glances directed my way–and not the kind you would want. Their stares just got my mind running even faster.

What if I'm not how she remembered me? What if war has changed me too much? It sure felt like it had. *What if I've changed too much?* It wasn't like I was exactly able to send her photos throughout the years of training and deployment. And I didn't know how much she had changed either.

Her postcards had become more sporadic lately. I'm sure it was just harder to get them through the post. I'm sure she'd done what she could do, but I was still disappointed when she didn't meet me at the bus station last night when I'd finally arrived in Atlanta. My fellow servicemen and I had sung "Midnight Train to Georgia" the whole way there in anticipation of our homecoming. Our bus was scheduled to arrive late and the song seemed perfect under the circumstances. And when the wheels stopped in the Atlanta depot in the dusk of the night, my heart started thudding sporadically. I knew she wouldn't be there, but it still burst forth with little hopes off and on.

As we loaded off the bus, a little pang of jealousy rippled through me as I saw my buddies greeted by their fiancées and wives when they got off the bus. The fresh Georgia air wrapped around them in a welcomed embrace as did their better halves. The crystal stars in the sky were shining just as brightly as I remembered them when I'd left last time. At least the night sky had shown up to greet me. I just stood by and watched as the other men were greeted by the special people in their lives. Well, at least by the few that did show up. I was already beginning to realize we weren't exactly popular here. I'd heard about it through the grapevine, but I hadn't believed it. But the ones that did show up had nothing but love in their eyes. And the kisses were hot enough to fry an egg on a sidewalk in July.

I stood there awkwardly, hoping she'd change her mind and would show up among the small crowd. I'd even stood there for an extra thirty minutes looking up at the large station clock, but she never came. My buddies didn't want to leave me, but one by one, they all went home with their beautiful other halves. *Who can blame them?*

So when Irene suggested meeting at the diner, I agreed. I felt sure she thought this would be a more private and intimate setting for our reunion. And after being away for so many years, I certainly wanted to do anything I could to make her happy. I wanted to build a life with her, and I couldn't wait to start. I honestly couldn't count the number of times I'd almost proposed to her in those letters, but I knew she deserved better. I wanted her to hear me say the actual words to her. I wouldn't settle for anything less, even if an answer to my proposal would have helped me survive those dark days of the war.

So I'd saved up my pay and asked my family to help me so I could buy Irene a ring. I took advantage of one of the bus stops along the way to locate a jewelry store. The shop owner hadn't been particularly friendly to me. I'm not sure if it was the uniform or something else. He was especially surly when it came to selling his merchandise, which seemed ironic since the store was empty. After much deliberation, I found a ring that seemed to encompass everything wonderful about Irene. Hollywood was always making movies about stuff like this, so I figured this romantic gesture would improve my chances.

I felt the little velvet box in my pocket, fidgeting with it nervously. I was mostly checking to make sure it was still there.

"Relax, she's going to say yes. Look at you. Who wouldn't say yes?" The waitress's steady and melodic voice broke my deep reverie. I looked up at her, taking in her mesmeric grin. It was infectious. The woman was stunning. She was going to make some man *very* lucky one day.

"Is it that obvious?" I chuckled nervously.

"Well, fidgeting with your trousers like that so often isn't helping. Either that or you have some sort of problem. I'm optimistic, so I'm choosing to believe the romantic notion is the accurate assumption here." She laughed, and it was so deep and fully rounded. It warmed my bones for the first

THE IRISH FALL

time since I had stepped foot on this soil. Here, I thought coffee would do that. Her deep auburn curls bounced softly as each note of laughter went up and down, falling around her in a perfect singsong harmony. And the dimple that appeared with it only made my stomach knot and contort itself even further.

I took note of her name tag, needing to address this woman by her proper name now. "Yes, Doris, your assumption is accurate. Thanks for going with the better of the two." I laughed my husky laugh. The one I'd been told sounded like I smoked a pack of cigarettes a day when I'd, in fact, never smoked a day in my life. "I tried on every fatigue outfit I own. I'm that nervous. I honestly don't know what response I'm expecting to get."

She set the coffee pot down on the booth's tabletop. "Oh, well you should know what answer you're going to get . . ."

"Carey," I interjected, more than happy she wanted to know my name.

"Carey," she said. And the way she said my name did something to me. "How about I sit down with you for a minute and you can practice? Do you have enough time?" I looked down at my watch, but before I could speak again, she slid into the booth opposite me and said, "Of course you do. I can tell you're the type of man that shows up twenty minutes early for a woman because you'd never want to make her wait."

I smiled at her words as I took in her frilly, lemon meringue-colored apron. I took a deep breath, actually now more nervous about what this woman thought of my proposal than the woman I was going to propose to. "Uh . . . Well . . . Irene," I began.

"Errrr." She made a buzzer sound like at a basketball game. I looked up at her in alarm. My eyes went as wide as the blue plate special.

"Excuse me?" I asked.

"Carey, you need to show the lady that you're sure. If you're not completely sure of her and your decision, then you might as well not start. Go again," she said, trying to instill some confidence in me.

"Right," I said slowly. "Irene, I know we've been dating a while–"

"Errrr," she buzzed me again.

I looked at her unbelievingly. "Really?"

"Yes, that's the most unromantic thing I've ever heard. Sweep. Me. Off. My. Feet," she said emphatically. "I don't want to hear pragmatic."

"You don't know Irene; she could be the most pragmatic person on Earth–"

"Errr," she buzzed me again. I threw up my hands.

"You can't buzz me for that. That was purely factual. I wasn't even attempting a proposal that time."

"Yes, but your logic was just all wrong, so I thought I'd go ahead and stop you." She laughed. "No woman wants to hear pragmatic when she's being proposed to. I don't care if she's Madame flippin' Curie."

I laughed so hard I had to collect myself before I began again. This time I looked into the woman's eyes. Her soft green irises invited me in and gave me unexpected inspiration.

Something inside of me seemed to unfurl. I came out of my shell, and this romantic soul took my place. "Irene, you're the most beautiful woman I've ever seen. And I've fallen more in love with you with each passing day. I would like to be given a chance to continue to do that every day for the rest of my life. As soon as I saw you, I knew there was nobody for me, but you." I reached for her hand that lay casually on the tabletop. "Make me the luckiest man that ever lived. Will you marry me, Doris? . . . I mean . . . Irene," I corrected as quickly as possible, my cheeks turning a shade of wild rose pink. *How embarrassing.*

I was worried because when I'd made contact with her hand, she'd flinched and pulled back, like she'd been scalded. But then she immediately said, "There's no way any woman would say no to that." Her physical reaction and words collided in such opposition that it confused me; but I loved the words, so I would take that victory.

I smiled as she got up from the booth, thanking her for her help as she walked away to check on the other patrons. The diner was busy that morning, although I noticed that people were avoiding my booth and the area around it. The way people had been acting around me and the stares elicited in the diner made me uncomfortable. Doris was the only person in here, well, the only person in America so far, that had made me feel normal–welcomed. And I was surprised she'd spent so much time with me, especially since customers were yelling and calling for her. Honestly, some of the men were so impatient that it was demeaning in manner. Their call of "toots" really set me off. I wanted to get up and put them in their place. But she didn't even flinch. Judging by her reaction, she was used to it. I really despised that.

I continued to sit nervously in the booth, watching Doris, wondering what her story was and what her life was like. I could see us becoming good friends. Anyone that would help out a stranger and take mercy on their soul was aces in my book.

At fifteen minutes past, I was beginning to worry Irene wasn't going to show, but when the bell at the front door jingled and her beautiful figure entered, I knew I was in for trouble. My heart stopped as I beheld her wavy mahogany hair and gorgeous complexion for the first time in two whole years.

Made in the USA
Monee, IL
29 January 2024